MW00587688

SEVEN DEADLY PLEASURES

HIPPOCAMPUS PRESS LIBRARY OF FICTION

W. H. Pugmire, *The Fungal Stain and Other Dreams* (2006)
Franklyn Searight, *Lair of the Dreamer: A Cthulhu Mythos Omnibus* (2007)
Jonathan Thomas, *Midnight Call and Other Stories* (2008)
Ramsey Campbell, *Inconsequential Tales* (2008)
Joseph S. Pulver, Sr. *Blood Will Have Its Season* (2009)

Michael Aronovitz

Seven Deadly Pleasures

Foreword by S. T. Joshi

Hippocampus Press

New York

Copyright © 2009 by Michael Aronovitz

"Passive Passenger" was published online in 2008 by *Demonminds* and *Scars Publications*.
"Quest for Sadness" was published in 2008 by *Metal Scratches* magazine in *Studies in the Fantastic* (Winter 2008/09).
"The Clever Mask" was published in 1993 by *Midnight Zoo* magazine.

Foreword copyright © 2009 by S. T. Joshi

Published by Hippocampus Press
P.O. Box 641, New York, NY 10156.
www.hippocampuspress.com

Cover art and interior illustrations by Thomas S. Brown. Cover design by Barbara Briggs Silbert. Hippocampus Press logo designed by Anastasia Damianakos.

All rights reserved.
No part of this work may be reproduced in any form or
by any means without the written permission of the publisher.

First Edition
1 3 5 7 9 8 6 4 2

ISBN-13: 978-0-9824296-0-0

Contents

Foreword

In a prefatory note to *Deathbird Stories* (1975), Harlan Ellison wrote: "It is suggested that the reader not attempt to read this book at one sitting. The emotional content of these stories, taken without break, may be extremely upsetting." Without attempting to compare a relative novice to a living legend, I would repeat Ellison's caveat in regard to Michael Aronovitz's *Seven Deadly Pleasures*. In fact, I would go on to add that it might be advisable to read only *one* of the stories in this book at a sitting, perhaps one a day.

The emergence of a writer like Michael Aronovitz is a highly interesting literary phenomenon. As we come close to the end of this first decade of the twenty-first century, the horror "boom" that began, more or less, with the simultaneous appearance on the bestseller lists in 1971 of William Peter Blatty's *The Exorcist* and Thomas Tryon's *The Other* has been over for close to twenty years. Stephen King and Anne Rice still make the bestseller lists, but the former remains there for shorter and shorter periods and the latter scarcely seems to be writing horror at all. The best writers in the field appear to have retreated to the small press, for it is only those presses that can take a chance that a Thomas Ligotti, a Caitlín R. Kiernan, or a Jonathan Thomas will be able to find an audience without generating that blockbuster (usually a bloated and gore-filled novel) which commercial houses appear to require of their genre writers. And so, when Michael Aronovitz submitted these stories to me—first one or two, then the entire volume— I could see at once that here was a writer who deserved his audience but whose intense, gripping, and emotionally wrenching tales would be sure to scare off—in the wrong sense of the term—any commercial publisher he approached.

What is impressive about Aronovitz's tales is their range of tone, mood, and substance. To be sure, such stories as "How Bria Died," "The Legend of the Slither-Shifter," and "Toll Booth" shows the author to be unusually attuned to the angst of teenagers—as is fitting for a high school teacher. But to turn from the dramatic tensity of "How Bria Died"—one of the most terrifying supernatural tales I have read in many years—to the sardonic humour of "The Clever Mask" is to wonder how a single author could be responsible for such wildly diverse specimens. And the philosophical depth that Aronovitz shows in stories like "Quest for Sadness" and "The Exterminator" makes one realise that he is far more than a mere shudder-coiner; rather, he follows the best traditions of supernatural fiction in making us ponder our tenuous position in the universe by means of terror and wonder. And the story "Passive Passenger" confronts us with the quasi-science fictional horror of the computer and the Internet.

This collection's capstone is "Toll Booth," a 40,000-word novella that seamlessly accomplishes many things at once. It is simultaneously a poignant tale of teenagers' ability—or inability—to face a moral dilemma, an almost unbearable tale of physical gruesomeness that any splatterpunk writer would be proud of, and a subtle tale of supernatural haunting in the unlikeliest of places—a highway toll booth. From Le Fanu to Lovecraft to Ramsey Campbell to T. E. D. Klein, the novella has been the chosen venue of many masters of the supernatural to fuse the intensity of the short story with the character development usually possible only in the novel, and in "Toll Booth" Aronovitz has fully realised the aesthetic possibilities of this hybrid literary mode.

It would be unjust to consider Michael Aronovitz a novice, for some of his stories have appeared either in print on online more than fifteen years ago. His surehandedness in prose, in character portrayal, and in the pacing and development of the short story also mark him as a veteran. This may be his first book, but I venture to say that most readers will fervently hope it will not be his last.

—S. T. JOSHI

SEVEN DEADLY PLEASURES

How Bria Died

Bria jumped rope all alone
And now her eyes are made of stone
She calls for Mommie from the grave
And crawls out of the drain
She drags her jump rope on cement
And calls you from the heating vent
Turn a promise to a lie
And you will be the next to die

Ben Marcus didn't like it messy, but it was that time of the year. His feet hurt. A ninth-grade boy in the lunchroom had not liked the fact that the volunteer serving girl with the hairnet had given him only one taco off the cart, so he had chucked it on the floor. Ben had walked over, retrieved the plate, and stuck it back on the kid's portion of the long brown table. After a staredown, the young man had taken it, a bit too slowly, to a trash receptacle in the middle of the room by a white pillar with a picture of Frederick Douglass on it. Ben had followed. When the kid tossed in the garbage there was some up-splash that got on Ben's sleeve. He hated lunch duty.

It was wrap-around Thursday and Ben had his homeroom for the second time that day. His legs were crossed. He was sucking on one of the temple-tip earpieces of his wire-framed glasses, and he had one shoe off at the back heel. He was sort of dangling it on the end of his toe. It was the time of the year when the kids started jumping into their summer vacations a month early. Right around May 5th, the boys started untucking their dress shirts and removing their ties before the first bell. The girls somehow found ways to roll their blue skirts far above the knee and show off a bit of bra strap up top, even though the uniform requirement clearly stated that they were limited to bulky, formless, long-sleeved white blouses. Suddenly, they all wanted to follow each other consecutively to the bathrooms like a parade, and trick you into thinking you had the due dates wrong for their final papers. You had to keep up the game face all the way through June or they walked all over you.

Marcus knew the deal, and his reputation as the most popular teacher at The People First Charter School in downtown Philadelphia usually carried him through these tough final weeks. All year, he was strict when he had to be and bitingly sarcastic. He was known for pushing the envelope and talking about controversial things in class, like sex and death. He made kids laugh and he cursed frequently. He was an expert at finding a student's one vulnerable moment and filling that moment with insight. The girls liked him because he could out-dance the boys in verbal confrontation, and the boys liked him because he was so popular with the girls. The school was set up first grade through twelfth, and given that Ben was the head of tenth grade and the sole English teacher at that level, most kids at People First looked forward to high school. He always found a way to make it interesting, often taking rude interruptions and turning them into stories. Then he'd wrap it all back into the given lesson.

Last week Rahim Bethea had activated a talking SpongeBob key chain in the middle of a lecture about totalitarianism in *Animal Farm*. Ben had stopped, rode the laughter, and gone into a rant about how Sponge-Bob's friend Patrick, the pink starfish, was really a symbol for the penis. The class had roared, and many defended the character. Marcus walked the room, one side to the other. He started the kids chanting, "Patrick is a penis!" so loudly that Rollins, the security guard for the second floor, poked his head in. Ben immediately mouthed, *"Johnson?"* the name of the school's chief administrative officer. Rollins gave a quick shake of the head, *"No, she ain't coming down the hall,"* and gave the thumbs up sign. Ben turned back to the kids and said that the human cock was the symbolic foundation of every story ever made, including *Animal Farm*. A conversation started, hands in the air. Half the class claimed that the story was clearly about money, and the other half argued that the story did, in fact, leave females to the side like a void. It became a discussion about which lens the story was better to build from, economics and exchange or feminstic absence. Marcus wrote those headings on the board, and as a class they filled it in. Yes, he was that good.

His wife Kim was a paralegal and kept a nice garden behind their comfy twin in Havertown. She had long red hair with a streak of gray in it, and slight age parentheses at the corners of her mouth. She had crinkles at the edges of her eyes that Ben still liked to kiss softly. He knew she adored him, but it had become clear that she thought his style was far too risky and inappropriate for an educational system so quick to slap teachers with harsh consequences delivered by stern lawyers and passionate advocates. It wasn't an issue. Ben had stopped discussing his methods with her years ago.

He put his glasses back on and rolled up his sleeve. It had come undone down to the last fold at the cuff, and the taco stain was showing. Behind him were some compare-and-contrast papers pinned to the cork board, their edges curling. His desk had been moved to the side almost to the end of the whiteboard by the hall door, and he was trapped behind some desks that had been pushed all the way to the wooden cubbies, those overflowing with hoodies, sweaters, old papers, binders, and ratty textbooks that looked as if they had been run over by an army of sixteen wheelers.

The parts of speech and number tables competition was tomorrow. It was Mrs. Johnson's baby. People First was a back-to-basics school, and while the elementary grades were required to chant the parts of speech in English class every day, Mrs. Johnson had the upper school kids unveil complex dance routines based on those drills so as to showcase her method for guests at the end of the year. At the last staff meeting she had handed out an official memo that instructed teachers to set a week of class time aside for rehearsals. The mayor was there for the performance last May, along with a representative from the N.A.A.C.P. It was no joke, and neither was Mrs. Johnson.

The woman ran a tight ship and everyone was terrified of her. She was six foot three inches tall. She wore her hair back in a tight bun and had eyes that always looked wide and wrathful. She was handsome in the way statues were handsome, and walked the halls like a general. She believed in old-school discipline. So did Ben. His vision of how to administer that discipline, however, was a bit off-color at times, and he was thankful that what went on behind closed doors mostly stayed between himself and the kids.

Ben put up his hands and waved them.

"No!" he said. "Yo. Yo! Turn the music off for a minute."

The kids stopped their routine and shut off the boom box. Monique Hudson rolled her eyes. A few boys sat on desks off to the side and Joy Smith popped her gum. Ben worked his face to a mask of gentle concern. Actually he had the beginnings of a headache coming on and he looked forward to his prep coming up in thirteen minutes. On Thursdays he had two free periods in a row to end the day, and he planned on putting his head down in the lounge.

"Guys," he said, "this is the last day you have to practice before the competition, and you're bringing in new dance steps all of a sudden. It's asinine. First off, the girls coming down in rows and doing the shoulder shake thing was great. You trashed that for this puppet-puppeteer pop-lock thing, and it throws off the group. Everyone is just standing and watching Steve and Jerome. It's like a big donut with a hole in it. I also have to tell you that my 'B' class is doing the same kind of puppet thing and they have Rob and Tiny."

"They ain't shit," Steve said. His tie was off and his shirt was dirty. Marcus hoped Ms. Johnson didn't do a pop-in right now. Most of the kids were out of uniform code at the moment.

"The hell they're not," Ben said. "They've been doing that routine longer than you, and you know it. Also, Rob is so tall that Tiny really does look like a puppet when he stands in front and they mirror each other."

Jerome made his eyes go to half mast and curdled up an angry grin.

"That don't matter. They gay."

"If I wanted shit from you, Jerome, I would have squeezed your head," Ben answered.

Everyone laughed. Marcus looked over toward Malik Redson. He was in the far corner of the room listening to his iPod, juking his head a bit, shirt untucked, hiking boots up on the desk in front of him. Ben made the sign to take out the ear buds. Malik did so reluctantly.

"What?" he said.

"You're the show," Ben said. "Your routine comes in after the girls hop down in their rows. Once they are in position they make perfect backing for you with that cheerleader thing they do with the hand-claps. You have to dance."

Malik yawned, then licked his lips. The peach fuzz moustache he had going was an illusion. He was as grown as any man out on Broad Street. He had two kids already, and he worked nights at the BP gas station on Market Street. His solo routine was also the best in the school.

"The music sucks," he said. "And I also don't give a Goddamn."

"Fuck the music!" Ben snapped. All the little side whispers stopped. He stood up. He did not like losing. Not even a trivial moment like this one. "I am aware that you think this contest is retarded, I'm not fucking stupid. But when the whole upper school is watching and the other homerooms have a better show than you, it's going to matter."

"The fuck it is."

"The fuck it ain't!"

They stared at each other. Malik stood up. He paused. He took off the gold around his neck.

"All right, Mr. M. For you."

Laquanna Watford, a two-hundred-and-fifty-pound girl with the face of an angel and a reputation for street fighting, walked to the middle of the room. She smiled and her big caramel cheeks bunched up. There were huge sweat stains on her white blouse, under her arms, and at the love handles.

"Ready?" she said. "OK. Now make the square and let me see you bitches gallop."

The door opened. It was Mr. Rollins. Ben got himself out from behind the maze of chairs and approached. Rollins winked.

"Y'all got to sub next period," he said.

Ben sighed. Don't shoot the messenger.

"Where?"

"Sixth-grade science. First floor by the Cherry Street entrance, one room in."

Ben cursed softly. He hated middle school. They were too young to really understand his humor, and too old for intimidating with the drill sergeant stuff. He thanked Rollins and went over to his black bag. He looked in the emergency pocket and got out a piece of paper that was a bit yellowed, almost falling apart at the fold lines. Writing prompts, slightly edgy. Usually kept kids in their seats for at least a half hour.

The bell rang and he hurried out to the hallway. The worst thing he could do was show up late. Impression was everything, and a teacher waiting behind a desk with an angry scowl on his face usually filled the chairs rather quickly. A harried guy with a soft leather brief-case coming in after the fact and pleading for order usually led to kids spouting off irrelevant questions, fighting over seats, sneaking out to the hall, chucking rolled up pieces of paper at the trash can, and plead-ing for constant trips to the bathroom, guidance, or the nurse's office.

He got down to sixth-grade science with about two minutes to spare. About half the students were standing by their seats in gossip circles. Other kids were still commuting through the space, shoving a bit, snaking through to get to the rear door leading to the social studies room. Three boys were back by the lab tables toying with dead frogs in jars. There were larger containers with what looked like pig fetuses on the shelves, and a skeleton hanging in front of an anatomy chart. Ben walked over to the boys. The tall one with the little crud rings at the edges of his nostrils started to exclaim that it was the other boys who had been messing with the frogs.

"I don't care about that," Ben said. "Look, I need a favor."

All three looked skeptical, but they were listening. Ben bent his head in and whispered, therefore making them lean in and make a huddle.

"See, I know some are going to try to cut because I'm a sub. I don't want you guys to snitch or anything, but I need for you to get all the kids in their chairs for me."

He looked from one boy to the next.

"Of you three, who was the last one to get in trouble? And don't lie, cause I'll know it."

They snickered and pointed to the tall kid. Ben raised his eye-brows.

"Look," he said. "I'm meeting with Ms. Johnson after school. I run the tenth grade up there and she listens to me. A good word to her and a nice phone call home wouldn't hurt, now would it?"

The tall one blinked, then glanced to the other two.

"Well, go on," he said. "You heard the man." He gave both a shove and the three immediately split up to tell their classmates to sit the hell down. Within about a minute, Ben had nineteen middle schoolers in their chairs with their hands folded, and that was the way that he liked it. He got out his prompt sheet and introduced himself. He told the kids that they were going to play a game of write for a minute and listen for a minute as other kids read back their answers. The first prompt was "When is it all right to lie?"

The writing part went well, and during the answer phase he was pleased to get a fair response. Hands in the air led to discussions and little anecdotal stories. Most kids were OK with his rule of not calling out and only two kids broke the atmosphere to go to the bathroom. There were a couple of instances where he had to goad a light-skinned boy with a bushy afro set in two large puff balls not to lean back in his chair, but altogether it wasn't so bad.

Half the period was gone when it happened.

Ben was on the third prompt, "What is your favorite violent movie and why?" and the kids were drifting a bit. Most were writing, but the illusion of order had eroded at the edges. A boy with close-set eyes was struggling with the girl who sat next to him over a red see-through ruler. A girl wearing a too much makeup for her age was texting on a cell phone she thought was well hidden in her lap, and the boy one seat up and across from her was crossing his eyes and making bubbles with his spit. About five kids had suddenly gotten up to sharpen their pencils and Ben was getting aggravated. Suddenly he shouted at the top of his lungs,

"For God's sake, close that book!"

He was pointing at a girl in the front row who had slipped her English textbook up to the desk and was looking at pictures of the *Titanic*. Ben walked a step closer.

"Shut it now! You've unlocked the door! Now the spirit can get in! Do you want to freakin' die tonight?"

She clapped the book shut and put her hands up to her mouth. No one was fighting over rulers now, and all the chair legs were on the floor.

"Sit down," Ben said. "Now." Those waiting at the sharpener scurried to their desks. Ben was in control again. In the back of his mind a warning flare went up. Were these kids too young for this? Too late. A lead-in this good couldn't go to waste.

"Don't you guys know the story of Bria Patterson, the third-grade girl who died right here in this school?"

Kids shook their heads. Eyes were wide. Ben's body and voice reflected a controlled patience, the elder who bestowed cautious forgiveness for a catastrophic blunder just this one last time.

"Don't you know about second-to-last period and how you never, ever open a book that's not the subject being taught? That opens the archway from hell and lets her in through every opening, every heating vent, every window, and every door."

A boy raised his hand. He had a smirk on his face.

"Put your hand down," Ben said.

The hand went down, the kid's expression now flat. No one giggled. Once more, Ben considered what he was about to do. He had told this story up in the high school many times; it was tradition. Once, at the climax, Leah Bannister had been leaning against the wall by the door and someone in the hallway had bumped right into that spot. She had burst across the room laughing and screaming.

Well, risk none win none, right? He walked back to the center of the room. He had never started the Bria Patterson story with the idea of an open book being a doorway. That part was improvised. Quickly, he tried to think of how he could tie it back in, but he came up blank. Would the kids notice the foreshadowing he left dangling in the wind? Too late now.

"Bria was a third grader," he started. "She lived up in Kensington, by L and Erie. She had a single mom, and she went to school here the year it opened back in 1999. Bria was a white girl, and she always wore her blonde hair in two pigtails on the sides, like the little Swiss Miss character on the hot chocolate can. Now, Bria was known for two things. First, you know the little cross-ties you girls wear? You know how Mrs. Johnson yells and screams when you leave them unsnapped and casual? Well, Bria started that tradition. Ms. Johnson used to fight with her about it all the time; just ask your older brothers and sisters."

A girl sitting in the second row with expressive eyes, corn rows, and braids to one side said,

"What's the second thing she was known for, Mr. Marcus?"

He stepped forward, almost touching the desk of the boy sitting up front. He was so short that his feet didn't hit the floor. He had been slouching way down in his seat the whole period, but he was not slouching now. His hands were folded and his mouth was open. Ben folded his arms.

"Close your mouth, son. Flies are going to get in there." The kid snapped it shut and there was some nervous laughter. Ben stepped back to his power position in front of the white board.

"The other thing Bria was known for was her jump rope," he said. "You know how every morning in front of the Korean hoagie shop on the corner the girl's play Double Dutch until the first homeroom bell?"

Heads nodded.

"That was not Bria's thing. She didn't have many friends here, and the girls out on Cherry Street never invited her to jump with them. Bria jumped alone. She had a single girl's jump rope that she had probably owned since she was six. It had red painted handles, but they were rubbed down to the wood grains where her thumbs always went. Its cord was a dirty blue and white checkerboard pattern that was worn down to a thread where it always hit the street on each rotation. And Bria was never without her jump rope. It was like that kid with a blanket in that cartoon."

"Yes!" a heavy girl with big golden earrings exclaimed from the back row. "Like Linus from the Charlie Brown stories!"

"Right," Ben said. "But think about our skinny hallways. If Bria dragged that jump rope behind her everywhere she went, what do you think happened?"

The short boy in the front row dropped open his mouth once again. Then his hand shot into the air.

"Ooooh!" he said.

"Yes?"

"People be tripping over it!"

"Again, right," Ben said. "Other students were always stepping on her jump rope, and Bria was constantly arguing with them. She was always in trouble and a lot of people wondered if she was going to make it here."

Ben paused for effect.

"Then, on March 9th, Bria Patterson turned up missing."

Silence. No one moved, and Ben knew this was the critical point in the story. It was the place where anyone with a shred of common sense could poke a hole as wide as a highway into the logic of the plot. It was time to really sell here. Ben walked a few steps toward the Social Studies room. He stopped at the corner of the first row of desks and personalized the question to a dark-skinned boy with bucked teeth, black goggle glasses, and big pink albino splotches on the side of his neck.

"I know what you're thinking. If a girl was M.I.A., why didn't any-one hear about it?" He turned to the class. "It is a good question, and my answer is this. Ms. Johnson is connected. She has her own radio show and she talks to Oprah on a regular basis, I'm not kidding. She knows the mayor and the chief of police. The news only reports on people that don't have the money or the muscle to put a stop to the tattle, you see what I'm saying?"

"That's right," someone offered softly.

"And I'm telling you, when a powerful person like Ms. Johnson doesn't want any bad publicity, the news does not make it to the boob tube. Bank on it, folks. Ms. Johnson used her relationship with the po-lice to cover this up. They investigated it in secret and when they came up with no new leads, Bria's mom went crazy. She moved down South and no one heard from her again."

He went back across to the entrance door, opened it a crack, and looked out into the empty hall. He could see the students leaning to-ward him out of the corner of his eye. He turned and spoke in a low whisper.

"Right out here, by this door, is where the horror most likely started." A boy near the back of the room buried his head under crossed arms and a couple of girls had their hands drifting up toward their ears. Ben walked slowly back to the center of the room.

"You know the alcove at the top of the stairs out here, right? That's where the juniors have those four little rooms all to themselves that everybody is so jealous of. What you might not know is that this place used to be an old factory, and that space wasn't fixed up in the first year the school opened. Back in 1999 the alcove wasn't four neat little rooms, but one big, dark room. It was filled with busted pieces of drywall and boxes of old, moldy shipping papers. There were stacks of splintery wood and piles of twisted sheet metal all over the floor. The ceiling was a maze of decayed pipes and dangling wires. There was a padlock on the big black doors out front, and everyone knew it was against the rules to go near the alcove, let alone in it."

A few sets of eyes drifted upward. This was perfect. The alcove was right above them.

"Don't look, for God's sake!" Ben hissed.

A couple of girls made the high-pitched "eek" sound. A boy was biting his fingernails, and a girl who had been sneaking corn chips out of her book bag had all four fingers in her mouth up to the middle knuckles. Ben sauntered back to the teacher's desk and moved aside a plastic tray bin filled with lab reports about the Ecosystem. He leaned his butt against the edge and folded his arms.

"Oh, they questioned everybody," he said. "Just because the news didn't get a hold of it doesn't mean they didn't try to discover the truth of what happened to Bria Patterson. You know the security guards here have sections they're responsible for, right? You know that Mr. Rollins has the second-floor high school rooms. Nowadays, old Mr. Harvey has the landing, the stairway, and this bottom area all the way to the lunchroom, but back then, it was under the watch of a guy named Mr. Washington. He only had two suits and both were this neon lime green color. Everyone called him 'Frankenstein,' because he was so tall and goofy, and he walked kind of pigeon-toed like a zombie."

Ben stepped away from the desk and imitated the walk for a minute. A couple of kids broke wide smiles, but most were smart enough not to trust Ben 's short moment of humor. He stopped.

"Mr. Washington was the last to see Bria Patterson. He thought he saw her standing up by those black doors, on the landing in front of the alcove. When the police went up there, they saw that the lock on the black doors had been stolen."

Ben supported his elbow on his forearm and pointed his index finger straight up.

"They took in their flashlights and floodlights and chemistry cases, their ballistics materials, DNA sample packs, and high-powered magnifiers. They dusted the place stem to stern for fingerprints, and do you know what they found?" He stopped. He put his hands in his pockets and shoved them down so his shoulders hunched up a bit. "The most frightening thing in the world of crime. They found that the evidence was inconclusive."

"What's that mean?" a paper-thin Hispanic boy with long black hair and braces said. Ben stepped into the isle between desks. He could feel kids shying away a bit as he passed.

"It means that Bria Patterson was most probably killed up there in that alcove, and then her body was removed." He made a quick path back out from the desks and back over to the classroom door. He

21

pushed it open and it squeaked beautifully. "See the Cherry Street entrance door here?" he said. The kids stretched in their chairs for the view. Two in the back stood up, thought the better of it, then sat back down quickly. He let the door creep back closed. "Many believe the perpetrator got access through that door, and it is common agreement that the door was open in the first place because of some member of the faculty who wanted to go catch a smoke. There are only two entrances to the building. There's this door right out here and the main doors up by the secretaries. If you wanted to sneak a smoke would you go all the way up front past the secretaries, who talk too much anyway, and smoke your cig right out there on Broad Street where Ms. Johnson could see you through her office window? Hell no. The theory is that this teacher or janitor or TA or lunch assistant slipped out through the Cherry Street door, stuck a pencil or something in at the bottom so the thing couldn't auto-lock, and went back to the teacher's parking lot for a quick fix. By the way, don't smoke. It's very bad for you."

No one laughed and Ben didn't mind at all.

"And so Bria vanished. We all think someone got in through the Cherry Street door and we all know that Bria Patterson was standing up at the top of the landing. How the stranger approached her, whether she ran back into the dark alcove, how he killed her, and where he took her, all remain . . ."—he looked from one set of eyes to the next—"inconclusive."

A few kids let out their breath. Two girls looked at each other, leaned in to whisper something, and then glanced at Ben. They decided the better of it, and both straightened up. This was Ben's favorite moment in the story, because it was the false climax. They thought it was over. Now, it was going to get really personal.

"So," he said. "You know that in 1999 we only went up to ninth grade here, right? When I was hired in the year 2000 to teach the new tenth graders there had to be a space for us. That summer Ms. Johnson had construction men to fix up the alcove, and yes, you guessed it, my room was through those black doors, first room on the right. I was there for a year. Since then, you know that I have moved into 209, the eleventh graders inherited those four little rooms, and the seniors lucked out with the fancy extension they built up front. Still, I am telling you, I never want to teach in that alcove again. In fact, if Ms. Johnson told me to go back there right now I would quit. There is something evil up there. Still."

Ben had never quite had this sort of focus upon him, certainly not up in the high school. It was more than strict attention. It was a submission that was almost divine in nature. They were lambs. There was an incredible cross-current of fear and trust. They were locked in with him, frozen, terrified. But he was a teacher, right? It was his job to keep them safe, right? They would all laugh when it was over, wouldn't they?

For a brief moment Ben considered derailing. For a moment he pictured the girl in front of him, the one with the hearing aid and the wide forehead, she who possessed only four of her top adult teeth, huddled tonight under the sheets in a blind state of fear. Bria was under her bed, scratching up to grab an ankle. Bria was in her closet slowly creaking the door open, on the chair staring at her in the dark, head lolled to the side, a silhouette in the doorway, arms extended, hair still dripping the dirty water from the Schuylkill River where her body had been dumped.

He thought of more than a few angry parents calling Ms. Johnson and asking why some substitute was telling high school stories to sixth graders. He dropped the storytelling voice.

"Do you guys want me to stop?"

"No!" The chorus was nearly unanimous. Nearly. There were two girls in the back who had not responded, in addition to a boy in the end chair, second row, left. Was it apathy? He couldn't tell. And again, it was too late now to make a difference.

"I brought my stuff in a week before classes started," he continued. "I've never been much of a decorator, so I had my parts-of-speech posters, a couple of pictures of Langston Hughes, an exploded version of a Maya Angelou poem, my file case, you know. And just when I am tacking up the verb-adverb board, I thought there was something in the wall. Something moving. I mean, have you ever heard something so faint that thirty seconds after it happens you wonder whether you really heard anything at all?"

Heads nodded solemnly. He walked to the wall.

"I could have sworn it sounded like this."

He made his fingers into a claw shape and scratched his nails down the plastered surface. A few kids squirmed in their seats.

"So I run out into the hall like an idiot, because I thought someone was playing a joke on me. But it was just an empty hallway. Later, when I went down to get my lunch I asked one of the other teachers if they played practical jokes on people here. It was then that he told me about the alcove, about the cover-up, about Bria Patterson. I didn't believe him. But when I went back upstairs to finish setting up, there was something sitting on my desk. It was something that hadn't been there before. It was a girl's blue cross-tie, laying there unbuttoned."

Lots of uncomfortable shifting. A boy was clawing his nails into his cheeks, eyes wide as saucers. A girl with multicolored beads in her hair had her knees knocked together and her hands in a finger web around the front of them. She was rocking and mouthing something unintelligible.

"I didn't want to touch it. Even though my common sense knew someone must have just stuck it there for a joke, my heart knew there was something unholy about it. Like it had come from the grave."

Someone was making a high-pitched moan up in her throat, but Ben hardly heard it. He had to finish and he had to nail this one. Damn the consequences, damn the torpedoes, damn everything.

"Now, I know for a fact that each and every one of us has a low grade level of E.S.P. I'm not talking about dumb stuff like bending spoons and reading minds and making flower pots fly across the room, but think about this. Have you ever been at The Old Country Buffet, or even in our crummy lunchroom, and you could swear someone was staring at you from behind? And then you turn, and they *are* staring, for real, for real?"

Heads nodded.

"That's the way I felt. I turned quickly, and I could swear that I saw the edge of a blue uniform skirt whip past the doorway. Then there was a swishing noise out in the hall. Like a jump rope dragging across concrete. I walked over, turned the corner, and she was there. I could see through her. She had blonde pigtails, and no eyes, just dark spaces. There was a line of blood coming down the corner of her mouth, and she was running that jump rope back and forth across the floor. She was moaning in the voice of the dead,

"'Mommie . . .'"

Ben was dragging the imaginary rope, playing the part, eyes far off, mouth slightly ajar. Here was where the story always ended. He had never figured out a proper conclusion, and he normally broke character, smiled and said something like,

"C'mon, guys. I was just kidding. You didn't believe that crap, did you?"

He did not get the chance. The fire alarm went off. Loud. It was a buzzer that was so overwhelming down here it actually made his skin vibrate.

Girls screamed. Boys jumped up from their desks as if there were snakes crawling on the floor. Three girls in the back row stood up, hands pressed to their mouths. They were hyperventilating. A tall girl with white stockings had rushed to the corner of the room, pulled out her blue sweater at the neck, and buried her face in the void as if she was going to puke into it.

Ben was terrified. Surely, he would hear about this from Johnson.

"Guys!" he shouted over the numbing buzz. "Out through the Cherry Street door! Go ahead, it's just an alarm! And I was only kidding about the ghost . . ."

No one really heard. They scrambled for the door. A boy was crying and rubbing the base of his palm against his cheek in angry shame. A girl with thick glasses and blackheads clustered around her nose was furiously punching numbers into a cell phone. Oh, Ben was in a shit-storm now. He wondered if he would be fired. He hadn't looked at his résumé for years. This was bad. The last thing he wanted was to be thrown into the system and assigned to a regular Philadelphia public school. They doled out positions by seniority. Charter schools did not rack up points, and he would probably wind up at some ghetto middle school where the kids took apart your emergency phone on the first day, ran in and out of the classrooms like mental patients, and found out where your car was parked before it was time for recess. Ms. Johnson ran a tight ship here with this charter, and he was lucky to have the position he did. He had never really been in trouble with Johnson, but he heard she was merciless if she had a cause. He supposed he could beg. At least he had that.

He walked out into the sunshine and crossed Cherry Street. It was tennis weather. Construction was going on down Broad Street and you could hear a dull pounding complemented by a slightly sharper ratcheting noise associated with cranes and oiled chains being rolled onto big pulley wheels. The kids were gathered in front of a row house with empty planters in front of the dark windows. There were faded white age stains shadowed up the brick. A couple of his tenth graders had migrated over and were sitting on the concrete steps one residence down. Ben waved to them absently and started working his way between children, pleading his case. It was lame and awkward and necessary. He had to do some kind of damage control no matter how slipshod it appeared.

"I was only kidding, guys. You know that, right? . . . I made the whole thing up. I tell it to my tenth graders all the time. . . . It's a silly story, really. . . . Didn't you see that I had no ending for it? Yes. It was just a joke. No girl like that ever went here at all."

Mr. Rollins got on a megaphone.

"Drill's over. Move on to your last-period class."

Ben had not worked the group in its entirety. He had gotten to the hyperventilators, joked it up, and earned a round of cautious, weak smiles. It turned out that the girl with the blackheads was simply supposed to call her mother at the end of seventh period every day and she had almost forgotten. Big relief there. Still, he hadn't made it to the crying boy or the tall girl who'd almost vomited into her sweater. There were a lot of loose ends here.

Ben went back inside with his head hung down.

This time he might have actually blown it.

His homeroom was up next. The brown tables were folded up and pushed to the back left corner of the lunchroom. There were rows of chairs set up in front of the steam table and the student council had put up crêpe paper streamers. There were some new plants suspended from the drop ceiling, and old Jake had hooked up a sound system. Ms. Newman's homeroom had just completed an oldies thing featuring the Electric Slide that the students laughed at and Ms. Johnson obviously preferred. A guy pretty high up on the food chain at Temple University sat with her at the judge's table, along with a man wearing thin rectangular dark glasses, close-cropped sideburns, and a long black overcoat.

Johnson had not called Ben in to the office today, thank God. He knew there was an unspoken code in the high school not to snitch about the wild stuff he pulled up there, but he had not expected the sixth graders to be so discreet. It had taken all his will power not to tell Kim about it like a confession when he got home yesterday, and he had woken in a cold sweat three times during the night. But he was pretty sure by now that everything was going to be all right. Ms. Johnson did not bide her time when she had to get something off her plate, so no news at this point in the day was certainly good news.

Laquanna walked to the center of the space, and the other girls followed. There was a hush. The boys filtered in and took positions between. Malik walked to the front, and there was a rousing cheer speckled by only a few boos from the small crew of guys from the "C" section that he had beaten in a parking lot rap battle last week. He looked over at Jake, and the music blasted on. The kids exploded in movement, and Ben grooved a bit where he stood. He was going to miss this homeroom next year. They had been a lot of fun.

Someone was pulling his sleeve. He looked down. It was a girl from the elementary school, short, probably fourth or fifth grade, long hair curled in sausage shapes and pulled back by a pink satin ribbon tied in a floppy bow. Her eyes were wide with terror.

"What?" he said. "What's wrong?" He had to nearly shout to be heard over the music.

The girl said something and he could not make it out. He leaned down, and her breath came hot in his ear.

"It's the dead girl. She's in the bathroom."

Ben pulled back a bit and raised his eyebrows.

"What?"

She made her lips frame the words in the deliberate manner one used when speaking to the slow or the deaf.

"Our teacher went out to make copies on another floor. Help us. It's the dead girl. She's in one of the stalls moaning, *Mommie.*"

Ben pushed past her and marched out of the lunchroom. The music was cut to a haunt the minute he turned the corner, and he felt his face going hot. This was *just* what he needed. Some jackass sixth grader squatting up on the toilet seat so you couldn't see her feet, then groaning "Mommie" like a wounded doorbell when a younger kid tried to take a piss. Wasn't this always the way of things? He was so sure he had dodged a bullet, and now in this strange backlash, he was still going to get nailed. He could picture the meeting right now, the teachers all at their tables looking innocently at each other, Johnson up at the podium.

"It has come to my attention that some middle school children have been frightening the elementary school students in the bathroom. Evidently, a story about an abducted third grader has been going around the school, and I would like to know where this started. From the bits and pieces I have heard, the story seems rather sophisticated for a student. I want to know what teacher was involved with this. I want that teacher to come forward and take responsibility for . . ."

You know the drill.

Ben reached the end of the hall and made the quick left. He paused, but only for a bare second. He had never been in the girl's bathroom. He walked through the archway (there were no doors for bathrooms at People First), and before passing the brown steel divider that blocked the sightline, he called out,

"Teacher coming in! Excuse me! I apologize!"

The bathroom was empty. Besides the strange lack of urinals to the left, it was the same as most institutional boys' rooms. Brown tiled floor, drain grate in the center surrounded by a shallow puddle of water in a shape that vaguely resembled Texas. There was a row of sinks and each basin had a mirror above it, the reflective material more like tin foil than glass so as to avoid cracking under the variety of incidents that were often far from delicate. The soap dispensers each had spots of blood-orange residue pooled below on the sink tops where quick hands had missed, and only two had been converted to the newer white units that rationed out foam by palm activation. There was a Fort James paper towel dispenser by the entrance just above an industrial plastic yellow trash can surrounded by the damp, crumpled sheets that had been poorly tossed. There were four stalls, the first three standard issue, and the last sectioned off in its own private area that spanned the width of the space. All three of the doors on the regular stalls were open, but barely. It seemed the floor was pitched in a way that kept them resting an inch or two in off the lock plates. The handicapped door was half ajar.

Ben pushed open the door of the first stall with the middle knuckle of his index finger. Vacant. The bowl was unflushed from what looked like nine or ten sittings, all number one thank God for small favors, and on the wall someone had written, "Shaneeka sucks monkey nuts." Stall number two was in the same relative condition, and number three, of course, was filled with a deposit Ben could not believe someone had the guts to leave out on the surface of this earth. He backed out, breathed in deep, held it, shouldered into the thin stall, and reached for the flusher with the sole of his shoe. When it whooshed down, he pulled back quickly. These institutional mechanisms were sometimes loaded with such strong jets that they kicked up a bit of backsplash off the suction.

After the rush of the initial violent whirlpool, there was that hollow, pipe-like refilling sound, and just underneath it Ben heard a voice. From the handicapped stall. It sounded as if it was in tow just beneath the running water, an echo, a faint ringing. It sounded like a girl's voice. Before he could really make out words, it blended with the receding sounds and thinned out to silence.

Ben walked into the handicapped stall. There was a runner bar along the wall, another behind the toilet, a private sink, and a separate towel dispenser. To the right there was also one of those tinfoil mirrors, and he saw something move in it. His breath caught in his throat. It was blue, and it had seemed to shoot through the mirror like liquid through a distorted syringe. He moved closer to investigate, and sighed. It was his shirt, picked up in the light and worked through the microscopic steel grooves in an hourglass effect. How did the girls adjust their makeup with these funhouse things? The boys had them too, but he thought the female breed would have demanded better. Personally, he always used the faculty lounge up front by Johnson's office. It was worth the walk.

The hair on the back of his neck was up.

He turned.

There was a hand coming out of the toilet. The seat was up and there was a hand gripping the rim.

Ben grit his teeth and smiled, despite the knocking his heart was still making up in his ears. It was one of those dollar store, plastic dead hands you could affix to door rims and bed edges. So here was the dead girl. Ha ha.

He levered down a fistful of towels and approached. The artwork wasn't even good on this thing. The sores had red spots half covering the indentations and spilling over about a quarter of an inch. Probably a misaligned factory stamp. The nail polish on the scabby fingers had already flaked partly off, and at the edge of the wrist, the press that had molded the rubber most probably had a small void, since there were two renegade nodules sticking off that needed to be pruned. Ben reached down to pluck it off the rim and stopped.

There was writing behind the toilet. It was written faintly on the wall tile in the spidery, uneven, block letter style of a young child,

"Turn a promise to a lie, and you will be the next to die."

"Fuck," he muttered. The written message had suddenly reminded him of a missed obligation. He grabbed the joke toy, held it off to the side a bit, and walked it out of the stall. His feet made hollow echoes across the floor. He had forgotten to put in a good word for the boy who had been looking at the dead frogs. It would have taken two seconds. He tossed the rubber toy into the yellow bin and sighed. His word was his bond.

Something splashed in the handicapped toilet.

Ben put his fists to his sides and stalked back to the stall. Enough already. He stopped when he turned the corner of the doorway.

There were two hands gripping the rim of the bowl as if reaching up from deep within it, palms down, fingers over the edges. They were girl hands, rotten and burst at the knuckles with yellow-graying bone sticking through. The skin was mottled, water-shriveled, and blue. The fingers released, and the forearms slipped back into the water, the hands following, down to the fingertips. Gone. There was a faint gasp, like the exit of breath.

Ben approached the toilet. "I did not just see that," he said to himself. His legs were numb, his mouth ajar. There was a brown ring at the surface edge of the water, and there was still the hint of faint ripples dancing above the submerged, funneled pipe orifice.

Something from the drain-hole exploded.

Ben saw a flash of dirty blue and white checkerboard just before it whipped across the bridge of his nose. The cold toilet water that sprayed him in the face was eclipsed by the sharp snap of pain. His glasses flew off to skid along the tile into the next stall. Ben's left eye had been struck bald and it was squeezed shut. The other was half open in a squint, and through the blur he saw the elongated jump rope whirling mad figure eights, its alleged wooden handles still buried in the depths of the drain. Dirty water snapped to the sides, spattering the dull yellow concrete block wall and the steel divider to the left. Ben put up his hands in a defensive posture, but the rope was quicker. It snaked out and hooked him at the back of the neck.

It spun mad spaghetti twirls and peppered drain water up his nose. He clawed his hands at the front of his neck and couldn't get his fingers under. The taste in his mouth was hot copper. There was a yank, and he was brought a foot closer and a yard lower. He kept his feet, but he was losing this tug of war.

Black spots danced in front of his eyes, and his lungs started screaming for air. He tried rearing back, but the pull was too great. He opened his eyes for the last time, and saw the toilet bowl rush at his face. And the last thought Ben had on the face of this earth was that the promise he had broken was far more fundamental than a forgotten bribe to a kid who was messing around with a dead frog in a jar.

The Clever Mask

I went downstairs for a cup of coffee and the Grim Reaper was sitting in my living room.

"Good morning," he said. His voice was gravel. He had bald, red eyeballs set in exposed muscle. He had lips, but they were diseased pieces of blackened flesh that dangled over his skull teeth. I snatched a quick glance to the stairs.

"Don't worry," he said. "She cannot hear us."

Thank God for small favors. Still, I was not going to take any chances. I sat down slowly, so as to make as little sound as possible. I could hear Tina moving around up there from bureau to closet. He folded his bony hands together.

"Still no talkie-talk? What a pity. I like a little conversation before I induce the coronary, or initiate the stove oil-fire that gets away, or cause the accident with the air conditioner that falls off the high shelf in the shed when you try to yank out the snow shovel jammed next to it." He sat forward. "For you, I was thinking of maybe an accident with glass! I was thinking about that picture window there, a fall, a shattering, and a decapitation. I could have Tina come down and find your body in spasm, hands still grabbing blindly at the jagged edges, your head, by God this is poetic, your head still held on by a single strand of neck tissue! What do you think?"

Sweat burst a bit on my upper lip. Just before this thing took over my living room, I had been thinking about the white, wooden blinds covering the picture window. The thin, cylindrical bar that you twisted to open and shut the blinds never stayed on the S-hook anymore. The metal had worn outward a bit from the continuous use, and the bar kept popping off. On a whim, I had been thinking about grabbing the pliers Tina had left by the stereo, climbing onto the back of the sofa, and giving the S-hook a squeeze. Why hadn't I done it over the weekend, or the last, or the one before that? Why did I decide to do it twenty minutes before I had to leave for work? A little, personal mystery. I guess I had always been impulsive that way.

"Impulsive guys die too, Joe," he said. "So, what will it be? Many of my clients like to have a say in their method of execution. It's in the contract that I ask and get some sort of response."

How did he know I was just thinking about my own impulsiveness? I thought. Tina dropped something upstairs, and I heard a quaint, "Oh shit!" I stayed where I was. I didn't think I was going crazy, and I was not foolish enough to wonder if I was dreaming. While asleep, one's dream could be mistaken for reality, but I had enough common sense to know it didn't work the other way around. Was I hallucinating? If so, this was one hell of a detailed manifestation. The Reaper pointed across the marble table that sat between us.

"I knew you were considering your own impulsiveness because I can hear everything you think the second you think it, Joe. Your little honey dropped the tweezers back into the bottom of the tin tangled up with the hairbrush, the two combs, the nail file, the clippers, and the three scissors that are too dull to keep in the kitchen drawer anymore. That's why she just swore. You're not crazy, you are not dreaming, and you are not hallucinating. That which is presently before you has too much vivid order for that, and you know it. Now stop thinking around me and think directly to me. It will help expedite things. I do have other calls to make."

"So, you can read my thoughts," I said. Tina did not respond, and a brush of new fear whispered up my spine. She should have heard me. It was a small row house. The Reaper clapped his hands together.

"Joy!" he said. "Actual discussion! My creation! The big lie! Go ahead, entertain me! Tell me you are too young to die even though you know deep down that when it is your time, it is simply your time! Say that you don't fear me when you are actually terrified!"

"What's the point?" I said. From beneath his cloak, the Reaper produced a long-handled sickle. He pushed himself up to a standing position and brought the weapon down with a kingly bang.

"Because I am the provider of your shield, and I like to see my work in action once in a while!" He paused, and leaned in a bit. "Don't you see? I am the creator of the mask. Without it, the human race would annihilate itself in a matter of days. Call it a loan. I supply your species with this safety device, this ability to screen, refine, and purify before going verbal so to speak. In return, I take lives at random. That's the deal. On the downside, I am the artist who so briefly gets to witness his product first hand because he must inevitably erase his subjects. It is life's ultimate irony."

"Then take back the mask."

"What did you just say to me?"

"Take it," I said. "I have nothing to hide."

He cocked his head.

"You reject my art? You dare to insult me?"

"Yes."

"You reject the gift I have given you? You reject the very essence of personal mastery?"

"Yes," I said. *And fuck you,* I thought for good measure.

His grin got savage and the air tingled. He pressed in across the table within an inch of my face, and I was overcome by an odor that drew up images of dead flowers strewn before gravestones under a pale moon. My head spun, and he spoke a last time.

"I always like a good wager, so survive this and your life shall be spared. Speak the truth for two short hours."

Then he was gone.

It was 8:00 A.M.

With every second that passed by, the "Reaper incident" dulled and lost potency. The bubbling sound indicated that the coffeemaker was on its last cycle, next to hiss the last of its water through in a thin stream. If there was any sound that could really ground you, that was it. I got down two clay cups, did the sweeteners, and added the half-and-half with the pretty Native American squaw on the carton. A bird chirped somewhere, but it wasn't that distinct sound cardinals made when spring had truly arrived.

I turned to the window and looked into the back alley. The neat checkerboard presentation of windows and brick face was betrayed at the bottom by small pockets of trash that had blown up and settled in various areas of fencing. Of course, everyone had a different idea of what color a garage door should be and how long between paint jobs was appropriate. Wires crisscrossed each other up and down the row, and there was laundry hanging off some of them. The family across the way had left their mongrel dog out all night, and he was circling his pen with his gray tongue hanging out. He sensed me, pawed up on the fence, and barked hoarsely. We really had to get out of the city.

I poured the coffees and strode back through the living room. Potted coleus and fern stood like handsome soldiers beside the wall unit stacked with television, cable box, DVD player, and state-of-the-art audio system. The sun coming through the blinds made glare bars across my Monets hanging on the east wall. From upstairs Tina's voice tinkled like those high piano keys little girls trilled in the drawing rooms of movies about the old country.

"Honey, we need toilet paper up here!"

The hairdryer kicked on. I switched the coffees to one hand, opened the downstairs closet, and snagged a roll.

"We could have used a jumbo pack of these at the office yesterday," I thought with a smirk. "The old man must have shit himself at the close of trade when he saw my profit and loss at eight hundred and ninety thousand in the black."

Then again, he probably thought it pretty much par for the course by now. After my third interview and the ceremonial handshake nine months ago, he'd said they hired me at Rollins and Howell Financial because I was the most serious young man they had ever met. They thought I was the dependable young mule they could keep in the wings, and what they got was a thoroughbred that shot out of the gate. They had planned a straight and narrow path for me, and now pretty much scrambled to get out of my way. I was a risk taker with an incredible poker face. I had a great sense of humor, but kept it to myself. I loved being an enigma, time and again dashing those lingering impressions of conservative stoicism with broad and sweeping strokes of precariousness behind closed doors. I always went long, and I never asked permission. I almost always won, and didn't even smile until I got home.

Tina called me an "old soul." Still, every oyster had to have a pearl to give up once in awhile. I did confide in her. I told her my dreams, confessed my insecurities, shared occasional frustrations, admitted the different angles and depths of my love for her. I preferred to do that in bed, under the covers with the lights off. I liked the warming effect of her cheek to my bare chest, and the hollow of my neck. I liked her lit-tle rosebud lips and the way she dryly brushed them along my jaw line. I cherished those intimate exchanges, breath mingled with breath. Whispers.

"Baby, I love ya!" I called out loud while climbing the stairs.

The hairdryer stopped.

"What did you say, Mookie?"

I smiled. We were still in the stage of little pet names in private. It started as a joke and we fell into the habit. It was cute for now, and it would pass. That was OK too. As long as we didn't turn into a quarrel-ing couple like *her* parents.

"I said I love ya! Whoops!"

"What?"

"My foot hit the base of the top step and I almost dropped the coffee."

She snickered.

"Klutz! You should work out or something."

"Cunt! If you keep sneaking handfuls of the Nestlé's morsels that are only supposed to be for baking, you're going to end up with a bitch-belly like your mother."

Whoa!

I straightened up and a hot dash of coffee spattered my wrist.

The vision was real!

And I was lucky. The ugly words had escaped under my breath just after Tina turned the hairdryer back on. Just. I stumbled into the bed-room and ditched the clay cups. Prickly sweat beads stood up on my scalp.

It was all real!

There was no filter. There was simply the primal brainwork here, immediately spit forth like sewage before it could be transformed into something witty.

I plucked a pack of Marlboro Lights off the bedside end table, stuck a smoke between my teeth, and absently patted my chest for a lighter. I was partly dressed, no shirt. My eyes did an erratic, bouncy search across the room and I made myself slow the glance down. On the bureau sat "the box" which Tina had conveniently forgotten to stow in the basement, and I snatched it down to dig through.

It was her old retro Gothic stuff, safety pin earrings, studded wrist-lets, spiked ankle bands, and junk jewels. It was her childhood hope chest, sweet nostalgic reminders of the fashion she sported long before I introduced myself, showed her the comforts of the corporate world, romanced her, swept her off her feet, and made her Mrs. Joe Kagan. The skull and crossbones lighter was near the bottom and I drew it out to thumb the small roller. The flame blew out before I could light up and I cupped my palm against the current of the ceiling fan. I popped it to life and took a deep drag.

"So," Tina said.

I jerked at the sound and she didn't notice. She was on her way to the closet to switch blouses for the umpteenth time, and she twisted her straight, jet-black hair up into a temporary bun. She scanned the overstuffed hanger-rack, shook her head, and reached for the small bottle sitting next to her pile of beret hats on the back shelf. She turned, pursed her lips, sprayed a bit of perfume into the air, walked into it, and spoke as if the conversation from last night had never been interrupted by seven hours of sleep.

"So, hon, if the kids play ball on the lawn tonight, it's your turn to kick 'em off, right?"

It was her slickest game. If not fully gratified, Tina would relent-lessly return to a subject until the answer brought full satisfaction.

"We discussed this last night," I said. She blinked thick lashes.

"Yes, but we did not conclude. They're always in our garden to use my flowering fig for first base. When I asked them to leave yesterday that older boy called me the 'C' word while his mother stood in her doorway across the street with a smirk on her face. It's not fair, and I think you should get involved."

"Fuck your flowering fig," I said. "That woman across the street happens to be married to the biggest, meanest-looking motherfucker I've ever seen and I don't relish the thought of pissing him off."

Tina's arms flew up to cross before her chest and my heart sank. Straight confrontation made for poor politics and the issue was tricky, especially since she had a good point. Our neighborhood was the far-thest borough northeast of town that still claimed an urban zip code. And it was littered with children, mainly two tribes. The nine-year-olds were the wild street rats who kept the avenue swarming with the violence of their Nerf bow and arrows, rubber dart pistols, and Super Soakers. Still, the real problem was the twelve-year-olds, that cruel clan that was quick to make captains and choose up sides. Whether it was a quick round of roughhouse, dodge ball, or nine-inning baseball played with an aluminum youth bat and duct-taped tennis ball, they claimed any section of unfenced property as prized, personal domain. Real champs. They swore like sailors, *fucking spastic, you suck!*, argued like lawyers, and slid hard and often into Tina's flowering fig.

"Stop playing the isolationist," she said. "I need your support in this because when I do it alone, I come off as the neighborhood witch." She bent to tug her black stockings and the smooth line of her cleavage jumped out to say hello.

"I want you now, baby," I said. "Shut your damned trap and bend over so I can do the nasty." As soon as it was out I clapped my hand over my mouth, but she read the motion as an act of sarcasm. She jerked up straight.

"I'm not your slut, Joe. And don't change the subject. Our life together does not just revolve around you."

"The hell it doesn't! Do you really think that the chump change you make at the boutique even comes close to—"

"Why, you slug," she said. Her eyes got weepy for a moment, but she fought it off with a quick sniff. I used the pause to the best of my ability.

"Honey! I made a bet with the Grim Reaper this morning and believe me, I'll be all right by mid-morning, please!" Her "hurt" look went ugly.

"Stop fucking with me."

"I'm not kidding! It's a curse! I just need two hours to get myself—"

She put her hands on her hips, and I jumped tracks.

"—that blouse makes your arms look fat, you pig."

Her eyes flicked to high beam.

"Fuck you, asshole!" She brushed past in a huff. "Today, I'll take the bus and the subway."

There it was. I had gone from "Mookie" to "Joe" to "asshole" in the space of two minutes. The room still held the muffled ring of hot words and Tina's voice wafted up the stairs just before the slam of the door.

"And don't chase me down the street, either! It would give our neighbors something else to laugh at, you bastard!"

I let her go. As badly as I felt about it all, it was clear that this would have to be patched up later over dinner and at the bottom of a bottle of fine burgundy. Wasn't there a really cool Italian place on Berkley that had waiters who played violins at the table? Yes, at the office I would make the reservation, order flowers, and maybe pick up a new piece of jewelry to sneak onto her cloth napkin. I reached into the closet for my double-breasted three-piece and frowned.

I could not go to work in this condition.

Still, I had to. Today, the unemployment report on which I had taken a few risky investment positions was being released. The old man knew it and I was under strict obligation to make an appearance.

"On the first Friday of each month you are to be here when the economic releases come across that news wire service. That means nose to the computer by 8:30 A.M., Eastern time, no exceptions. Pull a no-show, and we will do the rough and tumble in my office like you have never seen! I only want you to show you care."

But I had to stay home nonetheless, even though I had actually seen the old man issue a pink slip over a principle. If he was awarded my company in this condition, I would be jobless and blacklisted by 9:07. At 10:01 with the curse lifted, it would be easy to rush in with some kind of story to explain my tardiness.

I reached for the phone by the reading lamp and stopped before my hand touched the plastic. A sudden vision of the receptionist, Jessica McQuade, filled my head, and I drew my fingers back as if I'd been burned.

Jessie was a strawberry blonde who loved to show off her pretty legs. Two years ago she was a cheerleader for the Philadelphia Soul. Now, she ran the message center at Rollins and Howell in a blur of sheer blouses and short, tight skirts. She never wore panty hose, and it was a special pleasure to watch her kick off a heel, cross knee over knee, and massage her ankle while taking a call.

I stared at the phone and cursed my newfound inability to communicate. What could I trust myself to say or keep hidden? What words would I have for good old Jess when she answered my call?

Hi, Jess, I won't be in until 10:00, but while I've got you on the horn let's talk about the X-rated side of my imagination that has me climbing you like a tree.

I began to pace the floor. In desperation, I tried to figure a way to twist truths without telling lies and felt like an idiot locked in a cage with Rubic's Cube. On my second pass across the room I stubbed my toe on the bed leg and the small spurt of pain brought an idea along with it. I grabbed the receiver and dialed the office.

Jessie picked up the line and said, "Rollins and Howell."

I reared back and kicked the bedpost, hard, barefoot, and arch first. A bright bolt of pain rocketed up to my knee and I yelped.

"Hello?" she said.

"This is Joe Kagan," I said through clenched teeth. "I won't be in, and I just cracked my foot on the bedpost."

"Oh Lordy!" she said.

I hung up before my thoughts could turn from the pain in the foreground. I fell to the floor wincing and laughing, a private victory that meant nothing to no one.

The phone rang back at me like a dark intruder pinging a black bell. I stared at the device in dumb horror and thanked my lucky stars for answering machines. I got up and limped to the hallway to sneak in a listen. After the fourth ring the machine clicked on and I heard the odd, displaced sound of my own voice taped from downstairs.

"Hello. This is the butler. Joseph and Tina are on the yacht right now, but if you must leave a message, I'll hop in my dinghy and get it to them. Thank you."

There was a beep and I heard a blast of traffic through scrambled voices, with a pneumatic jackhammer deep in the background.

"Joe? Oh God, Joe, please pick up!"

It was Tina. She was crying. I rushed back for the bedroom phone and jerked it to my ear.

"Tina! What's wrong? Where are you?"

There was a long sigh and I could picture her looking at the sky, thanking the powers of heaven for finding me at home.

"Joe, honey. I'm at a pay phone. A couple of guys—"

A big truck or something roared past.

"Hold on!" I shouted. "I can't hear you! What the hell did you say?"

The large vehicle faded out and her voice came back in a gush.

"Two guys jumped me and stole my purse! I fought them, Joe, I tried but the big one knocked me down and they got everything. Credit cards, bank card, all my money, my cell."

"Then how did you make this call? You can't call collect to an answering machine! Why haven't you called the police? Why—"

"Because I've memorized our calling card number and I want to get out of here before Christmas!" She erupted into a fresh rush of tears and hiccups. "Why are you grilling me? I'm scared, Joe."

I looked at my feet.

"Tina, I love you so much. I want you to know that."

"I don't need you to love me right now. I need you to come and get me."

"Where are you?"

There was a pause.

"Well, there's a crab shack on the corner, a check cashing store next to a tattoo parlor, and a beauty shop called *Slick Divas*."

"Look for a street sign, Tina."

There was a clunk, and I knew that in defiance Tina had dropped the phone to go take a better look. My mind's eye could see the stained and chipped receiver swinging on its metal cord like a dead thing on a rope.

"Sixth and London," she said.

It was the worst section of the city, a war zone smack in the middle of the fastest route to the downtown business district. Together, we drove down Fifth, a block over, each day with our windows shut and doors locked. And now, Tina was trapped, out in the open, exposed to the wolves. She had probably been mugged on the short walk between the bus stop and the overhead subway trestle. The animals.

"I'll be right there," I said. "Keep an eye out for the car."

On the telephone's quick trip from my ear to its holder, I heard Tina plead a last word.

"Hurry."

*   *   *

The streets of my neighborhood flew past as I cheated one yellow light after another. Peripherally, I could feel the sun rays spangle across the Kennedy Middle School's football field and glint off the steel goal posts closest to the road. To the right was a blur of stores and lots that led to the cluster of buildings before Fifth Street, then the Blockbuster Video, Keystone Beer Distributor, and Rosenburg's Auto Tags. I cracked the window, lit a cigarette, and registered in some deep and far-off place that I really had to quit these foul things.

After the quick right on Fifth the properties withered and the buildings closed in on each other. Long zigzagged cracks in the sidewalks sprouted gnarled clumps of weeds, street signs were bent at odd angles, and plywood-covered doorways wore layers of unintelligible graffiti. I took my eyes off the road for a moment to flick an ash and almost slammed an old woman jaywalking a group of young girls to the Flemmings Ballet School on the far corner. I screeched my brakes and she glanced back at me with a sour look of distaste. I rolled down my window.

"Hey, pelican face," I said. "Next time, move your fat, wrinkled ass! Don't you have a duty to die or something?"

There was a spatter of laughter from the children and I drove on feeling lower than dirt.

I hurtled down the one-way, straight into the side of town most broken-down. Garbage bags billowed from the paneless windows of dirty tenements. The wind had knocked over a few recycling bins, and they barrel-rolled at the front of an alley like cars on a short-circuited Tilt-a-Whirl ride. Across the street, a pit-bull on a chain gnashed and slammed against a rusted, diamond-link fence.

I cursed out loud.

A block ahead I could see the two hookers that worked the corner of Fifth and Walsh. Tina and I passed the pair every day and had slowly numbed ourselves to them, made the whole thing into a joke. We even gave them nicknames. Thelma and Louise.

Today, Thelma had on her Friday colors, black mini and heels with both legs sporting a roadmap of purple bruises. Louise, the stockier one with fire-red hair hanging in dreads, boasted yellow hot pants and a matching bikini top. The girls looked feisty. They were in the middle of the street prepared to block traffic.

I drove between them just fast enough to make them shove over, and couldn't help but forfeit a grin.

They howled.

"Look at him with the piss-face laughing," Thelma said.

"Where's the little woman?" Louise said. "Come back here, baby. Ain't there something you want to ask me?"

I slammed on the brakes. I couldn't help it. I threw the car into reverse and squealed backward to a halt. Thelma approached, and the car behind me honked long and loud.

"Go around, muthafuckah," she shouted. "This is business!" He put on his signal and squeezed around like a good little boy.

"Hey there, sugar," she said into my face, arms folded on the lower window rim. Her breath stank of peppermint Dentyne and stale gin.

"There's something I always wanted to know," I said. "How much for what?"

She grinned brown, crooked teeth.

"I got two programs, sweet thing. Regular and High Octane."

"What's Regular?"

"For a hundred dollars we go to a room above the Y across the street. I light a cigarette and put it in the ash tray. Then you get to possess this body like the Devil himself, but when the smoke gets down to the filter, your time be over."

"And what's High Octane?"

She reached in and slipped a hand under my lapel to rub my chest.

"Not recommended for a little punk like you. The only thing left would be your belt buckle and a puddle of sweat."

There was a clunking sound and my car bowed down in front. It was Louise, crawling on all fours up the hood. She slipped down a strap and popped out her breast.

Thelma's hand became a strange shape under my suit jacket, and she made a play at stealing the gold Cross pen in my pocket.

"Hey!" I said. I pressed the heel of my hand to her forehead and pushed. She fell backward on shaky heels and landed butt to the asphalt. I hit the gas and Louise smacked the glass cheek-first before rolling off to the right. I burned rubber and eyed the rearview. Thelma was in the street shouting obscenities. Louise was looking for something to throw. I sped away as if the hounds of Satan were snapping at my tires.

Something was burning. It was the smell of tobacco and smoking fiber. I had dropped my lit cigarette during the scuffle and something was burning and my crotch was on fire!

I spun the wheel to the left and peeled curbside behind an old abandoned Buick that had been torched and picked clean of just about everything but the steel skeleton. I pushed open the door and scrambled to the street where the warm wind kicked up angry whirlwinds of newspaper, scraps, and plastic debris. I rubbed off my fly and bent in to brush the hot ash off the seat.

I heard laughter. I shut off the engine, backed out, and turned to a sea of eyes from across the sidewalk.

It was a welfare line, a smorgasbord of all the races and creeds that defined our own wretched refuse. There was a lot of flannel, cheap sneakers and soiled T-shirts covering pot bellies. Course sprouts of facial hairs grew from wart bubbles and the men looked even worse. My face brightened.

"Hi!" I said. At some deeper, more intellectual level, my brain was telling me not to do this, but that rational captain of industry was locked in a dark office in the back of the building somewhere. The mad elves were loose in the factory now, yanking the gear knobs, bending the crankshafts, pounding on the buttons, and pinning all the meters.

I stepped away from the car and walked toward my rapt audience. The intersection of Sixth and London was just one city block to my right.

"I just want to know how my employees are doing," I said. I unbuttoned my blazer and put my knuckles on my hips. "I pay taxes so in a sense you all work for me."

No one spoke back. They did not even speak to each other. And no one moved. They didn't want to lose their places in line. Yet.

I began to walk up and down their flank.

"Do you know who I am? I'm Joe Kagan. I trade stocks. I pull short or go long on the unemployment figures. Do you know what that means?" I slapped my hand to my forehead. "It means we make money off you whether you're working or not. And lately, it's been pretty easy to predict, let me tell ya."

"Shut up," someone said.

"Yeah," someone answered.

That broke the line. They began to converge in a follow-the-leader domino effect; I was surrounded. Rough hands grabbed and pinned back my arms. There were shouts and hoots. A thin, scarecrow bag lady type wiped her nose, licked the back of her hand, and spat on my headlights. A wiry dude wearing a back turned Mets cap grabbed a saw horse that had "POLICE" stenciled up the supports. He struggled it over to a blue dumpster and swung it around in an arc. There was a splintery crack and he was left with a busted two-by-four that read "LICE." I struggled and went nowhere.

"So this is how it is?" I said. "Gang up on the rich kid? Whatever happened to one on one? How about a fair fight, huh?"

What am I saying? I'm five foot six and couldn't bench a hundred pounds on a good day, oh mercy, please.

Something had changed. I was still held fast by my captors, but it had gone quiet. Then the crowd started to chant,

"Blood, blood, blood."

Someone was coming.

He pushed through the crowd, long hair, rawhide headband, lots of gold chains, and a mangled nose that appeared to have been partly bitten off in a bar brawl. Probably half Injun, a third Jamaican, and part wild animal, he was huge, a Redwood tree with feet.

He pressed his way into what had now become a semicircle and took loose hold of his prick.

"Set the brother free and let him express himself," he said.

The crowd roared.

I was thrust forward and I purposely hit the pavement, knees first.

"Please don't hurt me," I said. That brought on a chorus of boos. "I'm frightened, I can't fight you, and I want my mother."

The monster lowered his fists in disgust of my absolute truths and there was a sudden shout from someone in the crowd. Heads turned and the mob miraculously began to edge toward something better going on in the street.

It was Thelma and Louise. They were hotwiring my car.

I shot to my feet, but the human *Titanic* seized a handful of my hair. He yanked my head back and slowly, very slowly walked me to the curb. He spoke to me through the side of his mouth.

"Don't you ever."

Thelma struggled with the ignition. The engine sputtered and quit.

"Come into my neighborhood."

Another choke and grind from beneath the hood.

"And be simple enough to leave your car door unlocked."

The transmission kicked in and my car jerked away into the street. There were cheers and whistles and Bigfoot reached back and crashed knuckles into my face. A jolt, stars, black dots in a swarm, and as he threw me forward I could already feel my right eye swelling shut. A wild toss of knees and elbows, I stumbled into the street and smacked palms first into the back door of a Yellow Cab.

"Get in," the driver said.

I threw open the door and bent in. Clutching hands tried for my arms and missed firm grasp.

"Go!" I said, door shut, faces in the window. The interior smelled like beer, puke, and Pine Sol. Heaven. The cabby gunned it and gave a half look back over his shoulder.

"Should I follow da whores?"

"God no! Get me the fuck home!" I dug in my pocket and snagged my money clip. "Here's fifty. 225 Byberry Street. Move!"

Don't you mean Sixth and London? What about Tina?

I fought myself for a moment and tried to force the words out of my mouth.

Sixth and London, where the pretty girl waits with her heart on her sleeve. Say it.

I could not. I couldn't lie even to myself. I was too frightened to save her, at least in this condition.

I am selfish, yellow scum.

The driver turned down an alley and shot up fourth.

"How about the stolen car, son? You want to report it? North Detectives Central is only two blocks over. " He was looking at me in the rearview, big roll of fat on the back of his neck, crewcut, brown derby hat, a blue collar, fatherly type who had found maturity and kindness through a tough paper route.

"Yes, I'll report it." I massaged my bruised eye. "But I'll report it by phone when I get home."

Send a rescue squad for Tina as well.

In my hurry I had left my Verizon Razor charging in the kitchen, and I had no intention of confronting the cops in person. They were in the business of asking questions, and my possible answers were frightening. I thought for a moment about asking Joe-cabbie here if he had a cell I could borrow, but nixed that idea the moment it tried to surface. The less I talked the better. Hey, maybe I was getting control of this thing after all.

"Christ!" I shouted.

"What's wrong, son?" The driver wasn't flustered by my outburst in the least, just mildly concerned. It made me wonder what kinds of losers he carted around on a typical day shift.

"I never checked the back door," I said. "I ran out of the house in a panic and hell if I can remember locking the back door."

"So? 225 Byberry, that's up on 'The Hill.' It's a good neighborhood."

"But those two slutbuckets have my car! My insurance card is in the damned glove compartment."

Easy, easy.

"To hell with 'easy does it,' the slip has my address printed on it in big, bold letters."

Stop babbling.

"I know I'm babbling like a girl, but there is a lot of expensive shit in that house. Stereo and video equipment, sterling silver service, artwork, Christ, my wife has seven thousand dollars' worth of antique jewelry hidden in the zipper cloth coat hangers in the bedroom closet. Isn't that the first place you would look if you were a hooker in a strange house?"

The cabbie laughed. "Cloth coat hangers, huh? That's not so bad, kid. My wife has a collection of gold thimbles, big deal, right? Well, she keeps 'em shrinkwrapped in plastic and stuck down the back of the toilet tank. Women and their hiding places, eh?"

I didn't answer and he let it fade. I was slumped down in the seat now. My neighborhood was getting close and to my alarm I was gaining an urge to shout truths out the window. I looked at my knees. Thank goodness I had nothing to say to them.

The back door had been locked the whole time and the basement was unoccupied. Still, I checked the deadbolt three times before marching up the dark stairway to the dining room. The main floor was silent, shadowed, thudding with dull, dead air. I pulled at the lower rim of the kitchen window to make sure it was shut fast, tested the lock on the front door, and then vaulted two stairs at a time to get to the bedroom. I went to the phone on the nightstand and dialed 911.

"309 Police," said her android voice.

"You sound like voice mail," I said. "Get someone on the horn with a pulse."

Her tone sharpened. "State your name, please."

"Joe Kagan."

"What is your emergency?"

"My wife had her purse stolen and she's stranded at Sixth and London. Send a black and white to pick her up, and step on it, bitch."

"Who is this?"

"Joe Kagan, I told you. Pay attention. Aren't you writing this down? Put on your boss."

"My boss?"

"Yeah, the captain or the admiral or whoever the fuck he is, hurry up."

Her voice got quite smooth and official.

"May I remind you sir, that this line is reserved for emergencies. It is also being recorded."

"Good! Sixth and London. Send a car and look for my wife. She's short with killer thighs and a real girly smile that would make you turn dyke if you're not there already. Now move."

She hung up.

I slammed down the receiver and gazed at the bedroom walls. Suddenly I had a raw urge to walk my block, pound on doors, and tell all my idiot neighbors what I really thought of them.

Don't leave the house again, Joe. You're a danger to yourself and a danger to others.

I looked at the digital clock. 9:25 A.M., and the intense need to speak my mind seemed to be growing exponentially as the hour of 10:00 drew nearer.

"Screw this," I said out loud. I grabbed Tina's box of punk junk off the mantel and dumped the contents on the bed. I sifted through for a moment and came up with the pair of stainless steel thumb-cuffs that she had bought at Zippers. Its thin link chain was six inches long and a tiny key dangled off one of the circular traps by a thread. Perfect.

I pulled off the key and chucked it on the bed. I slipped out of my suit jacket and made sure I had a good supply of cigarettes with lighter. I snagged an ash tray and hurried into the bathroom before my mind could turn back toward the need to verbalize my thoughts to the world.

I took a seat on the tub rim and noticed that the toilet needed a scrubbing. I shoved the shower curtain to the far side by the towel rack, set down the ash tray, then leaned in to close one of the cuffs around the metal pipe of the cold water faucet behind the four-pronged knob. I gave it a strong pull and it held fast. Carefully, I put the other cuff around my left thumb and gently pressed it shut between the joint and bottom knuckle. A soft squeeze and it ratcheted down to lock into its tightest setting. There was a tug of pressure, a tight bind, but not quite enough to cut off the circulation. I gave a test yank and the cuff dug hard into my top, wrinkled thumb joint. It held fast.

I was going nowhere, thank God. I took out my cigarettes and shook up a smoke. I lipped one, set the pack on the tub, and dug in my pocket for the lighter.

There was a creak on the stairs and I froze. Another creak. Closer, a definite footstep.

"Who's there!" I shouted like a fool. I tried to pull loose but I had screwed myself real fine. I tugged three more times and drew up a trace of blood. I looked into the foyer and almost fainted as the growing, slanted shadow on the wall now appeared to be hooded. I scrambled into the tub, got to my knees, and shut my eyes to pray.

"You're cheating," the Reaper said.

My eyes flew open and I banged my head on the soap dish when I tried to shrink back. He was looking down at me, his horrid face twisted in fury. Black streams of smoke poured out of his nostrils. His lips were drawn back above spotted gums; he was not smiling. A hot, silver drool dripped off his teeth and turned to spats of fire upon hitting the tub rim in front.

"Mercy," I said.

"You are a coward!" he roared. "You have learned nothing. You have not yet really faced your aggressors. Did you actually think you would come clean of this without sacrifice?"

"Please," I said.

His tone changed.

"My friend, can you imagine what it would be like if you were not able to retreat into shock? Can you fathom the pain you could endure if your body would not allow your mind to black out? Can you picture the torture of surpassing your own ability to faint?"

"What? I don't understand."

"Stay still, my love. I want to kiss you."

My mouth dropped open. So did his. From between his teeth a sudden eruption of black vomit shot forth and sprayed between my parted lips. Obscene. The taste was bitter and the plume was a juggernaut of force. It was either choke or swallow.

I swallowed and the room immediately became brighter. The details around me focused into a vivid, pronounced reality. I understood. It was a supernatural drug now alive in my veins. For whatever was about to transpire, he wanted me awake. My face dripped and he spoke in a hoarse whisper.

"If you can bend the rules of our wager, then so can I. It is time for redemption. It is time for choice."

What choice? Oh, my fucking God!

"It is simple," he said. "If you are not out of this bathroom in five minutes, Tina dies."

He vanished.

On the sink, there was a white timer set on five minutes, already ticking off precious seconds. And something off the rim of the tub glinted at the corner of my swollen eye.

It was a razor blade.

I turned on the hot water with shaking fingers. I grabbed the soap, slopped its film across my left thumb for lubrication, and found it was futile. I wet it, jerked, pulled, jogged, and turned, but the cuff would not slip over the joint. I tried cold water, got the same result, and had already wasted a minute and ten seconds.

I stretched back for a towel to dry off my hands. I knew what was necessary here, there was no time left to deny it. My eyes were wide. I carefully picked up the razor in my right hand and tried to gain the motivation needed.

To cut off my left thumb.

I sliced through the top tendon in one sweep and my thumb jerked down to the palm as if snapped off a rubber band. A thick well of blood boiled to the surface and dripped down to the rubber tub mat.

Small needles of pain, live wires, I had cut it to the bone. Careful not to let the razor slip, I pushed it along the inner side with a forceful swipe and the left half of my thumb went numb. A jet stream of crimson burst sideways and spattered the wall tiles. A droplet of sweat slipped over my eyebrow and danced off the back of my left hand. I cut through the outer side and almost dropped the razor down the drain.

I was moaning, spitting phrases of gibberish. My thumb had become a foreign object, alien, a disease; obsessed, I was focused keen on its removal.

The entire appendage had gone numb and it was becoming difficult to keep it in place.

The bottom side was tough like old gristle. I slashed at it three times and through the runners of red I could see whitish-yellow pebbly things that must have been small fat deposits or something.

I stopped. My breath was hot and rattly. I was down to bare bone on all four sides and I had lost what seemed about half a cup of blood. The bathtub was a strange, inverted marshmallow with lots of cherry syrup. I did not feel faint. I eyed the clock, two minutes and ten seconds left, I dropped the razor and gripped my thumb in the towel. The compress bloomed dark red instantaneously. And I was far from finished.

But I can't hack through the bone with that razor. I can barely hold it as is.

Tick tock, Joseph, tick tock.

I knew what had to be done. I needed leverage. I put the edge of the towel in my mouth and bit down.

Carefully, I stuck my thumb up the spigot, braced my feet against the base of the tub, and wrapped my right hand around the left's knuckles. The greasy blood made it hard to take hold, so I pulled as slowly as possible.

The bone was spry like a green tree limb. It started to bend and I screamed. I screamed Tina's name into the towel.

The bone finally snapped and a hurl of momentum threw me against the back of the tub. Shampoos and conditioners that had been perched on the edge rained down on me and hot clouts of pain swarmed my left hand in an angry rush. On the other side of the tub my thumb was dancing a bit in the air, doing small twists and pendulum swings from its chain. It looked alive and I looked away. I curled my mangled hand in to my stomach and crawled to grab hold of my lighter.

I am not going to bleed to death in my own bathroom. I have to cauterize the wound.

I glanced back at the clock. Twenty seconds.

I flicked the lighter's dial to the highest setting. I gripped the towel in my teeth a second time and thumbed up a flame. Slowly, like a mad chemist, I brought the flare to the gaping wound.

There was a fusion of fire, torn flesh, and bone. My eyes blurred over and I shrieked myself silent as the gash was burned burgundy black. It popped and sizzled and I forced myself to keep the flame in place for a full five seconds.

I dropped the lighter. There was a hard pulse of anguish between the area of my recently evicted thumb and my forearm, and I wanted to curl to a fetal position to cradle the hurt. But my time was almost expired, so I heaved myself out of the tub, fell on my face, and made a three-legged shuffle for the door.

The timer went off as I was half through the archway and I gave one huge lunge.

I fell to the carpeted floor of the foyer and sobbed at the ceiling.

"Was it good enough, you bastard? Have I come clean? Did I get out in time? Fuck you!"

I heard something strange, a sound quite loud and out of place. At first I thought it was the mad ringing of the timer in my head, but it was not. It was a car horn honking and honking outside of the house. It sounded close enough to be coming from the welcome mat. I got up as quickly as I could, stumbled down the stairs, and threw open the front door.

My car was backed up on the front lawn, almost to the door, and rocking back and forth in Tina's flower bed. The Reaper was in the front seat and laughing in a broad display of rotten enamels.

"Wouldn't it be funny if everyone lost the mask?" he said. "Wanna see what that would be like? This is going to be fun!"

He melted. Bone and black cloth merged and swam like a mass of cartilage tornedoed in a slow-motion blender. The wet lump shifted, cracked, and made sucking sounds as it reformed.

It became Thelma.

"Hi, sweet thang." She gave a parade wave that jangled the many silver bracelets on her wrist. Then she spun the tires in a harsh, rubbery roar that kicked up dirt, mulch, and small stones to pepper the walls and shutters. I half closed the screen door and took cover behind it as she tore donuts into my lawn, sending up a confetti spray of grass, tulips, bulbs, and lilies to the warm summer breeze. Just before her sharp turn across the sidewalk and over the curb, she ran down Tina's flowering fig for good measure.

A horde of children had been watching and the weird event made them go mad with glee.

No masks!

It became a dirt-pile free-for-all as they infiltrated and began sliding, stamping, kicking, and rock throwing. I still had not moved. The pain was too close, the visual chaos outside too surreal, like the symbolic representation of something I could not quite put into focus.

I snapped out of it when they started to break my windows. Two small boys in OshKosh B'Gosh overalls aimed for the panes upstairs. A girl with pigtails and horn rims walked the plowed up garden and stamped her Mary Janes down on the flowers that remained standing. The bigger boy who lived across the street hefted a large cornerstone and waddled it over to the wounded flowering fig. He dropped it and broke the small tree at its base with a wet snap.

The sound of it was similar to my thumb's last words, and I marched outside. Children scattered. The woman across the street was standing in her doorway and shaking with laughter.

I strode down my soiled walkway and broke into a run to tell her my thoughts. My thumb stump was still smoking. I was covered with blood.

By the time she looked up and registered my approach, I was right in her face. There was no choice for her but to step back and suddenly I was in the strange house, backing her into a corner.

"You rotten witch," I said. "Do you know how hard my wife worked on that garden?"

"Get out of my house," she said. I had to lean in a bit because she was whispering. She backed from me farther but kept the low tone through her thin lips. "I've despised you and your wife from day one, it's obvious you hate women, and deep down I know you've always wanted my body."

What?

She had mean-spirited eyes but now looked a bit too frightened to make them work their magic. Her shaky voice seemed to complement the cheap, outdated wallpaper and the pastel furniture wrapped in vinyl slipcovers.

"I'll call the police," she said.

That turned my momentary confusion back to rage and I was tempted to stamp my foot and cry, "I called them first." Instead, I said,

"Try this."

I reached for my pants button but my lack of a thumb denied me firm grasp. She brought her hands to her face and screamed,

"Rape! Rape! Help, Oh God, rape!"

"Shut up," I said. "I was going to flash a moon, don't flatter yourself." She kept screaming and I moved even closer. "Believe me, I couldn't lie to you even if I wanted to. I was going to shine a moon at you, that's all."

She kept screaming.

I turned my back to it, ran out into the sunshine, and made a path straight back to my house. A score of neighbors were watching from lawns, walkways, and patios, and I could feel their greasy eyes on me right up until I threw myself into the living room and slammed the door tight.

"Jesus," I said.

The odds are all even and I'm still losing.

I heard the drone of a siren in the distance. My hand had settled for a dull, pounding throb and I climbed the stairs with weak legs. Then I halted in the bedroom doorway. There was a strange form leaning into the opened closet with a rag-tag pile of ripped cloth hangers at his feet. His coat was stuffed with Tina's antique jewelry and by the bulges in his pockets it looked like he had just about gotten it all.

It was my buddy the cab driver and part-time cat burglar. He turned and, with a gloved hand, leveled a pistol at my chest.

"Don't try anything stupid, kid. I don't want to waste you."

My bladder cut loose. He saw it, gloated, and rode the fear factor for all it was worth.

"This is loaded with hollow points. They would pierce your stomach like a dime and come out your back the size of a basketball. By the way, kid, you look terrible."

There was a peal of tires outside. Our eyes jerked simultaneously and he waved me over to the window. One-handed, he snapped the lock and lifted the frame. Now the gun was pressed to my temple as we both looked through the screen.

A weather-stained red pickup was parked in the middle of the street. On its side was a phone number and block letters that read "D'GIDEO PLUMBING." The thick-browed, tattooed bruiser who owned it was rooting through the job box bolted to the back bed. He was red faced and pissed.

"Who's that?" the cabby said.

"It's my neighbor from across the street," I said. "Probably got a distressing call from his wife about a rapist."

The plumber lifted out a long crowbar and started for my walkway. His fickle wife leaned out of her doorway and begged him to stop. Over his shoulder, he shouted back at her in Italian. The cabby shoved me away.

"Sit down," he said. "Now! On your butt Indian style. Hands in the back pockets, move!"

I complied and muffled a scream when my left-handed wound scraped the top pocket band. The cabby spoke through his teeth. His voice had a sort of whistle to it.

"From that position, you won't be able to get up in time to jump me clean, and if you move I'll shoot you like a dog."

"Please, no."

He punched out the screen, walked back a step into the shadows, and pointed the gun downward. He fired twice out the window. There was no roar and echo like the movies, just a pair of hearty pop sounds. I heard screams and moans outside and noticed that the sirens were closer.

My captor walked over and sat on the bed. He rested his forearms on his knees.

"Go take a look, son."

I struggled up and made it to the window. The plumber was flat on his back with his eyes open. There was a jagged area where his forehead used to be and the balance of his scalp lay in the grass like a hairy, down-turned soup bowl.

"I killed him," the cabby said. "It's your duty to turn me in." I turned and he had the gun offered out to me butt first. He nodded at it. "This is useless to me now. Go on, take it."

I came away from the window, snatched away the weapon, and aimed at his forehead.

"Just stay right there. The cops will want a big story out of you."

He laughed. He stood. He bolted for the door.

"Hold it!" I shouted. I aimed at the ceiling and pulled the trigger to fire up a warning. I got nothing but an empty click. His voice was a teasing, receding call from the stairway.

"You think I'd hand you a gun with bullets left in it? Boy, are you stupid."

I looked at the gun in my hand and realized how badly I'd just been screwed. He had been wearing gloves. Now my blood and prints were on the weapon. I even had motive.

His last words were muffled, but I heard them from the basement.

"Better get a new lock system, kid. This deadbolt was a piece of cake."

There was the faint slam of a door and then other slams of car doors out front. I looked through the window and gasped.

There was an army of cops outside in the street, cruisers criss-crossed on the pavement and angled up both sidewalks. Orders were being shouted and the troopers were falling into patterns, real cowboy shit, long-barreled guns two-fisted across roofs and hoods. I blinked. Members of a S.W.A.T. team dressed in military black were assuming positions on rooftops parallel to my small fortress which was now considered hostile. They had big rifles with scopes and a couple of men were positioning cannon things that looked like small missile launchers.

I backed away from the windows and ran downstairs for the door, to throw it open, to run out and blare the truth to them all, to go down in a blaze of glory.

Tina's clipped and amplified voice stopped me. They had given her a megaphone.

"Joe? Joe, please come out slowly with your hands held high. I love you so much."

She's alive.

I fell to my knees and wept into my palms.

The mask came back. It forced its way into my brain with such force it was almost physical. Relief swept through me and already I was beginning to sort the mess and fabricate stories. I got to my feet and looked at my watch. 10:01. I sighed and looked around for something white to wave.

There would be an investigation and I would have a lawyer, maybe a team, good, strong masks all around, thank God.

In the kitchen, I grabbed a handful of white paper towels. Peace. Truce. At last. Still, on the short trip back through the living room I was not mentally focused on my lawyers, my newest excuses, or the pain in my left hand. I was not thinking of the impending trial or how much bail or whether it would hurt when they threw me face down in the dirt to cuff me.

I thought of none of these things, for my mind was on Tina. Sweet Tina and whether I would ever again feel the taste of her rosebud lips through the thick skin of both our clever masks.

Quest for Sadness

I ordered my butler to fetch me a shotgun. To this he raised an eyebrow and revealed the trace of a smirk.

"Uh huh."

"Just do it," I said.

He stuck a long green blade between his teeth, even though I had told him not to chew grass in the house. He hooked one thumb under the dirty blue strap of his overalls and used the other to push the Marlboro cap higher up on his forehead. He smelled of Pennzoil and gas-powered gardening tools.

"Winchester or Smith & Wesson?" he asked.

"Something with a kick. Meet me by the west wall and don't tread dirt on the foyer carpet." He was usually careful, but it never hurt to remind him after his morning chores. I took long strides toward the main staircase and had just rested my hand on the banister.

"Hey there," he said.

"What!"

The old coot stood under the archway and stroked his beard.

"Whatcha want the heavy iron for? There ain't nothing in the west wing but breakables."

"The glass," I said. "I am going to shoot the stained glass."

He sunk his hand into his deep pocket and scratched the back of his right calf with the left boot tip.

"The whole wall is gonna be rough there, fella. That there glass is thick as a swamp and stands ninety foot high by seventy across. Took them artists six months of hard labor to install and it won't come down easy."

I flexed my jaw.

"Bring extra rounds."

*   *   *

The madness began yesterday on my private six-hole golf course. I was ten feet off the green and chipping for par when the gun went off.

That cocky old swine. He brought a .44 Magnum today instead of the starter pistol.

With a slight frown, I stroked through the ball and landed it in the cup. Touch of backspin. I turned.

"You fired late." He did not respond. He just sat there in the golf cart, feet up, toothless grin, firearm aimed to high north with gray wisps of smoke floating around the mouth of the barrel. My voice was patience. "I told you that the most sensitive point of concentration is needed an inch before contact with the ball. You shot on the follow-through."

"Well of course I did," he said. "By now, you've come to expect it like an old hog waiting on a slop-bell."

"Then we need a new game," I said.

"Looks like it."

I set my seven iron in its holder and crossed my arms. He scratched his temple with the muzzle of the .44.

"Can we think of nothing else?" I said. He leaned over the coffee can he always brought with him and spit a long brown runner into it. He wiped his mouth with a sweaty flannel sleeve and smiled.

"Let's play Antichrist," he said.

"What?"

He nodded at me slowly. The smile stayed.

"You know."

"No, I don't. Explain. You're no Antichrist."

"'Tain't about me," he said. "Every dime-store book of prophecy says the Antichrist comes to glory by age thirty-three. Seems time for y'all to be doing the thinking."

My thirty-third birthday was in two days, and the glint in his eye was constructed of things other than jest.

"You are permanently dismissed," I said. "Be off the grounds by five or I will have you bodily removed. Start packing."

He did not stir.

"I'll call the police right now," I said.

I went nowhere.

59

He tossed the pistol to me. It cartwheeled through the air and I caught it by the handle.

"Go ahead," he said. "Aim and pull the trigger. Put a slug right between my eyebrows."

I did nothing. He stretched out his legs, crossed them at the ankles, and clasped his hands behind his head.

"Now you must ask yourself why," he said. "Why do you choose not to fire the weapon? Is it because you give a damn about your fellow man? I don't think so. Y'all got more money than God and don't feel nothing for no one. Only way you keep ties with a man is by owning him and you won't pull the trigger 'cause it makes no sense to toss away your property."

"That's ridiculous," I said. "You are my employee, not my property."

"That so? Did you hire me or buy me with purpose? How much does it take to purchase a soul? What's your definition of slavery?"

I had no answer for that. He had been a patient in one of the retirement homes I had sold off. He seemed good with machines so I offered to take him in. His response was,

"Give me back a life and a pair of work pants and I'll do it for free."

I viewed it as a gesture of charity, the start of a strong bond of trust between a pillar of wealth and the salt of the earth. Now I was being forced to view it as something else. I studied him closely, my butler, my handyman, my lone companion who sat in the golf cart, the one who was brought on to expedite my will, he who would do anything for me because I owned him. I got a sudden whisper of fear in the small of my back.

"So, I bargained for your loyalty," I said. "Why is that so wrong?"
His smile vanished.

"Because I'd break the knees of a baby or take a bullet in my side for you. Go on, now admit who *you* are."

"No. You're the one with the problem and there's really no challenge in this. It is too easy to prove that you're wrong."

"Then do it," he said. "Prove me wrong." I hesitated and he went on with words that seemed treasured and rehearsed. "Children of Satan don't feel sadness, friend. They are incapable of any sense of loss. Tell me one thing that makes you feel sorrow for another."

I shifted my stance and crossed my arms.

"Game's too easy. I could lie."

"Why would you lie to me? I'm nobody."

"And I'm not a machine. I feel like everyone else."

"Do ya? When's the last time you shed a tear?"

I had no response, and the fear came to the forefront like a black bird flapping loose in the attic. Weeping was one particular release that helped define the human experience, I knew that, I had certainly read about it, seen it in film, observed it on the news. And though I had never actually come face to face with woe, I just assumed all along that this kind of thing existed in those more connected.

What does sadness feel like? The impact of a difficult moral choice?

You'll never know. It has been fully unlearned and now remains too easy to buy off with your money, more money than God.

I stormed off the golf course. Though it was too early, I retreated to the confines of my second-floor study to fix myself a vodka martini with three anchovy olives.

What am I?

Things I had known about myself were altered in this new tilt of light. Apathy seemed cruel. Lack of emotion seemed evil. Calm, cool, and collected seemed sociopathic. And why did I not just have my butler thrown off the grounds, no more questions asked? He was obviously disturbed.

You knew that from day one. You bought him so you could keep him as property. Now you refuse to let go what you own.

It ate at me all afternoon. It was an unsolvable round-about.

You have enough money to buy off sadness. Enough to purchase souls.

Wide-eyed in the dark, I stared out through my bay windows and searched for feelings of pity about anything. There were none. I did not give a damn about the homeless, not one shred of grief for the starving, not a single crumb of ache for any of the damned living outside of my isolated world.

What am I?

I was going to find out. I was going to scratch up some kind of humanity from deep within. I was determined to prove the accusation false.

*   *   *

Those lovely, massive windows.

I aimed high and the first shot back-kicked my shoulder so hard I almost fell on my ass. The large face of the Virgin Mary shattered into a thousand sharp glass raindrops, most of which landed outside on the grass. Others smashed the marble floor before me, skidding and spinning. Morning sun stabbed through the ugly void and the glare lanced off the steel barrel as I cocked another round into the chamber.

My butler followed as I moved behind the display of Persian vases. He was laughing. I went back on my heels, steadied myself against the wall, aimed low at the wide reproduction of The Last Supper and let the buckshot fly.

The second *thwack* of gunfire seemed louder than the first, but it did less damage. In somewhat of a rage, I grabbed the other shotgun and pumped five successive explosions at the stained glass mural, bursting it out at the bottom in thick sprays of calico shrapnel.

The entire middle section caved and we both dove for cover.

A huge chunk that was most of a thirty-foot version of the fourteen Stations of the Cross toppled inward. I sneaked up a peak and saw it crash down on my antique Ford, mint condition, museum quality. It crushed the roof, blew out the windows, and flattened the tires in a roar of destruction.

Smoke churned in the air and spare tinkles of leftover falling glass mixed with the faint calls of birds outside. I got up and approached the wall that was now no more than a vacancy with jagged edges. My shoes crunched in the glass, my gun dangled down toward the floor.

It was still there.

In the bottom left corner was the little treasure, originally hidden within the larger piece. I had spotted it a day after installation, I do not miss much. It was a tiny, nearly microscopic picture of a woman's head made with fragments. Below it and barely legible without a magnifying glass stood the letters, "Mama, R.I.P."

I brought up my gun and blasted that little piece of history into oblivion. I turned to my butler.

"Clean up the glass, get an exterminator, tell the security company it was a false alarm and make arrangements with a local contractor to temporarily patch the wall until the stained glass can be replaced. Now, you will excuse me. I have a phone call to make."

*   *   *

I was convinced his reaction would make me feel regret. The artist. The one who custom-made the stained glass wall piece by piece and spent the next half year of his life installing it.

When I told him of the senseless act there was dead silence.

"Why?" he said.

"I wanted to destroy a piece of your art. And I felt the need to obliterate the testament to your mother. How dare you include that within something I own. She will never rest the same."

"So, why call?" he said. "You want your money back or something?"

"No, I want you to fight for your mother's memory! I took it, and it can't be replaced."

He laughed.

"I'll buy her a park bench or plant her a tree, asshole."

He hung up. I stared at the phone, listened to the silence, then the dial tone.

Art meant nothing; it was merely a way to get paid. The authenticity of memorial was illusory; blind ritual, dumb obligation. The importance of the matriarchal matrix was a mirage and the mother was ultimately meaningless; she performed her function and was easily erased. This was going to be even harder than I had thought.

I told my butler to bring me a deer.

*   *   *

I watched.

He drove it onto the south grounds in a horse trailer, ignoring the car path and rolling straight onto the open lawn before the hedge gauntlet. Even through the expansive pantry window I was close enough to hear the animal bucking and kicking within its mud-stained steel prison. Locked in the dark. Frantic.

Don't fret, love. You'll be set free soon enough.

Bowlegged, my butler ambled out of the pickup and went around back to lift the drift pin that held shut the trailer doors.

They blew open.

Headstrong and frenzied, the deer galloped upon the smooth metal bed, slipped and banged down its proud white chest on the tailboard. It jerked up then and lunged out to the grass. Like a statue it froze there.

I raised my Nextel.

"Leave us," I said into it.

The transmission must have been loud on the unit hooked to my butler's belt, for it broke the spell cast over the deer. It bolted and my butler shook his head before driving off. He did not specifically understand and I did not need him to. Yet. All he had to know was that he was shielded if he had attained the animal illegally. Simple fact: through political contribution I supplied the police most of their radar devices, firearms, and computer equipment. It kept me well protected.

But there would be no protection for the animal-thing. The south lawn's forty acres were fenced in, it would not get far.

I palmed the leather grip of my Proline compound bow and ventured out into the sunshine. There were birds in the warm breeze, squirrels in the trees, beings of beauty, God's creatures.

Lower than you on the food chain. Insignificant in the vast scheme of things.

Were they? I thought I had formed an alliance with anything that lived or breathed. Or was that all inbred by the mass media, inserted, incubated, and sculpted over a lifetime in order to form a false system of values? Was I conditioned? Had a mental parasite with an exterior of high morals eclipsed my true being?

I was going to find out. Though my butler was required to provide me bi-weekly instruction on various styles of weaponry, I had always shot at targets. As far as I knew I was against killing for sport.

Really?

The only way to know for sure was to do it. To become involved in the act and gauge my responses. To hope the (power of God) execution brought on feelings of remorse.

Like a traumatized dog that pawed up to lick the boot of the one who kicked it, the deer had circled back to its original point of release. It stood about thirty feet away now with a sheen of nervous sweat blanketing its soft fur. Slowly, I reached and slipped an arrow from under the hood of my bow-mounted quiver.

It was an XX75 tipped with razorback 5, needle-sharp point amidst a cluster of five steel arrowheads all arranged in a circular pinwheel. Straight on, it looked a bit odd.

Like a five-pentacle star.

Odd feather out, I mounted it on the string, careful not to pinch but just hold gently between the fingers. I drew back on the eighty-pound resistance of the pulleys and my butler's voice twanged in my head.

"Let it go easy, don't snap away your finger pads. And go for the vital area behind the front leg. It's the best way to a fast kill."

But I did not want the thing to die quickly. I wanted it to suffer. Carefully, I aimed at its stomach and in my ears the outdoor sounds seemed to magnify behind the drum of my heart.

I let go the string.

The arrow split the air, a silent merchant of doom. It struck the deer flat in the paunch and there was a smooth sound of penetration similar to a hatchet sunk hard into a wet stump. The thing lurched with the contact, sprang high into the air. It was beautiful.

Wrong emotion!

I bit my lip, not willing to face my inner rush of joy as the deer shot across the lawn in its ecstasy of pain and confusion. The arrow shaft stuttered and bobbed from its flank and grass divots kicked up from beneath the blur of its hoofs. The beast tore straight away and then smashed through the pantry window.

Damn. Not in the house.

I drew another arrow and ran to the side door. Upon approach, I heard a riot of clapping hooves amongst crashes of wooden shelves, trays of silver, and stacks of fine china. By the time I entered the fresh rubble of my pantry, the thing was lying by the far wall in a state of jerks and spasms. I set the bow down and stepped forward, trying to fend off the nag of annoyance I felt as a result of the damage done to my kitchen.

The deer died with a guttural moan and I stared into its lifeless gaze.

I felt nothing.

There had to be something: guilt, sadness, anything. There was nothing, and I moved slowly around the dead thing. The fatal wound had spattered green intestinal juices across the ribs and it stank. Were this a two-dimensional DVD presentation my reaction might have been different, might have been, but all I felt was disgust.

What is wrong with you? Look at it!

The blind stare. The tongue hanging out of its muzzle, the rich blood that seeped across my Pietra D'Assisi beige ceramic floor tiles,

65

all visually and intellectually pathetic. So where was the pity? The feelings of shame?

Nowhere. Considering the damage it did to my kitchen and the stench, I was glad I killed it.

I pulled the Nextel from my belt.

"Get in here and clean up the mess," I said.

The tone of my voice barely hid the panic rising up in my throat.

*　*　*

I ran past the garden to the yard's south edge. Inside I felt scorched, blackened.

What am I?

I stopped to catch my breath. My nostrils were flaring and I looked down at my shaking hands. They seemed huge, smooth as bone, manicured nails, baby-smooth skin.

Flesh that thinly covers a dark beast whose inner eye just opened.

No! It did not mean anything, couldn't have! Lots of people hunt!

You don't.

I squared my jaw and marched down the grassy knoll toward the building I frequented the least, my butler's tool shed. I needed to see his domain, the castle I had built for him, the cold, hard proof that I had done some good for a fellow human being and blessed him with purpose, *time bombs of dark purpose waiting for ignition,* that I had rescued him from an existence of despair, *purchased his soul,* and made him into the kind of man, *Devil's henchman,* that he wanted to be.

Tool shed.

An ugly word that drew up images of work benches, dirty blue rags, and grease guns strewn across a cracked, oil-stained concrete floor.

Devil's playpen.

A place where men, *salt of the earth,* reigned supreme and broken machines became female. The frozen hex nut that would not budge was a *bitch.* That stripped screw that refused to budge was a *whore,* and the engine that blew an o-ring was dubbed a *fucking cunt!* For the first time in my life I felt something like lust. The feeling was ice, far from the warm touch of remorse I yearned.

The door was open. Just outside on the grass, there was a scattered array of railroad ties, framing lumber, gas compressors, and high-powered air nailers, as it was my butler's latest project to build a gazebo to be erected abreast the outdoor pool.

The door to the shed stood open. Inside was discovery. A single flood light poured its beam to the floor leaving to the sides a periphery of gloom.

I was hesitant to enter.

I was hesitant to walk between the long shadows of shelved equipment and stand in the spotlight, afraid of what would be illuminated there. My mind streaked to its farthest corners in search of a direction, a guidepost, some testament of how to start and where exactly to begin, a visible cornerstone to dent the steel shroud that lay cold on my heart.

I needed a symbol.

I fired up the compressor as I had seen my butler do, and picked up a large framing nailer. With the hose snaking behind, I bent to set two thick wooden planks at perpendicular. I depressed the gun mouth down and fired a three-and-a-half-inch nail through the beams. It banged through to flush with a sharp pop. I set five more nails into the same general area.

Now I had a huge wooden cross.

I dragged it into the shed, leaned it upright and stood before it, desperate for answers before this vision of purity.

I felt nothing.

No sparks, no quench of enlightenment, nothing.

Instead, I thought of the graphic crucifixion it represented, the vision of pain we had twisted to a commercial science of love. In literal terms, we celebrated the murder of a man, he who was nailed to a cross with a javelin stuck between his ribs. We framed the picture. We propped it over the fireplace, made it into earrings, and hung it off the rearview mirror. A man was nailed to a dirty wooden beam and left to die in shame. The scene filled our minds from our tender beginnings. We were impressionable children looking up with open faces as the violent was reconfigured to translate to the beautiful. I blinked. Suddenly, the cross looked wrong.

Top-heavy somehow.

Of course! I am not the one who has gone numb! I am the one who has come of age, become aware! We have all gotten too used to the image this way! Though the

Lord's death must have been ultimately painful, he could have been punished . . . more effectively.

I pushed forward and wrapped my arms around the cross. Careful to lift with the legs, I slowly turned it upside down. I backed off and stared. Now it seemed right, a rack of pure torture as it should have been from the beginning. I pictured the pain of having the ankles spread at bottom and hands, palm over palm nailed overhead like a victim in a medieval witch chamber. This is where sadness could live. This is where woe could be born.

I needed to feel it now more than ever. I was so close, so near to ripped tendons, torn muscle, shattered bone, the pain that resulted from three nails fired straight through the flesh, one step away from the ongoing path of true remorse.

I told my butler to get me a girl . . .

The Legend of the Slither-Shifter

1.

Denny Sanborn was the type who was always in trouble and the grown-ups at school had tried everything on him. There were warnings he ignored and lectures he didn't understand. There were conferences set up with teachers and counselors, but Dad never showed up anyway.

Denny was a pistol. He busted farts in the auditorium during moments of silence and melted crayons on the radiators. He drew on his desk, clapped erasers in the cloak room, called out, made noises, laughed out loud during sustained silent reading, and often fell from his chair on purpose.

He also took the blame for stuff other kids did. Once, Kimmy Watson poured out ten McDonald's salt packs into a last row desk Mrs. Krill used to coach kids who were slow. When Denny fibbed that he was the one who did it he lost computers for a week, but in return Kimmy gave him a black plastic spider, half a soft pretzel, and a fake barf cushion she won at the St. Mary's church fair. Latif Johnson once dented a hall locker playing pushy-pushy with a fourth grader, and when Denny claimed responsibility for the damage, Latif awarded him with a glow in the dark skull and crossbones pinkie ring.

Everybody loved Denny. They greeted him with high fives and low-down double pump slap-slaps. They laughed at his foolishness. They followed him around at recess and always wanted to know what he was thinking. Denny was a hero, everyone's friend, the class clown, and always knee-deep in hot water.

But Denny didn't really know trouble. He hadn't even a clue what the word meant until that wintry evening two days before Christmas, a week after his tenth birthday precisely at 4:09 P.M. For that is when all hell broke loose.

And what would become this absolute, supernatural terror began with a babysitter, some charcoal sticks, an empty picture frame, and one innocent little ghost story.

Earlier That Day: 2:54 P.M.

With the last buzzer the dented back doors of George Washington Elementary School burst open and children made a scramble for buses. Benjamin Rahim slapped Bobby Nagle on the back of the head and knocked his hat onto the pavement by the 18th Street railing. Three girls squealed and began a game of keep-away. Someone bounced a blue superball into the air and a flock of hands poked up at the gray sky to claim it. A new kid with little white bumps on his forehead hunted on his knees for something while a fifth grader in ripped white stockings and a plaid skirt pulled the girl's hair in front of her. Old Mr. Martin, the school policeman, stood over by the west gate thumbing the handcuffs at his side and jerking his head back and forth for better views. The veins in his neck showed. His fat cheeks and overgrown chin gave him a severe case of puppet-mouth.

"I see you!" he shouted. "You're right in front of me, all of you! Have some respect, huh? You ain't foolin' no one. Now cut it out or you'll spend the rest of your waking lives in the accommodation room and that's a promise!"

"Yes, Mr. Martin," a few scattered voices said back. Feet tramped up the bus stair grids. Some children made faces in the windows while others fought for the better seats in back. The pavement was clear for all but some stragglers.

Back at the school, Denny pushed through the doors and strolled toward 19th Street. He shook the long blond hair out of his face, closed his eyes, rocked up on his toes, and paused a minute right there on the empty playground to savor the wind. It was one of those deep, early winter breaths that felt keen in the lungs and tasted like dripping icicles. Images of wet snow, misted store windows, soaked sneakers, and roaring bonfires swept through his mind, followed by a sweet kind of sadness. Grown-ups didn't slow down to drink up the breeze. They were too serious. Too busy. And even a fourth grader could not stay this young forever.

"Yo, Denny! You can't be running ahead like that, man."

It was Stevie Ramano, Denny's T.S.S. from the Connect Program sponsored by the school district. If you lived within a four block radius of George Washington and your folks couldn't pick you up at the end of the day, you were given an escort home. Romano was one of the better ones. He cocked his winter hat a bit to the side, pulled together the flaps of his coat, and jogged up next to Denny.

"At least let me get you to the corner of 19th so you ain't taking off in view of the windows," he said. Denny shrugged and walked the short distance in silence. His chaperon stuck in some ear buds and sang with his iPod tonelessly.

"See you," Denny said. He slipped through the playground's far gate and made for the cross-street.

"Be good!" Romano called back, and Denny was suddenly in a footrace with this old, mustard-crudded hot dog wrapper caught in some running gutter water. He passed the check cashing store and ran through the warm, perfumy smell of Goldberger's dry cleaners. A mud-spattered bus threw on its blinkers and a Yellow Cab made a wide sweep around it. Denny turned the corner and ran down Cherry Street. At first glance, one would have thought that this was a burst of joy, a race for the sheer fun of it as growing boys were so often known for. A closer view, however, would have shown a grim, determined frown on Denny's face, a scowl usually reserved for adults with complicated responsibilities, problems, and debts. It was an expression that had hardened over time, like old leather.

He raced through an abandoned parking lot and hop-scotched through some uprooted cement tire bumpers. Between the empty lot shanty and a Porta-Potty, he did a tippie-toe across a narrow board covering deep hole made by the Philadelphia Street Department. He climbed a dumpster, scaled an iron fence, and ran along the top of a brick wall. He jumped down and turned a corner. *The* corner.

His chest was heaving, and his stomach cramped up a bit. The arrival always felt horribly new even though he repeated this tradition every day of every week, and that was why he rushed into it so. It was like diving into cold water or ripping off a Band-Aid.

There was a rusted mailbox, a bent stop sign, and a graffiti-covered newspaper box at the curb where the two cross-streets met. A tool and die company sat in the background with its windows barred up, and the gum factory under the train trestle still poisoned the air with that distinct, high stink of burnt sugar and machine oil.

It was a smell that Denny both hated and was drawn to, a signal that lovingly and at the same time cruelly preserved the importance of this particular corner. For Front Lane and Barrington was the third to last stop for the northbound subway, it was a block from the Veterans Administration Building, it remained a hot spot for Greek and Asian street vendors, an unofficial taxi stand, and the very place where Denny Sanborn's mother had been killed seven years ago.

2.

It was all a crazy accident and Denny did not really remember it except for some bits and pieces. Dad had been pushing him in the stroller and Mom had been walking out front with their little two-wheeled grocery cart. They had been on their way to the Acme and she had been hit by a car, not one driven by some drunk or runaway robber, but a regular lady in a station wagon.

Denny had a foggy recollection of his mother negotiating the cart over a spalled patch of curb. He had a dreamlike memory of a station wagon leaning to one side and hurtling through the intersection, but then it went blank for awhile. There was a scratchy vision of his father with his face in his hands, a woman with a ponytail and a baseball cap saying, "I just took my eyes off the road for a second," and an African American woman with a purple feather in her hat blurting something like, "Someone comfort this child!" Everything else was just a blur of what Dad refused to talk about from that day forward.

Denny walked across the street toward the sewer grating on the far side. He usually loved stomping on sewer gratings, and sprinting across subway street gratings, and spitting down the vent gratings that blew steam up into the cold air. This one, however, he always approached with respect.

He stepped carefully on the diagonal groove-cuts and looked down. Old leaves and a gritty run of mud had formed a long wavelike pattern that curved in a mild S-shape. Rust-colored water flowed over in rills and bubbled off into the dark recesses of the cavern. There was a museum of bottles, both broken and not, gathered on the near side of a piece of wood with five nails sticking out of it. On the far side of the makeshift wooden divider was Denny's collection of trinkets, only tainted by a torn Burger King bag that had caught on the edge of the Buzz Lightyear shoulder-launch missile attachment he had tossed down there last Monday.

Denny had been making sacrifices down the drain for three years now. There were tiddlywinks, tennis balls, Lego pieces, and Livestrong wristbands. There were marbles, Chuck E. Cheese gum balls, jigsaw puzzle pieces, and candy-necklace strings. When he couldn't find anything good, he hooked a crayon from school. Once he had thrown in a rubber band he found in the street. He always gave something.

Denny reached into his front pocket and pulled out his Mike Schmidt rookie card. It was faded across the back where he had once tried to annihilate the statistics with a pen eraser, and the front right corner had been torn off. He slipped the card between the bars of the grate, watched it drop, and sighed. Mom's favorite '80s Phil had been Bowa, but Denny couldn't find his card anywhere. He hated substitutes.

Denny sulked away from the corner of Front Lane and Barrington and made his way toward 20th Street. He stared at his bouncing sneaker laces. His mother was buried in Plot #7 in the St. John's Cemetery in Pennsauken, New Jersey, next to her mother and a stepbrother named Patrick that Denny had never met. The headstone was small and only said her name and the dates. Dad used to take him there every Sunday morning, but they hadn't been out there for years.

Denny jogged through the small grassy plot splitting Creek Drive, C Street, and Wyoming and suddenly thought how nice it would have been if he'd worn a hat. Briefly, he pictured the shelf in the hall closet at home, but only saw Dad's bowling ball, hard hat, and slush boots.

Denny broke into a run. Did he even own a winter hat that fit anymore? If he did, he could not place the thing in his mind. And Dad never seemed to have a clue (or a care) where to find Denny's hats or socks or book bags or underwear, at least not until the socks had holes or his ears had already gone cold. The man just never seem to remember in time.

Mom would have remembered.

Denny slowed to a walk. He approached 20th Street and his breath felt thick in his throat. On the corner an unshaven fat man wearing a Christmas hat with white trim-frost and a pom-pom on top muttered swear words to himself, hiked up his pants, and lifted a tray of soft pretzels off the warmer to pack them away. Denny skirted around him and noticed that a few people on his street had their holiday lights up. The stringed bulbs looked like cheap smiles in the growing dark. There was a mini-electric Santa doing the twist dance in a window, a fake snowman smoking a cigar, and a few wreaths hanging on door knockers. Suddenly, Denny had a strong urge to hook some of them, switch them around, and see if his neighbors would notice.

At the end of the day, Denny always found himself at war, half dreaming that he would hold so tight to the scattered memories that he could somehow bring Mom back, and half wishing for some magic non-stop thrill that would make him forget all about grocery carts, hurtling station wagons, purple feathers, and numb ears of the world. But magic was for nerds and wishes for babies. Weren't they?

Denny Sanborn was about to find out. For sometimes magic floated in the air just out of sight and other times wishes came true. They just didn't wind up exactly like the wisher pictured them to be.

It was 4:01 P.M.

The stranger was waiting for Denny on his front steps.

3.

"Hey there," she said. She moved her small purse to the other shoulder. "You Denny?"

He shrugged. The tall girl standing in front of him was about sixteen years old. She was African American, bone thin, and dressed in Catholic school clothes. Her teeth were slightly bucked, but it worked for her in a cartoon rabbit sort of a way. She chewed her gum hard. One hand was knuckled to her hip. She shrugged back at Denny and dug into her pocketbook.

"Here's my I.D., so you know I'm not some street freak or something."

Denny gave a glance to Josephine Thompson's temporary driver's license and shrugged again. Grandma Rosetta had been a much better babysitter, that was for sure. Grandma Rosetta always let him do what

74

he wanted while she played with the downstairs remote and ate microwave popcorn all night, so any rules this Josephine Thompson was about to lay down were sure to be major league bummers.

But what could he do? Grandma was getting older by the minute, no, by the second, and had recently started calling Dad by the names of old relatives she had not seen in ten years. And though it was no secret that Bob Sanborn never much liked the Cleveland cousins to begin with, it became quickly clear that he liked even less a sitter (even family) who couldn't remember his first name, write down a phone message, or scrub a dish or two while she was at it. The whole thing had been building for weeks.

And so here stood the golden answer, chewing her gum and flashing I.D. like a pro. Josephine Thompson, daughter of Mr. Jarell Thompson, friend of Dad's from Core Cutters Concrete and Demolition for four years running, or so Denny had heard. Oh sure, if you worked the wreckers and dozers with Bob Sanborn on late shift you were the man. You were the bomb. And it gave your daughter full dibs to snag a house key, push Grandma out the door, and boss around a fourth grader all night.

"Well?" she said. "You got a key? It's cold out here."

Denny sniffed.

"What's a tampon?" he said. She didn't even blink.

"Every month a girl bleeds from her private place. A tampon's a sponge. Anything else?"

Denny's jaw dropped. Even though he had not known the exact answer until now (and awesome it was after all!) he had been quite aware that this particular question was a doozy. He had asked it twice before, once to the snack lady at the roller rink and the other to a meter maid giving his Dad a ticket outside the State Store at 30th and Arch. Both women had gone wide-eyed, tight-lipped, and flushed, the first spouting, "Never you mind!" and the other going off about Jesus, spoiled children, spare rods, and lead paint.

But this Josephine had given it to him up front and straight. He felt a small part of his heart warm to her, but he wasn't ready to show it off just yet.

"What's that stuff?" He was looking past her to the knapsack on the stoop and the large, square-looking zipper bag leaning against the screen door. She gave a half-turn back, swinging her long, tightly woven braids.

"It's my homework, some books, a few charcoal sticks, and a portfolio case filled with blanks. I draw. If you want I can show you, make a picture or two."

Denny moved to the first stair.

"Maybe and maybe not."

"Suit yourself," she said, and as Denny brushed past he realized that by her not seeming to care whether he checked out her drawings or not, he would now just explode if he didn't get a chance to see at least one. But again, he did not need to show this just yet. He turned the lock and pushed into the dark living room with his new sitter lugging her stuff in behind.

Dad had cleaned, but Josephine curled her lip just a bit once the lights were turned on. Sure, the couch was swept clear of last week's newspapers and the coffee table stood free of soda cans and other various recyclables, but Denny realized how stale the place must have seemed to a girl. Mom's curtains had been long taken down and replaced with gray blinds that were easier to maintain. There was an old brown chair but no footstool. There was an end table with nothing on it. There were no flowers, no books, no scented candles, and the imitation wood-panel wallpaper looked worn. The place was missing those soft, womanly things that made houses into homes, and being reminded of it in this unexpected way seemed unfair. Denny felt an unexpected responsibility and guilt for it as well, and that didn't seem too fair either. Denny slumped onto the couch.

"You can turn on the heat if you want, but it shouldn't go past sixty-two. If you look, you'll see the line my Dad put on the wall above the thermo-thing with red magic marker. Just match the arrow with the line,"

and you'll help keep a roof over our heads, he silently finished. Josephine walked over to the thermostat and Denny stared at the blank TV. He could have flipped the heat on himself. But he was not quite tall enough to do it without dragging in a dining room chair and climbing on it. No thanks. The sure-to-be awkward moment would have pegged him for a baby in his own house, and he felt strange enough as it was.

"Pizza money's right there," he said. He nodded toward the twenty-dollar bill in the hotel-style ash tray on the coffee table. "It's just a first night thing, so you may as well go for it while you can."

"You having some too?"

"Nah. I'll just heat up some of Dad's left-over franks and beans."

She laughed through her nose.

"Do I get a say in this? Old beans could be deadly. Silent and deadly. In fact, I think you busted a fart on the way through the door."

Denny looked over his shoulder and grinned.

"Did not."

"Did so."

"He who smelt it dealt it."

"I'm not a 'he,'" she said. "And the one who denied it supplied it."

Denny turned and dug his knees into the sofa's back cushion.

"The one who first whiffed gave the gift."

"Yeah, but the one to first blame laid the flame." Her return answer had snapped back like whiplash. She was good. Denny paused, then scrunched up his nose.

"Did not."

"Hmm." She tossed her coat on the chair and folded her arms. "Now seriously, what else is there in the fridge for you?"

"Nothing."

"Yeah right."

"Really."

Her look was hard to read, but for a second Denny saw strange emotions pass through her eyes. Did she think he was lying? He could walk her into the kitchen right now and prove the fridge held nothing but a half-loaf of rye bread, some ketchup, some French's mustard, an unopened tub of whipped butter, some old Hi-C, Dad's beer, and some crusted jars in the door that were a million years old. It was never stocked up. Dad called that a waste and besides, there were always leftovers from his last take-out lunch to throw in the microwave. Leftovers were the best, didn't she know that? Any guy knew it at least. Dad said so all the time.

"Draw me a picture," Denny said in a blunt effort to switch subjects. She surrendered a bit of a smile then, but the strange look in her eyes still left traces.

"Really?"

"Yes!" he nearly shouted, suddenly bouncing on his knees. The couch creaked beneath him. "Yes, yes, yes!"

She paused only a moment more.

"All right, then. Move the ashtray."

Denny did it and then made room on the couch for her to get settled. From her zippered bag she removed three different sizes of paper and carefully placed them an inch apart, side by side on the table. Next surfaced the thin black case that, when laid open and flat, revealed charcoal sticks of various lengths. Each was set in its own individual leather pocket and each had been honed to a different style of point. The knife had a sewn-in sheath and its sharpening stone sat in a half-moon shaped pouch.

"Can I have a paper towel, Denny?"

He hopped to it, intrigued to be part of the ritual. She folded the paper in half, placed it on the left side of the table, and proceeded to take off her rings, all eight of them. She arranged them in a circle with the left thumb-ring in the middle. She webbed her fingers, turned them outward, and stretched.

"OK, now what do you want me to draw first?" Her hands were floating above the art case, ready to select the right tool for the job. Denny shoved back, sat on his hands, and frowned.

"I changed my mind."

Josephine raised an eyebrow but kept her hands hovering over the charcoal sticks.

"You're playing me now, right?"

Denny shook his head and struggled to bite back the grin. He knew the game better than anyone, and Josephine Thompson was not going to march right into the Sanborn house and take over that easily. If she wanted to come back she would have to survive the report to Dad, so Denny was proving right here who was boss. Oh, he wanted to watch her draw in the worst way, but wanted more to see how far he could push. After all, it was her job to make nice-nice and he was just here for the ride.

"Tell me a story," he said.

"You're playing me," she said for the second time. "Tell me you're playing." Denny shook his head and smiled at his sneakers.

"Nope. Not playing. Don't you know any stories?"

"What kind of story do you want to hear?"

"A scary one." He looked back over. She was smiling now, not so much in a sweet way, but more in a knowing one. Her hands had migrated to her lap but the rings were still on the table.

"Do you want me to tell something like *The Monkey's Paw*?"

"Heard it," Denny said.

"What about *The One-Armed Brakeman*?"

"Too stupid. Why don't you make one up? Do you know how to do that? Make one up?"

She blinked a few times as if in pure disbelief at Denny's smart mouth, then looked away, thought for a moment, and turned back. Her voice went creepy.

"Turn off the overhead light, Denny, and flip on that table lamp over there. We need atmosphere to do this just right."

He obeyed and the room wore its shadows a bit deeper. The thickening winter darkness outside seemed to press against the windows and Denny got ready for a thrill. He had asked for it.

It was 4:09 P.M.

4.

"Stand over in the corner, Denny."

"Why?"

"Just do it."

"But you're drawing. I thought you were going to tell me a story."

"Don't worry about what I'm doing just yet."

"I wanted to hear a story!"

"The story has already started. Just stand there quietly and whatever you do, don't touch anything. It's a matter of life or death."

Denny tried lifting his chin, going up on tip-toes, and jumping in place, but he could not see what Josephine was creating from his angle by the dining room archway. She was bent over the coffee table with one arm covering the work and the other drawing sweeps across the page. These broad motions were intertwined with little flicks of the wrist, rapid back to forth straight-hand, and various moments of smudge rubbing. Every ten seconds or so she would switch charcoal sticks and with each stick, she changed the grip at least twice. Her eyes remained hidden behind dangling braids. She was good. Denny knew this without even seeing the picture, for he could tell by her arm technique alone that she was a machine.

"C'mon!" he said. "Show me! What is it? How is it part of the story? What are you doing?"

She raised her head slowly. The lamp light caught her eyes and made mirrors. Her voice had gone toneless.

"I'm going to use the picture frame. Don't try to stop me."

She turned her drawing face down on the table, rose up, and made for the short mantel above the fireplace. The old, dusty picture frame she was going for sat at the back of the narrow shelf, wedged behind Dad's upstairs toolbox and a Rayovac security flashlight.

The article in question was Denny's first attempt at making straight lines, back from age one and a half. His mother had made a big deal about it by setting the paper into the oversized twelve-by-sixteen frame, but through the years the importance of the whole thing had faded. In fact, Denny had sort of forgotten the picture was there in the background until Josephine brought it up.

"Nice," she said, once the copper pinch-borders were removed and the pre-school scribbling was slipped out from between the thin glass face plates. For a moment Denny thought her tone was sarcastic, but her face was one of appreciation. She carefully placed the ancient page on the chair and set the now-empty frame next to her drawing on the table. She sat, clasped her hands, and looked over.

"Turn away while I frame my page, Denny. This is it. One peek while it's not caged behind the glass and both of us could be killed. For real, for real."

Denny spun toward the kitchen as fast as he could. Not only was the set-up getting better by the minute, but there was something about Josephine Thompson herself that was actually starting to spook him a bit. She was deep with this, no laughs and no smiles. She really wanted to scare him.

Cool.

"OK, you can turn around," she said. "The danger is locked up for now."

Denny raced back into the living room, eyes wild and ready, but the picture frame was still laying face down. Not fair! Bogus times two, and he was about to stamp, whine, and complain about it when Josephine asked him a question.

"Ever kill a bug, Denny?"

His eyes widened. Most ghost stories started something like, *"Deep in the dark woods outside this summer camp in the Catskills,"* or *"Years ago in this old house on the hill,"* but this one was going to be personal.

Double cool.

"Yeah, I've killed bugs."

"Ever kill bugs just for fun?"

"Yes, yes!" he shouted, thinking about the ants he'd torched with a magnifying glass last spring by the old dumpster behind the 15th Street Pep Boys. Then of course was the hot July afternoon when he was hiding under the Wilton Avenue Bridge, plucking the legs off daddy long legs spiders and watching the wriggling oval bodies cut across rainbow patterns in the oil slicks. And who could forget the countless lightening bugs he got by handclap, the houseflies he got by *TV Guide*, and the basement waterbugs he got by the old-fashioned sneaker. Oh, he was guilty of the crime all right. He was guilty as all hell.

"Yes. I kill them! I kill them all the time!" His eyes were shining and Josephine's eyes were shining right back.

"Sit down and chill, Denny."

He sat.

"Breathe deep."

He breathed. She folded her hands and leaned in.

"We kill those little pests because they're small and ugly. They crawl, they buzz, they bite, and they sting, so we squash the life out of them every chance that we get."

Caught in the trance of her eyes, Denny suddenly felt his skin come alive with a sick rush of the creepy-crawly itchies. He scratched his arms and legs furiously.

"They hate us," she continued. "We kill them by the thousands and think of them as helpless, but they are not. From the beginning of time the souls of all dead bugs have been gathering in the deepest pit of the earth, growing and forming a nasty demon-king, the dark spirit of all insects that waits for revenge in a hot puddle of slime."

"Revenge?"

"That's right, revenge. And if its soul was ever released the beast would keep on coming, never ever to stop." She picked up the picture frame and started to turn it around. "This is the Slither-Shifter, never before seen by human eyes."

The portrait came around to full front and for a moment Denny was speechless with awe. It was a horrid picture of partials and pieces, all drawn in fine detail. There were ten slanted eyes, all without pupils and each made up of what seemed like hundreds of miniature black bulbs. Below them was a lipless mouth overrun with jagged, uneven fangs. There was no body, but the proportion was cleverly hinted by two half legs, barbed at the joints and reaching out with dripping pincer claws. The one drawn wing had poisoned-looking stingers poking out at the veined cross-sections of webbing, and the whole thing looked mad as blazes.

Denny put on the best tough-guy face he could muster.

"Where's the rest of it?"

"It's not full-bodied," she said. "It's a spirit. But if it ever gets out from behind the glass, you're a goner."

"Why? What does it do?"

"It joins with things to become whole."

"What things?"

Josephine put her finger against Denny's chest.

"Anything you touch with both hands." He sat back and tried to treat the fascinating picture on the table as casual background while he hashed out the new boundaries.

"So, if I touch a pencil . . ."

"It becomes a pencil-bug. The point would turn into a stinger, the eraser would become an eye, and the body would sprout a thousand scrambling legs. Then it would start to slither. It would come at you until you were trapped and then it would get you."

Denny frowned and made laughter come through his nose.

"I'd lock it in a room and run away. That's too easy."

"No, no," Josephine said. "It's a Slither-*Shifter*. It shifts and changes. The very next thing you touch with both hands becomes a new monster. The 'shift' is forever stuck in your fingers and that's how it follows you."

"How do you kill it?"

"Can't. It never dies."

Denny squinted a bit. Every monster had its weakness. Those were the rules and it was up to him to uncover the flaw.

"How do you stop it from shifting?" he said.

Josephine hesitated.

Got her! She's got to think of an answer or the story is a major league boner. I'm going to win and laugh at her picture and laugh at her.

But she made a mental rally. She grinned and stood up.

"The only way to re-cage the Slither-Shifter once it cuts loose is to make it like you."

Denny grimaced.

Girly ending, gross but legal.

"Yuchh," he said. "How do you do that?"

"It's a riddle."

"Hmm."

He offered out a bit of a smile, and Josephine returned the gesture. Her story had been a good one and in their brief moment of smiling at each other, like it or not, Denny felt himself and this newcomer becoming something like friends.

"OK, Denny. Let's go. It's time to put this thing in its place." She grabbed the picture and set it under her arm. Denny sat on his hands.

"What do you mean?"

"You know."

Denny snorted and mimicked her doorbell-like tone.

"No I don't."

She put her free hand on her hip and rolled her eyes up at the ceiling.

"Where's the scariest place in the house?"

"The basement!"

"Well, lead the way, mister."

Denny sat where he was.

"Why?"

"What's the matter, you scared?"

"No!"

"Then let's go," she said. "We have to find the darkest corner of the scariest room and cover the monster up for the night. That is, unless you're chicken to have it actually growing two floors beneath you in the dark while you sleep."

Denny jumped up and raced for the cellar door. Totally cool! She made it so her story could go on all night in a lingering creep-fade. He flipped the butterfly bolt lock, grabbed the copper knob, and swung open the door so hard it banged the wall of the short kitchen archway.

The light high in the basement stairway winked on, and when Denny released the pull string a cone of tiny dust pieces swirled up toward the bulb. The wooden stairs led down to a furl of black shadows, and Denny vaulted to the bottom. Behind was the creak and groan of the steps as Josephine fought to keep up, and when she reached the basement floor she was quick to say, "Where's the next light?"

She shielded her eyes at the brow as if it would help her to read the new blindness, and Denny covered his mouth to muffle the giggle. He stood but two feet away from his babysitter and though it was her mission to scare him, it was now Josephine Thompson who had no clue a rusty water boiler was parked three feet to her right. She could not see that a roll of chicken wire sat directly to her left beside two rescue pick-axes, a spaghetti mop, and a pair of floor brooms with worn, curled-in bristles either. All she saw was Mr. Strange Darkness, and he was a stranger nobody liked especially during first visits to cellars.

"Over here!" Denny said. She jumped and Denny let go his laugh. He was closer than she had anticipated and fifteen years old or not, his sudden call had given her a kindergarten sort of a fright.

"Turn on the main light, Denny."

Her voice had gone out of story-telling character, and Denny went up on his toes for the string. The bent hanger, twisted onto the short length of clothesline that was tied to the light chain up at the bulb's base, soon came to his grasp, and Denny promptly gave it a yank. After all, it was in his best interest to do what she said. It was her picture. It was her story. And hadn't she promised that the best was still coming?

Maybe the scare he just gave her guaranteed it.

The overhead light made a weak yellow oval on the dingy floor and Denny turned, ready to guide her to the farthest corner of the basement. To the left just outside the dim ring of light was a haphazard arrangement of cardboard boxes next to a Westinghouse washer and a dryer missing its label plate. To the right sat a grouping of gray metal shelving units filled with paint cans, turtle wax tins, shoe polish, and varnish. On the wall behind, there were rows of power tools hanging off nails. Denny reached in between Dad's two-speed Sawzall and the cordless drill for his finger flashlight with the soft rubber grip.

"It's scariest back here," he whispered over his shoulder.

"Solid," Josephine whispered back. Denny's light cut slashing lines into the room's thickest darkness. Back by the heater, Denny stopped and shone down his beam.

"Here," he said. "The place for the picture is here."

Her hand fell on his shoulder then, and it took everything in Denny's power not to jerk at the touch. He had not expected it. Oh well, she got backsies on him. No problem. He supposed he'd had it coming.

Still, her voice was not filled with the triumph that he had anticipated. It was flavored with something he didn't quite get, quiet on the high edge of weird with a protective cover on top of it all.

"Denny, what is that stuff?"

He turned but could not see her eyes in the dark. He turned back and looked down into what the flashlight was showing. There was nothing there, however, except a few of his comics, a sleeping bag, and a bottle half filled with some Mountain Dew from last night.

"What stuff?" he said. "It's nothing, just some of my gear for basketball nights and Lady Weekends."

"What?"

He turned and aimed up the flashlight beam so it rode between them. Her eyes seemed strange and focused and hot, kind of like before when he had spoken of eating leftovers for dinner each evening. Or maybe it was just the lighting.

"It's my basketball gear," he said. "When Dad watches his games, he'd, I mean I'd rather play down here by myself. It's my doom-room, my bad-pad. Comics are best read in the dark with a flashlight anyway, right?"

"And what the hell is a 'Lady Weekend'?"

Denny looked back at his sleeping bag and twirled the flashlight so it made tight little circles on it.

"You know, Lady Weekends. Dad calls this special number and a lady shows up. He helps them. It's his weekend charity. The ladies always wear a lot of perfume, and Dad says I could catch something from it if I'm around. When I was younger I used to cry, but I'm a lot bigger now. A month ago I even went a weekend and a Monday without ever coming up, even for food. Dad gave me a dark chocolate Hershey Bar for that."

He put the flashlight right under his chin and gave a monster laugh.

"Mwahh, hahh, hahh!"

Josephine said nothing back for a moment, and with the light in his face, she looked like a burning, white outline. Then her breathing seemed really loud.

"Come, Denny, now!"

She spun and marched back toward the stairway. When she noticed that Denny hadn't followed in tow, she spun back.

"Now, I said!"

"Why? I thought the Shifter had to be put in the darkest, scariest—"

"Plans have changed. It's got to be put elsewhere or the magic air currents won't match up with the stars. I forgot that it's different in the winter, so c'mon, hurry up."

She was standing under the light now and her smile looked about as fake as the new, slipshod twist to the story. And as Denny dragged his feet across the floor he wondered why Josephine seemed not to want to be friends anymore.

5.

When he emerged from the basement Denny was surprised to see that Josephine was not waiting for him by the couch. Instead, she was standing at the foot of the stairway that led to the second floor and hugging the large picture frame, drawing side in. She pivoted, walked up the first four stairs, and turned back.

"Ready?"

Denny approached and rubbed his toe on the first stair.

"Ready for what?"

"It's got to go in your room and you have to survive the night alone with it, Denny. And there's no sticking it under the bed or inside the closet either. It's got to stay in full view, that is, if you've got the guts for it."

Denny did not trust the new deal and he stayed where he was. The integrity, rhythm, and essence of the ghost story had been clearly discarded, and this new stuff had everything to do with Josephine Thompson's obvious need to be shown the upstairs. It was creepy and Denny just couldn't figure out why it had all become so important all of a sudden.

"You know I ain't scared," he said.

"Then let's go. Straight ahead, then to the left or the right?"

"The left," his distant replay. He sidestepped up the stairs, pretending to study the paint chips in the banister, and a light beckoned down proving Josephine had found the hall switch. Denny looked up. She was studying him from the landing.

"Coming or what?"

He glanced down and by the time he raised his eyes the landing was empty. She had made her way down the hall without him.

"Hey!" he said.

Nothing.

"Not funny," he said, forcing a laugh into it.

Nothing still, and he made himself trudge up the stairs. Why was she playing possum at this point? What did it mean? He turned the corner and saw her frozen in his bedroom doorway, facing in and away. The bare bulbs of his combination ceiling fan/ceiling light stretched her shadows down the hall almost to the bathroom.

"Well?" he said.

Silence. She remained a statue in the doorway and Denny took a cautious step toward her. His breath quickened.

This was all starting to spook him for real.

Denny had it figured by the time he shuffled past her and he tried to cover his sigh of relief. Mystery over; Josephine Thompson was just a bit shocked by the mess, nothing more, no reason to freak. Denny hadn't cleaned in a while; in fact, he could not remember the last time he'd reshelved a magazine or wiped off a table. Oh sure, everything looked just peachy to him, but Denny tried hard to put himself in his babysitter's place.

To her it must have seemed pretty gross.

The bed was unmade and rumpled with an old yellow checkered summer sheet balled in a blanket that had faded pictures of tugboats and trains on it. By the footboard, a pillowcase popping lint balls along the seams was crammed to the gills with gadgets, toys, and rolled-up Monster Truck posters. A bit farther up on the mattress there was a stadium air horn turned down on its bell, and next to that a Stomp Rocket Load Launcher with a busted tripod. The place of honor atop Denny's pillow was occupied by the PlayStation controller and an empty case that read "Twisted Metal II," while in the darkness beneath the box spring an ancient, half-deflated kickball could be seen next to an orange squirt rifle that had a snapped trigger from two summers before.

And from there it all really crumbled.

Clothes were strewn around the bed area like a ring of drowning children, all reaching for the lifeboat that kept afloat their captain's best interests. Past that was the clutter of obsolete playthings that crawled for the wall shadows. Tonka trucks were jackknifed and up-ended across sections of warped Brio train tracks. Two Hot Wheels talking road lanterns sat by a toss of baseball cards, key chains, C batteries, and Mega Bloks Lego pieces. Pogo foot rests, streamers, extended forks, and other bicycle parts lay stranded by the TV, and a heap of greasy chains curled themselves into the remains of a ripped T-shirt in the corner by the closet. Stuffed animals of the past were abandoned by the heating vents. Pocket change, crayons, CDs, spitball straws, and other littery things spotted the rest of the floor, and at the room's farthest edge there sat an unfinished rolltop desk that had a bunch of used-up Wendy's Frosty cups stuck across the top in a line.

Josephine entered the space and walked from one side to the other as if in a dream. By the far window she finally paused and reached toward Denny's only room plant, a large tub-shrub left from the days of his mother. It sat on a rickety bar stool and had a sweat sock stuck in the branches. She plucked it out, let it dangle, and then dropped it.

"What is all this?" she said. Denny shrugged.

"Nothing."

"Nothing?" Her eyes had gone wide and her voice started to rise. "Nothing? It seems like this room has been left on its own to rot,

Denny! This is worse than I thought it would be. It's not just ghetto in here, it's funky and nasty like a live nightmare. There are things on your floor from your baby years. How do you live like this?"

"It's OK."

"OK? Are you out of your mind?" She looked up at the ceiling, blinked, and looked back. "What does your father think of all this? The refrigerator was suspicious and the basement was a horror show, so set me straight one thing at a time. Explain his angle. What does he say about the disaster in here?"

It was Denny's turn to blink.

"Nothing."

"What?"

Suddenly, Denny wanted to scream, *"Did I stutter?"* but thought the better of it.

"He doesn't say anything," he said. "He tells me to keep my stuff to myself and out of the hallway, that's all. He doesn't care. It's cool. It's OK."

"No, it's not OK!"

Eyes wild, she paused there for just a moment, then marched across the room and slammed the Slither-Shifter picture down on the flat part of the rolltop desk. The sound made Denny jump and the picture now stared out face front catching glare. Josephine stepped back in close and spoke in a tense whisper.

"It's not cool, Denny. It's not cool, it's not OK, and it's a case of neglect. The question is what do we do about it."

Denny stared. She was using adult words that stood for bad things, and he usually ignored all that crap. Finally he gave up, frowned, and looked down at the floor.

"Right," she said. She put her hands on Denny's face and raised it so he would look at her. She smelled nice, like soap. Her hands were smooth and cool and her eyes had gone soft.

"I have to make a phone call, Denny. I have to call my father. It's going to be all right in the end, I promise."

"But why—"

"Shhh."

She put her shoosh finger against Denny's lips and he spoke through it.

"What are you going to say? What are you gonna say about me and my Dad?" Tears were springing in his eyes and Josephine backed away.

"I'm going to use my cell phone. I'll be right outside on the stoop."

"We've got a phone downstairs. What's so wrong with our phone?"

She shook her head and made for the door.

"This is private, Denny. You stay here. Do not move, understand?"

Josephine's quick turn on her heel cut off his chance to answer. Her footsteps then marched away down the hall and went quiet as they hit the carpeted stairs. Denny raced for the window, sickened now with the feeling that he'd somehow gotten the remains of his family in real trouble. Down on the step Josephine soon appeared, cell phone to ear. At first she seemed to be waiting. Then she paced, talked, and made big arm motions.

But what had Denny done to earn all this? What was so bad that Josephine Thompson, a teenager who was almost full grown, felt the need to call her Daddy on a cell phone outside? His breath made a hot oval on the glass, and suddenly she looked up from the stoop. Their eyes met. And it was then that Denny could have sworn he heard a scraping behind him. Just one little scrape.

He spun around and looked to the rolltop desk in the corner of his room. He gulped. Blinked his eyes twice.

The Slither-Shifter picture had changed since Josephine created it and brought it into the light of this room. For the lines now looked darker. The eyes seemed brighter, and in the bottom left corner about an inch off the frame there was now a small crack in the glass.

6.

It's only a drawing.

Denny crept toward the picture on the rolltop desk, his head cocked to one side and eyes squinted down with suspicion.

It's only a drawing.

His heart was pounding and he was ashamed of it.

It's only a drawing.

Of course the sketch now appeared sharper and darker, for anything would look sharper and darker under unshaded bulbs like those in the overhead ceiling fan.

But what about the scrape from behind?

Good question, and Denny fought with it for a moment. Cripes, about thirty seconds had passed since "the noise," and it was already hard to imagine what it had actually sounded like in the first place.

Did it happen at all?

Another good question. In fact, as time trickled by the whole business seemed sort of silly. Still, Denny was almost positive that Josephine had smacked the frame dead-nuts center, and now it was parked a shade right. With his toe, he nudged aside a ribboned coil of weather-spotted caution tape he'd recently found in the street and stepped in close to the glass. The crack itself stemmed from the picture's bottom corner and split to a fork at its peak. The new flaw was tiny. A sliver. In the background behind it, Denny's shadowy reflection wavered in the glass atop the dark lines of the Slither-Shifter. Suddenly he was aware of the sound of his own breathing and he noticed his neck hair was up. Dang, it felt like those bug-eyes were watching him! They almost tickled. Denny raised up his glance and by instinct he also sucked in his breath.

So did the picture. Denny jerked back and almost stumbled over his heels. A sharp breath or something just like it had vacuumed into the frame a split second after Denny's own whooshed back through his lips. Was that thing actually alive under the glass and echoing the patterns of Denny's breathing for camouflage? He took a step forward and the glare on the eyes followed. He took a huge breath and held it fast.

Was there overlap just then?

He could not tell. It was too close to be sure.

Denny made a scrambling rush for the bed, climbed up, and pawed at his pillow. One of the limp, weathered corners was poking a feather and he grabbed it out, jumped back to the floor, and stamped across the room as fast as he could. Close to the picture again, Denny breathed deep twice and then held one in with all that he had. His hand rose and he let the feather fall on the desk just in front of the crack in the glass. His lungs were starting to beg for air but he had to be sure. He backed all the way to the window, focused, and let out his breath as hard as he could.

The picture did not blow back even a bit, for the feather had not moved an inch.

Denny paused, stared, shook his head slowly, and then almost laughed out loud at himself. Whew! Breathing pictures? Spirits alive under glass? How old was he, four? He leaned back, turned, and rested his forehead against the cold window. The little grin that had surfaced on his face faded. Down below, Josephine was sitting on the step and comfortably deep into her conversation. He bumped his head lightly against the glass pane. *"At least that picture ain't really alive,"* he thought, and when he rapped his head once more for good measure, a noise came again. A noise from the desk area. Loud this time and unmistakably real.

"Wwwwhhhoooo!"

Denny whirled and almost gagged. The feather was dancing on the air, cutting half-moon sweeps toward the floor before the rolltop desk. He eyes went wider. Behind the glass there was now a third claw and the faint outline of a new tail fin growing in the background.

Denny burst into a run for the door, and the picture scraped sideways along the rolltop's surface as if tied to him by an invisible wire. He threw on the brakes mid-stride, one sneaker still in the air and the picture halted as well. Now the corner of the frame was way out over the desk's edge, teasing, promising that another fraction of an inch would make it spill over.

Denny struggled for balance, brought down his foot, and then tried retreating a step. Slowly.

The picture did not slide back one inch and its ice black eyes seemed to sneer,

"I don't play Monkey-See-Monkey-Do when you wimp out going backwards. And it's still your move, scumbucket."

Denny pounded a mad break for the door. The picture then launched off the desk, cartwheeled across the room on a slant, flattened out, and crashed to the floor in a loud burst of shattering glass.

Odd-shaped pieces mushroomed up and showered the floor before Denny's feet. The fierce buzz of a thousand insects then filled the air and he was hurled back by a blast of cold wind that erupted up from the gutted picture frame. It smelled like wood-rot and its force rattled the window, flickered the lights, and slammed shut the door with a clap.

Denny was lifted off his feet, his hands flew overhead, and while coming down in a half-turn he noted that his body was headed toward the old wooden stool by the window. He tried to land it running. No dice, the spin threw his balance and dropped him. Sliding now, still turning, Denny Sanborn bowled knees first into the stool and reached out to grab hold of something to cushion his spill. His arms closed around the big potted plant in a bear hug. The weight of the heavy clay urn spun him, lifted him from the knees, whipped him around a last time, and returned him to the floor on his bum. He skidded and then crashed backward into the wall, all breath knocked out in a whoosh. Black stars swirled and danced in his eyes. He blinked at them and noticed something tickling under his chin. It felt hairy, rough, and, of all things, alive.

Denny looked down at the plant between his palms and his mouth fell open. The branches were moving. The ball-jointed stalks were bending and reaching like spider legs, and what had been small, white flowers at the tip of each axil were now black claws that snipped open and shut.

A scream rose up in Denny's throat.

Deep between the branch-legs, the pot soil had grown a ribbed, uneven skin and its small, gray pebbles were now spotted lids. They flew open and ten black eyes smiled upward.

Denny broke the stare and shoved the thing away as hard as he could. It somersaulted end to end across the floor and screamed an angry, high-pitched whine with its multiple legs thrashing up at the air. When the tumble-flip brought it down flat to hard wood, the huge flower pot smashed in two beneath the beast, spraying fire-hardened clay fragments and shards toward the door. Immediately, these razor-edged pieces turned grayish-white and began to curl. Maggots now, they wriggled on their backs, sprouted rootlike, uneven legs, and struggled to get upright.

The original Slither-Shifter was stuck under the two main halves of the busted urn, with the crack between the clay pieces sitting directly over its knotted spine. Something moved slightly and then the curved hunks of pottery began to flutter and lift. Now they were wings, webbed, sectioned, and flapping to a milky blur.

The huge insect rose off the floor and let down its branch-legs in the dangling, bent-in position for flying. It buzzed over to the far wall, landed, and scampered for a high corner.

Every muscle in Denny's body was frozen. The small, white, squirmy things had grown up fast, most now thumb-sized replicas of their master on the wall and swarming inside the torn T-shirt on the floor. In addition, a few of the biggest were crawling up the busted twist of bicycle chain and practicing jumps off it. They got more sure-footed each round.

Denny glanced back to the wall. The beast was bunched up on its haunches in order to expose a small opening in its bloated underside, and from beneath those folds there was a sudden spitting of white. Denny ducked and heard a suction of contact above his head. He chanced up a glimpse. A long thread from the monster was now stuck to the wall, taut, and melted in at its contact point.

Denny went to his knees and rolled, while in his ears there was the rapid clicking of many claws crawling the wall for better positioning. When he came up, the Slither-Shifter was dead on, a few feet above the bed's headboard, and the babies, now hand-sized, had formed blockades by the window and door. Some remained crouched there while the ones most matured jumped for the walls to crawl up toward the room's highest creases.

Denny reached out his right hand and groped at the floor for a weapon. Already the growing larvae, now the size of Nerf footballs, had turned themselves upside-down from the ceiling and were trindling down from above, crooked legs curled up and skittering along sticky ropes. They looked like paratroopers or Navy Seals repelling a wall. Denny groped around harder. They *had* gone military, for the window crew was webbing checkerboard sections of rope to the right while the door crew had cut off escape to the left.

He was trapped in a death triangle with the big one waiting to wrap him.

Denny's hand closed on a handle of sorts, and right away he recognized the grip of that ping pong paddle he'd found in the trash outside of the 18th Street Y. He pushed up with his left, found his knees, eye-balled a "swinger" about a foot from his head and reared back.

"Die!" he shouted while whipping around the paddle with all of his strength.

The contact was sure and the *crack* from the initial swing was not nearly as sweet as the *splat* when the thing hit the wall. For a moment

Denny grinned. The mini-Shifter burst into about seven pieces, spraying gray guts and leaving a blotch of black dripping slime. Denny's smile faded. The gory pieces immediately took form, turned grayish-white, curled at the edges, and started to sprout rootlike legs.

Denny had created seven new monsters. He looked up and saw that the webs on either side of him were nearly complete, stuck fast to the rolltop, the far wall, and the bed at both ends. And some of the beasts, now as long as an arm, had come off the walls to nestle into different things on the floor. There was one with its bottom side stuck in a pair of Nike sweat shorts and another squirming under an old beanbag chair. They were laying eggs. Denny was done for.

He looked across the room and saw that the main monster was bunching up for the kill. Paddle in hand, Denny shot to his feet and sprang to the bed for a last-ditch, Kamikaze run at the master. To the side, a larger of the replicas turned up on its bottom at the last possible moment and sent out a shooter. Mid-jump, Denny felt the paddle get knocked from his hand and his balance got screwed in the process. He landed the bed on all fours, absorbed the slight bounce, and looked up, fully expecting the big Slither-Shifter to be twirling a snare right into his face.

It was doing no twirling; in fact, it was dead. Nothing but an uprooted plant again, the mess of dirt, roots, and branches fell off the wall, glanced the mattress, and met the floor with a *thunk*.

All around now came similar sounds, as wads of dirt came off the walls and plopped around the bed area. What had been wriggling vermin now tumbled down as small bits and chunks of old pottery. Denny peered over the edge of the mattress to see for sure that the big one was dead. The wad lay still in a muddy tangle of branches and dirt, but Denny suddenly noticed that something had grown warm and wet beneath his palms and knees.

He looked down between his thumbs. Now his hands were pressed to some sort of gross-looking body part that floated in a pool of black phlegm.

It's a tongue! I touched the bed with both hands!

Denny dove from the bed and rolled off his elbows toward the closet. His shoulder bashed into an ancient Phonics Bus and the old speaker wheezed "A is A and Ahh," while spinning and flipping to its side. His back just caught the edge of a mini-firetruck's cherry picker, and through the sharp pain Denny tried to recall in a flash every video or computer game he'd ever set hands on.

Nothing came to mind, at least nothing like this.

He crashed to a stop by the closet and turned. The entire bed frame had gone leathery. There were layers to what looked like gums and each ridged level dripped spit. The short bed legs were now knobby stingers and the only thing missing were teeth.

Solved soon enough.

The "bed" split itself width-wise at center and snapped up like a large mousetrap, the top half coming down with a crash. The headboard splintered and what remained of the jagged spindles formed quickly to fangs set fast in a pair of mammoth jaws.

It didn't wait long to make its first move. The huge thing came forward like a giant set of chattering joke teeth with razors, stilettos, and poison spikes stuck in the gums. Hot black venom sprayed off its jowls.

Denny rolled to the side, found his knees, and looked around for an out.

Touch something small!

His eyes fell on the PlayStation controller sitting on the floor where the bed had just been. He cut back, sprang in, slid on one knee, and grabbed it two-handed in passing. Score! From the corner of his eye he could see the bed snap back to its original form and bang down to the floor at an odd angle.

Yes!

But the thing in Denny's hands was already squirming, and he did not want to waste time saying hello. He shot for the door and at the same time, threw the new Shifter as far behind him as possible.

He heard it land.

He heard it hiss.

He didn't quite make it to the door.

A barbed coil of sorts whipped around his ankle, brought him to the floor, and dragged him backward on the elbows. He winced, turned back a look, and saw that his PlayStation controller now towered above him, balanced on its wire like a large-headed cobra or thinned-down, limbless black mantis. The left and right button boards had sets of cruel eyes and the palm rests were horns made of bone.

The wire tail that had torn itself loose from the console now whipped from the bottom of his right ankle, circled both Denny's shins, and wrapped all the way up to his knees.

It was binding him cocoon style.

He tried to dig his fingers under the tail but the thorny scales spiked up at his touch, puncturing both thumbs and the inner side of his left index finger. He was bleeding now. As if from a dream he began screaming for help, shouting, and thrashing around on the floor.

"Denny?" someone said. "Denny, what's going on?"

It was Josephine standing in the doorway, phone still in hand and a look of amazement spread across her face.

In response, smack in the middle of his current struggle on the floor, Denny felt a bizarre embarrassment strike up inside. He was never one to ask favors. He was never one to beg for help. And regardless of all this, he was still Denny Sanborn the hero, wasn't he? He was still Denny the clown, the one who took the blame for things other kids did, and always made out best on his own.

Wasn't he?

Or did he have it wrong all this time?

"I need you," he said despite himself.

And she came forward. Josephine Thompson came forward in order to help Denny Sanborn, and it was the biggest mistake she ever made in her life.

7.

Josephine made her way into the room and broken glass crunched beneath her shoes. In response, the Slither-Shifter lifted up and cracked down its tail circus-whip style, twirling Denny a number of times in mid-air and sending him spinning toward her in sudden release.

She instinctively hurdled up, but on the way past underneath, Denny's elbow caught on the toe of her shoe. She tumbled forward, swore out loud, and landed in the glass palms first. The swear words became shrieks of pain. She made it to her knees and raised bloodied hands as if making prayer.

No one upstairs was listening.

The living PlayStation controller head swiveled, focused, juked back, and sliced in hard through the air.

It bashed Josephine square in the face. Her head snapped back with the force and when she turned back toward Denny, her eyes were huge. She pressed her hands to her nose and blood squirted between her fingers. She brought her hands down to inspect them and then went back to the wound twice in a touch and look, touch and look. Denny could do nothing but stare at her, hunting for the tough young woman he had met earlier that night on the stoop.

She was gone. And the one left behind in her place was no more than a baby-girl now. A small child lost at the mall. The brave one, the one talented beyond measure and a bit too old for her years was long gone.

As if to prove this, the Shifter twirled its lower end in circles above Josephine's head. In a flash the barbed cord wrapped her throat like a lasso and the beast yanked her up to her feet. It pulled her toward the hall door. She kicked out her heels, clawed at the noose, and her eyes showed nothing but fluttering white.

Denny got to his knees.

By the time he gained a standing position Josephine's flailing feet had disappeared around the corner and into the hallway.

Denny hunched for the run, for the heroic chase scene, but then he just stopped where he was. What possible good could he do for her out there? Was he strong enough to loosen the coils around her throat when he couldn't even budge them an inch off his leg? Who was he fooling?

Shift it again!

But to what? The closest things were the bed, some trash-trinkets, and the hard floor itself; three options that looked pretty bad when you realized that the bed was sure death, a tiny Shifter made of, say, a glass sliver would be small enough to get in an ear for a brain invasion, and a touch to the floor held the horrid possibility of a creep to the walls that went to the ceiling that supported the attic which led to the roof. A house-sized monster by connection-infection! No way. That would put them both inside the nasty thing's gut with nowhere to run, and the chance to run was about all they had left.

Josephine's kicking sounds had faded down the hallway, and Denny realized he was sweating, panting, and doing nothing while the precious seconds slipped through his fingers. He had to do something fast, and the idea of doing something "fast" linked suddenly with the thought that the chance to run was really their last.

Denny had to stop it from moving. He had to trap it somehow and lock it down long enough to save Josephine. He looked up at the ceiling fan and thought about what Dad had said years ago when a much younger Denny was scared it would fall on him.

"Don't be stupid, kid. It's fastened down with toggle bolts. That sucker ain't comin' down, not now and not ever."

Good enough.

Denny jumped no hands to the bed and just before he made his first upward leap, the connection-infection theory again raced through his mind. Would touching the overhead fan-light spread the beast to the ceiling? Where did the disease begin and when did it stop?

He had no choice but to find out the hard way. If she wasn't cooked already, Josephine was damned close to getting there. In fact, right about the time Denny made his first bounding spring there came the sound of a body falling down the hall stairs.

Denny stretched with all that he had and just managed to brush a light bulb with both middle fingers. Instantly, the room was transformed to blackness and Denny stumbled off the bed to get away from the rank garbage wind that whirred from above.

His eyes refocused and on his way out the door he chanced a brief look over his shoulder.

The blades of the ceiling fan were spinning like mad. The four black bulbs, now eyes, arced back and forth in their pivoting hoods, casting thick black beams all around like searchlights on prison walls. The blades spun faster and the new demon began beating those propeller wings up and down with a fury. There was a squeal of steel anchors tearing through ceiling board and a spray of plaster dust that snowflaked the bed.

Denny ran for it.

He ran through the shattered glass to the hallway and slammed shut the door on his way out. He tried to call out Josephine's name but was drowned out by some ripping sounds that came from the room just behind.

It didn't take long for that thing to cut loose from the ceiling. Geez!

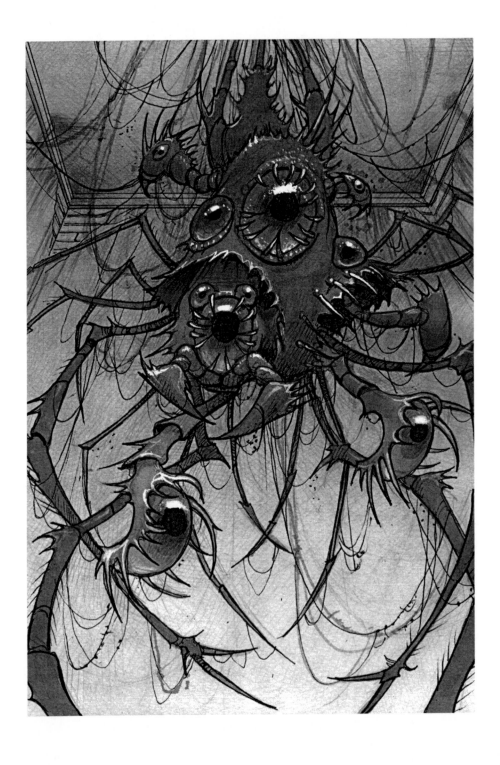

There was a muffled, rapid-fire chopping noise.

It plowed into the bed with its propellers!

There was a crash that was too close for comfort.

It's hacking through the door!

Denny reached the corner and peered down the stairs. He was moaning a bit and he froze where he was. On the downstairs landing jutting out just past the handrail was a twisted foot. Unmoving. Obviously, the rest of her was spilled into the living room. He was too late.

Another splintery bang from behind made Denny jump, and he turned just in time to see the edge of a wing-blade poke out, yank back, rev in a high pitched scream, and punch back through like a hatchet head.

Get down there, if not for her, then just to get out of the house!

Denny tried, but his feet disobeyed. He did not want to see Josephine dead. He hated to admit it but he was scared of the body, scared to approach it, scared to step over it. No, he did not hold his breath while passing by graveyards. He never avoided cracks in the sidewalk nor cared one hoot if he'd stepped beneath a ladder, but there was something about this dead girl that creeped him out something fierce.

"Real live dead girl," he thought and laughed out loud at the way it kind of made sense. Then he laughed at the way his laugh made him sound like a mental patient from *Tales from the Crypt*. Then he laughed at the way his laugh made him laugh . . .

Suddenly the door down the hall exploded off its hinges in a crashing of steel, wing, and wood pieces. The Slither-Shifter, a lunatic helicopter now, blew out sideways, straightened, and came flying in low and hard.

Denny broke down the stairs, taking two at a time. It was not going to be enough. The blades whipping behind him were a hair away and he was only three quarters of the way down. He made a leap for it.

He jumped, stretched, and reached.

Both of Denny's hands closed around the large handrail knob and his momentum swung him over Josephine, into the living room. The hunk of metal that had been the Slither-Shifter bumped loud somersaults the rest of the way down the stairs, bending metal and breaking bulbs. It passed the kitchen archway with a roll and a bang, finally bashing the cellar door and leaving a dent in the wood nearly two inches deep.

Denny landed on his knees and forearms and slid backwards. He upended the coffee table and then came to a stop. He looked back at the stairs.

The handrail knob had become a huge eye, the banister behind it had turned into a long spine, and the spindles beneath soon became slime-dripping ribs. One by one they ripped up from the stairs as the Shifter fought to get mobile.

Denny elbowed over to Josephine. Her eyes were shut as if she was sleeping but Denny knew not to believe that one. Her head had been wrapped three quarters of the way around her shoulders. She was gone forever.

And Denny almost cried when the Shifter's frantic shadows danced across the lifeless form of his babysitter. Still, the cold shame in his heart twisted his emotions a different way. He just stared for a moment, face ashen, mouth open as his mind pointed the finger of blame.

You could have done better, Denny. You could have saved her.

And it was nothing but the horrid truth so help him God, for he had laughed like a hyena at the worst possible moment up there, hadn't he? Hell, he had stumbled down the stairs with a freakin' smile on his face! And the ceiling fan? Why, he should have touched the bed again, hell, it was closer. It would have turned the monster back before Josephine took her fall down the stairs, giving her a fighting chance on the landing instead of a broken neck by the banister!

Yeah, and the thing would have gobbled you whole for your trouble.

Denny grit down his teeth. Sure, he could always be the hero at school and take the blame for things other kids did. But when it came to the real deal here in the house he'd delayed in his room like a coward. When it came right down to it, he'd wanted to live.

Mom didn't get that choice, did she?

Denny looked up at the ceiling, mouth open and neck strained, all in a buried scream that refused to come out. He was no hero, Mom was never coming back, he did not save Josephine, and he had not solved the puzzle. He had only succeeded in running for his life and that race was coming to a close.

That thing was still going to get him.

Suddenly, he lowered his face, took in a deep breath, and did something not too many would ever have expected from the likes of Denny Sanborn. He shouted. He shouted straight into the face of a dead girl.

"How do I win? Why did you have to end the story with a riddle? If I can't kill it, then how do I stop it from shifting? Look at it, huh? How do I make that thing like me?"

It was almost free of the stairway now, a huge and wriggling centipede with clawed spikes for feet. It had but two spindles to go.

Denny's lips formed blubber-bubbles as the weakness of surrender crept toward his heart. Then he stopped cold. Swallowed. The monster had one spindle to go.

How do you stop it from shifting?
You have to make it like you.

Once more, Denny ran those two sentences through his head just to be sure he'd thought it out right. Then he added a third sentence. A sentence that answered the riddle.

How do you stop it from shifting?
You have to make it like you.
Well, Josephine likes me.

At least he hoped that she had. He was, after all, betting his life on it. Denny reached out both palms and cradled her cold cheeks between them. Immediately, the handrail turned back to wood, creaked, yawned out to the side, and hung there.

Josephine's eyes fluttered open. They were pupil-less, bulbed up, and black as midnight. Her broken nose healed and became a slate of uneven scales. Tiny antennae poked from her nostrils and flicked in small, inward arcs. She pushed up and brought her head around in a series of stiff, jerky twitches.

Denny shrank back in horror and at the same time realized that both of his hands had just been to the floor. But there was no tongue beneath now, no sticky legs, just the floor as it always had been.

"I've recaged it," he said from his new position a few feet from the live thing. "Oh, man."

"That's right," Josephine whispered. "Your anger always needed an interpreter."

"What?"

She cleared her throat and laughed at full volume.

"That's right. You've managed to recage the Slither-Shifter."

Denny cringed, for her voice was an awful, inhuman whine that droned with insectile vibration. If he was better off than five minutes before, the difference was too little to measure. There were no hiding holes deep enough for this stuff and nowhere to run anymore. He had invited it in. Now it was his.

"Oh, don't worry, Denny," she said as if reading his thoughts. "I like you, heck, I liked you from the moment I met you."

She stretched over, made a purring, buzz noise, and reached out a claw to pat his cheek gently.

"But I have one big surprise for your Daddy when he gets home from work. One big surprise just for him."

Then she smiled.

She smiled a mouthful of fangs.

The Exterminator

Evan Shaw was lanky. He had a lean face and boyish sandy hair that was always hanging just enough in his eyes so he could give that haughty jerk of the head to clear it off if the moment suited him. He was a sweater-and-jeans guy, a casual guy, the kind of twenty-seven-year-old that had joked his way through high school, breezed through college with a degree in communications he had no use for, and put himself on track to become a thirty-something man's man, king of the golf outing, lord of the watering hole. He was the phone-tanker at a power tool distributor in West Philly, and it bored the hell out of him. He rented in the 'burbs and cooked a mean paella. He often painted on Saturdays. Oils on canvas. He never showed that stuff to his co-workers, but he and Eddie Boylan, the shipping assistant, sometimes held bachelor parties for no reason.

He had a '96 tan Toyota Corolla passed down to him by his mother, and he always had his stuff tossed around in there because it was a shit-heap. His chest pad, knee protectors, and face mask from the over twenty-one summer hardball league were all still strewn across the back seat along with a dirty squeegee, a black umbrella, an unread copy of *How Football Explains America* by Sal Paolantonio, and a AAA map that he had never taken out of the plastic. Up front, there was a red canvas Staples bag on the floor of the passenger seat crammed with three empty half-gallon jugs made of brown glass. He could still return them to the Iron Hill Brewery if he wanted a discount on some very expensive and very potent Belgian Triple. There were a bunch of old cash receipts and straw wrappers in the change-holder between the seats along with some pens, a clay man figure in a reclining position that his little brother Robert had given him for his twenty-fourth birthday, and a bunch of pennies that looked as if they had been on the bathroom floor of every truck stop in America.

It was the day before Halloween and Evan was driving sort of fast. He'd originally intended to stop at the gas station on Haverford Avenue and do a quick vac job to the old rustbucket, but Horowitz had pinned him at the loading dock with questions about how to properly tag some repairs. It held him up for thirty-five minutes. Evan prided himself on the fact that he got along with everyone: diesels, wise-asses, and even the sensitive intellectual types (usually electricians and specialty carpenters) who came along once in a while in the trades. Still, his sincerity with Horowitz had come off a bit condescending. He would have to work on that.

He hawked up and spit out through the open window while curving past the bowling alley. Now he was going to miss the first hour of Comcast Daily News Live. The T.L.A. Video was way up Lancaster Avenue almost to Villanova University, and by the time he returned the DVD and doubled back to his small apartment in Wynnewood, Michael Barkan would be long done talking about the Phillies and their miracle run. They'd be into that "Quick-Six" bullshit where the reporter looked right into the camera to answer some "funny" little question, as if that wasn't the creepiest thing in the universe, and then they'd digress to the dregs, like interviews with retired basketball coaches from St. Joseph's or LaSalle, or some such dumb shit.

Evan flipped on the radio and hit the four programming buttons in succession. Super Tramp, too queer, Three Doors Down, too predictable, Papa Roach with that annoying way he curled his "R" sounds, and a Journey song that made him want to scratch his eyes out with a fork. Nothing. He had installed a CD player last June, yet anything but Puddle of Mud's "Famous" or Metallica's black album came through the speakers with too much bass no matter what combination you threw on the dials, and he had killed both records with overplay weeks ago. Someday, he would buy a long American car with soft seats, a smooth sound system, and shitty gas mileage. He did have plans.

His nose was bleeding. He recognized it immediately; heavier and quicker than snot, and he could feel a runner drop over his upper lip like a stone. He sniffed in hard, tilted back his head, and felt along the seat for a tissue or something. He'd had a Kleenex box with the cartoon rat from that Disney movie on it, but to the best of his memory it had migrated to the trunk for some reason, there along with an old hubcap, a cheap red and white blanket, a mini-stepladder with rubber tread on the stair grids, and a million plastic water bottles he'd forgotten to recycle.

He strained his eyes down at the road and looked for a place to pull over. He had just passed the D.M.I. Home Supply, and the parking lot for the commuter train was on the far side of the street. The trees were a red and orange blur and the asphalt a slick black mirror with leaves stuck in the wet gutters like paste. Evan almost knocked "Vantage Point" on the floor, and he caught it just in time. He was co-ordinated for a big, lanky guy. In fact, Jimmy Savoy in accounts payable told him that he was a ringer for the dude who had done those "There's only one October" commercials this year. That guy caught a baseball coming out of the television.

Evan snorted a laugh at himself and instantly regretted it. Hard breathing in any way, shape, or form was not the wisest idea right now. He pinched the bridge of his nose between his thumb and index finger and cursed himself for not setting up his humidifier earlier in the month. He'd had nosebleeds in the cold weather since junior high school, and he knew better. It's just that he seemed to forget every year whether he was supposed to dig out the humidifier when he brought his sweatshirts out of the closet or when he started actually using the heat all night. He suddenly thought that it would be a good idea to keep a notebook for that kind of stuff. He hated nosebleeds. Even when they stopped, they fucked his confidence for a day or two.

He passed Ardmore Avenue and felt a sneeze coming. This would be an interesting test. Sometimes he had a bleeder for just a minute or so, but now it would be determined whether or not he was going to have a gusher. He moved his head down a bit, studied the road, memorized his position as opposed to the oncoming vehicles across the double yellow line that made *whoosh* sounds on the wet street as they passed, and let his mouth come open.

His nostrils flared out, his eyes squeezed shut, and he sneezed.

No blood, no gusher. He would have felt it immediately.

He opened his eyes to check and possibly realign his position on the road, and he saw something in the afterimage left by the sneeze. It was right on his eyes, like a brand. Behind the image, the road was clear through the windshield, the drooping trees with huge L-cuts in them to let through the electric cables, the dark sky pushing black clouds behind a traffic light suspended on a steel cord, but this thing, this "face" stayed superimposed on all that for a good few seconds.

Evan had two immediate thoughts. First, why is this image in my head, and second, how is it so goddamned vivid?

The shape was the bust of a circus clown with fat cheeks that had red dots on them. The thing was wearing a white party hat with red and blue stripes going up to the tip like a barber pole. There was a golden star at the top on a thin post. The shape wore a skull cap that was as powder-white as the face paint, but there was a clear line where it ended at the top of the forehead and along the temples. Wide eyebrows drawn in arches were colored in solid blue, but that was where the jolly stuff ended.

The brow arches were not located on the front of the face. They were in three-quarter view, almost as far back as the ears hidden by the skull cap. They sat above bulging eyes, wet black eyes bursting out of the head on the sides the way they did on birds. There was no nose, just a furrow with two seed-shaped breathing holes slanted inward. The entire bottom portion of the face was a mouth with no chin. There was a red lip drawn across the top of the maw, and there were teeth, so called. At first, it seemed as if the top row was made of dark, slithery streamers for lack of a better word, like small versions of those rubber strips that dragged over your windshield at the car wash. They were snakes poking out of the gums. The bottom, where the grinding teeth usually stood, was one wide piece of curved bone, sparkling in an idiot's grin. Around the neck, there was a ruffle piece with blue trim and crescent moon patterns. The image stood on Evan's eyes for a moment, then started to fade.

Evan shook his head, hard. He blinked twice and widened his eyes. He touched his upper lip, checking for blood almost in afterthought, and banged a right on Bryn Mawr Avenue. He passed the hospital and the library, then doubled back a block on Lancaster. When he parked in the handicapped spot in front of the video store, he realized he was sweating.

What the fuck *was* that? He wasn't one to like carnivals, and he'd never actually been to a circus. He knew that clowns were also a cliché horror thing, but they had never really interested him in that way either. Political thrillers tickled his fancy more than those jack-in-the-box slashers. He shut the car off and put both hands up on the steering wheel. He'd never paid attention in that high school psych class about Freudian stuff, but he had to wonder how this thing with bird-eyes and greasy-looking snake teeth had made it into his conscious awareness. For something to come into the conscious, didn't it have to be planted somewhere in your experience?

He got the movie and pushed open the door. He stepped in a puddle and soaked his sneaker. He cursed softly. Then he laughed. It was drizzling. He ran his free hand through his hair and it comforted him. He stuck the DVD in the drop slot and by the time he got back to the car the memory of the image had already tapered off. Maybe it was the wind on his face. It felt good. Sweet and damp. Evan loved the autumn. It meant burning leaves, and Thanksgiving, and bare trees scratching art onto a cold, naked sky. Made you want to stop for a moment, cross your arms across your chest, and marvel at the wonder of things.

He pushed back into the vehicle, turned the key in the ignition, and started thinking about change, about possibilities. Maybe he would take a class or something, go back to school, go into teaching. He went for the back exit of the parking lot because there was a light there after you wrapped around. For some reason he liked going home via Lancaster Avenue, and he hated making that left out by Bertucci's against the flow of traffic.

He passed the Viking Culinary Center, pulled up, and waited for the light. Across the street in the Walgreens parking lot, a woman with blonde hair braided in long pigtails got out of a maroon Dodge Caravan with a soccer magnet on the back window. She was wearing a white back-ring halter top, cowboy boots, and a short brown leather skirt with a slit in it. She dropped her keys and bent over. Something in the background moved, and Evan's eyes drifted upward.

There was something in the second-floor picture window. Movement. Colors.

For the second time that day Evan blinked. The Walgreens used to be a Barnes and Noble bookstore. The second floor where the sports books had been along with the children's racks, the brown tables with the wooden chairs only a foot high, and the gourmet coffee shop, was now dark and vacant.

There was a clown up there. He was there in the window. This one had on a big fireman's hat and a mop of bright orange, frizzy hair sticking out to the sides. He had a huge, red bulb of a nose that was tied around the back of his head with a rubber band, and a reflective silver collar piece that rose up almost higher than the back of his head. He was wearing a baggy tinsel-green jumpsuit with oversized buttons that had propellers that moved. His shoes were enormous duck-foot cushions with sparkly, coiled circular twirlers on the toes that gave the optical illusion that they were disappearing into themselves and simultaneously growing as they spun. He had white face paint and black arches drawn high above the eyes that protruded out the sides of his head. There were short black mime lines drawn vertically on the lids and below the lower rims, and that gave the immediate impression that the black eyes were smiling.

There was a kid with him, a little boy of around five or six, in sweat pants and a navy blue pullover with a hood on the back. He had brown hair in a bowl cut and his eyes looked almond-shaped. He could have been Asian, but it was hard to tell. The two looked like they were playing "Catch Me If You Can." The kid ran to the left and out of sight deeper into the space. The clown looked one way, then the other. He put up his hands and gave a big shrug. Then he brought his elbows up twice, leaned down a shoulder, dug at some imaginary dirt with the sole of his foot, and galloped out of sight into the darkness.

A moment later the boy was back at the glass. His face was wet with tears. He looked over his shoulder and tried to run to the right. The clown then emerged and grabbed him by the back of the hood. Clotheslined, the kid's feet almost kicked out from under him. The clown yanked him across and lost his grip for a second. The kid fell toward the glass, then pressed up against it, his face a wide grin of terror. He pounded the window with his open palms. Evan saw it shake with the contact.

The woman by the minivan did not hear a thing. She shut her door, adjusted her purse, and reached up the sides of her ribs to straighten her bra with an exasperated little tug and twist with both hands. Evan usually took his time to savor that particular move, but was compelled to glance back up to the dark glass. The kid was facing sideways now, trying to run, clawing at the grip the clown still had on

his throat through the hood. With his free hand, the huge circus creature drew something from the back of his jumpsuit. It was a meat
hammer. He raised it up and looked right at Evan. He nodded his head
as if they were sharing the cutest little secret, and then he brought the
weapon down.

The head of it disappeared into the boy's skull. Something dark
splashed the window, and wet matter sprayed the clown on the cheek.
A black tongue squirted from the thing's mouth and lapped the splatter off his face. The boy was going through convulsions and a milky
discharge was coming out of his mouth. The clown yanked out his
weapon, and slyly looked out at Evan. The head was sideways. One
black eye winked. Then he lowered his face to the back of the boy's
head and let the snakes in his gums start the feeding process.

The light turned green and Evan hit the gas. He screeched across
Lancaster Avenue, bumped into the parking lot, took up two spaces on
a slant, and jumped out of his car like a plainclothes cop in a TV movie.
Still, the moment he passed through the doors of the store his courage
withered. He was going to blurt out that there had been a murder up on
the second floor, but he had not planned for the change in atmosphere.
The dark sky and wet streets lost their mystery in here under the fluores-
cents. It was like watching old "Twilight Zone" episodes in the living
room with the lights off, then having Mom come in, flick on the over-
heads, and start grilling you about fourth-period calculus.

Up one of the rows there was an elderly man wearing an arm cast
that was dirty and yellowed at the edges where his fingers poked
through. He had a brown scarf around his neck with one end almost
brushing the floor as he bent over to check out the laxatives. There
was a fat African American woman in a caramel-colored pants suit
waiting in front of the photo counter. She had blue eye shadow and
heavy triangular earrings that kept jangling back and forth while she
spoke through her teeth in an angry grin to a bow-legged teen who
wore new-creased blue jeans low enough so you could see the shape of
his butt through an old pair of black running shorts. There was a small
grouping of mainline moms over by the pharmacy having an animated
conversation in a blur of jogging spandex, ponytails, raised sunglasses,
and freckled cleavage.

There were two counter girls up front in blue smocks with name tags, but the shorter one with all the face piercings was counting her drawer. The plainer one with the mild acne and auburn hair tucked behind her ears was managing a line five customers deep.

What was Evan supposed to say?

"Hey y'all! There's a dead kid upstairs with his head bashed in! The clown with the snakes in his mouth did it!"

Couldn't you get in trouble for bringing out the cops for what seemed like a prank?

He walked toward the middle of the store and noticed that his wet sneaker was squeaking and squelching a bit on the hard white floor. The blonde woman with the cowboy boots was squatted down, sifting through the Clairol, Redken, and Essensity products on a low shelf. Evan noticed that she had pretty fingernails, half blue and half white, with silvery trim.

"Hey," he said.

She pushed up and balanced the thin steel handles of the shopping basket on her forearm. She had nice eyes and heavy mascara. Her nose was a bit too big, but she had that hourglass thing going for her. Evan suddenly wondered if there was any blood left on his upper lip. In all the excitement he had never checked in the rearview.

"So tell me you didn't hear someone pounding on the window out there," he said.

"What?"

"When you got out of your car. You dropped something and someone was banging on the second-floor window. You're telling me you didn't hear anything?"

She stopped chewing her gum for a second and put all her weight on one leg. With her free hand, she took a long, braided lock of hair and tossed it behind her shoulder.

"Fucking stalker."

She brushed past and Evan felt his face redden up. He balled his fists and moved to the back of the store. They had only really used about a third of the ground floor. There was new drywall in the rear by the auto parts, and a thin hallway that led to a locked door with a steel keypad on it. Evan peered through. There was the old Barnes and Noble first-floor bathroom, some blue chairs, a microwave, and a row of temporary lockers. If there was a stairway it was not in this sightline.

And Evan could not remember where it had been anyway.

He strode back to the front of the store and approached the counter. The girl counting bills didn't even look up.

"I'm closed."

The stud in her eyebrow looked like real diamond. Her hair was tied back and thrust through a leather Concho, or whatever you called that oval piece with the stick running through it. She had some brown moles at the peak of her forehead that were going to look really hideous when she crossed the age of fifty or so.

"How can I get upstairs?" He bent down a bit. "Hello?"

"You can't."

"I left my jacket up there."

"No ya didn't."

"Yeah, I did. Yesterday—"

"It's locked and they knocked out the stairway. Ya got to take the elevator and it's out of service."

She looked up and cocked her head. She had a wide face and dimples. The nose piece was subtle but the two ball-studs through the upper lip were just a bit too much. She smiled a little.

"Watcha want, anyway?"

Evan was suddenly attracted to her and he did not understand it in the least. He sensed that she sensed this and he looked away, past her shoulder. His eyes settled on a folding chair, set behind her to the right beneath the cigarette display. There was a green jumpsuit laid across it and on the floor was a big fire hat with frizzy orange hair stapled to the brim. She turned to look where he was looking, her eyes staying with his as long as possible. When she turned back she had her mouth opened slightly. She was curling her tongue around the silver stud that was pierced through it.

"It's a return," she said. "The kid said it was too baggy."

Evan went up on his toes and leaned across a bit. The suit was nowhere near big enough to have fit the thing he saw in the window. And this hat had a golden label on the front that said "Engine 52." The one he had seen was blank.

Maybe someone stuck the label on for show.

"Can I see that?" Evan said.

"Sure."

But as she turned he changed his mind. The momentary pull she'd had on him was gone, and he didn't want his fingerprints on that thing on the chair. He walked toward the glass doors and looked along the ceiling for surveillance cameras. He didn't see any and it did not really matter. The guy did not come in through the front entrance and he probably wasn't even up there anymore. If the counter worker was unaware of an access point, the escape would be just as invisible as the entry. There was probably a ladder back by a cutout behind some piping near an old emergency exit or something.

Even if the thing cleaned off the window and took the kid's body with him there had to be some trace of DNA left up there. He'd get in his car, call the police on his cell, and anonymously report what he had seen. Then he would have done his duty. He'd just ignore the question of why the kid was up there in the first place. He'd just leave out the part about the eyes on the sides of the head and the moving teeth. He'd let the professionals figure that garbage out for themselves.

But he never called the police.

He swerved back onto Lancaster Avenue, went around an old bat in a Volkswagen going about three miles an hour and got stuck in the turning lane two blocks down. Just before hitting the last digit in 911, something made him glance to the left.

What he saw in the dark windows of the building across the street was not of this earth.

It was a violent infestation.

It defied rational definition and made his skin crawl.

The huge glass windows were sectioned off by three-by-three white square frames. Through them, Evan could see that the "things" vertically filled the first four to five feet of the space from the floor up and went wall to wall about fifty feet across. They were man-sized and swarming over and across and underneath and between each other. Evan had once seen news footage of rats that had overrun a section of a downtown junkyard, crawling across the bodies of their mates, and this was the same plague on a larger scale. The movement was a constant and violent blur of bright satin colors, arms intertwined and writhing through legs mixed in with flashes of red painted smiles, and stretched balloon pants. There were ball noses and squirting joke flowers and bowler hats being crushed and popping back into shape and

French berets slipping in and out of the cracks along with white gloved fingers and leggings with stripes on them all knotted up and wriggling between and around wristlets with bells, neck frills, gaudy vests, and ruffled-up cummerbunds.

There were people walking on the sidewalk in front and no one was noticing.

Evan jerked the wheel to the right, hit the gas, and sped away down the avenue. He knew he wasn't crazy. If he had gone insane he wouldn't recognize all the normal stuff. He'd be in fairytale la-la land, dribbling on his shirt, picking at his hair, and believing he was someone like Gandhi, or King Henry the Eighth, or Marilyn Monroe.

This was something different.

There was a tear in the fabric here and the virus was getting in.

The face of Rudi DiDomenico flashed into his mind. Rudi was a counter customer who came in with a batch of homemade wine every year around Easter. He was short and always wore overalls and flannel even in the summertime. Rudi drove a van with a model of a huge bug on top of it. They called it the roach-wagon. Rudi was an exterminator, and Evan had worked out a deal with him where the guy bought his twenty-four-inch straight shank carbide bits in bulk for just a thirty-five percent markup twice a year.

Rudi had once said that the key to stopping an infestation was to find the "point of entry."

Evan raced through the intersection at City Line Avenue and sped back toward West Philly. He wouldn't be home for a good while.

By the time he opened the front gate and pulled it shut behind him it was almost dark. Mr. Jarvis had given him the alarm code for the sake of emergencies, but that was a year and a half ago. He hoped the boss hadn't changed the combination.

He walked past the red bay doors and rounded the corner of the building. The steel door to the shop had a small glass window with diamond wire inside it. There was no light coming through it, and the overhead halogen in the back parking area was off. Good. Sometimes Joey Sanantonio liked to stay late and tinker with his vintage Camaro out under the corrugated overhang so he could save money on garage space. Tonight he had cut out at closing with the rest of them.

Evan took a last look around. There were dark row houses behind the building and a high back wall made of cinderblock with razor twine curled in at the top. A dirt plot choked with weeds and occupied by a couple of arrow boards they tried to rent to PennDOT every now and again sat to the left, and the power station across from the front lot was dark and quiet for all but a nearly inaudible hum. He could smell someone burning trash. He opened the door, disarmed the alarm, and turned on the back office light by the head mechanic's work area. The dull glow made long shadows come off the plastic invoice trays, the red repair bins stacked in steel racks anchored to the wall, the calendar with the girl in blue jean shorts and work boots posing in front of a miter saw, the row of bench tools neatly arranged on the wooden slab. He reached over for the Metabo four-and-a-half-inch grinder and flipped it over. It had an eighth-inch cutting wheel on it. OK. So now he would have to go into the first aisle and get a grinding wheel as well as the other stuff. He grabbed a flashlight and went out into the warehouse.

When he returned to the bench he set down a jigsaw with a metal cutting blade, a four-and-a-half-inch grinding wheel, some rivets, a handful of number twelve self-drilling screws, and a fourteen-inch diamond blade still in the cardboard. He unpacked it. He put it in the bench vice. He reached across for the mallet and a file with a thin end on it. He started knocking off the segments. They were only good for concrete. When he had a bare edge, he put on a pair of goggles and plugged in the grinder.

After burning up three abrasive wheels and trashing seven jigsaw blades, he was ready for welding. He went out by the forklifts and approached the scrap pile to the side of a pallet of generators. He found a length of two-inch-wide pipe that was about five and a half feet long. He brought it to the shop and got back to work.

By the time Evan pulled up in front of his apartment the moon was at its highest point, and some DJ was talking about how you could do late night radio in your underwear with a fifth of Jack Daniels by your elbow without management ever knowing it. Evan shut off the car, gathered his stuff, and went up the short stairway. He entered his small foyer and left the lights off. He didn't need them anymore.

*　　*　　*

"Hey, ma."

"Why ain't you at work? It's eight o'clock in the morning."

"I called out. I had to take care of some things. Did I wake you?"

"I was doing a crossword puzzle. What kind of things?"

"Shopping."

"What, do you need money?"

"No, ma. I'm good."

"What's that mean, you're good? You want to talk to your father?"

"What's he doing home?"

"His back went out again."

"Naw, that's OK. Tell him not to believe everything he hears."

"What's that mean?"

"I love ya, ma."

"What?"

"Dad needs new glasses. Last time I was over I saw him squinting at everything."

"Hey, are you sick or something?"

"Bye, ma."

Evan Leonard Shaw looked around his apartment. He hadn't slept. He didn't remember not sleeping, but had no recollection of lying down. He had no recollection of anything.

His fingers were aching.

His tubes, solvents, hog's hair brushes, and pallets were littered across the black dining room table that he bought two years ago at IKEA. The red canvas director's chairs that went with the long black table were shoved in his coat closet along with his down comforter, his four pillows, five trophies (one back from his nine-year-old little league team, The Angels), and thirty-seven novels that had recently shared space with the trophies on the set of inlaid shelves by the fake fire-place. There was paint on the bed sheets. Lengthwise, there was now a pair of eyes, a bulb nose, and a grin. The forehead was cut off by the rectangular limitation, but the tongue was continued down the side of the bed so it could spill out onto the carpet.

The inlaid shelves, those that had been one of the primary reasons he took the place for such a high monthly, were now bare. They helped form a picture of a clown-giant as if seen from under water, huge balloon-like feet across the bottom, then legs with ruffles at the knees, all pyramiding up the slats like waves until the head was but a dot on the front edge of the top mantle.

The exposed bottoms of the pots hanging off the rack in the kitchen were covered with dots and smears. At first it looked like random, yet somehow organized, paint splatter. From the stove five feet away, however, it was a close-up smiling Bozo, red hair burst to the sides, wide eyes, and a grin that stretched along the bottom frying pans. From the dishwasher at the far edge of the space, then, the nose became a medal hanging around the neck of a hairless clown wearing a chef's hat and flipping red pizzas. In the bathroom, there were clowns riding bicycles on the three sections of mirror, but when the two outer pieces folded out, the reflections joined to make a smiling elephant clown that turned into a frowning hippo clown if the angle was altered a fraction of an inch.

The television was on, its screen painted over in thick strokes that formed a smiling clown with silver dollar blush dots on his cheeks. The inside of the mouth and the eyeballs were not painted in, so the moving images beneath made it seem as if he was communicating with the wall clowns across from him. They wore striped shirts, suspenders, and white flood pants and they were painted on either side of the stereo unit, each with a sledgehammer raised in the ready position. The rest of the collage filled the balance of the wall space, one portrait bleeding into the next. There were clowns with big bow ties and clowns with red smiles. There were clowns with checkered bibs, and clowns that were pouting. There were Fedora hats and police hats, and little British hats, and pirate hats perched on bald heads, and heads with wooly hair sticking out over the ears. There were fat clowns and thin clowns, and clowns with teeth and clowns with mini-trumpets that had little rubber squeeze bulbs on the ends.

He did not recall painting them.

They stared at him and he knew what to do.

He went to the bathroom and got out his beard trimmer. He removed the comb-head attachment. He shaved off his eyebrows and then used his razor to erase the stubble. Then he began to remove the hair above his ears. First, he had white-walls, then a Mohawk, then a burr. He picked up the razor for the second time. When he was finished, he started painting again. They wouldn't even see him coming.

* * *

The clown strutted down Lancaster Avenue, and when he passed the college kids who spilled out of the Subway sandwich shop, all four of them cheered.

"You da man!" Andy Pressman called. He was a sophomore, philosophy major, buzz cut, wire frames, head shaped like an egg. He was known to cross his legs, click his pen up by his ear, and in the silkiest of tones deconstruct whatever paradigm the professor had just spent a half hour building in seminar. Even his friends admitted that they thought he liked to hear the sound of his own voice too much. Tonight, he was dressed up for the Halloween party as a cowboy. He'd borrowed the Stetson and the brown chaps from a techie in the theater department. He had just eaten two large Italian hoagies. There was going to be grain punch with dry ice in it, and he didn't want to party on an empty stomach.

Mandy Rivers was wearing a black leotard. She had straight strawberry blonde hair, funny teeth, and an ass that had gotten a bit bigger this semester. Too many late nights reading for her Modern American Lit. survey course, and too many jumbo bags of peanut M & M's to get her through. She was wearing cat ears and had drawn whisker lines on her cheeks. She had painted the end of her tiny, upturned nose silver with product from a cheap makeup kit that she picked up at the Acme, and she tried not to think about how badly it itched.

Terry Murphy, the Murph monster, had gone the economical route. He had on a corduroys blazer, jeans, and a cap. He had drawn in a square, black moustache above his lip, and around his waist was a wire stuck through a potato hanging in front of his crotch. On his back there was a sign that read "The Dictator."

Rachel Silverstein surprised them all. Throughout the semester she had always worn baggy army pants, oversized sweatshirts, and dark black eye makeup. Real Emo, for all but a mane of curly brown hair that would have made any female country singer jealous. A lot of kids thought she had an eating disorder. Tonight, she was wearing a nun's habit, a tight halter top, and black hot pants. Skinny yes, but all legs, hips, and muscle. Andy Pressman couldn't take his eyes off her.

Except when the clown strutted by. That got everyone's attention. The four partiers spilled out onto the street to cheer. Mandy held up her bottle of Deerpark spiked with vodka and spilled a bit on her pink ballet slippers. Across Lancaster Avenue a group of suits elbowed each other and laughed out loud, while a woman wearing ear buds, a fanny pack, and a sun visor turned her baby carriage around, squatted, and pointed.

Later, Andy Pressman would tell the police that the dude was born to be a clown. He was made for it. He was lanky and humorous. He was strutting and swaggering. He would take two steps forward, and one step back. He would prance in circles and wave to onlookers. He did the "Farmer-John-Doe-See-Doe" thing with his elbows, yuck, yuck, and made all the exaggerated facial expressions. He had his entire head painted bright white. He had a Charlie Chaplin hat about half the size of his bald crown cocked to one side. There were blue brow-arches painted all the way up to the top of his forehead. He had black liner around his eyes and they made big teardrop shapes at the outer edges. He had a red nose ball that honked when he squeezed it and fake ears that were about nine inches long. He had on a green and red jumpsuit, Christmas colors, with buttons shaped like horseshoes.

And of course, he had that sick executioner's axe. It was humongous, with a five-foot handle and a fourteen-inch blade cut in a half moon. It was covered with crinkled tin foil, as if there was cardboard or something like that underneath, and it had a red ribbon tied around the shank in a big bow.

He was the scary clown, perfect for the Halloween party in the McDonald's next door.

When asked why he followed the clown, Pressman said that he saw something strange. When the dude passed by, Andy noticed that there was a small rip in the tin foil on the blade of the play-axe. But the material underneath the rip was smooth silver, not cardboard brown.

When asked what he saw when the clown entered the McDonald's, Andy Pressman took off his wire-framed glasses and rubbed his eyes too hard. A bit of saliva bubbled at the corners of his mouth. He said that before the doors shut behind the dude, he could hear the screams of children. The scary clown-thing, you know? Then, through the dark windows sectioned off by those three-by-three white borders, he saw the guy raise up the axe and bring it down in a rush. It flashed. It seemed as if he split a white-haired lady straight in two, forehead to crotch. Pressman thought he may have even caught a glimpse of the inside of her head for a second, marbled T-bone steak in a half-shell kind of thing, as she was turned sideways on one leg and the other half fell away into the shadows like a domino. Or maybe it was a trick of the light. It was really hard to see anything with the angle and the glare of the low sun. Then Andy had hustled back to the sandwich shop to dial 911.

His cowboy hat was now behind his head, the rubber band stuck under his Adam's apple. He rubbed his nose on his index finger and then asked the cop if anyone made it.

Officer Scott McMullins went under his cap with his pen and scratched his forehead.

"After we put him down we found four," he said. "Three employees who hid behind a deep fryer, and a six-year-old girl dressed like a fairy godmother. Like you said, son, he was born for this."

He looked down at his notebook in a quick review.

"Is there anything else you saw, son?"

Pressman shrugged.

"Not really. Just a flash of something, like afterimage. I'm waiting for it to fade, but I don't think it ever will."

"What exactly?"

Andy Pressman looked off toward a picture of Ryan Howard in front of a Philly cheese steak on the wall by the restrooms. His usual honey voice was shocked and dull.

"After he did the old lady, I watched through those windows for an extra second before I ran. I saw them all trying to get away. And for a second they didn't look like people anymore. They were bristling all over each other, like bugs when you upend a rock in the woods." He looked Officer McMullins in the eye. "He made me forget all the stuff that we pack on to make ourselves into complicated geniuses. He forced me to revisit the fact that we all urinate like dogs no matter what kind of fancy porcelain we make the bowls out of. He reminded me that we hate for no reason, and shit on each other more often than we pause to offer one of those 'how ya doin's' that we don't really mean."

Pressman got up.

"He tricked my eyes, don't you see? Just for a moment, he made me look at kids and grandparents as if they were a swarming disease."

He walked to the exit and stopped. Talked to the wall.

"Then he erased them, and I'll never forgive myself."

He pushed through the door and the little bell at the top tinkled in a small fanfare that followed his exit into the night.

Passive Passenger

She was starting in again, and he was well used to it after all these years. Same old tapes played over and again. It was all because he never got that doctorate. He couldn't finish the thesis, and his mere master's in mechanical engineering translated to thirty years of community college work. The pay had been OK, but they'd raised the boys amongst neighbors who were better off. It was not the way of life Dorothy had pictured when she married the number two ranked student overall, first in the sciences, from Brooklyn's Washington Academy and Technical Institute for Boys. Grainy memories from the black-and-white days before the Beatles. She must have thought he would clean up in government work. He preferred the classroom. When they moved to Broomall Pennsylvania for his assistant professorship at Delaware County Community College, she stopped caring about the ins and outs of Melvin's contributions to society. When he failed to complete the Nova doctoral thesis in 1983, she assigned him the back den by the bathroom as sleeping quarters. Melvin had no real argument for this. She'd backed the wrong pony, and now they were limping toward the finish line in their golden years.

Melvin pulled the damp towel a bit tighter under his bloated paunch. The towel was cranberry red, with flower designs on it. He disliked the towel. It was a cheap, short towel that did not absorb the water well. Seemed to run moisture across the skin, leaving a sheen. Dorothy had picked out the towels. She picked out everything. She demanded to do so, and hated Melvin for the drudgery of the responsibility. She cloaked her hate in a mask of annoyance that boasted only slightly blunter fangs. The mask had dug itself in permanently. Her eyes were shock blue, and red at the edges. Her hair looked like a perm, but had taken on the hard consistency of old steel wool. She was very skinny, and the veins on the back of her hands were raised like gorged bloodworms. She had not aged well. Neither had Melvin. He had a nesting of bags under his eyes, thinning hair falling in limp strands over his ears, and pipe-stem arms.

He had goose bumps. It was cold in the hallway. The wallpaper just above Dorothy's head, in the catty-corner between Brian's old room and the bathroom, was starting to curl down at the top edge. It was an ancient, peach-colored wallpaper with a repeated copy of some Impressionist painting of men with bowler hats, tuxedos, and canes. The decorative scheme put the figures in alternating poses both upside down and right side up. Dorothy's taste for a dizzying show-tune world of ladies and gentlemen. Melvin vaguely remembered helping Dorothy pick out the pattern, some time in the early nineties when Douglas was still in middle school learning to play the clarinet that he would give up soon after (he much preferred smoking pot, listening to The Stone Temple Pilots on volume ten, and masturbating for what seemed like hours on end). Melvin dimly recalled shopping with Dorothy when he had lab books to grade, shopping with a smile at the Wallpaper Plus that sat next to the Dress Barn, next to the Kids Cuts, next to the Blockbuster Video. Back then, Melvin had been good at acting interested in wallpaper, and knowing which designs to keep hesitant about. He knew just how long to play hard to get, and then zone in on Dorothy's real first choice. He knew that she knew he was faking interest, and he had long lost the talent to play that particular clarinet, so to speak. It had been a slow process of intricate, quiet protest to convince Dorothy that their little illusions had truly worn down, but that moral victory led to constant, explosive confrontations. The price for the breath of freedom. And he well knew he would somehow be blamed for this current curling in the corner of the ceiling. This unexpectedly raised up an old, helpless anger in him, and he swallowed it. Dorothy always won those things. She was just too darned fast.

"Move over, Mel. I've got to get in there."

"OK."

"You slept in again."

"I know, but it's the weekend."

"It's almost nine o'clock!" Melvin looked down.

"I know."

"Comb your hair."

Melvin brushed the lock that had fallen across his cheek back over his bald spot. She pushed past, and her voice snapped from behind the door.

"Wipe off the sink after you shave, Melvin. We discussed this."

"OK."

"And call the plumber today. That rattling heater kept me up all night."

"Right!" Melvin entered his room. He hung the towel on the doorknob. He slipped on an old T-shirt, and sagging underwear with rips and tears beneath the band. "Right-O!"

But he would forget. He always forgot. Dot was bound to come home and ask up front if he had gotten it done. Melvin would look up in guilt and surprise. "Gosh, honey. I forgot!" Then she would explode and do it herself. It was an old, familiar routine. Melvin pulled his glasses down to the end of his nose and mimicked Sigmund Freud under his breath.

"It is a vicious cycle of reciprocal punishment that dates so far back we fail to expose its very origin, silly, silly."

He reached into the closet and got out plaid trousers and a wool sweater with tan patches on the elbows.

"Practicalities get in the way," he thought. "They work against the very fabric of creative thought." He stroked his chin. "But we must always make room for greatness, mustn't we?" Melvin turned toward his home computer and his eyes danced with lust. Was it still there? The naughty treasure hidden inside the terminal, was it still there?

Of course it was. It had to be, for Melvin had kept the computer running all night. He hadn't dared shut it down for fear of losing it forever. He approached the dark screen, flipped the dimmer switch to bright, and was greeted by words on a electric green background:

WELCOME TO PASSIVE PASSENGER

"Melvin!"

The voice came from behind his closed door, but he still jerked up and slapped the dimmer button across so to blacken the screen. "Yes, mother?"

"Stop calling me that! I'm your wife, Goddammit!" Melvin stared at the carpet and made no reply.

"I'm going out," she said to the silence. "I'll be back later." Her announcement did not require a response, so there was no hesitation in her footsteps that marched down the hall.

"Go ahead, stay out all day," Melvin said to himself. "Out all day so Mel can play." He slid the dimmer again to bright and the letters surfaced, cat's eyes with black lids. How he had stumbled on PAS-SIVE PASSENGER was a bit of a mystery, all starting with a website address that he had downloaded onto his flashdrive yesterday before lunch, and subsequently forgotten by dinnertime.

Innocent. That morning he'd signed on for a fellowship offered through the college by the U.S. Navy. The same as last year, the program commissioned two thousand dollars to the candidate most quali-fied to chart the voice patterns of dolphins. The website was an innocent little orientation page, and the announcement received on his school e-mail was jammed on his already overloaded flashdrive that was slung on his lanyard with his college ID, tucked under his jacket, and out of mind as he shuffled through his daily routine. After classes, he stopped at Kelly's for a chocolate donut with rainbow sprinkles. He flipped through some science magazines at Borders, lost track of time, and wound up back at the house after six.

"Sorry I'm late," he called out at the door, as if it was not standard practice.

"I'm in here," Dot said. She was watching the tail end of the eve-ning news. Melvin stood at the edge of the room.

"Well, I'm home," he said. "Anything for dinner?"

"I already ate."

"Oh. Time just kind of passed by, and—"

"I know."

"Oh."

Melvin still had his coat on. He held his hat in his hands, fidgeted with it, and considered joining his wife in the living room for the nightly ritual in which they viewed the news together and passed it off as communication. He watched his wife watch TV for a moment, the image reflecting off her emotionless face.

"Melvin, either come in or go out. You know it annoys me when you stand—"

"Hey, I know him!"

"What on earth are you talking about?"

"They just said Engine 38, look!" He pointed at the television. It was a firefighter, dirty, tired, and at the conclusion of what seemed a strained interview.

"Here with Captain Hugh McNulty, I'm Marylin Chang for Newswatch."

Melvin took a step farther into the room. "So that's his name, Captain Hugh McNulty! It's his mobile unit that I pick up on my radio scanner. By God, I've heard his voice a thousand times!"

Dot sniffed and rubbed her nose.

"Melvin, why don't you toss all those contraptions into the garbage where they belong? That room of yours is an eyesore."

"But—"

"Melvin, it's a junkyard in there."

His shoulders sagged. He had constructed his radio scanner of parts from an ancient radio, digital clock, and Press-N-Play record player. Yes, it was locked onto one lone frequency. It was true that his electric trains only ran in reverse and he had to concede the fact that the automatic pencil changer couldn't be run on 110 without blowing a fuse. He sighed. Originally, he had built his scanner with the hope of picking up a variety of weather stations, and what he had gotten was Engine 38 of the Philadelphia Fire Department. It was a lot of code words, background sirens, and probable D.O.A.'s.

Suddenly, he remembered the stuff on his flashdrive. He straightened up and cleared his throat. "I'm going to work on my computer." With her eyes, Dot gave the cold permission for him to sneak back to his room.

It's a junkyard in there.

Melvin closed the door and searched for a place to toss his coat amidst the disorder of games and gadgets that were scattered across the room on tabletops and milk crates.

Yes, but it's my junkyard.

Melvin got his last yellow post-it note, found a pen, and wrote the name "Captain Hugh McNulty" on it. He stuck it to the top plate of

127

his radio scanner, the name behind the voice. Then he turned, smiled, and approached his computer. His coat went to the floor, his briefcase to the side. Some things never spoke back at him. He gently pressed on the power to his electric friend and ran two fingers down the screen. It winked on with quiet obedience.

It's my junkyard and here, my little subjects hum and buzz and radiate like music.

With an artist's flair, Melvin inserted his flashdrive. The checkerboard of files came up, but the announcement for the orientation page was missing. Melvin backed out and went online. After a bit of tooling around he found the website and clicked. Then came the sudden pop and coppery smell of overloaded wires.

"Balls," Melvin said. The screen shut down to a rude shade of black. Melvin sighed and reached down for the power strip. He flicked it off and on in quick succession and bolted upright when his computer made a sharp beeping noise he had never heard before. Melvin rested his fingers on the keys, ready to log it off and start over again. But atop a strange green background, words were materializing that had nothing to do with Annapolis and the songs of dolphins.

MCGILLICUTTY / DELSORDO
PROJECT SOKAR
DEAD FILE
PRESS ESCAPE TO CONTINUE

Melvin snatched his fingers off the board. Ryan McGillicutty and Angel Delsordo had not been front page news since the seventies, but they were as much a part of the cultural fabric of the greater Philadelphia area as was Rocky Balboa. They were mobsters who had demanded protection from more than a third of the small downtown businesses back then. It was rumored that by 1982 they had taken control of the plumbers' and electricians' unions as well as the Department of Transportation. But hadn't McGillicutty died of lung cancer back in '87? And wasn't Delsordo serving multiple life sentences at Graterford now? If anything, this was a new generation. Melvin looked over his shoulder, turned back, and read the screen again.

PRESS ESCAPE TO CONTINUE

He stared at it and it stared back. Could they trace this to him through his cookies, or whatever they called those things? Too late, he was already in. And what the Dickens was "Project Sokar" anyway?

PRESS ESCAPE TO CONTINUE

Melvin rubbed his chin thoughtfully. It was in the "dead file," right? How often did people really check back into closed dossiers? He pictured the basement level of a huge warehouse, crammed down there to its dark corners with boxes of old, rotting invoices. It was the same kind of thing, right? Melvin hit the ESCAPE button and new screen winked up. A title page of sorts.

WELCOME TO PASSIVE PASSENGER

"That's interesting," Melvin said. He hit the ESCAPE button again.

INSTRUCTIONS—OPERATOR WILL ENTER HIS SOCIAL SECURITY NUMBER. NEXT, ENTER THE S.S. # OF SUBJECT AND STRIKE ANY KEY TO ACTIVATE. OPERATOR WILL THEN JOIN WITH THE MIND OF THE SUBJECT AS A PASSIVE PASSENGER FOR THE LAST FIVE MINUTES OF TIME PASSED. ACTUAL TIME ELAPSED FROM POINT OF ACTIVATION UNTIL CONCLUSION IS ZERO HOURS, ZERO MINUTES, AND ZERO SECONDS.

It had to be a gag of some sort. Melvin hit the ESCAPE button again.

O—ENTER SOCIAL SECURITY NUMBER

"O" is for "Operator," Melvin said. "OK, what the hell." He entered his own number. He tabbed to the next screen and gasped. Under the bolded words

S—ENTER SOCIAL SECURITY NUMBER

(and a space to enter the nine characters) was what seemed the first page of a massive subject-directory; a glossary of names, occupations, and social security numbers. Melvin punched the ESCAPE button again and again, but it seemed an endless sea. Screen after screen, there were thousands, no *hundreds* of thousands loaded into the program.

This was no gag. Melvin scanned the H's and saw that his own name was listed.

Melvin felt a sudden shiver run straight between his shoulder blades. The planets were named after Roman god figures. Pluto was the Roman god of the underworld and "Sokar" was the Egyptian equivalent. "Sokar" must have been Pluto's brother planet located in a different solar system! The offspring of McGillicutty and Delsordo had gone into research and development, for God's sake. They'd reached out and touched someone. Did they really have the money to do such a thing? Melvin supposed that if AIG could go on a week-long junket for four hundred and forty thousand dollars without blinking an eye, anything was possible. Those bastards were selling names. And the payoff? A simple trade. The outworlders got to invade the human of their choice for the sake of study and the mobsters got to learn everybody's secrets. Clearly, the subject would not be aware of the operator's presence so as to insure that "Big Brother" could keep on watching, and Melvin Helitz had caught this tiger right by the tail.

Yes.

The program was his now, was it not?

Melvin fought with this question. Part of him wanted to shut the thing down immediately for the sake of legality and morality. The other side of him, however, the professor, the theorist, and yes, the inner child, could not help but marvel at the possibilities of this device. Could it actually work? Did he have the courage to give it a test run? Would he get caught?

He thought of that big, dark warehouse again. Garbage in, garbage out. And the mobsters were nothing but conduits anyway. Stooges working the sale. The ones in charge came from beyond. It was even possible that they did not have the corrupt intentions that their association with McGillicutty and Delsordo suggested. Did they understand our system of law and ethics to begin with? Didn't the presence of the program itself suggest a certain need to be educated in the ways of humanity? They were most probably scientists, and it was entirely possible that they were under the assumption that those with the power to make first interplanetary contact would have been our world leaders.

Melvin gave a scan to the subject directory and found no mention of McGillicutty or Delsordo. Of course not. Moreover, there was probably a failsafe even if their social security numbers were discovered, that which would keep them forever immune to scrutiny. The circumstance that built this relationship across worlds was meant to remain secret.

And whether the alleged aliens were aware that they were in league with criminals was not finally the point. While Melvin would have dearly loved to have had the opportunity to unravel the politics of all this, chart the history of the initial encounter, and communicate with beings from another world, he did not have McGillicutty's nor Delsordo's initial exploratory technology on hand. He had the spawn, and the question was whether or not he had the balls to use what he had accidentally pirated. Friendly aliens or not, Melvin was trespassing. And stooges or bosses, those "conduits" did have nasty reputations for taking matters into their own hands. At least their fathers had.

On the other side of that, the horse was already out of the barn now, wasn't it? The thing was *on* his computer. What difference would a test run make at this point?

Melvin spent the evening tabbing through the subject directory. He saw plain people, rich people, famous people, faceless people, beautiful people. What would it be like to read their thoughts for five minutes? He ran scenarios through his head of various journeys, and countered them with possible consequences. His eyelids were drooping. He needed a fresh start here. He needed to sleep on this.

Melvin backed out to screen number two and dimmed it for safe keeping. He killed the light and climbed into bed with the residue of fluorescent green still dancing in his eyes.

It's mine as long as I wish to keep it. I don't have to use it. I can just . . . possess it.

That thought tailed Melvin through the first stages of sleep and followed him into the R.E.M. state. All night, he tossed and turned, in and out of erratic dreams in which he became a melodramatic, cartoon villain. He wore a top hat and black coattails. He had a thick, waxed, handlebar moustache. He wrung his hands, twisted his lips to a sneer, and gloated over his evil machine. His shoulders and arms then began moving against his will. His dance became erratic and violent. One of his hands ripped off at the wrist, the other at the elbow. From the shadows above, blue alien fingers worked the strings. He'd woken in a cold sweat.

Out all day so Mel can play.

Melvin cracked a window to breathe in the smell of the pines, winter's kiss on this crisp morning's breeze. He buttoned his sweater. Now that he was showered and Dot was gone, he was free to consider the mind-melding time machine that sat amidst his clutter of private projects.

It's a junkyard in there.

"Oh, bug off," Melvin thought. The recurring memory of her criticism distracted him.

She was unable to share in the thrill of creation because her eyes could not see past the bald results. To her, the room was not some storybook playground laden with the very landscape of her husband's potential, but rather a metaphor for failure, a wasteland of bogus inventions that refused to function properly.

The hair suddenly rose on the back of Melvin's neck as if he were being watched. It was the computer with the words **WELCOME TO PASSIVE PASSENGER** smiling across its screen.

"I work properly," it seemed to whisper.

"Let's find out," Melvin said. He sat down at the terminal. A final vision of himself as a fifth grader reciting the Pledge of Allegiance came into his head, and he combated the vision of purity with cold logic.

I won't do this for gain, and I won't invade someone famous. That would be rude somehow. I will do this scientifically and democratically.

He backed off to the Subject Directory, closed his eyes, tabbed multiple screens in, and pointed his finger. He opened his eyes.

"Floyd Lynch—Truck Driver."

Melvin tabbed back to screen number four.

O—ENTER SOCIAL SECURITY NUMBER

Melvin entered his own.

S—ENTER SOCIAL SECURITY NUMBER

Melvin looked at his watch. Ten seconds until 9:10 A.M. He counted it down. At precisely 9:10, Melvin hit the RETURN button and activated Passive Passenger.

It was immediate. There was no sense of travel, no supernatural feeling of exit and entry, but an instant exchange of physical presence. A moment before, Melvin Helitz had been sitting in his bedroom, but now pushed through the doors of Lucy's Bar and Grill, hungry, pissed off, and ready to drink anything that would smooth his raging hangover.

In the back of his mind, Melvin had imagined that the experience would be somehow removed, like being in a theater and watching a movie shot in first person. But he was there, not only with Floyd Lynch, but as Floyd Lynch, the finest West Virginia had to offer, thank you very much. He felt the greasy perspiration that had built up already that morning around the dirty inner band of Floyd's Mountaineers baseball cap and down the back of his underwear. He had a cut on the ring finger of his meaty left hand from breaking down cardboard and carelessly slipping with a box-cutter last week on Bay #2, and the small of his back was killing him. The thick smell of sausage, lard, and home fries doused in onions sickened Floyd in a vague, friendly sort of way that made Melvin know that Floyd isolated the smells as those of preferred breakfasts most mornings after a run. Not today. American firewater was going to do just fine. He walked heavily past the seating area and its steel booths with maroon, plastic cushions. A busboy moved out of his way.

The place was so busy that there were a few stragglers eating breakfast in the bar at dark tables by the windows. The shades were pulled, and Floyd's eyes adjusted to the shadows. He ambled past the pool tables on the right, and approached the long mahogany bar. Three green paper lampshades hung above it with old tobacco smoke suspended underneath like veils. Though Lucy's advertised all-night service, the idea of cocktails at 9:00 in the morning only seemed to appeal to an old-timer at the far corner of the bar wearing old gray overalls, weathered boots, and a John Deere hat pulled over his eyes. A Garth Brooks song came from a vintage jukebox that actually played vinyl.

"Double, Jack Daniel's," Floyd said. The bartender, a stiff, quiet type, set down the Pilsner glass he had been wiping and chucked down a cardboard coaster. A rock glass followed, and he filled it two-thirds.

"Two-fifty."

"Tab it," Floyd said. The barkeep left the bottle within reach, and Floyd grabbed his glass. He downed it, refilled it, and Melvin had a sudden, clear understanding of why alcoholics drank for the purpose of remedy. The jolt of whiskey was like dark fire, deliciously burning the throat, warming the stomach, and coursing into Floyd's throbbing headache with kneading, soothing fingers. Everything loosened, and suddenly Melvin felt Floyd's arms and thighs come to the forefront of his perception of personal physicality. Gone was the idea that the stomach creeping over the beltline defined "Floyd Lynch," and the backache from lifting fifty-pound crates from concrete dock to rusty truck bed slipped far into the background like a dream. The ghost of a teenage Floyd, starting center for the Jarvisville Panthers, rose right up behind the eyes, and concentrated old feelings of power in the junctions of the knees, the elbows, the hips, and the balls of his feet. Floyd sat up straighter and glanced to his right. A thin woman with straight black hair had just taken a seat two stools down. Her back was to the bar, elbows propped backward upon it, and she watched the game of pool that began to unfold in front of her with mild interest. She pushed out her lower lip and blew upward to fluff her bangs.

She wore a sleeveless black T-shirt and cut-off blue jean shorts. She had those silver and turquoise Injun earrings and a braided ankle band. Black mascara, purple gypsy eye shadow, no lipstick, she had the face of a thief and the legs of a hooker.

"Oh, let this get good while there's still time," Melvin thought.

"Hey there, sister," Floyd said, as if in response to Melvin's plea. "When I wake y'all up tomorrow morning, should I nudge you or call you?" She looked over, and let a half-smile tug at the side of her mouth.

"I don't know, baby. The day is still young."

Floyd felt his mood brighten, and he was glad for it. This morning had been a shit-poor experience, and he wanted nothing more than to forget about it. Melvin laughed silently. It was like that old joke, "Tell someone not to think about pink elephants, and that's all they can think about," for the morning Floyd wanted to push out of memory projected through to their shared present like a technicolor movie. The flash took but a moment, barely enough time to equal a breath, but Melvin was amazed at how well it familiarized him with the heart and soul of Floyd Lynch.

The day had started fair to middling considering the raging drunk Floyd hadn't quite slept off from the night before. He had shown up bright and early at the Red Arrow Trucking Depot with a pounding headache, a steaming cup of black coffee, and dark glasses. He got double overtime on Saturdays, and he needed to make these two deliveries to cover some bad online bets he'd made on college hoops the week before. The rig was pre-loaded, and Floyd had headed toward Clarksburg with nothing on his mind but making it through the run.

"Base to Lynch, over."

Floyd grabbed the radio mike, stretched the curly cord, and pressed in the button. "Lynch here, over."

"Ahh, Floyd, uh y'all got to double back here right away, over."

"What the fuck for!" Lynch shouted into the radio despite the FCC violations he had been warned of. He could almost feel the dispatcher cringe on the other end.

"Uh, Scutter Drywall called the vendor for the pro number of that ceiling wire that come in late yesterday. The guy chewed me a new butt asking where it was, over."

Floyd smashed the mike back into its holder and looked for a place to turn around. This was bad news three times over. First, Scutter Drywall was in Glenville, a hick town that sat at the tail end of Route 33 West, the twistiest, turniest stretch of back road in all West Virginia. Second of all, Floyd had spied the Scutter invoice back in the warehouse and noticed that the rig assigned to it was #3, an old 1982 International cab-over shitbucket with a 6V-53 Detroit engine and two-speed rear end. This meant a trans so full of slop that finding gear was like sticking a cold virgin with a limp pecker. And third and most finally, the Scutter order was still piled by load dock 5, and since Floyd wasn't union, he'd now have to help load five hundred bundles of twelve-foot wire like an African slave-boy.

Things got worse quick. Route 50 Westbound was under construction and cut to one lane. And the moment Floyd pulled on he got stuck behind an old Toyota Starlet that refused to break forty. Floyd ran right up its butt, close enough to see the weather stains on the bumper stickers. One said "Save the Trees," and the other said, "Lick Bush."

Floyd bristled with rage since this flatlander got to display dirty shit about our commander-in-chief whilst he had been forced by a statie to scrape off his own that read, "I shoot Muslims on sight." He squinted and saw the frightened eyes stare back at him in the rearview. The kid had small circular wire frames and hair all over the place. The little fuck was probably the type to parade the White House steps and hand out leaflets defending the rights of faggots to marry each other, adopt little Asian rug rats and collect benefits. Floyd suddenly ached to spy just one piece of left lane so he could sneak up, run the little shit off the road, blare the horn and yell "God bless America" as he passed. When the kid turned off exit seven in fact, Floyd almost followed him to carry through the urge. Almost. After all, he was a professional.

The rest of the run was a slushy haze. The extra labor, the back and forth, and the complaints and questionings and demands of the given warehouse managers receiving his shipments blurred in a vision of a headache that had began as a hot needle in the middle of his forehead and spiraled out to a massive pounder. But he had made his runs without puking. At least he had that. After all, as long as a man could hold his liquor, it never really had a hold on him, now did it?

With that thought, the memory faded and Melvin found himself once again with the present tense of Floyd Lynch. The big trucker downed another shot of J.D., hauled up, adjusted his trousers and plopped himself down by the thin woman's left elbow.

"What's your name, darling?"

"What's yours?"

"Floyd Lynch, ma'am."

"Well, mine's Elaina Mayberry. My friends call me 'Lay-May.'"

Floyd winked.

"Lay-May, your legs are so purty I'd drag my balls through a mile of broken glass just to hear you piss in a tin cup." Her full smile revealed a gap between her two front teeth.

"You're a dirty ole dog, Floyd." She punched his arm, and it was the opening Floyd was looking for. Any woman who initiated physical contact was a piece of fair game. He shoved his stool closer, slung his arm around her shoulder and with two fingers fiddled a bit with a partly exposed bra strap. If Melvin had been connected to his own mouth it would have been frothing.

Oh boy! If you're going to shtup her, I'll pop in through Passive Passenger all night until I catch the moment you do it!

"We got trouble, Floyd."

Lynch removed his arm and looked around. The pool game had stopped, and one of its players was leaning on his stick, staring. He was a tall, haggard man in red untucked flannel. His long hair was in a ponytail, and his red, deep-lined face looked like weather-hardened leather. Floyd reached back to pour another drink.

"Is that your boyfriend or your brother?"

"It's my husband." Floyd did not return her grin.

"Now why would you be flirtating me with your husband standing right there?"

"I'm mad at him," she said.

"Why?"

"He's losing the game."

The skinny dude obviously disliked being talked about as if he was not in the same room.

"You'd best move on, fat boy," he said. "Ain't your woman to be groping like that." Floyd turned to face him and put his hands on his knees.

"Now looky here, boy. I'm gonna take your wife and I'm gonna do her. I'm gonna do her right here on this bar. You get to watch." For emphasis, he grabbed at her bra again. This time, he yanked the strap over her shoulder and she slapped at him, the joke now dulled in her eyes.

The song on the jukebox faded to its conclusion. The machine ejected the record, and its motorized shift was a lone cry in a room gone dead quiet. A waitress stood by the entrance to the front seating area with three plates balanced up her arm. A pair of pool players wearing wide-rimmed Stetsons set down their sticks and moved their drinks. One fumbled to snuff out a smoke. A couple at a four-top scrambled for their coats, and the bartender stood by the cash register, phone in hand, ready to dial 911.

The jukebox flipped the next record to the turntable. An amplified scratch turned into the first notes of "The Gambler." The man with the ponytail bared his teeth and snapped his pool cue in two across his knee. Melvin tried to read Floyd's next move, but it was impossible. His mind had gone a cool, predatory blank.

Ponytail spat on the floor and tossed the light end of his pool stick into an ash can that doubled as a chaw bucket. Heavy end up, he two-fisted his weapon and came on. Floyd let him approach, almost counting the steps. Their eyes remained deadlocked. At the last possible moment, Floyd sprang up and danced to the side, dragging his bar stool with him. He swung it back across in an arc, and dead air hissed through the oak legs.

Wood met skull. Ponytail moaned as the pool cue flew behind the bar along with three of his teeth and a chaser of bloody spittle. He hit the floor, and Floyd dropped the busted stool next to him.

Another broken bat homer.

Lynch reached back for his drink, turned, and raised the glass to propose a toast.

It never came out. Someone punched Floyd in the back of the neck (and fucking hard too) before it could be vocalized.

"What the hell," Floyd tried to say. Instead, a hideous gargle escaped. He tried to swallow, but his throat was blocked by something. There was a thick spurting of blood driving up against the roof of his mouth. Melvin shot out of Floyd's body, and hovered unseen by a ceiling fan.

Wait! I haven't been here five minutes. The exit is too early!

He calculated it so to be sure.

Walked in, ordered a drink and chugged it, one minute at most. The flashback was instantaneous, then we talked to Lay-May and fiddled the bra strap, another minute. We smart-mouthed the husband and bashed him, another sixty seconds maybe, if that. That makes three minutes, so where are my other two?

Melvin realized that he was not alone. He was still connected to Floyd Lynch, who for the life of him could not figure out why he was floating up in the air. The trucker looked down then, and Melvin silently shared his disbelief. The body of Floyd Lynch lay in a puddle of his own blood with Lay-May's switchblade stuck out the back of his throat.

"Get up!" Lynch soundlessly shouted down at himself. "I ain't ready to die, please!"

None of the patrons had moved. Floyd and the ponytail man were huddled in a rag-tag pile of arms, clothes, and hair, a strange embrace, but Melvin did not enjoy this dark humor.

Is time ticked off the same in the hereafter? What if one second of human time equals a thousand years of spiritual time? I had two minutes left.

A deep brilliance of color with a hue indescribable by the blunt tool of human vocabulary closed in from the corners of Floyd's perception, a flood from beneath, behind, and within. It quickly became everything, save one point of dazzling light in its center.

"Looks like a headlight on Route 9," Floyd thought. "What's next, drag racing?"

Floyd shot toward the bright sphere.

"So you do actually shoot toward a bright light," Melvin thought.

It was some kind of doorway. Floyd could not see it, yet he perceived it, like eyesight, but fuller. Like touch, yet more intimate, as if all the senses were combined in a new kind of vision. It was a circular cascade of fragrance, of warmth and absolute beauty. It was the thunder of a thousand voices in harmony. It was a shimmering storm of waterfall colors that formed rivers and rainbows.

Floyd burst into the sphere and joined its powerful warmth. It was a sweet flotation, the loving embrace of the beginning and end of all things. He had felt it before, once in his mother's womb. He had entered his world kicking and howling. Now was his exit of silence and wonder. He passed through the sphere.

Floyd was at the far end of a long corridor, and he had been given back his sight. It was not a gift. Erected through a thick fog of bluish mist were two white pedestals, and atop each sat an entity, not alive in the earthly sense of the word, but present in forms Floyd understood on a fundamental level. The beings began to take form as wavering outlines, the inverse of images in the visual sense, existing on the periphery of what Melvin would consider "perception," and filling in the grounded center of focus with suggestion. For a moment, Melvin tried to describe this phenomenon in scientific terms, but the best he could come up with was, "It is what it is, and Floyd manufactures his version of what it is to fill in the stuff between the lines for the purpose of base recognition." It was a crude rendition of the experience, but here the human was a crude slave in the palace of his betters.

The entity on the left pedestal spun itself into a tornado of red flame that turned and twisted at the edge of Floyd's version of a nightmare. It tossed sparks, spit lightning, and slowly opened its eyes, terrible orbs that were slanted with rage. They were bottomless caverns of agony that held reflections of torment, ageless and unforgiving. Floyd looked away and was made to look back.

The flames hardened into a body that formed around the slanted eyes. It was a huge jackal with fangs as long as the pedestal was high. Its tail was a whip with razor quills and its tongue was a serpent.

Floyd was suddenly allowed to break the glance and he silently thanked it as if it was God.

"No, not God," Melvin thought. "That thing cannot be the Almighty because it does not know that I am here."

Floyd was allowed to look at the pedestal on the right. It was bliss. It was a warm, white cloud that seemed to ebb and flow with the very fabric of tranquility. It opened a pair of eyes that sang to Floyd in a chorus of voices that defined its outline as the shape of a dove. It reached out its huge wings to Floyd in a glorious gesture of hope.

Floyd was not comforted. The dove and the jackal merged colors and combined for a moment in a tone that by the power of its own design was capable of cracking Floyd's very being.

"*Bladnestannabellshannah*," they said, in a reference to what must have been Floyd's name before a human mother reconfigured the title into that generic, shared form that began the long, inherited process of reshaping the individual into the stagnant patterns of "culture." Man's decorated prison, his savior, and his tragic flaw.

"*You are in the corridor of deeds*," they said.

Then began the construction. Every single thing Floyd had done in his twenty-seven years of service on the land surrounded by the seas, one at a time and with deafening speed, shot toward the pedestals. It was not difficult to figure out the purpose of the activity. What was viewed as "good" went to the dove, and the "evil" actions were consumed by the jackal. The deeds were filling in the wavering lines, and Melvin had pretty much come to the conclusion that the dove and the jackal were finally to fight for Floyd's soul.

Some of the deeds were recognizable, and some Floyd had no

memory of. Most of his early childhood actions filled in portions of the dove, yet the insignificance of the given action was measured proportionally in reference to the amount of fortification it provided to its host. At six months, Floyd was in the dirty powder blue car seat stuck in the dark corner of the living room inside Mama's mobile home on Burnt Lick Road. He usually behaved himself in the car seat, yet now he cried out in a passion of hunger, small arms jerking and flailing at the cold, silent darkness. At three and a half, he hid in the broom closet underneath a low shelf that supported a few weathered pairs of work boots, a large Sears security flashlight, and a red toolbox with its top tray littered with screwdrivers, hammers, dented steel tape measurers, and an array of homeless fasteners. He hid in the dark closet because his uncle Jimbo was watching him today, and Uncle Jimbo thought it was funny to chase little Floyd around the yard with a steel-tined rake. At five, Floyd sat on a sloping, uneven stone wall and tossed pebbles into the creek that ran below him. His head itched and he had no socks, because Mama had to work a double at the mill, and she didn't have the time to throw in a wash. At seven, Floyd got a game-winning inside-the-park homerun in little league that was called back to a single because it nicked the pitching machine. At eight, he read aloud to his class a poem about the shapes clouds make, and at nine he crashed his bike into a willow tree because Freddie Smithers dared him to ride blindfolded.

The dove grew and fattened with each instance. Still, the balance of Floyd's years seemed to hold more weight, and most of those actions went to the other pedestal.

When Floyd was twelve, he stole a fishing rod out of the back room in Gorton's general store, and at fifteen, he robbed the same place blind as its cashier, hitting "No sale," writing up dummy receipts on a spare pad he kept under the drawer, and pocketing the cash after the customer exited the premises. At sixteen, he and Bubba Nichols regularly bullied Harvey Wallson, finally making him lick toilet water in the handicapped stall in the second-floor bathroom, and at seventeen, he hit Ma the first time. The contributions to the jackal seemed endless. The drinking, the fighting, the reckless driving, the cursing, the side-comments to co-workers, the endless stares at women even in church, all culminating with the argument he had with his common-law wife Jessie last year, right before she threw him out for good.

Two final images danced before the dove and the jackal, then shot forth. Though the circumstances leading up to Floyd's murder belonged to the jackal, the act of the murder itself greatly enhanced the intensity of the dove. Still, the conclusion of Floyd's all-night shouter with Jessie was devastating. It was 3:09 in the morning, and Floyd had her by the hair. He had her bent over the kitchen sink with her nose scraping into the dried remains of some baked beans on the plate on top of the pile. He was leaning over her, and yelling into her face, and grabbing a spoon, and threatening to dig her eye out with it.

The jackal took this last image in one swallow and then devoured the fragile white head of the dove. The spiritual victim beat its wings and the jackal snapped the white body from side to side. It smashed its prey against the right pedestal, leaving dark blue spatters of blood and feathers. The sound was deafening.

The jackal dropped the lifeless body of the dove and gnashed at the hot blue mist that poured from its wounds. The coarse hairs of this beast stood straight and lathered, like wet knives. It turned to Floyd with blood dripping off its teeth.

"Come with me, Bladnestannabellshannah. For now, you are mine. Your deeds have given me the right to escort you to the hall of thoughts. It is the second of many . . ."

Melvin began to exit Floyd's consciousness. The retreat was achingly slow. The jackal tensed on its haunches and looked. Its ears whipped back close to the head. It bared its teeth, showing spotted gums.

"It sees me!" Melvin thought. "Oh hurry, please!"

The jackal howled. It snapped at the air and clawed at its own nose. Melvin was almost to the archway. The jackal screamed and elongated its face. The jaws stretched and chased Melvin the length of the hallway by themselves. Melvin felt its scalding breath. Then it was gone. The whole corridor was gone.

Melvin was back in his bedroom, floating behind the version of himself that was about to press the button to initially activate Passive Passenger. The clock ticked right up to 9:10 A.M., but just before the rejoining he heard something. A voice, faint like an echo on damp cobblestone.

I'll be waiting for you . . . Melvin.

The joining was complete. Melvin shrieked, shoved his chair out of the way, and crawled under his desk. He curled to a ball and jammed his knuckles into his mouth. His eyes stayed wide open.

He did not come out for a long, long time.

1:40 P.M.

Melvin reached for the carton of Tropicanna. He would simply go back to his room and unplug the computer. End of conversation. He popped the bird-beak of the container of orange juice and brought it to his lips. He wiped his moustache on his sleeve. The side door opened, and he heard Dot come in. He heard the crinkle of brown bagged packages being thrust onto the kitchen table a few feet behind him, and he slowly took another swig of juice.

"Look at you," she said. "How many times have we talked about leaving the refrigerator door open? And if you are going to drink your juice, the rule is to use a glass, remember?"

He heard her start reaching into the bags and then heard her stop.

"Did you call the plumber like I asked you to?"

Melvin kept his glance focused into the fridge. The door shelves boasted a museum of crudded Dorothy shit; old balsamic vinaigrette, a quart of soy milk with dried wavery stains around the opening, a six-pack of Promise Activ peach drink that actively lowered cholesterol, and a Tupperware tub filled with salmon croquettes floating in two levels of oil, one gray and the thinner one on top almost maroon with small white fat-bubbles skimming the surface. Melvin took another slow swig, then spoke at the fridge.

"Fuck the plumber, fuck the orange juice, and fuck, y'all."

"What?" she said. "Wha . . . what did you just say to me?"

Dorothy's voice was a symphony, an auditory kaleidoscope of emotions, all the colors. There was anger, frustration, righteous defense, and absolute disbelief, but also undercurrents of doubt. Melvin liked that texture very much, but he was filled with complex emotions of his own. Clearly, Floyd Lynch had left a residue. That was a concern. Slowly he turned to face his wife.

Her mouth dropped open.

"My God, what happened to you?"

Melvin looked at her in disgust and her right hand flew up to her face. It fluttered around her cheek.

143

"What?' he said. He pushed an impatient whistle through his teeth, slammed the fridge door, and bent to look at himself in the reflection of the toaster. He nearly gasped. The image was warped and slanted like a funhouse mirror, but the distortion did not alter the facts. Some of the little hair he had left hanging over his forehead was simply lost, and his eyebrows had gone from graying to bright white. His wrinkles had deepened and his eyes were sunk back in their sockets. He looked insane, as if he had recently seen something not meant for human eyes.

"I want you out of here, Dorothy. I don't care where you go or what you do, but I want you gone now. I want to be alone today."

She put her hands on her hips.

"You know, Melvin, this is all a result of the way you feel about yourself. If you had stuck with engineering and dismissed these silly ideas of becoming an academic—"

Melvin's eyes got huge.

"Don't y'all try that ole psychologic bullshit with me, girl! I said get out, so git the fuck out!" He reached into the sink and grabbed a table-spoon. "Just don't make me use this, you hear?"

Dorothy retreated to her bedroom, eyes locked on Melvin, feeling her way like a drunk. She slammed the door. Melvin could hear the nervous bumps and shuffles of clothes being yanked from hangers. When she emerged, she was wearing an older, heavier winter coat than she had used for the trip to the supermarket. Probably going on an outdoor shopping spree now. The witch. She brushed past him toward the side door, and he growled at her. She slammed that door behind her, oh yes, a great ole door-slammer was she. He watched through the laundry room window. She backed out of the driveway haphazardly, and then she was gone. He tossed the spoon on the counter and stomped back to his own room.

I'll get some order around here, just wait and see!

He opened the bedroom door and the computer was waiting for him.

You'll have to get past me first, you leech!

Melvin shook his fist and stormed through the room. He dumped drawers, upended boxes, and routed the shelves in search of his Stanley clawhammer. He crawled on his hands and knees and swiped at the piles of *National Geographic* and *Scientific American* stowed under the drafting board. He shoved over a few Hills Brothers coffee cans that threw splashes of bolts and ball bearings to the carpet. He spied the hammer stuck under a snaked pile of twelve-gauge extension cord, and gripped the handle. Face red, he backed out and stood up. His knees popped. He approached the computer and raised the hammer over his head.

You paid two thousand dollars for that computer, don't smash it. Be sensible.

Hard breath swelled in his chest and he dropped the hammer.

I'll unplug it right now. Boom-boom, out go the lights, Passive Passenger gone for good.

He did nothing.

Suddenly Melvin threw back his head and laughed like a stoned junkie who had just gotten a crazy urge to go straight and dump an ounce of prime blow down the toilet. But Melvin knew better, hell, he'd seen all the movies.

You don't quit until the stash is gone.

Melvin sat in front of the terminal and let his mind wander the path it truly desired. It took all of three seconds.

What's next? No, who's next? Who is my next subject?

But that was not quite right either. Entertainers, daredevils, politicians, pick a card, any card, they all seemed insignificant. Hell, who's next was not even the right question.

The right question was lurking beneath the surface and Melvin almost dreaded its acknowledgment. Almost. True, this morning he had been frightened straight through to the marrow, but the events had been a surprise. Now, he was better prepared—that was a cold hard fact. And was he not a symbol of education? Did he not stand right here, right now at the very state of the art, at the cutting edge, at the brink of greatness? Did not the movers and shakers of history press on through the unexplained until it was reshaped by their genius into manageable terms? It was his duty to press on. It was his duty to ask the question,

How many corridors are there, and then, what's beyond the dove and the jackal?

He put his hands on the desk to push up, go get the newspaper, and scan the obituaries. His face went red hot. He fought a dark urge to strike something.

I can't use the names in the paper because they will have been stiff at least a day already. Passive Passenger only goes back five minutes in time. That leaves twenty three hours and fifty five minutes of post mortem that I'll miss.

145

He grabbed both his earlobes and pulled.

A true scientist observes the entire process from front to back. A true scientist returns to the experiment at the exact place he left off!

Melvin balled his fists and rubbed his knuckles in his eyes.

Think! We left Floyd Lynch at the point of two minutes into the hereafter. To logically continue the process we need someone freshly dead, seven minutes dead to be exact. But how will I know when the right moment hits? I'm not clairvoyant.

An old, buried exasperation washed through him. Melvin turned and swept a wild glance across his collection of inventions. In disgust, he went to shove at his radio scanner and noted the yellow tag on it. Captain Hugh McNulty.

He knows.

Melvin froze.

McNulty can show me "who."

Melvin smiled and turned back to his computer to tab through the subject directory of Passive Passenger. He found Hugh McNulty's social security number and entered it into the Subject mode after entering his own in the Operator space.

The scanner will tell me "when."

His system was ready. He fired up his homemade radio. He sat. He listened. He patiently waited for someone to die.

"Box 2173, Five Star Refinery. Reported to be oil tank on fire. The following companies will respond. Engines 38, 44, 29, 32, Ladders 15 and 23, Medic 4, Battalion 6, Deputy 1, respond, over."

Melvin bolted upright in his chair. It had been a two-hour wait, but the fire at the oil refinery was perfect.

"Engine 38 responding to Five Star Refinery, second in, over."

"McNulty," Melvin whispered. He scrambled to the computer and hovered over the RETURN button. The scanner was silent for twenty minutes.

"Engine 38 on location. We have a heavy fire, one tank. Unit has been ordered to northwest side to lead off with master stream devices, over."

Ten more minutes ticked by. Melvin was salivating. McNulty's voice suddenly shouted over the tinny speaker,

"Fireman down! Northwest side! Send rescue squad now! Fireman is down, respond!"

Melvin silently cheered.

I'll see it happen all over again through McNulty's eyes. I'll know the circumstances of the accident and the severity of the injury. And if the poor guy does kick the bucket, I'll know that dead man's name!

Melvin struck the RETURN button.

Captain McNulty hopped out and watched Zac pull a five-inch hose from the back of the truck.

"Tie it tight, kid," he said. "Signal when it's firm." The young fireman ran to put a wrap on the hydrant and Tommy Green followed with the wrench. The kid had forgotten it. McNulty turned to his driver.

"Eddie, once the hose is secure drive straight eighty feet up to that big black gate valve by the cooling tower there. Get parallel to it." Old Eddie waited for a thumbs-up from the kid and McNulty turned with the stiff wind to eye the tank of crude that was active. It was the worst fire he had ever seen. Oily heat blanketed the air in ripply waves, and flecks of black ash swirled in the sky. Melted snow ran down the gradual three-inch grade and made small whirlpools under the grid work of piping. The oil tank towered over it all and was speaking in smoke signals.

It's my party and I'll bitch if I want to!

A football field high and ninety feet across, "Crude #43" vomited upward a furl of black smoke thick as chocolate mousse. The two-inch-thick steel at the top was melted, split, and bent inward with the iron spiral staircase swung out to the side like a loose strand of hair.

The wind shifted and a dense wave of smoke splashed the equally large naphtha gas tank thirty feet to the left. The thick plume stained it spotty black.

"Just in time," McNulty thought. It was their job to protect the exposure of that tank of naphtha, so close to #43 that they shared the same dike. Seven engines were already on the front side of #43 with deluge and foam units, and McNulty had been ordered to put up a defensive stream on the neighboring tank. Fast.

McNulty spun around to check the progress of his two field men and glanced up to the Rt. 95 overpass. A news van had pulled up on the shoulder and its crew was setting up tripods.

Great. To the uneducated eye it will look like we are spraying down the wrong tank.

It should not have bothered him, but it did. He still had a foul taste in his mouth from being selectively edited on channel 9, and his boys deserved better. Tommy Green had been with him for fifteen years, he was family. Old Eddie was six months from retirement and though Zac could be a bit of a wildcard, he listened pretty well under pressure. They were a rare collection of men that this business hadn't turned sour. They all deserved better than this and they were heroes just being here.

Melvin agreed. Though he felt relatively safe inside the brave exterior of Captain McNulty, there was something absolutely terrifying about that smoking tanker. It was a god, and Melvin could draw enough from McNulty's experience to know that the neighboring tank of naphtha was the angel of death.

Still, the scene was mostly chaos to Melvin's unpracticed eye and the old professor understood only parts of it, especially as McNulty began running his drill. McNulty's mind was far advanced when compared to that of Floyd Lynch, and much of his decision making was based on an instinct of expertise rather than a visible hierarchy of principles. Melvin went through the motions and only caught some stuff on the surface. Time flew.

Eddie drove the truck and that motion unsnapped the hose. They set the pressure at 220 psi. With help, McNulty struggled a thing called a "Stang Gun" off the roof of the truck. Zac went to set up the water cannon and Tommy Green shouted orders at him concerning locking devices, wheel locks, and pins.

McNulty was checking off Tommy's commands in his head, and he stole another peek at Naphtha #2 and Crude #43. The conditions had not changed, but the sloped eight-foot dike surrounding the bottom perimeter of the two seemed awfully full. McNulty went up on tiptoes. The water and foam units from the other engines had been over-pumping Crude #43 and the collected water in the dike was far too high. It was five feet deep at least, with a layer of foam floating the top.

It seemed significant for some reason, but McNulty could not nail it.

"Pressurize," he ordered. Eddie worked the controls and the hose fattened with water. Thirty feet east of the truck, a burst of spray suddenly came through the nozzle in Tommy's hands. Zac helped him stabilize and McNulty looked at his watch.

Four minutes. Battalion Chief Romonosky would be proud.

"Four minutes," Melvin thought. *"Here we go, oh boy, oh Jesus."*

Commotion. Tommy and Zac were shouting in each other's faces and fighting for control of the live nozzle between them.

"Report!" McNulty yelled into his radio. The plea was ignored.

"They're not fighting for control!" Melvin shouted to no one. *"Tommy's trying to hand it over, and Zac won't take it. Oh boy, which is going to get it, the vet or the kid, oh Lordy!"*

Zac lost the argument. With obvious protest, he took hold of the nozzle and fought for a moment to keep it controlled. Tommy broke away to a run and made straight for the tanker, his boots kicking up dirty splashes. McNulty looked to where Tommy was headed and frowned. A refinery yard worker in brown coveralls was crawling atop the lip of the dike.

"Damnit Tommy, hurry," McNulty thought. His best fireman reached the foot of the dike and pawed up the slope. The yard worker cradled a scorched hand and made his way along the crest in a three-legged crawl. Disoriented, he went up on his knees. His hair was matted with blood.

Tommy straddled the lip of the dike, ran along it and reached out his hand. They clasped palms, and that is when the top of Crude #43 exploded.

There was a *whoosh* and a huge *thwack*. The ground shook and an orange, mushroom-shaped flare rocketed up against the gray sky. Then came a hearty *bang* that pressed McNulty's eardrums and rattled his skull. A tremendous wave of white heat followed and he fought to keep his eyes open against it.

Shrapnel flew everywhere. Small pieces whizzed overhead and a star-shaped hunk at least twenty feet square spun across the parking lot like a jagged Frisbee. It smashed into a guard shack and turned it to splinters.

A boiling sheet of black crude rained down over the dike area and ignited the ground in a ring of blue flame. The yard worker went up like parchment and rolled down the slope. The hot blaze swarmed the crest of the dike, grew, and caged Tommy Green in a wall of combustion.

The very air was on fire. Tommy's dark outline of headgear and long black fire-retardant coat danced and jerked within the orange shroud and even back where McNulty stood, each breath tasted like a hot spray of Quaker State. He gave a desperate look back to Zac and saw the young man working the Stang gun to an alternate position.

"Yes," he thought. "It's our only chance."

"No!" Melvin thought simultaneously. "Whatever it is, futz it up please! We are so close!"

Zac aimed the bullet-like spray and hit Tommy square in the chest. It knocked him into the dike and he haphazardly splashed through the foamy surface of water. But what happened next made no sense to Melvin or McNulty. A flame at least thirty feet high shot up from the water where Tommy had broken the surface. It whooshed up like a huge torch and then vanished.

"But water and foam are not flammable," McNulty thought.

He dropped the walkie-talkie and threw his hands on the stepladder.

"There's a leak in the naphtha tank! There's a layer of flammable gas in the dike between the water and the foam!"

McNulty mounted the top of the truck and shaded his eyes. Tommy came up for air and broke the plane of foam. He'd lost his helmet and mask, he was exposed, he became a fireball, and McNulty caught a glimpse of skin melting on bone just before Tommy went back under. But the Captain's mind did not allow him to move toward sorrow. Not yet. He was steel. He jumped off the truck, he twisted his ankle, he threw Eddie aside and reached for the engine radio.

"Fireman down! Northwest side! Send rescue squad now! Fireman is down! Respond!"

McNulty fumbled for the dashboard controls. He hit the siren, threw on the flashers, and put the high beams on alternate blare. An audio-visual epitaph.

Tommy was gone. It hit him and he fell to the ground on his butt. He felt his throat closing with grief.

Melvin left McNulty's body and began his ascent. At the top of the raging tanker he looked down and silently applauded. Tommy Green was floating face down. Fire pools still burned the ground all around like jungle death candles.

The scene disappeared.

Melvin wiped away the tears that flooded his scalded eyes. His hands felt as if they were greased and his tongue held the taste of a crudded dipstick. He looked at his watch and it read 3:45 P.M. He took his kitchen timer, set it on seven minutes, and hit the ground running, his fingers in a mad chase across the keys to hunt down Tommy Green's social security number. At last, he found it.

It did not make him smile. There were hundreds of Thomas Greens, and eighty-nine of them were listed as firemen. The vein in Melvin's forehead throbbed. He clutched at his hair and some of it came off in his hands. His watch read 3:48, four minutes to go.

Melvin squeezed shut his eyes and tried to force his mind to march in a pattern of logical thought. It was not easy. Anger and frustration were a bright red blockade, and it took a supreme effort for Melvin to guide his brain toward the one identifying factor at hand, the social security number. He put both palms against his temple and tried to rush his thoughts through the tangent they were trying to explore.

My students are listed in my grade book by their social security numbers. Most of them are local and the first three digits are common to this geographical area. By god, I've seen the exchange a thousand times! 223 through 302!

Melvin's eyes flew open.

Chances are that Tommy Green was born and raised here. I can identify him, ha!

He scanned the screen and blinked. His jaw dropped and he crashed both fists to the desk. There were two Thomas Greens with the common exchange and a third just one digit off. All three were firemen. Melvin shut his mouth. For a moment his mind soared to calculate the sorry odds of actually finding three Philadelphia-born firemen with identical names.

Time Melvin, time!

He looked at his watch. 3:50 P.M. and thirty seconds. A minute and a half until kick-off and his mind was an angry traffic jam. He scratched his head furiously.

I've got to do all three! Passive Passenger doesn't burn any real time. It's instantaneous. The only seconds I'll lose are those used to punch in the numbers. I can do this, but I've got to move fast.

Melvin took his last index card, wrote down the three social security numbers, and checked his watch. 3:51, one minute to go. He made himself punch the keys with care, and backed out to screen number four.

O—ENTER SOCIAL SECURITY NUMBER

Melvin entered his own and hit the RETURN button.

S—ENTER SOCIAL SECURITY NUMBER

Melvin glanced down at the first number on the index card and raised his fingers above the keyboard.

"Melvin! It smells like smoke in here. What on earth are you doing?"

Melvin whirled in his chair. Dorothy's eyes widened in response to his appearance, but she looked ready this time. She took a step forward.

"We have to talk."

"You're in my room," Melvin whispered.

"Yes, and it stinks in here. What have you been doing?"

"You have interrupted me." Another whisper.

"You bet I have, and it's high time—"

"Get out! Get the fuck out of here, now!"

Melvin was on his feet, body shaking, fists clenched, tears flowing. His ankle hurt where McNulty had twisted it and he shifted his weight to point a finger.

"Out!" he roared. It hurt his throat.

"No, I will not."

"I said—"

"No."

The alarm on the kitchen timer sounded. Melvin looked at the device and then at Dorothy. His mouth made babbling motions and the rage in him was so hot it felt religious. Dorothy was oblivious.

"Melvin, there is something wrong here. There is something terribly wrong with you and I'll be Goddamned if I am going to let you—"

She stopped in mid-sentence. Something had changed, something new in the air, thick and heavy. The room still held the aftertaste of distant smoke, hot voices, and something else.

Melvin was smiling.

"Dorothy, I want you to assist me in a scientific experiment."

"What?"

Melvin shuffled past her and into the hall.

"Wait here," he said. "I'll be right back."

"But—"

Melvin put up his hands, gave his head a gentle shake, and re-lit the smile.

"The situation is under control. Wait right here and we'll talk, I promise." He hobbled through the kitchen and out the side door. The cold felt good. He laughed into the wind and made his way to the back yard shed.

To get his ax.

Dorothy Helitz felt the pang of danger, real danger the moment Melvin left the room. Her mind told her to flee the house while she had the chance, but she fought it. This was her house too, damn it, and hell if she was not going to get in the last word. Besides, she was dying to tell Melvin face to face what she had done, dying to see his expression when he was informed that she had phoned Gentle Giant Movers, that she had pre-paid by credit card for a pair of brutes to pack all his mechanical crap and cart it to the dump. She looked at the room and rubbed her arms.

I feel soiled just being here. And where are those moving men? I called them an hour ago.

It was too quiet and Dorothy had a sudden apprehension about confronting Melvin alone. It was a childish yet real sensation that bordered on terror. She tried to shake it and couldn't quite do it.

Weak men are the one's who cause the worst domestic crimes, I've seen it in all the magazines. And I really think he has gone crazy. Maybe face to face isn't such a hot idea.

Dorothy smiled.

I'll write him a note and go straight back to the car. If I see him in the hallway, I'll run right through him.

She approached the desk and took up Melvin's pen. It was slick with a oily film of sweat, and she frowned. No tissues in sight, no paper, and the index card file was empty. On the floor was a lone card with numbers on it. She picked it up, bent to write on the back of it, and looked up at the computer. She giggled.

Now there's poetic justice. I'll type him a message on his precious computer. That will show him.

Melvin reached for the ax and yanked it out from under the wheelbarrow and aluminum stepladder, that which had spider webs floating between the rungs. The weapon in his hands was a long-handled affair with old smudges and paint drops splattered up the shaft. A long split in the hickory just beneath the steel head was bound with old frayed duct tape and the micro-finished cutter was dotted with rust. Except at the tip. The keen edge was roll-beveled and sharp for added strength and increased splitting ability.

"The right tool for the right job," Melvin said. He hefted the ax, left hand at bottom and his right up at the head. His smile had not faltered.

I'm going to kill you in the name of science, my sweet, and follow wherever you may go.

Melvin limped back to the house.

Dorothy look up at the screen and cursed. She had just typed "Dear Melvin," but the letters were not showing. Aiming carefully, she hit the "D" key again, but it did not take either. The cursor just jerked in its place below the words,

S—ENTER SOCIAL SECURITY NUMBER

"Ah," she said. "It doesn't take letters. It's a code. I've got to log on just like in the movies." She read the screen again and smiled.

Oh, you're not so clever, Melvin. All I have to do is enter your social security number. And it's just like you to come up with such an easy password, too.

Dorothy typed in Melvin's social security number. She snickered and raised her index finger above the RETURN key.

Melvin tiptoed up the hall. The element of surprise was key and the splat of wet feet on hardwood would be a dead giveaway. He heard Dorothy snicker and quickened his pace, careful not to bang the ax head along the wall. He rounded the corner of the doorway and geared his muscles for the rush, the set, and the downward stroke.

I'm going to put my legs and back into it, Dorothy. I'm primed and ready for sport, Dorothy.

Melvin loped around the corner and froze. Dorothy's back was turned, that was good, but she was also bent over the computer keyboard, and that was very bad.

"Dorothy, don't touch that! You don't know what you're—"

Dorothy had not heard him coming. His harsh call from behind was startling, but her mind had already commanded the motor function of her finger. It was on its way down and there was no stopping it now. She hit the RETURN key.

The ax in Melvin's hands vanished. His feet were not cold or wet, and he was limping back down the hall to the side door. For a moment he was disoriented, as his body had been magically turned ninety degrees left and five feet to the East, set in motion against his will. Still, the overall sensation was familiar. It was the eerie feeling of becoming a Passive Passenger.

Melvin felt himself open the side door with his thoughts from five minutes before on replay. A keen anticipation of grabbing the ax was at the forefront.

"I'm in myself!" Melvin thought. "I'm the Operator and the Subject!" He tried to shout a warning to himself as he crunched out barefoot into the snow, but of course, he was "passive." The original Melvin had taken his sweet old time.

Melvin re-experienced pulling out the ax, appreciating the craftsmanship of the head, running his hand along the crude shank; it seemed to take hours. Finally, he was back inside, limping up the hall and quickening the pace upon hearing Dorothy's snicker. He rounded the corner, raised the ax and felt a new panic.

Why aren't I floating behind myself for the re-entry? Why is this journey not completing its cycle?

He felt himself shout at Dorothy. He saw for a second time, her finger punch down at the RETURN key.

Maybe it is in the "dead file" because you can't do yourself! Oh please don't hit that button!

Dorothy hit the RETURN key, and Melvin found himself back in the hall, ax-less and limping toward the side door for a third pass. This time he could feel the thoughts of two Melvins, the first tickled with the thrill of the hunt and the second obsessed with the five-minute-old fear of becoming his own Passive Passenger.

The thoughts of the first two Melvins clashed and overlapped. They made harsh echoes and squealed against each other like electric feedback caught in a closet. Back outside, back inside, up the hall and around the corner. Dorothy again struck the RETURN key as he knew she would.

Again, Melvin joined himself and he howled into the deafening roar of three Melvins plus one. His head had become a torture chamber, overcrowded with multiple, dizzying, collisions of thought.

Melvin endured the cycle fifty-eight times.

On the fifty-ninth, his heart exploded.

Dorothy struck the RETURN key and spun around. Melvin was in the doorway with an ax and for a second, she just could not buy it.

You may as well show me an infant smoking a cigar and driving a tractor.

Dorothy gasped.

Melvin is in the doorway with a Goddamned ax!

He screamed in agony. To Dorothy, it sounded like a vast number of voices in unison, and again she questioned her sense of perception. She brought her hands to her face.

Melvin turned in his hands to clutch at his chest and the motion turned the ax blade inward. He fell over face forward and the butt side of the ax met the floor first. His forehead came in a close second place.

There was a loud *thunk* and a wet *shuuck* as Melvin Helitz became one with cold steel. The computer whined, sizzled, and gave a loud *pop*. Its screen shut down to dead black.

And Dorothy screamed. She screamed and screamed and . . .

Melvin shot out of his body and watched his wife scream.

"I never filled out the life insurance forms at school, Dorothy! I forgot! What do you think about that! I forgot!"

The deep and brilliant colors of Melvin's final journey began to close in. He opened his arms to it.

"I'll finally know," he thought. "I'll finally know."

And somewhere off in the distance, a jackal was laughing.

Toll Booth

Anemia: a condition in which the blood is deficient in red blood cells, in hemoglobin, or in total volume.

My name is James Raybeck, and if you are reading this message I am already dead.

It most probably took about two weeks to work through all the young hard-asses, younger jackasses, and older disbelievers trying to make it all night in the booth just once for the thrill of it. It probably took another pair of weeks to put feelers out past Westville and come up absolutely empty in a serious search for long-term toll collectors to work the graveyard shift. I would estimate it was another three or four working days to rush through paperwork issuing the green light for removal, and a couple of business lunches to secure a deal for the dismantling the booth itself, the demolition of the concrete pad beneath, and the excavation of the ground under that.

It is no secret to the townspeople of Westville that the Siegal Group claimed back in '74 that the footer under the base was never properly surveyed and assessed while Runnameade Engineering gave the quicker OK for the construction of the pad, and later, the single toll booth at the base of the exit ramp off the Route 79 overpass. Everyone and their mothers knew that Siegal never really cared so much about that initial pour (small beans) or the possible flaw in the footer (a technicality to be used for leverage). Their real interest was in the contract for an entire toll plaza, a complicated network of lighting systems, road signs, a restaurant complex, a gas station complete with plumbing of its own, and a double-lined two-way straight through to Main Street. It was Goliath's vision. Risky, gargantuan costs up front, and when it all came down to whose bid was chosen, Ed Runnameade was the now late Mayor Smitherbridge's second cousin, and his middle boy was just starting out on his own with Runnameade Concrete, Road

Systems, Builders, and Wreckers. The easiest (and most expeditious) solution was dumping in the backfill, pouring the concrete, and enjoying the highest initial profit margin that a simple guard shack, traffic signal lamp, and barrier gate arm would bring despite the horrible things that happened right there at the edge of Scutters Woods.

Since the present-day removal of the booth itself will be the first item of business (the current governor is married to a Siegal) and certain individuals in current positions of power downtown have been waiting for an excuse to move forward with the closure of this particular chapter in Westville history no matter what the cost, I would estimate you are reading this approximately five weeks after my demise, six at the outside. A new contractor recommended by the conglomerate now known as Siegal/TriState Industries, initially agented by some twenty-five-year-old kid with a hangover from last night's adventures at the Pleasure Chest Gentleman's Club out on the Pike, will have found this packet of writing long before his team has taken out the safety glass, disengaged the roof support channels, and used mini-grinders to cut through the welds bonding the wall panels. He will have found this writing in its manila envelope under the storage cabinet that I bolted to the floor with wedge anchors last February. I kept the night-time stuff in that steel case, the lot consisting of a pair of Embury Luck-E-Lite Kerosene traffic lanterns, a Streamline Fire Vulcan flashlight, and a pair of PF 500 power flares, so as to absolutely disinterest the dayshift employees: Tim Clements Monday through Thursday, and Frank Hillboro the long weekend crew chief. And just in case one of them had gotten a wild hair up his ass, unscrewed the bolts, and moved the cabinet before I died of "natural causes"? Well, I do carry a Ruger LCP .380 for protection. I would have had no problem turning it on myself. It has been a long road, my friend.

Since the age of seventeen I have dedicated my life to this toll booth, this literal sanctuary, this metaphorical prison, Monday through Monday, 6:00 P.M. to 7:00 A.M. Cal Ripken's got nothing on me. If you entered the town of Westville, Indiana, from Route 79, down Reed Road and through Scutters Woods between the years of 1979 and 2008 after the sun dipped below the horizon, you did it on my watch.

I am the one who endures.

When this structure went up, the first collectors on graveyard shift initially complained of feeling faint. Then came rumors of severe palpitations, followed by stories of visions in the windows, always at the edge of sight, teasing the periphery of the given operator's view of the 360-degree sliding glass safety panels around him. Some claimed it was a boy laughing maniacally and then being decapitated from behind, while others swore it was a woman ripping apart an embryo. After two short weeks, the booth almost came down. I dropped out of high school to save it. I had no choice.

Within days of my first moments on the job, I started taking Geritol to up my iron and B vitamin counts. It was like a Band-Aid on an amputation. The visions were bad enough, but the blackouts were disastrous. In the first month I was woken up from a dead faint three times, twice by customers laying on their horns, and once in August when a young waitress from Kulpswood actually exited her vehicle, opened the portal door, and helped me off the floor. I approached my doctor and was refused medicine for anemia, which I showed no signs of in my life outside of the booth.

I thickened up my blood the old-fashioned way. I went on a "diet" including high-fat stuff like liver and whole milk. Since my late teens I have consistently eaten breakfasts made of a minimum of five egg yolks, three large links of Hatfield sausage, home fries smothered in onions, and Jewish hallah covered with butter. My lunches have been constructed of various red meats, and my dinners have always included drawn butter, fried side dishes, and cheeses. Between meals I've pretty much settled with deep fried Cheetos and good old-fashioned vanilla chocolate chip ice cream, but have been known to go off the beaten path with Hot Fries, Ranch Doritos, and Ring-Dings. There is no physician worth his salt that would ever tell you that there is a correlation between cholesterol and anemic need, but please believe me when I say that you could not survive the booth with an LDL or triglyceride count under 330. When I started there I was five foot-eight inches and a cool one hundred and fifty-four pounds. Though I have quietly cheated any overt sort of obesity with a lightning metabolism passed down from my mother's side of the family, my small pear-shaped paunch and respectable weight of one eighty-four is deceiving. Stuff like this catches up with you, and I have been a poster-boy for a stroke, blood clot, or heart attack for some time now.

That which you are reading at this moment, I composed on my Dell. It took me four months to say it exactly the way it needed to be said, and since I wanted you to get the whole picture I put the thing in story form. I even added italics at times to express inner monologue and recent flashbacks. Though I am no professional, everyone knows that even a high school dropout can up his level of discourse through reading. And I have had nothing but time on my hands. I have had time to read, to write, to mourn, and adapt to the unthinkable.

Reed Road is a one-way thoroughfare that cuts through Scutters Woods for five miles and eventually opens out to Main Street. To use Reed Road up until now, you would have had to come off the Route 79 overpass and pay me a toll anywhere from fifty cents to two-seventy-five, depending on where you originally picked up the turn-pike. So to all my customers, to my acquaintances in the past, to my mother God rest her, my relatives, and those of you that will hear of this through the media, know and try to understand my story.

And to you, my contractor friend with the hangover, he who has just found this packet under the bolted-down cabinet. I finally want to confirm something before you dismantle the walls, stack the safety glass, put my cash drawer and F9 500 POS touch screen on eBay, and start busting out the concrete pad below your feet.

The toll booth still erected around you is haunted.

I am going to tell you how it got that way.

This is my confession.

1.

She's a gay, faggot, pussy-dog, and you know it, Jimmy.

No she isn't.

Is! She looks like a leprechaun.

She's half beagle and half fox terrier. That's why her ears stick up like that. And she's really nice.

Nice! Dog's ain't supposed to be "nice." They're supposed to be faithful. They're supposed to have big paws and lots of hair. They're supposed to chase after sticks, guard the house, and flush rabbits and pheasants out of the brush and shit.

She barks when strangers come . . .
She yips! She's a yip dog.
Well, I like her.
I know you do, Jimmy. Hell, I like her too. I was just kidding.
Really?
Yeah, she's awesome. For a gay, faggot, pussy-dog.

Kyle winked, pushed out of the pit, and crawled under the caution tape. On tiptoe I peered over the lip of our new hiding hole and watched him strut across the abandoned job site. He stopped by a stack of cinderblocks and a pile of long steel bars with grooves in them. He turned and scratched his head. He stroked an imaginary beard. He hawked up and spit into a red wheelbarrow with a flat tire, then spun away, spread his feet, and fumbled with his pants. He started pissing down the side of a dented fifty-gallon drum. His shoulders were shaking as were mine, and his stream went through a number of unsteady spurts in rhythm with his laughter. He started gyrating his hips and the urine that dissolved the old dust in shiny splatters became a pattern. He was writing his name.

"Kyle, don't."

He zipped up and climbed into the cab of a bulldozer.

"Don't what?" He grinned and started yanking on the gear handles. He was not quite tall enough to reach the floor pedals with his feet.

"Don't mess around."

"But Jimmy, this piece of shit won't move."

I giggled a bit. It was forced. He knew it was forced and he challenged me to say exactly what was on my mind with a hard, watery stare. Then more yanking. Hard. His teeth were clenched beneath the thinnest of smiles and sweat ran through his dirty blond crewcut. The scene was becoming a familiar one. It was a hot summer day in Westville, we were thirteen years old, I was Kyle's new pal, and we were out making mischief.

"C'mon," I said. "You're gonna bust it."

He stopped.

"So? What are they going to do, take fingerprints? Next you're about tell me that the chief of police is going to connect some busted dozer gear with my name written in piss over there on that can. You're one paranoid little jerk-in-pants, ain't you?"

I shrugged. He shrugged back and we both laughed. It was the usual standoff. My base instincts screamed "foul" long before we chucked apples at the Levinworths' tin roof, or doused the church doorknobs with bacon grease, or lit up a bag of dogshit right by the umbrella stand in Mr. Kimball's front foyer. I was the worried voice of what could go wrong and Kyle would twist around my illustrations to prove we wouldn't get caught. He always had ironclad proof and a way of presenting that proof that left me speechless.

I rested my forearms on the edge of the trench and looked for a place to draw pictures in the dirt. There was a half-buried tube of liquid nails and a scuffed-up red gas cap next to a fanned-out toss of broken green glass pieces. The bent-up Genesee Cream Ale bottle cap was a foot to the left, and I made note to possibly flip it at Kyle if the moment was right. I rubbed my index finger into the ground. It was good dirt. Soft, with pretty little mica specs in it. I drew a cartoon penis and a cartoon vagina. A stalk with a bulb and an oval with an upside down "Y" in it. Why did vaginas look like peace signs anyway?

"So," I said. I scratched out a dot where I imagined the clitty thing would be. "This is the big secret?" I looked up. "We rode bikes five miles just to trash some old dozer? You said you had some new surprise out here that was ultimate pisser."

Kyle put his elbow up on the steering column.

"Still drawing pussy instead of getting it, Jimmy?"

I yanked up my finger as if burned. If Kyle had heard, it was pretty clear that more had gotten in on the story over the summer.

Mr. Ferguson had caught me drawing weird stuff in my notebook on the last day of school back in June, and I'd gotten a weirder lecture in the hall after class. He told me all about respect and being appropriate and careful and all. He'd colored up while telling me, reddened right at the neckline, and when Miss Royer came around the corner from teaching her gym class he'd gone scarlet. As all the boys in school had been doing since the beginning of time, we both ignored her horse-face, peeked at her long mane of straight brown hair that went nearly down to her waist, and then shot a quickie glance right to her Olympic legs. We looked back at each other, and his finger was right in my face.

"Now look, Jimmy. You're a good kid, but you're a bit lost. You've got one more year of junior high school and I want you to fly straight. I've seen you looking at the girls sitting next to you and across from you, and it's getting a bit obvious. Other kids are snickering about it. Keep your eyes out front, all right?"

Now *I* was scarlet. The fact that he was looking at Miss Royer's legs just as I was a second ago seemed suddenly petty. His accusation was true. I couldn't keep my eyes off anything female. They were all so . . . sexy. Since last year I couldn't help but always stare at the girls in their swishing little field hockey kilts, and the cheerleaders in their green and white "Go Wildcats" sweaters and matching black miniskirts, and the girls in gym class with their high-cut white shorts. How could I not stare? They were a dizzying carousel of feathered hair, shags, tight pants, blue jean skirts, strawberry lip gloss, and light blue eye shadow with sparkles in it. I studied them every chance that I had!

The urge had been so overwhelming that I had not considered the possibility that others were watching me watch the skirts and all. Weren't other boys doing the same thing as I was?

Maybe, but they weren't showing.

And I'd initially thought I was lucky. Even though I was pretty sure Melinda Thomas had seen the pictures I was drawing and actually heard bits of the conversation as she passed us in the hallway, Ferguson had confronted me after my second-to-last class on the day before summer vacation. There was no detention, no phone call home, and no lunch period for the rumors to fly through the student population like a bad disease. Still, the story had obviously gained legs over the last month and a half, painting me as the world's worst heavy breathing sex addict.

I rubbed out my dirty cartoons.

"So, how much kootchie are you getting?" I said.

"Enough. Just ask Billy Healy."

I had heard the stories. Supposedly, Kyle had copped a feel of Jeanette Wallman's crotch at the Thatcher Park Shopping Center, in an unlocked pickup parked behind the Briarbrook Deli. The legend was that she was wearing tight white jeans and his dirty hand left actual prints. Suddenly I wished for a magic scale that would weigh my "staring problem" against his little episode in the pickup and somehow come up with a comparison between us on the perv-o-meter.

"Got any gum, Jimmy?"

He was staring. It sort of hurt to look back at it. For the millionth time that day, I looked down, and to my dismay, started drawing in the dirt again.

"You know I don't," I said. My mom didn't let me have gum. She didn't let me have Twizzlers or corn chips either. She was a health food mom and stocked the house with granola, wheat germ, and soy products. Of course that didn't mean I couldn't sneak to the Acme or the Drake Emporium on 7th, and cram an entire Plenti-Pack of Doublemint in my mouth every now and then. The problem was that Mom did regular room checks, I wasn't good at hiding leftovers, and today, as always, I was flat broke in the munchie department.

"That's OK," he said. "I do."

He fished a square of Bazooka out of his pocket and chucked it to me. It fell a bit short and I reached to pinch it from the dirt. It felt like Christmas when you could scarf up a freebie. I ripped it open and licked the sugar powder off the comic no one ever read anyway. I jammed the pink square deep between the back molars and had chewed it three good times before I realized that Kyle was still wearing that hard, blank expression.

"That's all right," he said. "I didn't want my half anyway."

I froze. Kyle Skinner was the rudest, hardest, most obnoxious boy that went to Paxon Hill Junior High School, but he sure had his cast-iron rules of etiquette. Figuring out these laws and boundaries was a constant source of pain for me, but it also fascinated me in some deep, secret place. Somehow, these were the real laws of growing up your mom never told you about. I just wish I didn't feel so stupid every time there was an infraction.

He turned away and gazed out at the woods that flanked the dirt road.

"Come up here and have a smoke with me, Jimmy."

My hesitation was embarrassing.

"My mom will smell it on me."

"Huh?"

"My mom will smell it!"

My voice carried louder than it had before, but I knew it wasn't going to do me any good. I used that excuse yesterday when he tried to convince me to light up in my room and blow it out the window. He did seem to forget about the whole thing when he found my school supply drawer and started a rubber band fight, but you just didn't re-gift excuses to Kyle Skinner. He was too quick for that.

In truth, I had no excuse to deflect the fact that I was absolutely petrified of tobacco. In truth, I had nightmarish visions of taking *that puff* and feeling that dirty ghost eat away at my guts. Its gray wisps would scrape at my throat and push through my nose. I would rapidly fizzle away from the inside out and become a spotty skeleton-child, destined to be buried in the back yard under the dandelions.

And all this was stupider than the "mommy" excuse. Kyle smoked all the time and was healthy as a greyhound.

"That's bullshit and you know it," he said. "Butt breath goes away in fifteen minutes."

"How do you know?"

With a jerk of surety, Kyle bent up his knee and slapped the sole of his foot flat to the bulldozer's control panel. He hiked up the bottom edge of his jeans and dug for the smoke pack hidden in his sock.

"Bobby Justice told me."

I was silenced. Just the fact that Kyle had conversed with Bobby Justice was an instant credibility. It made me feel young, and un-worldly, and again one step behind the parade.

Bobby Justice was seventeen. He took shop classes half the day, majored in raising hell, and even got arrested once for selling grams of Hawaiian pot under the bleachers on the football field. He drove a jacked-up black Mustang. He wore shit-kicker boots, and a chain hanging out the back pocket in that half-moon that said in its dumb, blind sort of grin, "Fuck off, Chief." Rumor had it that he once pulled a sawed-off shotgun out of his trunk at a Hell's Angels biker party, somewhere between the tube-funnel beer-chugging contest and the motor throw, because some dude was wearing a Lynyrd Skynyrd T-shirt that he wanted.

And it was mind-boggling to picture Kyle extracting this informa-tion from Bobby Justice in casual conversation. The only reason this bully ignored kids like us was that we were still too young to beat up.

Kyle drew out the pack, ripped away the cellophane, and let it float off on the wind. With a mild sort of alarm I noticed that the brand in his fist was the filterless Chesterfields. Last time I'd looked it was Marlboros.

He scratched at the foil cover and shook one up.

"Come here, sit down, and have a smoke with me, Jimmy." He held it like a pointer for emphasis. "I'm not asking you to steal the change from your mom's purse like I did. I'm not asking you to go down to the Rexalls and tell the old fart that the butts are for your old man, neither. I've already done all that myself. The only thing I want is for your first puff to be with me. Ain't you my new best friend no more? Don't ya want to hang out with the big boys?"

I climbed out of the trench and edged toward the dozer, my face burning, my mind racing. In the past two years friendships had suddenly twisted around by definition, and it was like I hadn't been paying attention in math or something. Up until third grade the fastest readers and the ones who brought in the most clever projects were the coolest. In fourth and fifth the best on the playground sort of shared the rule of the roost with the fast talkers, and the only ones picked on were those accused of being quiet, bookwormy, unpopular gay birds. It seemed I had tons of friends and we told each other everything.

But things shifted in seventh and eighth. Suddenly friendships seemed built on what you could bring to the table, not who you were or the thoughts you could share. A boy who had regular access to his father's *Penthouse* and *Gallery* magazines was far more revered than the "nice" kid in the school choir. Anyone with a steady supply of Pop Rocks, cherry bombs, pump BB guns, and exploding gag cigarette loads stood head and shoulders above those with straight A's and no allowance like me. Cool kids were building monster album collections with the complete works of Zeppelin, Sabbath, Kiss, and The Who, while my only eight-track was a commercial, pop anthology you ordered from TV called *Autumn '73*. Every day it seemed like I was losing ground. I tried talking to Ma sometimes, but her response was always to supply me with thick doses of values after methodically rejecting my requests one by one.

I walked to the dozer.

Kyle scrambled from the big bucket seat and sat on the dozer's thick tread strip between the two side wheels. He slapped the area next to him and I took my place at his side. Our weight bowed the track pad down a bit and it brought our shoulders together. I cupped my hands between my knees. His arm was across my shoulders.

"Now listen," he said. "Don't suck it down like you're gulping a Pepsi. And don't use your teeth. Take a small puff, hold it in your mouth for a second and then breathe it in slow. And when you blow it out don't try to do smoke rings. That shit is for girls."

I nodded. With all the steps and instructions I was more worried about doing it wrong than the effects of doing it in the first place. I guess that was a good thing.

"Go on then, Bozo. Take it," he said. He was holding the pack out over my lap with my cigarette jutting up about a half inch from the others. It was a sentinel on guard duty with Kyle's arm holding me in place. No escape.

I reached for the cigarette. My fingers were shaking a bit.

"Breathe," he said. "Breathe, baby. Stay with me." In a far-off way I noticed that his arm had disengaged itself. I put the cigarette between my lips. Took it back out. Wiped off a little drool. Reinserted. "OK, OK," he said. "Here we go."

He struck a match, cupped it, and brought across the two-fisted treasure. I leaned in going cross-eyed in my trance before the dancing flame. Close up it looked beautiful and deadly. I sucked in carefully and got braced for the hot, nasty swallow.

It was awesome.

Sharp, it hit the back of my throat and rolled into me like a chocolate cloud. It was potent and rich. Forbidden. I blew it out and watched the gray smoke make art on the air, a mushroom cloud spreading to the gauzy, three-fingered hand of a beckoning witch, to thinning curlycues, drifts, trails. My head spun a bit in a friendly sort of a way, and I knew I could handle this. I was older now. Better. I spit my gum out and took another deep drag.

"Now you're ready for the surprise," Kyle said. He was studying me, smoking one himself now. His eyes were thin, but his expression was otherwise neutral. I leaned back.

"Show me."

He hopped down, went to his knees, and reached behind the dozer's front roller. I couldn't see his arm from my angle, and I had the sudden premonition that he was going to fake like something grabbed his hand. He would open his eyes in wide surprise and jam his shoulder into the front of the dozer, giving the illusion he was being yanked really hard from something lurking in the shadows under the load bucket. Of course, this did not happen. If it had, however, I would have been ready and it made me smile. I really was changing for the better.

He came back with a cardboard box about half the size of a car battery. It was old and stained with what was either coffee or puddle splashes, and the front had a sticker that said "16D."

"What is it?" I said. He carefully set it down on the tread a few feet to my left.

"This here is a fine example of why most grown-ups have shit for brains, that's what it is," he said. He gave the box a half turn so we both could view its front label. He took a deep drag of the smoke he'd been lipping, then pointed to the box with the lit end for emphasis.

"Notice, James, the '16.' This stands for three and a half. The 'D' stands for 'penny.' Put them together and the '16D' means three and a half inches of nail. But please explain to this dumb-ass kid what 'D' has anything to do with 'penny,' and what 'penny' has to do with hand nails which are so obviously made of steel and not copper."

I let go a nervous titter which hung in the air for a moment. I took a deep drag off my Chesterfield to fill the space when Kyle didn't respond, and marveled at all the social uses these cigarettes had. During the exhale I reasoned that I wasn't really supposed to understand Kyle's joke yet, but was more there to prep him for the punch line. Another breakthrough. I was really on a roll.

"Where did you get—"

"I clipped them from my Pop's tool box," he said. "Look." He flipped open the top, dug up a nail, and held it outward. It was bent and a bit jagged.

"Why's it all screwy?" I said.

He frowned. I had not kept up with his storytelling rhythm and he didn't want to backtrack. He tossed the nail back into the box and shut the cover.

"When my Pop's done framing a house he walks the job and yanks out all the bent nails."

"Why?"

"He brings them all back to the toolhouse and pulls a major bitch and moan. Gets paid back for each and every one of them."

"Then he'll miss that box!" I had jumped to my feet and chucked away the smoke. "Geez, Kyle, why did you go and do that? He's probably going to kill you and then come for me!"

His eyes went wide.

"I ain't that stupid, James. I found the empty box in the garage two months ago and stashed it in the closet behind my old board games and Lego garbage. I've been filling it up one nail at a time. Cripes, don't be such a fucking dipshit!"

I forced a wounded grin.

"You're the one with a dipshit pal and that makes you a total bonehead."

"Yeah," he said. "I must be freakin' bonkers." He was smiling but I found it hard to mirror it. Just because Kyle knew how to handle his old man didn't mean I'd cracked the code.

Mr. Skinner was Westville's definition of a good ole boy. He drove a mud-splattered, light brown Chevy pickup and always had the back bed filled with ladders, lumber, metal scraps, upside-down wheelbarrows, and garbage barrels filled with square-mouthed shovels, street brooms, steel-tined rakes, and nail-ripping pry bars. He had a chainsaw, a gas-powered chop saw, and a circular saw with a continuous-rim diamond blade on it. He had pickle barrels filled with drills, Sawzalls, nails, and a million miscellaneous hinges, Y-fittings, PVC junctures, and wall anchors. He had an American flag on the hood-side opposite the antenna and a bumper sticker that talked about ripping his pistol from his cold, dead fingers. On the driver's door was his company logo, "One-Truck-Johnny."

I knew the ass-end of that vehicle because Mr. Skinner had grudgingly driven a couple of us home from practice once when our moms were too busy to come by the field this past spring. Kyle, Lars Maynard, and Tommy Birch made me sit out back in the "junkyard." Before we set off, Mr. Skinner had told me to be careful not to "mess up his office back there." He touched his leather belt as if he wasn't afraid to use it, opened a quart of Miller by snapping the cap off in a notch he had cut into the wheel well, and pointed the mouth of the bottle at me meaningfully. Then everyone in the truck-cab had laughed. And if you think the veiled threats and the booze were disquieting, you should have seen old "Pop" on the baseball field.

The Skinners, Kyle as player, Dad as coach, had won the Westville Central Championship two of the last four years, once with the nine-year-olds and once with the elevens. Mr. Skinner was a town fixture at the edge of the diamond, coaching third base in his clam-digger shorts, black socks, Converse All Stars, gray sweatshirt with the sleeves ripped off, and NASCAR cap turned backward. He had a beer gut hanging way over the belt, big arms with curly hair all over the biceps, and a thick scar running from his collar bone to the base of his left ear. His hair was thinning, but he wore bushy sideburns to the jaw line. He had what looked a bit too big to be a mole and a bit too leathery to be a birthmark in the form of a long brown oval along one cheek, and his eyes were the coldest pieces of flint you had ever seen.

Some guys are book smart and some guys work around the campfire in other ways. Mr. Skinner never got past the tenth grade, but he was certainly no dummy. And he didn't like losing. Up until this year, I had always been on bad teams that my mother loved, made up of nice boys (for the most part) playing their best with volunteer coaches encouraging the successes and soothing the failures. When I was ten, Mr. Solomon actually threw us a pool party for not coming in last place, for God's sake.

This year I was ranked sixty-first in a draft of one hundred and thirteen boys and was Mr. Skinner's seventh-round pick. (I know, because Kyle showed me the draft sheet. He came in second by the way, one behind Ray Bradbeir, a big boy at a buck ninety who could catch, pitch, and regularly hit a ball two hundred and seventy feet in the air). It was the toughest two months of my life. This was not about fun, or learning, or even winning. It was about the absolute thrill of the kill, or on the other side, the horror of being utterly demoralized.

Skinner went outside the league rules and had us practicing back in early March, on the vacant lot behind the old paper branch. We did soft toss with thin metal poles and multi-colored golf Wiffle balls. Mr. Skinner would throw up three at a time and call a color. If you didn't get at least eight out of ten, you had to sprint to the edge of the quarry and back. I did a lot of sprints. He hit grounders at you as hard as he could, and if you shied away from knocking the ball down even on the goofy hops, you did pushups. I did a lot of pushups. When the season started, it was quickly determined that I was no more than a below average hitter, and really susceptible to off-speed pitches. Unfortunately, you saw a lot of curves and change-ups at thirteen, and it was common for Mr. Skinner to shout at me down the base line, *"C'mon, Raybeck! You're stepping in the bucket and your shoulder's flying open! This ain't girly softball! Keee-rist, I seen a better swing on a playground!"* I was the cause of his ejection for kicking over a bucket of balls in the dugout when, in the fourth inning against the Renegades, I came in on a fly ball to center field before realizing it was over my head. Still, he was the hardest on Kyle.

In our third contest, Kyle check swung a looping line drive to the second baseman to end an inning. Mr. Skinner made him go off by the porta-pottys in the parking lot and take five hundred full swings before coming back to the dugout. The next time Kyle was up, he cracked the game-winning double to left center. He joined in the celebration by the pitcher's mound where we did that hop-and-tap-each-other-on-the-head thing, took off his helmet, walked by his old man and said,

"Fuck you, asshole."

His dad looked away and let it stand. It was at that moment that Kyle Skinner became my idol. He came up beside me in the dugout and started packing his gear.

"Nice," I said. He clapped me on the shoulder.

"Thanks, Bozo."

It was then we also started becoming friends. Our team won almost every regular-season game with Kyle batting third, playing shortstop, pitching every other game, and breaking a township record by hitting .827. I ran a meager .223 batting average and tried my best to shag every fly ball that I could on defense. It always amazed me that my mom didn't complain about Mr. Skinner's hat-throwing, dirt-kicking, scolding, and taunting, but I believe she thought it was some rite of passage. Or maybe he reminded her of her father. Or maybe she was actually perceptive this time, not *mom* perceptive as in predicting who would fail at life because of their lack of being *verbal* or *being in touch with their feelings,* but real-life perceptive enough to see that in a very practical way complaining to this guy was, first, useless, and second, detrimental to my playing time.

I struck out looking in the title game. Last ups for us, two outs, bases had been loaded, Kyle on deck. I was still standing in the batter's box with my head down when the crowd dispersed. Mr. Skinner walked up to me, put his hands on his knees, his face up close, and said through his teeth,

"You cost me a championship, son."

I let the head of my bat dip to the dirt and I leaned on the knob. Mom wasn't even there because she had her "Divorced Ladies Let's-Share-Our-Inner-Issues Meeting" at the junior college on Fridays. A tear ran down my nose and I felt a hand on my shoulder. It was Kyle.

"It was a foot outside, Jimmy," he said. "You didn't cost us nothing."

It was then that we became *best* friends. It was then I realized that Kyle was the only one who really had to deal with Mr. Skinner full time. My service under the monster's watch was not only temporary, but completed. It became the unspoken rule that me and Kyle would always hang out far away from their house over in the Common. I only wished I didn't feel so vulnerable to his meanness, even now, long after the season was over.

I sat back against the tread and kicked a bit at the dirt.

"So, what are the bent nails for?"

Golden question. Jackpot. Kyle was glowing.

He brought the box to head level and gave it a shake. The nails clacked inside and he moved to the sound in a sarcastic rendition of the "Do-Si-Do" we learned in gym class two winters ago. His head was sort of sideways, one eye regarding me in a sly sort of observation. He was doing a circular motion with the box now like the Good & Plenty choo-choo boy on TV. He shuffled past me. He stopped. He pulled up the box top, drew out a nail, and tossed it into the middle of the dirt road that cut through the job site.

He turned back with raised eyebrows. I was sorry to disappoint.

"What are you doing?" I said.

He took out a second nail and flipped it to the road from behind his back. He grabbed another, lifted his leg, and chucked it up from beneath. That particular one landed with its sharp point angled straight to the sky.

I shot off the tread.

"You can't do that!" I looked back to the Route 79 overpass that spanned the horizon to my right. "If someone takes a wrong turn off the highway you know they'll be trucking, shit, they're gonna run over those nails and pop a tire!"

Kyle looked up at the sky with his arms spread out.

"By George, I think he's got it!"

The taste in my mouth was electric. Three months ago the construction men had blocked off exit 7 up on the overpass while completing the off ramp, but the job got delayed before the new extension could be finished down here. Dirt road city. The plans for pouring and paving had come to a dead halt and long since, all the road barriers up on the turnpike had been stolen or moved. It was an old joke by now, that bum steer on the overpass and everyone knew not to take the deep, unmarked turn. Everyone.

Unless they weren't from Westville.

Every now and again some goober took the exit by mistake and barreled down the ramp to the dirt road. It was a major pain too, as the rough detour stretched for five miles through the woods before hitting the outskirts of Westville Central. Bumpy ride. Slow as all hell.

Soon to be stalled out and stranded.

I looked up at the overpass and, from behind its triple guard rail, heard the cars shooting past. They couldn't see us and we couldn't see them. A double blindfold.

I pictured some huge tattooed bruiser with a ponytail tied up in a leather shank throwing open the door to his muscle car and shouting curses into the fresh swirl of raised dust. He would chase us for sure, and I didn't run so well when I was scared. He would grab us and punch in our faces. What if he had a tire iron under the seat or a hunting rifle in the trunk?

"Pick 'em up, Kyle," I said. It sounded like a command backed at least by a shred of confidence, and of that I was glad. Kyle replied by flipping another nail into the road.

"You sound like your mother." His voice rose to falsetto. "Let's talk about you and how you feel about yourself, James. Let's have a big pow-wow."

His tone went back to normal.

"Damn, Jimmy. Your ma just won't leave you be, will she? The lady has you turned pussy is all, hell, why does she have to know everything anyway? She don't even give you an allowance."

"What does that have to do with—"

"Well she don't, *does* she? Does she?"

My eyes felt suddenly hot and bloodshot.

"She gives me money."

He slapped his thigh.

"Exactly! But ya got to ask for it every time. That's how she keeps tabs on what you're going to do with it. Don't you see? Anytime you want to buy something fun she gets to shoot it down. She wants to keep her little baby-boy, don't she? She won't let you have secrets. That should be a crime or something."

He nodded at me meaningfully.

"I know you're a charity case of the apron strings, Jimmy. That's why I want to help ya. That's why I *like* ya." He held up a crooked nail. "This ain't gonna cost nothing. This here secret is gonna be a freebie."

My mouth opened and I shut it. Like always, Kyle had twisted my mother right into the crux, and though the correlation was clumsy, the effect was potent. Oh, it had everything to do with the matter when you really paused for a gander. It made you stop still. It forced you to look, to judge up your life, and to stew.

Sure, Kyle played it up real nice in front of my mother, being all charming and verbal and "forthright," making up some allergy to softly admit he "was having to wrestle with," or quietly confessing he was "working through something with his father." Oh, he knew the language all right! Ma thought she was cutting edge, while her whole deal was already cliché. And in terms of how this trickled down to me, Kyle's accusations were right on the mark. Mother made me the oddest one out and it had been so for a couple of good years now.

And since she kicked Dad out the door, the woman had turned downright sour. When I was way younger she used to sing out loud in the house all the time. She used to hum "Michael Row Your Boat Ashore," and "Puff the Magic Dragon" to me before bed, but Dad never liked it. He called it "sensitive man bullshit," and made her feel like a dumb hippie all the time. He was always telling her a thing or two, proving her wrong and making her cross. Then he'd be gone for months at a time. Dad was a traveling sales representative. He sold gourmet coffees to restaurants. Sometimes I even liked him OK when he was around, but he spent too much time moaning at Ma and practicing his pitch in front of the mirror. He was a big fake-me-out, Dad was. One second he would be sitting at the table playing the all-American father, next to be ranting about how *"Maxwell House was whoring up the industry,"* or how Hills Brothers had all the *"market share,"* or how Judith (Ma) *"had really pulled a boner this time."*

In 1971 they got a divorce and he officially became "The Bastard." We moved out of Westville Central and bought a house out on Weston Road, where the plots stood acres apart from each other. Ma really cleaned his clock.

The problem is that she never stopped being cross. Her red hair went a bit gray and the dimple marks at the sides of her lips deepened around a nearly permanent scowl. All of a sudden it seemed that everything tensed up a notch and she wanted to know all I was thinking and the whole long road of what I was feeling.

She made me tired.

And kept me poor, trapped in the fold, and begging. Most of my friends were starting to get out more, like after dusk and all, but I still wasn't allowed. I had to stay home with mother so we could talk. Talk-talk, some nights she had me at the kitchen table until eight o'clock, asking about the details of my day and hanging on the words. She was lord, judge, and jury, always cramming my head full of her *interpretations.* Oh, she was a regular code-cracker all right. I always got a technicolor version of just "who I really was" at that particular moment, thank you very much.

And no allowance, lord, it was a big responsibility being the man of my family! A responsibility I was starting to resent.

Kyle pushed the box out toward me and gave it a shake.

"Go on, Jimmy. Do a nail, man."

I scooped my thumb and index finger into the box and drew out a nail. I underhanded it out to the road and felt an immediate speckle of the guilts on my face. My nail looked like a crooked finger pointing back at me in dark welcome. It was an invitation, leading me to my next step down the dark path. I looked to Kyle and he was nodding. I turned my glance back down at the road.

This was not the way I imagined I would turn out. Maybe it was fun to make crank calls and play knock-knock zoom-zoom, but this was big time. I didn't belong here, and I suddenly didn't care what Kyle said.

I took a step forward and bent to one knee so I could grab back my nail.

"Too late for that shit!" Kyle said from behind.

There was a *shhhuuuuckkk* sound followed by a flock of shadows spinning madly across the road. A shower of nails then pelted down to kick up a scatter of small, dusty clouds.

The lane was covered.

I had every intention then of picking nails from the road one by one, but I stopped. I realized I had made fists at my sides. I was not the one who dumped the whole box. It was not my idea to leave someone stranded out here with a flat, shit, I was the one who wanted to pick up my nail and get out of here!

I decided to let him get his own Goddamned nails and pick mine up in the process. What did I owe him? A Chesterfield and a piece of gum? I didn't care. I wasn't going to do this. I had enough guilt dumped on me at home. Weren't friends supposed to be your relief from that stuff?

I spun around to face Kyle and somehow stammer my thoughts out to words, but he was not even looking my way. He was looking at something off to the right. Something absolutely mesmerizing.

I followed the line of his gaze and saw the car coming down the ramp.

It was coming fast, yet everything seemed to be caught in slow motion. The air suddenly tasted rusty and harsh. Kyle grabbed my arm. My stomach was a lead ball, my ears hot as branding irons.

We scrambled behind a red dumpster and there was the gritty sound of a car bumper banging from roadway to dirt. Kyle dropped to his knees for the low view and I stayed up high.

Sharp sun lanced off the chrome and plastered a hot glare to the windshield. It was a dull orange Honda Civic, already swerving, plumes of dirt spitting up behind in huge turkey-tails.

My mouth was working the word "no" silently.

There was a series of sharp "pop" sounds. The car did a rapid back-and-forth, left to right to left to right, then shot straight toward us. Like a yanked sheet the glare on the windshield vanished, and I was

176

eye-to-eye with the driver.

She had straight blonde hair. I thought she was wearing one of those plastic, red, three-quarter-moon hair bands that formed her bangs into their own separate little statement, but I couldn't be sure at the moment. Her face had a long, sharp sort of beauty that was almost regal, and of that I was quite sure. Then the moment was gone. She overcompensated for control and yanked the wheel the other way. Now I saw the back of the car and the huge oak tree rising up ahead of it to the left of a long jobsite trailer.

There was a hard clap. The butt end of the car actually jumped, and small fragments of bark and glass burst to both sides. The car bounced twice and settled. The raised dirt split into threads and blew off into the woods like ghosts.

The car horn sounded.

Its steady wail fingered its way into the afternoon sky and spiraled up to an accusing, hot summer sun.

2.

We both spoke at once, and then took a moment to absorb what was voiced by the other.

"Run," I said. This was Kyle's problem. It was a bad dream that could not possibly have happened to me. Mom's specialty was trashing news flashes like this. She taught me to be concerned on the outside, and to turn up my nose just beneath the surface. We were above people who got caught up in dumb legal stuff. The proper response was to purse our lips gently and trade knowing glances when the trailer trash acted up. Dinnertime war council was all about our superiority and our ability to interpret the world around us. Surely, this would all go away if I ran fast enough and promised not to tell.

"We killed her," Kyle had said.

We.

One of those nails was mine. The fact that dumping them was not my idea in the first place did not matter anymore. We were in this to-gether.

I still thought we could run. I did not have time to consider what the slightly older boy I was on the verge of growing into would call "social responsibility," and what the boy I was on the verge of leaving behind would call "owning up." The car horn was a danger. Though we were five miles from Westville Central, there was bound to be someone passing by on the overpass with the windows down. And perpendicular to the dirt road, through the front leg of Scutters on the other side of a shallow, wooded valley of sorts stood my own house. Was it a quarter-mile from here? A half? Was Lucy out on her lead, up on her back legs, front paws scratching at the air in response to the si-renlike sound coming from this side of the trees?

I opened my mouth to argue what I thought was the obvious, and was denied the opportunity. Kyle was walking away. He was not running, but walking with casual purpose in the last direction I would have expected.

He was walking toward the Honda. His hands were in his pockets just to the fingertips and his shoulders hunched in just a bit toward his neck. He gave a cool glance to the side and I saw his future. In one hand he had a crowbar and in the back of his waistband was a Colt .45 with the safety flipped off. The Honda's horn was now the alarm in a jewelry store downtown after hours with a shattered storefront window and three smashed display cases inside. Kyle casually glanced down both sides of the avenue to see if the cavalry was onto him yet, and approached the getaway car. And he didn't approach it on the run, even though one of Westville's finest was just rounding the corner of Ludlow and Main. He walked toward it with casual purpose.

I expected Kyle to look through the window of the Honda and give himself a "one-two-three," but he didn't. He simply yanked open the door and leaned in. Through the short rear window I saw his elbow piston backward. The horn stopped as if it was cut by a blade. He backed out, slammed shut the door, bent, and puked into the dirt.

I suddenly wanted my father, and a cramp of loneliness and hopelessness opened me up inside. Mom couldn't help me here. Mom pushed morals and preached lessons and soothed stomach aches and provided verbal simulations that *proved* mean people were insecure on the inside, but this was out of her realm. It wasn't even in her universe.

When I'd had man stuff to talk about I used to approach Dad and beg for "Boy's Club." As busy as he was, he always seemed to make time for these moments, most probably because it both excluded

Mother and also helped him see himself for a moment as "Dear old Dad" with the pipe and the confident smile you saw in Fifties movies or the sugar tins and cookie jars with Norman Rockwell prints on them.

Once, back in fifth grade, I asked his advice after breakfast when Mom went to check the laundry downstairs. It was Saturday.

"Dad," I'd whispered.

"Yeah, Skipper." He turned down the corner of the paper and peered over it. My eyes were wide and earnest.

"I have to ask you a *question!*"

"Right." He put the paper down, folded it in thirds, and looked at his watch.

"Let's go."

We slipped out through the sliding glass doors and went to our spot on the log bench by the tire swing. I proceeded to tell him that yesterday when I went back to the school to get a social studies workbook I'd left in my cubby, I caught Spencer Murphy stealing Mrs. Levitz's science test from the top drawer of her desk. It had me frozen in the doorway. I looked over my shoulder for a janitor and saw nothing but empty hallway.

"Hey, dork!" Spencer said. He was a tall, thin boy with disheveled reddish hair. He had what seemed a permanent cowlick on the back left side of his head, early acne, an upturned nose flooded with dark freckles, and ears as small as quarters. He was wearing a light blue shirt with the Copenhagen tobacco logo written across the chest in cursive. There were stains of sweat under his arms. His face had paled, and the pimples on his cheeks shone out like stars. He took a menacing step toward me, the test between his thumb and index finger.

"Tell anyone, Raybeck, and I'll say you were in on it. I'll tell Principal LaShire you dared me to do it, I swear."

Mom would have hit the roof. She would have called Spencer's parents, demanded a meeting with LaShire, rounded up all the other kids involved, and lectured them all about "ethics." If she didn't get satisfaction, she would have gone to the board, and after that, the county paper. I would have been labeled the world's worst snitch and banished to the special ed. lunch table for life.

Dad just got out his calculator.

"What's your average in science so far, son?"

"Around a 95."

"More a 93 or a 97? Be precise, Jimmy."

I closed my eyes. The in-class report on the nervous system didn't go so well last week. I hadn't gotten a grade sheet for it yet, and I had been riding a 94 up until then.

"Maybe a 90."

"How many questions are on this test Spencer *borrowed*?"

"Fifty, I think."

He punched a bunch of numbers into his calculator.

"You're going to get eleven of those answers wrong. Make it every third or fourth, then clump a few together in a row. That'll leave you a 78. Considering it's a big one at the end of the marking period, I would imagine it might be worth fifteen or twenty percent. You'll wind up with a 'B' for the semester that you'll have to live with. If Spencer gets caught you never knew anything about it."

He tousled my hair.

"You're my tiger."

It was pure survival in its most practical form, and I needed that kind of logic in the here and now. I needed my Dad to hit his calculator, snip the goodie-two-shoes stuff to its bare bones, and map me a way out of this.

Kyle wiped off his mouth with the back of his forearm and came up to me. He stopped a few feet before me, put his hands on his hips, and looked around. By default, his logic was the only logic that was going to be heard around here, and he voiced it in a tone almost as cool as my father had done out by the tire swing three-odd years before.

"Listen, Jimmy, and please listen good. We have to get rid of her. We have to make her vanish like fucking Houdini. See, yesterday Barry Koumer called you a pussy while we were checking out his dad's compound bow, and to defend you I told him we were coming up here today to raise all kinds of hell. If someone finds this wreck, Koumer the Rumor is going to point it straight back at you. So there ain't gonna be any running, Jimmy. Stop standing there with your mouth open and start picking up nails."

Nothing left but me, Kyle, and the street logic. There would be no "tsk-tsk" over the rims of our herbal tea mugs and no quick fixes totaled up on the calculator. We were two young boys who had been left no choice at the crossroads, scarred, hardened, and under the gun to hide a dead body by sundown.

3.

The nails were everywhere. A small colony of them had remained in the strip between the dumpster, the dozer, a few stacks of three-foot-by-twelve piping, and various pieces of construction equipment. Still, the Honda had scattered many of them into trickier nooks and crannies. I found two under the rack of a gas generator and seven in the shadow of a huge compressor that said "Emglo" on it. There were storage boxes and gravel troughs gated off near the green construction trailer, and I found six nails playing chameleon with the bottom of the chain link fence. The were three nails hiding under a long roll of razor twine that had caught on a wooden surveyor's marker with an orange strip-flag on it, and I cut my middle finger on the withdraw when I finally managed to coax out the third bent fastener.

I'd filled all four pockets and I widened my sweep. On the far side of the trailer, toward the oak tree now directly to my left, I found a good many clever ones that had bounced into the dead grass that split the dirt road from the woods. I found five more in a patch of wild ivy below a trio of birches and then I backed on all fours into the dirt road. I took my time with the bloody horror only a few feet away. I sifted my hands back and forth for leftovers beneath the dusty surface. Sweaty hair dangled in front of my forehead.

From behind I heard Kyle open the car door for a second time. There was that wheezing sound that happened when a knee got pressed down to an old seat, then muffled shifting and knocking about.

"Jesus Christ," he said. "Get the fuck *off* me!"

I got to my feet and turned.

The passenger side of the car was smashed in, and I really had no window to look into. Not like I wanted to study the damage or anything, my eyes just sort of fell there at first. It looked like a smunched-in picture frame with turned edges. I moved around the back of the vehicle to get a view of Kyle's side of it. Ass in the air, he was buried in the driver's opening all the way to the waist. The car was rocking a bit, and it was clear that he was struggling with something on the floor.

He backed out and his face was a twist of aggravation. A smear of the woman's blood zigzagged across the chest of his T-shirt and a wipe of it stained his left cheek in a shape like the Nike logo that came out three years before. He shrugged his shoulders like the dope I must have looked like, paused, then looked to the side and threw up his hands.

"Well, don't just stand there," he said. "Try shifting your ass and helping me out over here."

I came forward a bit. My wrists were throbbing from the doggie-walk and my eyes were burning. I got close enough to touch the back left corner of the Honda's fender with my knee and stopped.

This was it.

Whatever Kyle expected of me it was sure to involve the dead woman, and I wasn't ready and it wasn't fair. While I had been picking up nails, Kyle had already hurdled a stage or two ahead of me, graduating with fast honors from looking to pushing at the dead thing and yelling. I hadn't managed my first solid glance yet.

I took a peek through the back window and made out the form of her head. It leaned to the right with that crown of blonde hair swirled around. It looked hot and disturbed. It looked like disbelief, rage, and disgrace.

I brought down my eyes to the back seat area and suddenly I knew her, or at least it felt like I did.

At an odd angle between the right side of the car, the void, and the back of the passenger seat, there was a picnic basket made of weaved bamboo. It had been filled with a bunch of stuff now vomited across the vinyl from the impact. There was a ground blanket with braided frays at the edges still half rolled up in the bottom of the basket, its other side unfurled. It had maroon stitchings of wolves and bears on it. There were a few paperbacks scattered across the blanket and the seat. One was missing its cover, and the others were face down and open like birds. In the far left corner was an upside-down bunch of dried roses tied with a rubber band. It had shed most of its dead petals in its trip across the seat and had left a trail that settled over the books and the blanket. Deeper in on the floor it seemed as if there was a pair of yellow flips-flops, a squeegee, a record album by Jackson Browne, and something with red streamers. Could have been a kite.

"C'mon, Jimmy!"

Right in my ear. I jumped and brought my hands to my throat. Kyle grabbed my elbow and pulled me around to the open door.

"I can't throw the clutch and bang it to neutral because my arm can't reach," he was saying. "And the bimbo is stuck right in the middle. The passenger side is crushed and I can't move her, ya dig?"

I did not "dig." We were right in front of the open door and I could feel the cab's sticky heat. Throw the clutch? Bang it to neutral? I knew he was talking about the gear shift, but wasn't sure whether the clutch was on the floor or by the steering wheel. My mom drove a Toyota and it was automatic.

"Neutral?" I said. I avoided the car's interior by focusing on the top rim of the door. Kyle sat down Indian style before me and pushed his hand in toward the floor mat.

"Yeah, neutral so we can move the car. When I push down the clutch pedal I need you to switch that gear shift to neutral. Pull it to the middle and just waggle it a second to make sure you're back to home base, all right?"

Easy for him to say. He had to fumble around with a pair of shoes down there, but I had to go in right over her lap.

I held my breath and bent into the car. The heat was an assault. By instinct I turned away from the close form beneath me and I felt something ever so slightly brush the hair on the back of my head. I jerked a bit and banged into what must have been her face. A bit of warm liquid oozed onto my neck and I lifted my frantic eyes from the wheel to the windshield. It was spiderwebbed with a series of cracks that roadmapped from the wipers clear to the roof side. At the center there was a marbled dent pushed into the glass where her forehead initially made contact. It was like the eye of a fly, with multiple cross-sections dripping tears of blood to the dash.

I let out my breath in a burst and gagged.

Caught between two scissored shards was a piece of her skin, dangling. It was big enough that I thought I could see a freckle on it.

My head swam. I could taste the aroma of her perfume on my tongue mixed with the heavier scent of shock, violence, and what might have been shit.

I bent in farther to accomplish my task in swift combination. From what seemed another planet I heard Kyle ask what was taking so long, and I fell a bit forward. I put my left hand down to the seat for support and it pressed the woman's bare thigh.

A scream whistled up in my nose and I groped to find the space between her legs. I stretched in with my right and made for the gear knob. In doing so I caught a glimpse of her right arm somehow outstretched and propped against the smashed-in right side of the instrument panel. I saw three thin gold bracelets down by her elbow, and one of her soft blue-painted nails that had broken off to a bloody smear.

I pulled at the gear shift and watched my fingers go white with the struggle as if from miles away. I yanked it as hard as I could downward instead of across and got nowhere. I jiggled, then threw a shoulder into it. I almost toppled in. I tried using some finesse and just wristing it. The bar went into its groove. It snapped in to rest at center, and I nearly tripped over Kyle in my peeling scramble away from the vehicle.

The hot wind actually felt cool for a second. I crossed the dirt road and went hand to knee before a square stack of bricks. I breathed deeply, then advanced to standing fairly straight with my hands on my hips. The brick pile was waist high and covered with a ratty blue tarp that flapped its edges and corners into the summer wind. The taut, roped-down surface was water-stained and covered with sticks, mud curls, bird shit, and a few acorns. Ordinarily, I would have liked to have chucked those hard little nuts at a sign or something just to hear the "ping." Ordinarily, I could have been distracted at any moment to jump up and see if I could touch a high archway, or tap a ball against a wall four hundred times for a record, or race someone through a field, past the last phone pole with the tar marks on it, and all the way to the little walking bridge over the creek that sat between Pennwood Park and the back side of the shopping center. Ordinarily. The word didn't exist anymore.

I wiped the back of my neck, looked at my hand, and almost threw up. Her blood and my sweat combined in a red slime. I rubbed my palm on the leg of my jeans until it burned. I thought of Kyle reaching in for the pedals between those hard, impersonal shoes while I had the open wounds in my ear and the bare thighs of a corpse surrounding my prop hand. I thought of his telling me to hurry up from the safety of the open air outside of the cab while I was stifled in the hot box, and I suddenly wondered if I could take him.

Kyle was bigger. I floated between one-o-eight and a hundred and fifteen pounds or so, and I would estimate he was about a buck forty-five. The problem was that I had never seen Kyle fight. Some guys were built for fighting and they dressed for it. There were the guys with the silk shirts and gold chains, the guys with motorcycle jackets and boots, and the guys with crewcuts who looked like they already pumped iron. Kyle was the closest to that last category in appearance, but didn't need nor bother with the actions that usually went with it. Where tough guys seemed to look for the weaker breed to build a footing on, Kyle made a living gathering troops of all shapes, sizes, and colors against the older generation. He was never challenged because he had everyone on his side.

There was, however, the thinly smiling (but not at all smiling) aggression everyone could sense beneath the broad grin of the ever-present wise ass, and I believe Kyle sometimes gave a demonstration or two, of course masked as a joke, just to make those with an ugly side think twice about crossing him. At the end of seventh grade, he brought a tape measurer with him into the hallway and bet Ronnie Shoemaker that he could put a two-inch dent in a locker with one punch. A crowd gathered in the traditional semicircle at the end of a line of thin lockers we called "The Gray Mile," and watched Kyle wind up, bash the steel, crimp it in about an inch and a half, and fall to the ground in gales of laughter.

At the end of the same year, Kyle became the hero of metal shop by cutting off the tip of his pinkie. I heard that they listed it as an accident on the school report, but I was there. This was not incidental. Kyle had been at the station with the portable band saw turned upside-down and propped to an angle in a set of huge bench vices, filled in their creases with metal shavings, dirt, and WD-40. His project was a four-post lantern shell and he was supposed to trim the scrolls down from twenty-four inches to a foot. Before doing so he walked the room with a whisper in a given ear at the soldering and welding bench, a hand to a shoulder at the drill press, face to face in front of the

185

bench grinder. Protective glasses were propped up on foreheads and safety shields were put in open positions. I set down my file. Kyle approached the Portaband, flicked it on, and turned a sly smile to us. He then ceremoniously raised his hands above his head, the triumphant prize fighter. He held the tip of his left pinkie in between the pads of his right thumb and index finger. He lowered it all slowly and then leaned into the whine of the machine. We craned our necks and went up on our toes. No one had a good angle for a visual past his shoulder, except, that is, for Junior Macenhaney over by the dual industrial wash basins who suddenly put a dirty work glove up to his mouth and pointed.

Kyle turned around. He was still smiling. A thin, spotty line of blood had splashed up his cheek and over the left lens of his goggles. He walked up to Mr. Ruthersford, who was bent over the tool drawer, and shouted,

"Hey dude! Want a Chiclet?"

After being rushed to the nurse and then the Children's Hospital out past Rutherford Heights, they sewed the tip back on for him. You didn't even notice the tiny scars nowadays unless you got right up close and personal with it, but he still got mileage from it. He claimed he couldn't feel it anymore, and on a dare right before last Christmas break he put it over a flame in science lab long enough to burn the nail black.

You would have to assume a guy like that was a vicious competitor if forced to fight. Some guys boxed real well, and others even laid down rules like no eye gouging or crotch shots, but Kyle gave the impression that he would do anything to beat your butt if he had to. I pictured kicking, bites, scratches, and worst of all, props if they were handy. What would stop a guy who cut off his own fingertip for a thrill from grabbing a rock and bashing your cheek with it, or snapping off a car antenna and jabbing your eye, or breaking a bottle and swiping it at your jugular?

I was no weakling myself, but my skills didn't apply here. I could wrestle pretty well, and had earned a spot on the B team last year. Though there was an ace at a hundred and ten pounds named Barry Cutlerson who knew all kinds of fancy ways to stack you up, put your head where your ass should have been, and twist you into a pretzel, I had my own reputation for being "a worm," rarely pinned, often winning my matches by a couple of points. But even if I could rush Kyle, get a single leg, and take him down, what happened next? What could I really do except hold him there? I needed to knock him out and run home, not tire myself out submitting him.

The cold fact was that I had to have the cold will to pick up a rock when he wasn't looking and sucker him. I had always wondered if those who bragged about keeping weapons handy actually had the gumption to use them. What did it feel like to murder someone if you thought you had the right? I looked down at my hands and pushed out a shaky breath. I just helped murder someone for absolutely no reason at all, and I deserved a bash on the head as much as did Kyle. A sneak attack just muddied and worsened the complicated equation.

"Hey Jimmy," Kyle called. "I want to show you something. C'mon, man, you're really going to like it."

I turned and spit into the dirt. There was blood in the saliva because I had bitten the inside of my lip without realizing it. Kyle stepped across the lane, took a position before me, and rubbed the sole of his sneaker over the place I had moistened. The thin streak of red mud blended, darkened, and vanished.

"What, did you cut yourself shaving?" he said. I sucked in at my lip to nurse the wound that was no more than a trickle. He licked his teeth, smacked his lips, gulped air a few times, and let out a tremendous belch.

"Whiplash!" he said. He then took a fistful of my shirt and dragged me across the road past the back side of the car. "Look."

We were on the far side of the road now, near the edge of the woods, and I saw nothing but a patch of wildflowers in front of a thick march of trees.

"What am I looking for?" I said.

"The doorway, man, the doorway!"

Now I knew. There was a space about nine standing men wide between two elms at the lip of the forest. A rough path pushed a short way in, quickly hooded and darkened by overhanging branches. The far side of the glade was a wall of ferns, vines, and brambles.

"Go in, Jimmy," Kyle said. "Walk through the doorway, make a sharp right, and find the surprise down at the end of the path."

I advanced into the shadows. I did not want to take the time to second-guess it. Dead vegetation crinkled under my sneakers and passed through my mind vague images of snake skins and insects. I shook it off. I had been in dark forests hundreds of times, hunting out salamanders, fossils, and arrowheads, and whatever was down here had to be better than what was waiting in the Honda.

The woods took me in like a cold womb. Stabs of sunlight slipped through at odd angles, and a spiderweb that had once spanned a two-foot nook between a trunk and crooked branch now fluttered with one side unfastened, a frail shroud pointing in stuttering rhythm the way of the breeze.

I followed the light wind and shifted right. I edged down the rooted path about twenty-five feet down as Kyle had advised and then it was there, waiting in silence.

It was a place where the ground fell off in a twenty-foot arc. A deep, black hole.

It was going to be the woman's grave.

Closest to the dark, empty shape cut into the ground were huge banks of dirt piled at the far side covered with what looked like low cut open air circus canopies. There was a digging machine to the left, and a score of rusted shovels scattered along the perimeter. I dragged my feet to the rim of the pit and peered over the edge. The drop was so deep I could not see the bottom. Edges of roots pushed out of the near inner wall like the knobby fingers of jailed witches. I reached into my right front pocket and fumbled out a bent nail. I tossed it into the hole. Once the nail winked out of sight I did not hear it land.

The other nails followed, all of them, mate joining mate down the black well of silence. No one had told me to unload the evidence here; I just sensed it was right.

All on my own I was beginning to think like a criminal.

I forced myself to pull my glance out of the blackness of the abyss and walk the border. The scene around the hole past the dirt hills and shovels was busy with "stuff" that made a haphazard background of things I passed on the roadway a thousand times and took utterly for granted.

Just beyond the biggest pile of light brown dirt was a smaller heap of crushed stone. At the far side of the clearing there were two machines with massive inner coils and big, flat bottom-pads. They were turned on their sides like discarded bicycles near an apparatus that looked like a standing ride mower with a nine-foot chain saw at the end. Five rolls of orange construction fencing were lying in some overgrowth between two trash cans filled with wooden stakes, and the mini-bulldozer now directly to my left sat opposite the position I had just abandoned at the front side of the hole.

The machine had "BOBCAT" stenciled in block letters beneath some dried mud caked to the back panel. Around front, the wide bucket was full of the whitish crushed stone in a pyramid shape and the whole thing was raised out about ninety percent flush over the lip of the hole. I stepped in closer. It seemed as if the driver of the machine had stopped cold just before getting fully squared in position to spill the rocks, and there was a thick length of old chain now holding up the bucket. It was padlocked through a hole between the digging teeth and figure-eighted into the high steel mesh of the cab.

The Bobcat was obviously busted.

So was the chain. There was a broken link halfway up that was rusted through, cloven on one side and almost forced straight by the pressure of its neighbors. The whole affair was held together by what seemed no more than a thread.

"Do you know what this is, Jimmy?"

Across the hole, Kyle was standing with his arms stretched out wide. He had followed me down to see my reaction and then give a lecture. His old smile was back like neon.

"It's a footer, James. Before my asshole dad started his own ass-hole company he poured concrete for Molina Industrial. He always talked about footers and stuff. Bored me to freakin' tears."

The smile left him. He reached down to his sock for a cigarette.

"Want one?"

I shook my head. He straightened, puckered his face, lit up, and dragged. He spoke through the smoke, aiming and directing the cigarette as a movie professor would do with a pointer.

"Footers are good, James. Footers are our friends. They pour cement to complete footers, and we're lucky we found this one half-baked. They dig these things for big columns that hold up bridges and stuff, and you can see that this one was a mistake. All we've got to do is put Blondie and her piece-of-shit car down the hole. We fill the fucker with dirt, throw on a light cover of crushed stone, and when the new guys do show up, they'll think the first team filled it back in a long time ago."

My nose flared out.

"What if they think it looks like it wasn't done by a real contractor? What if they decide to dig it back up?"

He snorted.

"Too much money, my man! Contractors are cheap whores by trade! Why would they dig around into a mistake when the help costs over twenty an hour? If they don't think the little bow we put on it is nice enough, they'll swirl around the rocks on top more professionally or something."

I crossed my arms in front of my chest. I was not good at this riddle stuff, especially considering that I was not as technically minded (or as willing to roll the dice) as Kyle. The apparent ease of all this was more than disturbing, and I still wanted to weasel out some way of running off, or at least delaying any more interaction with the dead thing up there, without Kyle literally beating me to a pulp.

"What if it wasn't a mistake?" I said.

"It was."

"But how do you know?" My chin was out and I was pleading now. "It looks like they had every reason to dig here and the foreman or whoever just blew the whistle in the middle for some reason. What if the job starts up again and the same guys do come back and try to pick up where they left off?"

Kyle took a sharp drag. Blew it out hard.

"They won't."

"How do you know?"

"First, because you don't have extra-fine dirt ready on the side unless you brought it in for repacking. Look at the piles, Jimmy. This dirt didn't come from this hole. There are no rocks in it, and no roots. Also, why the crushed stone? That stuff goes on top of a repair. You don't use it when you're going to put in a pillar. And even if this turns out not to have been a mistake originally, it won't be the same guys working off those old plans that never came together in the first place. It's been eight months since this job shut down. Look at it, Jimmy!" He put up his hands. "I know you're not a diesel head, but look around. Doesn't this hole seem funny to you?"

"Yeah."

"And why?"

"Because it's in the middle of the woods. It doesn't fit."

"Right!" he said. His hands were both offered out to me now. "The guys digging the holes didn't work for the same company cutting the trees, or pouring the 'crete, or grooving the road. No one got along and no one ever knew what the other was doing. It was a big fucking mess and my dad used to laugh about it regularly. Every night. Believe me, I'm an expert on the subject even though I never wanted to be until right about now."

"Oh." It's all I had left, really.

"Let's go," Kyle said. "We've still got a lot of fun stuff to do."

I walked around and put my back to the hole. Kyle's arm was around me immediately. The smoke from his cigarette twisted up a hooking shape at the rim of my head and struck a chord of familiarity in me, the sensory trigger of my concept of "friend," of "not mom," of "other," of the "not me" that was becoming more of the latest "me" every second.

Side by side, each absorbed in thought, we made our way back up the incline toward the open air. Below our feet, the roots along the path pushed up and across, and I caught a toe at one point. Of course, Kyle held me up. It was nice and at the same time crushing, since it reminded me again of his superior strength. We turned the corner past the floating spiderweb and walked into the heat and the brightness, through the two elms that made Kyle's doorway. We stopped. The car was waiting for us. I noticed that from this angle I had to tilt my head up slightly to look at it. The path from it to the trees sloped downward ever so slightly.

"Jimmy."

"Yeah?"

"How ya doing?"

"'Kay."

"Do you think that you're strong enough to shove the back bumper and move the car by yourself? The right front tire is flat but the other three are OK."

My answer was automatic.

"No. I'm not big enough, Kyle. I'm sorry."

"No problem." He turned me to him and put his hands on my shoulders. He looked at me with full, sincere eyes.

"I can move the car or at least get it going, Jimmy, but the rest of this is on you. Just promise not to fuck it up, all right?"

"What do you mean?"

"What I mean, James, is that this whole thing will be fine if you can pull through."

"How?"

He glanced up at the Honda.

"I'm going to push. You've got to steer."

My breath hitched. I blinked. The picture became clear, and it was not pretty.

I was going to have to get in with her and shut the door. The space between the two elms was barely enough to fit the car through, let alone allow me the luxury of trotting beside with my hands reaching in to the steering wheel.

I was going to have to sit in her lap and feel her press against me. Or more realistically, I was going to have to sit in *its* lap and feel *it* press against me while I tried to maneuver the entry, pull the turn, hold it steady over the roots, and bail at the last second.

Suddenly I heard something, faint and sneaky like a whisper. It could have been the wind or the traffic droning past on the overpass, but I knew that it wasn't.

It was the corpse. She was waiting for me in that hot vehicle, baking, letting a horsefly run over her crushed lip, the gash in her head, an open eyeball.

And on some dark wavelength that only existed between sinners and the vengeful dead, I could hear her say something. It flickered between us but for a moment. A message in the static, barely on the radar.

"I dare you," she said to me.

I swear it.

4.

The right corner of the Honda's fender was turned up and embedded in the tree. At first, Kyle wanted to piston out his foot and kick it loose with the sole of his sneaker, but there wasn't quite enough fender to kick on the outside edge. He tried wedging himself between the tree and the crimped hood, but the car was too close. He could not summon the power needed for the push with his knees up in his chest like upside-down V's. We removed our shirts to be used as makeshift gloves for our fingers and actually crawled under the car. Kyle had the one-inch nub to the far right and I hooked my hands more toward the center where there was a lip in the steel to grab. We both straddled the trunk of the tree from under there like a horse, Kyle on ground level, my legs splayed above his. Something from the engine dripped on me three times, but it wasn't quite hot enough to leave burns.

There was a squeal and a stuttery moan like a door creaking open. The fender had come loose. It gave about an inch. We crawled out from under the car and brushed off. After a couple of misfires and determined "one-two-three's," we really put our backs into it and managed to push the car backward a few inches more from the tree in a hesitant, lumpy sort of progress. Now that there was a bit of room, we both mounted the hood, backs to the tree, shirts now used as buffer cushions against the hard bark. We pushed with the soles of our feet and actually managed to extend our legs.

The new placement had the vehicle about three feet from the tree's base, and I got a full frontal view of the corpse from between the shadows of overhanging branches.

Her head was facing downward. Blonde hair stuck to her jaw on the left side in a glaze that looked like matted red paste. Her hair band had been thrust a few inches backward and drew rakes of thin, red trails behind it. Bangs clumped with sloppy strokes of red hid the top of her face, but her mouth was in sight, burst open, swelled, and caught in a scream. Her tongue was out and dripping off of it, she had a long dangler, a spindle of blood, snot, and drool that went past her chin all the way to the chest.

I stepped down, turned away, and crossed my arms.

"I can't do it, Kyle."

He stepped in front of me.

"You have to."

"No way. You do it."

"Go ahead and move the car one inch by yourself and I will."

My mind raced.

193

"Why just me? We can both get it going and then you could jump in to steer."

He pointed at the car.

"There isn't enough room. One of us has to bang a hard right on the wheel from the start or it will end up back at the tree."

"Fine," I said. "I'll take the back and you lean in to the front through the open door. You can work the wheel and help me get it rolling too. As soon as you hit the patch of flowers there, it's downhill. You could take it all on your own."

He looked at the ground and shook his head.

"Won't work. The guy who leans in the front don't have the leverage. The bigger kid has got to be at the back. And once it gets moving there won't be time to switch places."

I went to the back of the car.

"Let's try it my way first."

"Fine." He shrugged, put his shirt back on, and walked toward the driver's side door. "Just hurry the fuck up."

"Fine," I mimicked, as if the last word really meant something. I retrieved my own shirt, threw my arms through the sleeves, and took a stance behind the vehicle. I started getting ready to get set, and my heart sank a bit.

Kyle's not going to push very hard.

Didn't matter. I had to try. I bent down and pressed my hands against the back bumper. I started to draw deep breaths. I pictured the thing rocking a bit in the starting groove, then making lumpy advance by the sheer force of my will. Think it—be it. Easy. No problem.

I heard the car door open up front.

"Ready when you are," Kyle said.

I tightened up and got ready for the push of my life. I counted it out really loud so there would be no false starts off the blocks.

"One, two . . . THREE!"

Nothing. No way. Dead weight going absolutely nowhere. I pushed again with every possible piece of strength and my back screamed with it. My face prickled and my eyes went scream-wide. Nothing. Nothing at all.

"Ready when you are," Kyle said. With a final gasp I dropped to all fours and hung my head. I pushed up on my fingertips and dragged

194

through my feet to cross them Indian style. I sat in the dirt. I stared at the red cauliflowers left blooming on my palms and heard the approaching footsteps.

Closer, then halted.

"Door's open for you up there," Kyle said. "Now try it my way. Just to see, OK?"

I got up and brushed by him. Our shoulders knocked together a bit in passing and I held up my jaw. I was angry and enjoying the feeling. I was also aware somewhere beneath the surface that I was feeding off the anger to manipulate myself away from the idea of approaching the horror in the front seat. By the time I registered this idea I was there at the opening, so I continued as quickly as possible before the little that remained of the power of my anger blew off.

I stuck in my right hand. The steering wheel was hot and I curled my fingers tight. I braced my left palm in a pushing position against the door's armrest and had a sudden feeling that the woman was going to clamp down her broken teeth on my elbow and sink them in as deep as they would go.

The car started moving. Kyle had gotten it going on his own, and we bumped about two inches forward.

"Turn the wheel!" Kyle said.

I spun it hard to the right and heard the tires beneath me creaking and scraping in the dirt. The car slowly moved away. I sidestepped in to keep up.

"Aim it!" he shouted.

I straightened back the wheel and walked faster beside the moving vehicle. Every time the wound in the right tire rotated to the bottom there was a skip and a clump, and that combination was getting less and less pronounced as we gained speed. We bumped off the road and went through the wildflowers. I had thought this was just a test, just to see . . .

"Keep going!" he yelled.

Now I was running beside the car, almost struggling to catch up with it. The "doorway" between the trees was looming a few feet before me. All options vanished and it was now or nothing.

"Do it!" Kyle roared. "Do it for real!"

I did it.

I jumped into the hot car and reached for the door that was flapping out like a broken wing. My nails scratched at the plastic and I found the void in the arm rest. I pulled the door shut and all sound around me snapped off as if by a switch.

The woman was a hot envelope stuck to my legs and back. Her hair brushed along my right shoulder and my neck. I was moaning, bending in low for a view beneath the bloody cracks in the windshield.

The front end of the car made it between the trees for a bald second, and then there was a terrific yet muffled screaming sound as the flanks of the vehicle scraped against the bark on both sides. We jarred through and the light wiped dark. It felt as if we had gone under water, and the heavy smell of death and hot vinyl filled my lungs.

I jerked the wheel to another hard right and skidded a bit, just missing the thicket on the far side of the glade. The car swerved and I straightened back the wheel, my scream rupturing through the thick silence as the woman's wet face fell against my neck. I screamed again when the knotted branches of overhung trees rushed in and elbowed the roof. The car picked up speed down the rough decline and the roots underneath wailed hard on the tires. The woman and I shucked against each other in hard, sticky frictions.

The wide hole approached fast. It was time to abandon ship. I reached for the door handle.

My fingers found it, pulled up, and then tried to shove outward.

Nothing. The impact with the trees had crimped the door and jammed it. I made a weak play at giving it a shoulder. Frozen solid.

The hole was everything now, huge and black and big as the earth. I jammed down my foot for the brake and found a jungle of the woman's feet. I stomped down haphazardly, got nothing, and felt a discarded shovel bang up under the car.

The hole was upon us. I could not even make out the front edge anymore, only its wide rim at the periphery and its yawning, bottomless center. I brought up my hands. The front tires fell away into nothingness and there was a shock and a bang as the undercarriage scraped across the dirt cut-away. There was a final thump from the back tires and bumper, and then we were jettisoned into the black.

196

5.

The dead woman and I were flung off the seat, floating and bumping around in the black. My knuckles scraped on the windshield. The body beneath me slipped out from under, bounced away, and hurtled back in. Her hair snapped in my eyes and my head banged the roof. My legs forked out, my eardrums popped, and then we hit bottom.

"Holy fuck!" were the wild words I could actually see spelled out in my mind as the impact hammed the nose of the car. *"Holy fuck!"* as the windshield ruptured across and above me and my head was hurled forward.

I had a quick vision in the pitch black, a glimpse of what my face would look like after smashing into the hard rim of the steering wheel. It was no work of art. In reflex, I thrust out my hands to block. The heel of my left hand caught most of the wheel while my right barely got in a thumb.

It broke my fall, or at least put a major dent in it.

I hit face first.

There was a loud *smooonch*. A slap of pain plastered out from the bridge of my nose, but what I did hit could not have been factory made. It felt like wet webbing over caved seashell plating. I felt it mold and contour, and a burst of liquid smeared between my lips.

It was the woman's face wedged between me and the wheel.

My first kiss in the dark.

For a moment I was too disoriented to scream. With the car's nose rammed to the ground, my ass was back where my head should have been and down seemed like up.

I sucked in a big breath to let out a holler and swallowed a throatful of blood. Her blood. Salty. Greasy and thick and inside me. I choked. I spit, I scrambled, and flailed. I fell waist-deep into the vertical void between the wheel and the seat and clapped my chin to something hard. The blow sang through my jaw making my teeth buzz and my ears ring. I twisted away and felt a cool brush of air at my face. It was my first clue as to where I was and which way I was facing. I gathered together a scatter of common sense and recognized that the impact had blown the door open.

I pawed for the shallow breeze.

I flutter-kicked, climbed, and doggie-paddled through the dark portal and fell out on the bowed-out door. I stood, wobbled, and grabbed at the wheel-well of the back tire. My eyes had adjusted to the deep shadows and I could see in gray, grainy snatches. I chinned up past the driver's side opening, reached up, hauled in, and put my feet where my hands had just been. I soon found footing on the rear hood, almost slipped backward, crouched, and froze there for a moment.

"Are you cooked down there or what? Jimmy-man, quit jerking me off and say something, huh?"

The voice was faint and dreamlike. I stood up slowly and felt a brush of fresher air. Still, I pictured the woman's eyes suddenly coming open in the darkness below me. She would jerk and twitch and then gnash and spit at the air. I could feel her desire to crawl out of the car in jerks and spasms, to reach up for a pant leg, yank me back down, and suck back the blood I had stolen.

I had my hands splayed out for balance and I saw my best chance sticking out of the earth, just above the shadows. The re-grown roots that had pushed their way through the higher end of the pit's inner walls hung about a body length away and three feet over head.

I jumped.

I stretched out and my feet made insane bicycle pedals in the open air. I forced my right hand into a last-ditch, overhand sweep and clutched out for broke. I caught the base of the nearest root and just managed to turn a shoulder before crashing into the embankment. A burst of dirt showered around me and I held on. I twisted myself to face front and my left hand joined its mate. I pulled my chin to my fists and then grasped out for the next highest root. The heat of the open air teased my forehead and I strove for it, arms burning, just like on the pegboard anchored to the polished block wall in the gymnasium at school. I really had to reach to the side for the next root, and I almost slipped back into the hole. I got it by the fingertips, shimmied it into a fist, swung out one-handed, grabbed with both, and pulled. Sunlight bathed across the base of my neck and my back. I was *in* it now with my chin again parked at my clamped fingers, and I could taste making it, and when I raised up a knee for a last thrust to the top, there was a hard tug on my ankle.

I shrieked.

I struggled and kicked and almost lost hold. Of course it was the pawing zombie that had followed me up the wall to pull me back down into the shadows. It was the beast, the dead-alive thing hungry for boy-guts, she who wanted to rip me to steaming ribbons and sniff at the remains for her shoplifted blood.

Of course it was just a root that had snagged on my pant leg. I tore loose, clawed up to the lip of the hole, and screamed again when a hand closed tight over my wrist. I was dragged up into the heat. The pit's edge scraped along my chest, ripped my shirt, and drove dirt into my underwear.

I was out of the hole. At the far end of my arm was a strange being that I believe on earth they once called a boy. He yanked me out the rest of the way and my wrist roared with Indian burn. His footing tangled and he let go of me. He fell flat on his butt and I almost tripped over him. He looked up at me in amazement.

"What the fuck, Jimmy? You look like the Creature From the Black Lagoon! Is that all your blood or what?"

"No!" I cried. He jumped to his feet and it looked like a blur. The light was overly bright, tinged with afterimage, and Kyle was a swirl of the woman and the hole. I fell on him with flailing fists and he knocked me aside with an easy, backhanded pass.

"No!" I cried, swinging at nothing. I was still deep in that grave, covered with darkness and kissing a corpse. "No!" as I stamped on the ground. "No!" as I clawed at my hair.

He hit me.

It was a nasty, open-handed wallop that caught me full in the face and cracked loud in my ears. My head turned with the force and my mouth dropped open. The sting gave way to a dull throbbing that worked itself into the sobering sounds of the wood; the call of a bird, the shrill of crickets, the sigh of the wind. I was free and I was alive. The dead woman was no longer the entire world, but a series of frightening pictures that flickered by slower and slower.

I let out a grunt of exhaustion and sat down. I was breathing in dry sobs. I hugged my knees and shook.

"Hey," Kyle said.

I ignored him. I noticed that he had moved closer, but not quite close enough to reach out and touch. I stared at his sneakers.

"Clean laces," I thought. I rubbed my arms to smooth the chill that stole over me. "Thanks for your help," I said to the sneakers.

"Don't mention it," Kyle replied. He had noticed my dry, toneless delivery, and his three-word retort clarified things. He was too proud to admit that he had not jumped down into the footer to help. "Don't mention it" meant, *"C'mon, Jimmy. Let's move on to bigger and better things. Of course I didn't fly after you down the hole. I probably would have landed right on your head and snapped your damned neck with my squeaky-clean sneakers."* "Don't mention it" meant, *"Let's not talk about it because I'll come up with a million excuses as to why it was better for you to go down there instead of me."* "Don't mention it" was Kyle's way of admitting that the two of us were never again to be friends.

"Help me fill it back in, Jimmy. We're almost done."

A spade-point digging shovel landed at my feet. It was an ugly, rusted old thing with the initials P.D.G. written on the wooden shaft in spidery black magic marker.

Kyle turned his back and walked up to a mound of fill piled at the far edge of the pit. He pulled up the stakes of the tarp canopy and let the canvas blow off toward the back of the clearing. It looked like some of the fine soil had run off over time, but there was still a massive amount left in a shape that vaguely looked like a large pair of camel humps. He picked up his shovel, sunk it into the pile, and tossed the first scoop of backfill into the opening. The sound of dirt scattered across sunken steel was gritty and final.

The horror of it all was now somehow diluted, and I was left with a hollow grief in the pit of my stomach. I pushed up and dragged the shovel to my side of the hole. To the immediate left was a mound of fill with a clear plastic covering flattened over it and kept taut with tent stakes at three corners. I took a moment to peer over into the dark tomb, my expression closed and flat. She was not a zombie. She was no monster. She was a once-pretty lady whom two bad kids had to make disappear before dinnertime.

"I'm sorry," I said. It was an empty whisper. I pried up the plastic at one of the corners, dug in, and threw my first shovelful of dirt down the hole. There was a tinkle of soil across the wreckage, and that led to another thrust, and another followed by another. The sounds of our shovels were flat accompaniment to the memory of the unlucky soul trapped beneath us, and though the sounds were anything but musical, they were rhythmic in their dumb regularity.

It was hypnotic. I developed blisters on my hands that had been mildly alarming when they formed, annoying when they broke, and then an afterthought when they finally went numb. The afternoon wore on and spun itself into gray, gauzy, thoughtless purpose.

We were fully entranced when I dug up the watch.

This pile of dirt is different.

I'd noticed but not noticed. I was on overdrive, a machine, shoulders and back aching in a distant way that was not really "mine" somehow. My shovel was making a different noise. The pile had rocks in it and was filled with trashy stuff amongst rougher dirt. There was a busted cup to a field telephone with the bigger holes in it for the ear, small pieces of wire with the copper sticking out, an industrial rubber glove that was black on one side and yellow on the other, an old, opened pack for a Trojan condom, and a million cigarette butts. I pushed up and put my hand to the small of my back. Kyle had exhausted four huge dirt piles and I had managed three. There wasn't much left to dump. I sunk my spade into the pile and it made a gravelly sound. Something winked up. I turned the shovel and scraped the tip over the area. It brought to the surface a Mickey Mouse watch with one of the bands torn off. The face was scarred by a jagged pair of nearly parallel cracks, and the colors and familiar shapes just under the deformities doubled like mirrors. The image brought up the trace of a smile. Red and black kiddie colors, big white gloves on those stick arms. The red second hand was continuous, and didn't do those little twitches across the background. One of Mickey's gloves was on the ten, and the shorter one was just shy of the five.

I jerked up and looked around in a wider view than I had taken a second ago. Had the cover of the forest screwed my sense of time flow that badly? It was not as if I was some expert like the explorers in adventure books who always seemed to know the time by the position of the sun, but I usually knew when the day was getting old. I looked back in the general direction of my house and then up toward the jobsite above us. The sun was filtered through the trees the same as it had been all day. Of course it was. The sun didn't go down until seven or eight at the end of the summer. I could have gone at least another hour and a half until I noticed any difference at all. My thinking was behind the eight-ball here, and I cursed myself for it. Worse, Ma had bought me a watch and I always forgot to wear it. I think it was on my bookshelf next to a ceramic mug I made in fourth grade, but I wasn't sure. It would have been easy to convince myself that I never wore the thing because it got in the way or I thought it looked snobby, but it wasn't that easy. I was simply too lazy to remember to put it on. Then, I was forever asking my friends what time it was like a begging little idiot. My whole life was one step behind, and it was self-inflicted.

I threw down my shovel. Kyle had ceased digging as well and he was gazing into the hole.

"Looks almost ready," he said. "Almost."

"What?" I said. "Uh, Kyle, I just dug up a watch and it's getting close to five o'clock here." I took a good look into the grave and saw that we had actually filled it three quarters of the way. It seemed good enough to me and I suddenly burst into action. Last-minute business, chop-chop. I was dimly aware that I hadn't asked permission or advice, but the time factor had forced me to independence. Kyle stuck the point of his shovel into the ground, and leaned on the D-handle with his elbow. I believe he was smiling.

I vaulted up the rooted path. The sun made me wince and I spread my index finger and thumb to make a visor. The Honda had left a trail of tire marks. I ran up and dragged my feet across the evidence. Dust rose. I coughed a few times. There were imprints running through the wildflowers as well, but I couldn't straighten all of the broken flowers of the world, now could I? With nothing leading up to the impressions they would be a mystery. An unnoticed one, I hoped.

I approached the tree. There was no time to pick up every shattered headlight piece, so I kicked dirt across the lot of them. Baseballs under a rug. It would have to do.

The gash in the tree itself was impossible to hide, but I tried to give it the illusion of age by scooping up soil and rubbing it into the wound. I stepped back to study my handiwork. It simply looked like dirt plastered to a fresh gash in a tree. Again, it would have to do.

I walked back down to the clearing and circled the pit. I picked up a flat garden rake with steel teeth and smoothed over our sneaker marks all around the perimeter. Next, I raked over the tire marks at the base of the path. The front fender had kicked up a wide spray of earth on its violent entry into the space and left behind an angry furrow that was an extraordinary pain to repair. I even had to retreat to the hole, scrape at the remains of an exhausted dirt pile, and shovel in filler to even the ground. Kyle never helped. He simply stood at the edge of the drop with a grin and a cigarette. I didn't care. I took my shovel and tossed it by the rake. I was about to ask Kyle to give me his tool so I could throw them all in the dumpster up on the site when he asked a strange question.

"When do you walk the dog, Jimmy?"

Everything kind of stopped. My breath was loud. It had probably been loud all along, but I noticed it now, and noticed myself noticing it. A drop of sweat made a runner down my jaw, and I wiped it off with the back of my hand.

"Why?"

"Just tell me."

"For what?"

"'Cause it's important. Trust me."

My eyes narrowed. He knew I didn't trust him and I knew he didn't give one shit about my dog. Double lies. His open, sincere persistence made it interesting though, like sticking your tongue in a mouth-sore.

"Right before dinner," I answered warily.

"What if you're late? What happens then?"

"Mom does it."

"She walks her?"

"No. She puts her on the lead in the back yard. She probably had her out there all day, actually. Why?"

"No reason," he said. "Here's my shovel. Don't throw them away up there because it'll look too obvious. Trash guys pick through stuff. Find a place where it looks like shovels and rakes should go. Maybe scout out some others and make a little family, hmm?"

I gathered the tools and headed up the path. It amazed me that Kyle somehow guessed I was going to toss the stuff away, and I was still puzzled about his concern for my dog.

By the time I set the tools in the middle of a group of others that were leaning against the top crossbar of a long sawhorse, I realized that

I didn't care what Kyle had to say. I strode back down the path. I didn't need any dialogue with my ex-friend, we were done here. I walked over to the Bobcat with every intention of banging loose the busted link in the chain that held up the bucket of crushed stone. I wanted to put a final covering across this nightmare and go home. I reached up to do so, and Kyle laughed.

"There's no time for that now, Jimmy. We'll do it later."

I turned.

"What do you mean, later? There is no later. I've got to get back."

He laughed again. Heartily.

"Like that? Jimmy, maybe there's no mirror out here, but I'm telling you there ain't no way you could walk through your door right now. You're covered with dried blood, man. It's in your hair and on your shirt and embedded in your pants. It's all over your face. Damn, how are you going to explain *that* to mother dearest, huh?"

I froze. Then I was the sleepwalker, stumbling off toward the path to look for a fountain or canteen or something to wash up with.

"Ain't no water up there," Kyle said after me. "When I was up here planting the nails yesterday I cut my elbow on some barbed wire by the trailer there. I hunted all over that damned jobsite searching for a cooler and a first-aid kit. It's bone dry. The nearest water is clear across town at Meyer's Creek and we can't chance someone seeing you like this."

I wanted to run up there and check out his claim, but the fact that my window of time was down to a hair made me put that suspicion on hold. And why would he lie about it? He wanted to get out of this as badly as I did. I turned.

"Maybe she wouldn't notice."

Kyle roared.

"Wouldn't notice? Have you lost your fucking mind? Christ, Jimmy. You come in from climbing a tree in the front yard and your mom checks your hair for ticks! We've got to do better than that."

Tears of frustration welled up in my eyes.

"I could sneak in and clean up."

"Are you serious? It's dinner time. The kitchen window faces the back yard, and even if she goes to the bathroom she'll hear you coming in. She'll be listening for you and you're going to be late as it is."

"How about the front door?"

He clapped his hands at me.

"Think, Einstein! That front door is one short room off from the kitchen. Her antenna is going to be up! You ain't gonna have the chance to get in, cross through, and run for your room. Those Fred Flintstone, one-floor jobs out on Weston Road suck for sneak-ins and you know it."

"Then what do I do?"

He walked over. Closed in.

"She puts the dog out back when you're late, doesn't she? In fact, Mommy never really liked little Lucy because your dad bought her for you way back when, right? She probably left that darned little yipper out all day so you could take her in when you got home your own damned self, right? Just to make a point?"

I nodded cautiously. That was Mom's game. It was my dog and if I was going to play all day, Lucy got banished to the back yard with the water bowl that wound up getting bug floaters and leaves in it. Old rule. Kyle came up a bit closer.

"Now, do the math. The way your house is set up, you can't get in unseen or unheard, but you would maybe have the time to race into the back yard and, say, touch the hose spigot and sprint back to the woods, now wouldn't you? I mean, even though she watches out for you through that back window like a hawk, she sometimes goes to put soap in the shower dish, or a bowl of nuts in the living room, or she slips off to the bedroom to take off that tight bra because it digs in a bit too much when she bends to do the dusting, ya copy?"

My eyes glanced away. I didn't like strategies predicting what my mother would do. It was first much more complicated than this little map-on-a-napkin presentation, and next, personal in a way that gave me high discomfort up in the neck bone. Though Kyle made a living busting on my mom, she wasn't his to interpret, especially when he started removing pieces of clothing. It seemed impolite, even for him. He reached out and placed a hand on my shoulder. His left palm copied the other and he made me look at him.

"Jimmy, listen to me. If we walk through these woods no one will see us. It's a pain in the ass with the gullies and stuff, but we could make your back yard in seven to eight minutes, fifteen at the outside."

"What about our bikes?"

He pulled his hands off.

"To hell with the bikes. It's not like we're going to leave them here. When we're done we'll ride 'em back down the dirt road to Westville Central like we came and go the long way. If we hurry we won't be going in the dark. Let's go."

"Go where?"

"Through the woods! Your old lady has already put the dog out back. The high weeds at the far edge of your back yard will give us cover until the moment dear Mommy goes to another room. Then we can make our move."

"What move?"

He gave a short laugh.

"That's when we can grab the dog, Jimmy. That's when we can bring her back here and do what we have to do. If it looks like a road-kill there ain't a parent alive that would question the blood on you. The story is easy. We were out here having a dirt fight with the shovels. That's the cause of the blisters. But then we stopped when you realized how late it must have gotten. Feeling all guilty, you ran back and snagged Lucy, because you knew it was time to walk her. But she ran away and got hit by a car up on the overpass. It knocked her into the muddy ditch under the guardrail and you had to crawl in and get her. There's the dirt and the blood in a nutshell. And I know you'll be bawling when you bring her back to the house. It's perfect. You've always been a crybaby and your little tears are going to be just as real as the blood your ma will think came out of the mutt."

It made such a strange kind of malicious sense that at first I could not work up the inevitable refusal. My mind had not geared up that quickly. I was still caught in the demented world of *Kyle's plans* and whether or not they could work.

"How?" I managed.

"Oh, I don't know," he said. "Does it matter? A rock to the skull or something. Anything that will do it quick. Then if you want to get fancy we could run her over with something up on the site with a wheel so it looks like a car tire did it. I would try to use this Bobcat, but it looks kind of busted, are you with me?"

I did not respond.

"Jimmy," he said. His eyebrows were up. "Are you with me? Time that we don't have is a-wasting."

I said nothing. He came toward me as if to give me a tickle.

"Jimmy, say it. OK? Are we ready? Check? Roger? Victor-vector? Ten-four?"

"I can't kill my dog," I whispered.

To this, Kyle threw his head back and laughed loud. He laughed as if I had misunderstood the whole thing and *boy*, would I be relieved when I finally got a firm grasp on the bottom line.

"Whew," he said, flattening his hands on his knees and shaking his head. "That was a good one!" He straightened and stretched. "God, Jimmy, no one would ever ask you to do *that*. Shit, you could never pull it off in a million years. All you have to do is sneak up and grab her."

His smile turned down to a thin line.

"And *I'm* the one who's going to kill her, Jimmy," he said. "I'm the one who's going to kill her."

6.

We wasted ten minutes in angry debate before Kyle gave up on me and tore off on his own for my house. I had tried to convince him that we could rub dirt into the bloody patches on our clothes, just enough to cover, and he said it would look just like that, dirt that was put on evidence to cover it up. I ripped off my shirt and tried it. He was right. The blood had really reached in, taken hold, formed its own surface, and removed the cloth's ability to "absorb." Even when I really pressed the dirt on with my palm like an old-fashioned lady with a washboard, it just seemed to flake and brush off. I then tried to convince Kyle to fly back to his house in the Common and bring me back a change of clothes. Straight refusal. His dad was waiting with a cold Miller in one hand and his chrome pitch counter in the other. Fall ball was coming up soon, and before dinner Kyle had to hit a hundred balls off the tee in the basement. There was no sneaking into his house either. I had even entertained the idea of burying the clothes and going home naked. Why not? Kyle was a joker, right? He would steal my clothes to razz me, wouldn't he? His response was to laugh in my face.

That wasn't the "Kyle" my mom knew, and she'd never believe it. Christ, he'd even nosed around lately in his mother's magazines to brush up on some weight-loss tip or gardening technique before coming to my house, just so he could get my mom in some "gentle-ass girly conversation" with his eyes all puppy-dog earnest before going back with me to my room, shutting the door, and busting into a laughing fit he covered up with two hands. Besides, as he claimed I very well knew, my mom would call the cops on him if he stripped me down in public. Is that what I wanted? A plan that *invited* the cops?

He was not going to budge on this. In the end a lie was best worn out in the open, and I was going to do it his way or nothing.

I chose nothing. I just could not watch my dog get slaughtered, so I sat down right there at the edge of the pit.

"I'll stay here all night. Bring me the stuff tomorrow."

"Fine," he'd said. *"I'll get the bitch myself. See you in twenty minutes."*

I sat there in disbelief for a moment and it was not until he was nearly out of hearing range that I jumped up to follow him.

The woods were not friendly. I aimed in the general direction he had taken and barreled on through. Stubborn tree limbs swung in at me and I forearmed them aside. I ran through patches of deadwood. I tried to dodge big jumbles of prickers and hurdled large rocks, nests of tangled ivy, and mounds of thorny scrub that came in my path. I took crazy chances, running blindly into the brush and headlong through shadows.

My lungs were screaming, yet it ironically felt as if I had made up some ground on the sudden elevations hewn into the forest floor. There were a few rocky crags that rose before me with some obvious (and rather luckily placed) ledges for finger- and toe-holds, and two nearly identical bluffs in a row draped with thick, hanging vines that I grabbed, trusted with my full weight, and went up hand over hand, back parallel to the ground, feet kicking up bursts of loose earth as they slapped their walk up each bank. Kyle couldn't have made it through those obstacles that fast. He couldn't have.

Still, the flat-out stretches between made it a footrace and things seemed to jump in from dark places just as I began to get a rhythm.

There was a bad moment when a low-hanging crook of a branch crossed in from nowhere and nearly separated my head from my neck.

I raised my forearms into an X and ran straight into it. Dull pain rang straight through to my shoulders and a flapping cluster of swallows burst out from their nest. They swarmed up like hornets.

I kept pushing.

I jumped over a rotted-out log with white fuzz growing in the bark and moss covering one end like a blanket. I had made the hill, and I caught sight of him down in the gully, scrambling across a wide ribbing of partly exposed steel sewer pipe. The thing in the ground looked like the knotted, rusted spine of some partly buried monster. Almost home. The misshapen landmark sat between two rises, the one I was on, and the far one that spread out of the forest and into my back yard.

I sidestepped down the embankment. My breath was a tired horse. Sweat ran through older sweat and dried blood, making sticky trails down my jaw and forehead. There were rocks in my sneakers.

I found the bottom, scrambled across the sewer pipe and snuck up a glance to mark my progress. Kyle was waiting for me at the top of the rise, elbows bending in and out with each heaving breath, his eyes pinned to me with dark regard.

I slowed. Each intake of air felt like the cross of a sharp scissors, and the more I clawed an advance up the slope, the more my resolve weakened.

He waited.

The strategy was so cool, so unexpected and obvious that it stole any of my remaining fumes of courage. I had gotten nowhere with this. First, from his position above, all Kyle had to do was give one push and I would tumble back down the embankment. More practically, however, Kyle had quickly and effectively gotten us both right where he originally intended. Seventy yards or so from my back door. The victory for him was cold and absolute. I hauled myself up over the lip and there was no helping hand to pull me across. Those days were done.

I fell to my knees on all fours in front of him so he could not sneak a push to my chest just to teach me a final lesson or something. I looked down and took in sharp draughts of air, hating myself, hating the world and its cruel little realities, the twists and slants on fairness, the imbalances. If another kid was stronger, I was supposed to inherit the smarts. Those were the rules, weren't they?

Kyle spoke first, but just before, he snapped out his arm and gripped the back of my neck with clammy fingers. He pushed down a bit so my face went about four inches from the ground.

"Just come with me and take a peek," he said. "Chasing me down to fight is only going to get you beat up and the both of us nailed. See if you see it my way first, that's all I ask, all right?"

An absolute insult. He was quite capable of charging in on Lucy and grabbing her for himself. I was no factor. The only possible difference was that my dog trusted me enough not to make a ruckus on the approach. But why would that matter to Kyle? As long as Mom was in a room away from a back window Lucy's barking wouldn't mean diddly to her.

I suppose he wanted to get off scot-free, take from me what I loved the most, and do it with my approval. Maybe so he could sleep better. The fucker.

I had not responded.

"All right?" he repeated. He shoved my head down farther. Now the ground was a pencil's width away my nose.

"Let go first."

"Promise to help me scope out what's waiting for us in the back yard and I will. Nice and slow through the weeds. We'll spy it together. Make the promise."

Yeah, fucker. With your hand on the back of my neck and the dirt so close I can smell it I'm just a rat in a trap, aren't I? Like this I would swear the world is flat, school is a blast, and chickens have lips, but you're still going to make me say it, aren't you? Aren't you, fucker?

"All right," I said.

He squeezed harder and I gave a short yelp.

"Say it like you mean it, Jimmy. And don't even think about pulling a run and tattle. You're the one wearing the blood, dig?"

"OK, I get it, Kyle!"

He gave one more hard press, then removed his hand. Then he helped me up, but made sure it didn't really feel like help. He hooked into my underarm and dug right up in there as if it was the bottom of a window frame that was stuck. I came up and looked him in the face, but my eyes wavered first. His grip had been like iron. The message was clear.

"Let's go," he said.

He crawled his way through the high grass and I followed behind as I was supposed to. A swirl of gnats followed above us in a cloud. We pushed through a long stretch of high reeds, pussywillows, and long ferns that bent quietly before us, and when we passed over a damp patch we detoured off to the left. My mind thought of everything and nothing at once, circling back to an image of Lucy curled up at the foot of my bed every night, little paws under her maw, a little sigh of satisfaction when my feet, the covers, the sweet semi-darkness, and the warm air made a perfect little pocket of physical comfort. I tried to jump that sentimental track and get real. I tried to scratch out alternatives, but came up with nothing.

Mutiny was not my game and the familiarity of the surroundings was distracting. We were on the outskirts of the world of Mom, the place in which I was nothing but a squatter. Here, uprisings were not tolerated and loud protests never given. I had never been a path blazer or a rebel, a fighter or even an underdog. I followed here. I followed and hoped one day to grow magically into my right to drum up alternatives.

Kyle was going to kill Lucy and I could not stop him.

The weeds were thinning a bit. It was happening fast now. Everything itched and my mouth was bone dry. We were at the edge of my back yard. Kyle took the last bit of camouflage, a stalk in the middle of a wide growth of prairie grass, and moved it an inch aside.

It was lucky that we had averted the muddy little run back there. If we had continued in that direction it would have brought us to the middle of the property and that is exactly where my mother was looking.

She was on the back deck, hands in fists on the hips. She stared into the woods just to our right. Her blouse was a soft pastel green, an absolute irony to the steel beneath drawn into high tension you could see in the tendons of her forearms, the cords in her neck. Strands of her reddish-gray, bobby-pinned hair had come loose and they flew around her face like sharp tendrils of smoke. Her nostrils flared and I immediately thought "dragon." Her shock-blue eyes looked both ice cold and blistering hot at the same time.

It was a bad sign. I was not permitted past the weeds and into the forest, and if Mom thought I was desperate enough to try a sneak-in from this angle, it surely meant dinner was long past burnt. How long had it taken for me to rake the area and dump the shovels once I had found the watch? How long had I argued with Kyle about strategy? How many minutes were lost in the wild sprint over here? I had not taken the Mickey Mouse timepiece with me to keep a running check, and it was one more piece of poor preparation. When was I going to get with the program and be ready for shit like this? My dinner was probably into that ugly stage between cold and crusted. It would be a massive badge of failure in my mother's eyes, and God help us all if a Raybeck dinner ended up in the *trash*. Lord have mercy on children of all ages, that lecture could go on until midnight!

A gust of wind swept across the yard and my terrier stretched out her paws. She was lying on her side at the edge of the patio with her snow-white chest aimed at the sun coming in from the left. She snorted a little breath through her nose and ran her tongue along her whiskers.

Mom ignored her. The nylon lead kept the dog out of her perennials and that was all she cared about. Lucy was out of the way, chained there, and basically out of mind.

Lucy was our best hope and it killed me inside. Kyle was right. There was no fooling the blue-jean queen at the door. I was amazed at the absolute power my mother exuded when you were displaced to the side and observing her as a stranger would. I thought she was bad in the kitchen when she was up in your face, but this was actually awe-inspiring.

A sudden shrill, mechanical buzzing cut into the breeze and Kyle tensed up beside me. A sick rush went through my stomach. Mom turned toward the sound and made for the kitchen door.

The clothes were done.

This was it. The dryer in the garage had completed a cycle and Mom would be tied up for ten minutes or so, folding shirts and piling skivvies. Our window of opportunity had arrived.

The screen door swept shut behind her and Lucy barely noticed the exit. Her ear flicked. Kyle gave me a shove.

"Go," he said. "Now."

I paused. I couldn't.

"Fucking go, Jimmy! What the hell are you waiting for?"

I did nothing and he exhaled in a way to make me notice the sound. He started to stand and I grabbed his shirt sleeve.

"No," I said. "I'll do it."

I did not want Kyle Skinner touching my dog. I would take her myself. Hold her one last time.

I took one more second to look between the stalks of wild grass, and Lucy crossed her front paws. She opened her muzzle, curled her tongue, and gave a yawn.

I swallowed hard, blinked twice, and rose up out of the brush.

7.

Lucy sensed me right away and sprang to all fours. Her ears perked up. I came across the lawn hunched over as if someone was about to strike me. It was a nightmare and a blur.

The silence about the house seemed to boom a sickly pulse. I could feel the threat in my throat. At any moment, Mom's face could swim into one of those windows, her surprise quickly spreading to a look of alarm. Then fury. Lucy dragged the lead taught. It caught on her water bowl and dragged it across the concrete patio deck for a few feet. She went up on her hind legs and pawed at the air.

I kneeled and she exploded into me, a flurry of paws trying to take me in all at once. She was jumping to get up onto my back. I grabbed at her collar and unhooked the lead. I had a moment of disorientation during which I saw what I must have looked like in symbol world. I was no longer a boy, but a demon with no face, wearing black with the collar up. Lucy started in with her licking and lapping. I did have a face and it was covered with the blood of a dead blonde. I almost threw up.

I turned away my face and gathered the awkward moving bundle. She was still trying to mash her muzzle against my lips, craning in, cold, wet nose. I turned and made for the woods. At any second I fully expected the squeal of that screen door, the sharp call of my mother, the footsteps in pursuit.

They never came.

I broke through the weeds and pushed down the hill, past Kyle, down the steep rise. I almost tripped and went headlong down the slope. I caught myself just in time and widened my steps. I heard Kyle's hoarse breath behind me. He was panting and I don't think it was just the rapid pace. I think he was excited as hell. Lucy was nervous now, nearly motionless for all but an occasional kick from a hind leg.

I reached the bottom of the gully and stopped. Lucy's nose was nuzzled into my neck and I could hear her curious sniffing. Her body felt warm with trust in the arms of her best companion.

My mind went red and I heard roaring in my ears. I could not do it, not in a million years, not ever. A hand fell on my shoulder. I shuddered so badly I almost dropped the dog. Kyle slipped in front of me wearing his fake-me-out smile. He reached for Lucy.

"Hand her to me, Jimmy. You've taken her as far as you can go. I can tell. Give her up. It's almost done."

He stretched a set of grubby fingers to the fur on her neck and I exploded.

"No, you fucker!"

I stepped to the side and tilted back my head.

I brought it down. The air whistled. Contact. A splatting sound. He was rocked back with the violent contact and my motion brought me just past his shoulder. In the corner of my eye I saw his palm race up to the middle of his face. I got my balance and took a good look. Bright blood squeezed through his fingers and dripped down his wrist. Got him square in the nose. Bull's-eye.

"Argghh," he said.

"Take that, you fucker!" I shouted back. I was fuming at a height so great and so new that the boundaries seemed endless. Kyle was hurt. I had caused it. Now *my* breath was starting to race and Lucy started to kick.

I held her tight.

Then I just dropped her. Maybe Kyle could chase me down in a dead heat, but he would never catch Lucy once she got going.

She fell between us and scratched for a footing. Kyle dove in at her and missed, landing hard on his forearms and pitching up dirt. Before he could recover I stamped on the back of his left hand.

"Run!" I hollered. "Go, Lucy, run!"

She skidded across the sewer pipe in a fast break for the far hill. Kyle clawed to his feet and spit blood to the ground. I shrank back and covered up. The rain of blows was going to be heavy and motivated.

But no punch was thrown, and by the time my eyes fluttered open Kyle was past the pipe and tearing up the side of the hill. He was going for Lucy. Thirty feet above him I caught a glimpse of her hind legs disappearing over the peak and into the trees.

And suddenly I knew.

I knew where she was going and Kyle did too. She was not running blindly. She was following our scent back to the pit.

I put down my head and pushed my aching legs as hard as they could go in chase of the boy who was stalking my dog. My heart was pounding. My lungs started to burn.

This was all far from over.

8.

By the time I crashed through the trees and down into the clearing it was almost too late. The unfolding scene was repulsive and odd, with Kyle bent over and making a slow tiptoe along the far lip of the grave. One bloody hand was pressed to his face and the other was dangling down and out, thumb rubbing against forefinger. His breath rattled. His voice was a muffled "come hither" from beneath the bloody hand and kept repeating "Here, kitty, kitty," between more muffled curses from the back of his throat.

Lucy was not buying into it. Yet. Her tail was down and her neck hair was up. Every time Kyle got close, she pranced away. Then she would slow and stop, never escaping but always keeping a cushion of a couple of feet between herself and her coaxing assassin.

I ran long to the left where they were instead of where they were going and wound up at the edge of the circle across from the rooted path I had driven a car down in what seemed another age. My hands went to my waist, then my knees. My shoulders were heaving up and down, my lungs raw.

"Lucy!" I gasped. "Come here, now!"

She stopped fast and twitched up her ears.

"Come, Lucy, come," I said, suddenly hating myself for having let my pet roam for her entire life as a wild child. She was never the type to sit or to heel. She had not been taught to obey like my inferior and now it was going to kill her.

"No, Lucy," Kyle said. "Come to me, little honey-bunny, come to me."

His eyes darted back and forth between me and my dog. Lucy cocked her head and eyed us both in turn. She had moved off from Kyle, but had not yet committed to me. Her tail was wagging. She thought it was a game.

For a moment the three of us held our positions at the rim of the abyss, Kyle at due west, myself claiming south, and Lucy at dead east.

Kyle jumped for me. I ran to meet him head-on. I ducked under the raised bucket of the Bobcat and it cost me a second. Kyle was coming hard. I passed under the steel tub and put on a burst of speed. He matched it, and we both closed in with such determination Lucy became a temporary afterthought.

We rammed each other chest to chest, and while his momentum was a bit stronger, backing me up two steps on impact, my grip around his shoulders was firm. I bear-hugged him and tried to throw my feet, to bring us to the ground. I would have been stronger there. He reared back and kept us standing. I clapped his ears hard and pushed off. Our hands slapped out and gripped at the shoulders of the other. Heads buried in the crooks of necks as we grunted and pushed and tried to gain superior holds. The footing was bad. We were atop a small spread of rocks and the sound of heels raking across stone seemed to fill up the world.

He was strong. His biceps were iron.

I was desperate, my limbs slippery and quick.

He tried to shoot his arm under to clamp onto my shoulder blade. I countered by flapping down my elbow like a chicken wing and pinning his hand in my armpit. Our heads were mashed ear to ear and locked there by pressing fingers. I was holding my own.

He yanked loose the hand that was trapped and got a palm flat to my collar bone. He dug in and pushed, shifting me a quarter turn and a full step backward. I tried to plant my sneaker flat and it slid farther back along the rocks. Then suddenly it was not the whole sneaker on the ground. It had become just an arch and a toe. I was at the very edge of the pit and Kyle had almost succeeded in pushing me over. Loose pebbles cascaded down into the void.

I suckered him.

I pushed as hard as I could, gained back two inches, then released all my pressure. He came in to me hard. I nimbly leapt to the side, a half-inch to spare from the drop, put my hand on the back of his neck in passing, and helped him right into the motion he initiated with a hard shove. He took a header into the hole. I heard him swear and hit the dirt we had thrown in there. It hadn't been a long fall. We had filled it up almost all the way, and he would be back out of there almost as fast as he went in.

I turned to make a run for Lucy. I did not know exactly where she was, but I was pretty sure she would still be at the hole somewhere. The fight had only gone on for a few seconds and I didn't think she would have wandered yet to go on a sniffing tour. I saw her up by the edge of the rooted path, and when I ran to get her I stepped on the business end of a square-mouthed shovel. The thick wooden handle snapped up and I saw it snapping up, just not fast enough to avoid it altogether. I jerked my head to the side and it whacked me just below the hollow of my throat on an angle. I didn't want it to stop to me, I *willed* it not to slow me up, but it put me down to a knee. I saw red and black stars dance in front of my eyes, and a wave of dizziness threatened to drop me the rest of the way. I shook my head hard. It cleared. I turned.

Ten feet back, Kyle's fingers came over the lip. Then a dirty face, a palm placed flat, an elbow and an arm propped to make a perpendicular angle, a foot sideways and ankle down, and a knee pushing into the dirt. I grabbed the shovel and ran at him. I was holding the thing like a soldier going through a swamp, flat across a bit above chest level, one set of knuckles out, one set in, but I was not moving slowly like a soldier pushing his knees through the muck. I was charging as if chasing the American flag down a hill in a blitz.

It happened fast.

Kyle gained his feet and I was on him. He was surprised. He threw up his hands and grabbed the shovel right before it blasted him in the face. His feet had no choice but to mimic mine and I ran him backward. A bicycle built for two, our feet in perfect synchronization with Kyle facing the wrong way. The Bobcat and its bucket filled with crushed stone came up behind us and when Kyle struck into it there were three distinct sounds that matched up with three graphic visuals. There was a rip, and Kyle's eye's jerked open to the point where you could see the nests of bright red veins along the watery rims. There was a light crunch as the bar of the shovel came in contact with his already flattened nose, and a piece of the bridge tore through the skin between his red, watery eyes. And finally, there was that sound that really has no fitting name, the flat and final sound known mostly to butchers, that occurs when something sharp at the edge runs through living matter. The front of Kyle's throat bulged, the foreign shape pushing out the skin like a book shoved into the bottom of a trash bag. The last digging tooth on the right side of the bucket had impaled him straight through from the back of the neck. Everything stopped. Just like that.

I was amazed that I did not feel even the slightest bit sorry. I dropped the shovel.

He froze there like a doll. His mouth was a forced grin baring teeth in an eerily similar copy of the shape the tine made against the outer surface of his neck. I looked into his eyes for a moment. Blind as stones. I marveled for just a moment more about how something round like an eyeball could look so flat. Then I moved around behind him, put my palm against the back of his sweaty head, and pushed.

He went over in a rumpling cascade of elbows, knees, and head lolling around like a balloon on a stick. His blood streaked along the tine, marbled, and beaded up. I had the vague impression that these claws would have been too blunt for this kind of event, and most of them actually were. This one, however, must have hit a big stone or two in prior journeys, because it was turned up to a sharp little edge in the middle and nicked worse in a divot on the outer corner that curled to a point like the end of a knife.

I was numb now. I was thinking in a far-off way, but not so far-off, that if the police felt their find was a layer deep there would be no reason to dig into the same hole twice. Could I actually explain away Kyle? Maybe. He tried to kill my dog, that fucker. And the woman? Never in a million years. I picked up the shovel and whacked the chain holding up the bucket. Dust and dried dirt gusted back in a small cloud and there was a "ping" when the broken link popped free. The taut lengths on both sides snapped and the dozer's bucket came down. It dumped the load of rocks over Kyle in a flat roar.

It didn't get all of him. An ear, two fingers, and the cuff on one of the legs of his jeans protruded. I jumped down into the hole. It had to look like I panicked and tried to hide the body. There had to be some-thing to *find*. I kicked rocks over him and smoothed the surface over one last time with my toe.

"Bye, Kyle," I said.

I climbed out and looked for Lucy. She was gone. I had nothing left now but Mother, my "story," and dumb purpose. I trudged up the rooted path to the jobsite to retrieve our bikes, because that is what Jimmy Raybeck would do if he killed his best friend for trying to kill his dog and he wanted to cover it up.

The last lap was a tough walk, but I did it. Sometimes I wheeled Kyle's bike and simply let my old Huffy crash down the embankments like a wild marionette. At other times I couldn't help but toss Kyle's Schwinn, but I tried to baby it when I could. He had a sissy bar that I didn't care about and extended forks that I cared very much about. They were fragile, and I didn't want to lose the front wheel. Dragging the bike up the steep parts would be a lot harder that rolling it.

It was cold at the edge of my lawn even though it was hot and I was sweating. With the jobsite behind and my fate out in front it felt cold in the space between nightmares. I let Kyle's bike drop into the thick grove of weeds and pushed forward.

The sun was finally on its last legs, deep into the clouds above the horizon and the back yard was vacant. Garden in a rough square to the right of the patio. Moldy birdbath with the stone dish set unevenly to the left. Empty leash. A harsh light from the kitchen window.

I let the Huffy fall to the grass. I walked forward and thought that in another life Mother would have scolded her boy for not putting what was his into the garage.

I opened the screen door to the kitchen.

Bulb light washed over me in an angry glare. The house smelt of burnt broccoli. The door clapped shut behind me and for the moment, Mother's back remained turned. She was reaching up for something in the cabinet over the utensil drawer and struggling with the weight it put on her wrist. Yellow Pages. She hugged it in and then said to the wall,

"Young man, you had better have a damned good explanation for—"

She turned at the neck and her voice died off. She looked at me over her shoulder and her eyes went wide.

"Jimmy?" A long strand of hair fell across her face and she ignored it. She finished her turn in slow motion.

"Mom," I said.

"Mom, I just killed a boy."

9.

I wanted to burst into tears but I was empty. I wanted my old life back, but it was gone. My mother and I stared at each other like strangers. Jimmy Raybeck didn't live here anymore.

I wanted something to snap, rip loose, or strike out, but that was not Mother's way. She reached out and set the phone book on the counter. I was wild inside with the sluggishness of it. The air was bright and hot. I looked away and took a dry swallow.

There were scuff marks on the floor by the kitchen table, black abrasions marred in by the legs of my chair as I had so often pushed back too fast after being excused.

My chair.

No longer mine.

I had a yellow report card displayed on the refrigerator. It was suspended by a magnet shaped like the democratic donkey and labeled with five A's and a C+ in math. In red pen my homeroom monitor (and first-period English teacher) Mrs. Fulviotti, had written, "Jimmy is verbal in class discussions and with more study, shows great promise."

But I was "Jimmy" no longer. I was the thing in the kitchen.

"Mom," I said.

"Who?" she said. "Tell me who."

"Kyle Skinner." My voice sounded feminine and false. Mom folded her arms as if chasing a chill.

"Where? Where did it happen?"

I shifted and tried to find a place for my hands. I had moved a step forward and Mom put her palm up like a stop sign.

"Where did it happen? Answer me."

"Through the back woods, at the Route 79 jobsite. By the overpass, but Mom, I—"

The stop sign flashed up again and she quickly whipped it back into the fold-pattern above her stomach.

"How did you do it?"

I wracked my brain in an effort to come up with the right little spell for her, the psychological reasons as to why I killed Kyle, of how on earth I possibly *could* have done it. Clearly my mother was past the point where lingering pauses were tolerated.

"How, Jimmy? It's a simple question. Tell me. Knife? Stick?"

"I pushed him. He banged his head against the metal tooth of a small bulldozer and it went through his neck. Then I was so scared I covered him up with rocks."

"You pushed him."

"Yes."

"You—"

"He was going to kill Lucy! I had to!" My hands were out in the begging posture, like Oliver asking for more. I snapped them back, but not before my mother had seen them. Her eyes snapped back to mine and for just a moment they locked there as if on a wire. Had she noticed the blisters? I could not be sure. I had not done an inspection lately, yet had a dim recollection of layers and splotches of dirt soiled and spotted all over my palms and fingers. There was another quick second then, during which she looked at me, all of me, not just with a gaze leveled at the eyes, but more, for lack of a better word, *comprehensively.*

I could guess that a lot was decided in those two seconds, but I can't be sure *anything* was actually weighed or decided. As far as implications or accusations or suspicions you might have, I go on official record here stating that my mother, Judith Raybeck, said absolutely nothing in reference to further implications, accusations, or suspicions.

What she did was spring into action.

"You can't walk into a government building and speak to an officer of the law looking like this. Take your clothes off and put them in the bag. Do it."

She had let down her hair and rolled it into a knotted lock between the shoulders. Battle guise. The place was sealed, doors latched, shades pulled, and Mother had not so much as let me twitch during the preparations. She had yanked open drawers to crash around the silverware in their plastic tubs and then rooted through the utility cabinet. By the time she found that old pair of dishwashing gloves her ears had gone an angry red. I tried not to wince when those scum-hardened Johnson

& Johnsons imitated big yellow spiders with my mother's fingers wriggling inside. She snapped the rubbery ends down to her wrists. She bent again and reached under the sink, breathing the anger hard through her nose, never pausing until the Hefty bag made its way into the light.

Double ply. Mother only bought the best.

Close before me she let the bag unfold and cascade down to its full length. There was a slippery gnawing when she fingered for the opening, a loud *whack* when she whipped it down to fill it with air, and a look of divine wrath as she loomed above me like a great white shark in a red mommy wig.

"You can't walk into a government building and speak to an officer of the law looking like this," she said. "Take your clothes off and put them in the bag. Do it."

I paused. In the past there had always been a tenderness in my mother's face, a kind of long-term sadness etched there as if the things she had wept over as a girl had left traces. Even when she dragged me through the typical lessons that dictated why *my judgment had been poor*, there had always been an opening for understanding. Acceptance. It would finally show in the softening of her eyes when she let loose the hooks and said,

"Now we've both grown a bit, Jimmy."

Not tonight. No softness behind the steel glare, friends and neighbors. That kitchen was closed.

I fumbled with my pants button and felt my face redden. Mom had not seen me naked for five good years. But the ways of our world had regressed. I was the new Jimmy Raybeck starting from scratch and the clothes were coming off. Mother held the trash bag front and away from her body as if I had lice.

"Sneakers first, Jimmy."

Of course. Footwear before pants, shit, everybody knew that. I bent and had trouble with the laces. There was blood caked in them. Blood assumed to be Kyle's. I worked at the hard knotting as best as I could and got nowhere. The double square on my right sneaker was frozen and I risked soiling Mom's shiny floor by crashing to my butt for better positioning. I sat. I hauled up my foot by the heel, rested it on a knee and twisted. My sneaker jumped loose and bounced on the floor. A gravely spray of dirt followed it and I leaned to scoop it into a neater pile.

"I'll get that later," Mom said. "Put your clothes in the bag."

Sneakers, socks, and shirt went swishing into the sack. I scrambled up and attempted to work my way out of the pants. It took forever and I almost fell over twice. I smelled of earth, of old sweat, and death.

"The underwear too," she said. "Move."

I slipped down my dirty Hanes briefs and stepped out of them. I wanted to hide but there was no escape from my mother's cold stare. I sensed myself swing open before her, and my balls felt like two hard pieces of granite in a pouch with the slip-string pulled tight.

I dropped the underwear in the bag and felt horribly cold. I stepped back and covered myself with both palms. I started to shiver. My mother was expressionless except for those wide eyes on high beam. Then she dropped her eyes. She pulled the red plastic cords of the trash bag and started tying them.

"Go shower, Jimmy. Then comb your hair, brush your teeth, and get dressed. We have to go do our duty now."

When I came back to the kitchen in fresh jeans, my backup Keds, and a nerdy shirt with a yellow smiley face airbrushed on the front of it, I saw that the kitchen floor was clean. The yellow gloves had been put away and the trash can by the sink was empty. Mom was wearing her white summer dress. There were dark, thin clusters of hair laying against her bare shoulders. Combed down, still wet. We only had one shower, so I assumed she'd washed up in the utility sink in the garage.

We drove to Westville Central and did not speak one word to each other for the entire twenty-six minutes.

10.

I don't have a good recollection of the Q-and-A downtown, mostly because the busy things that unfolded all at once, the slamming shut of file drawers, the ringing of incoming lines, the static patch on the two-way radios, and the orders being barked between officers were foreign to me. It was like a science trip to a museum containing exhibits we hadn't yet learned about in class, or better, a visit to a hospital, with orderlies, nurses, doctors, and a number of specialists entering and exiting on an established system of cues amidst machines that beeped at what seemed random intervals. I was also busy playing the boy in shock (I think I still was a bit in shock really) and the insistence that I be attended in some kind of medical facility was shot down by my mother faster than you could say, "The queen bitch is in the house." I do remember that, and the way she signed the waiver so hard it almost ripped the top sheet. The rest is a bunch of grainy flashes.

I dimly recall that the station was oppressive in a vaguely masculine sort of way, with a lobby floor that had dull rainbow stone in it, and thin chrome dividers making long rectangles of the smooth flat polish. I remember a thin woman with a long face and features that were rather extreme, hawk nose, scars from past acne, and wire frames with lenses that looked too small working the phones from behind a half partition, but I don't remember where the set-up was in reference to the lobby. There was a ceiling fan turning slowly enough to make absolutely no difference in the vague shape of cigarette and cigar smoke hanging beneath it, but I don't recall what room that was in.

I do remember Mother walking me up to a counter and saying, "Excuse me, officer. My son murdered a boy and we would like to make a full statement." That officer was quickly replaced by another, then yet another, and we were moved away from reception. When I revealed the location of the incident there were wide eyes, buttons pushed on intercoms, and orders barked from hallways around the corner. I heard snatches of conversations that mentioned the mayor, a fear of red tape tying up "that mess out there" for another eight months, the new construction going live at 7:00 A.M. the next morning, a desire to have it all tagged and bagged by 10:30 P.M., and the fact that two black-and-whites and an ambulance would have to do. There were desks, and forms, and a parade of officers of various ages, ranks, and serial numbers. At one point I was in a bright interrogation room with a detective who had combed-back black hair and an avocado blazer. I recall that he was rather dislikable. Snotty and irritating. He sat with his legs crossed, eyes often half lidded, and a slight, soft preference for his "s" sounds in a near lisp. He also used vocabulary in a way that made you think he felt working for the police department was beneath him, but I don't have a good recollection of where in the timeline this occurred as opposed to the questions asked at the desks in more public spaces.

I remember a coffeemaker on a folding table with a stained, red checkered plastic cloth, a big old kettle of a coffeemaker that smelled as bad and as old as those that cook all day in the waiting rooms of shops that change your tires and do alignments for no extra charge. I remember talking in a monotone, yet the *sincere* monotone of a boy in shock who has categorically given himself over to clearing the air with the absolute truth. I admitted that I tried at first to hide the body under the rocks because I was in a panic. I told of my immediate confession upon returning home, and claimed that confession came because I could not bear to lie to my mother. When asked over and again in a thousand different ways as to why I killed my best friend, I responded over and again in a consistent voice that he tried to kill my dog. My violent response was prompted by instinct and the result was a horrible accident.

When asked why he would want to do such a thing to Lucy in the first place, I remember having a bad moment. I was unprepared for the question. Hell, if you knew Kyle you wouldn't have even thought twice about his wanting to do any sort of damage for a thrill. Still, it wasn't my automatic assumption (and miscalculation) that my story-listeners would be as up on the background stuff as their storyteller that bothered me. My mind had been working on two levels, one answering the easy questions being asked out in the live, real world, and the other below the surface calculating the unattended variables that could get me pegged for the murder of the woman.

I had just been thinking about the pressure on the officers to be done at the site quickly, and the gash in the oak tree. Had it been dark yet when we arrived here at the station? I thought it had been on the cusp. Two black-and-whites meant that there would not be a flood of headlights up there, and whether or not they noticed that gash depended on which direction they approached from and where they decided to park. When the interrogator asked about Kyle's motivation to kill Lucy in the first place, I had just been reassuring myself that I had been at the station for a good while now with no interruptions, so I could only assume everything out at Route 79 was going according to plan, no questions about gashes in the trunks of old oak trees. It was then that I suddenly thought about the body of Kyle and had a premonition of the future question that was bound to be raised by those doing the autopsy. What would they say about Kyle's hands? Sitting there, I knew I would be able to fill in the blanks concerning the current question on the table, but what would I say later about Kyle's blisters? I had kept my hands palm down all night because I didn't think Kyle's initial idea about a dirt fight with the shovels was good enough. I hadn't thought about *his* wounds being exposed and it froze me.

Then I actually smiled. When Kyle initially mentioned the dirt fight I had assumed he was covering for both of us, but he must have been talking about my hands alone. He wouldn't have had the same problem. His dad made him hit a hundred balls a night off a tee in the basement. His palms were already calloused as hell.

I used my smile to my advantage, dipped down the corners of my lips, and made it the predecessor to a wry response. In the driest tone I could manufacture, while still staying respectful, I proceeded to say that Kyle tried to kill my Lucy on a dare he claimed another kid made to him. It was a kid he refused to name. Though we had spent most of the day racing the dirt road from Westville Central to the site on our bikes, there was a good portion of the time devoted to Kyle's mischievous genius.

Mom raised her eyebrows at me when I told about smoking the Chesterfield, and I think that helped my case all around. Then I spilled *"everything."* I told about Kyle's pissing on the fifty-gallon drum and his pulling on the gear shafts of the big dozer. I told about the way he stole money from his mother's purse, and how he taught me to light bags of dog shit on people's porches. I revealed how Kyle set off firecrackers in mailboxes down in the Common, I told about the way he greased the doorknobs of churches, and I snitched about how he was the one who snuck the piles of cow shit up in the drop ceilings of the elementary school last year, yes, go check, he still had a piece of the soft tile that he broke off for a trophy hidden under an old box of clothing in his garage. Another Westville mystery solved.

After an undetermined amount of time, yet a long and drawn-out undetermined amount of time, they let us go home. I got the feeling that most of the officers felt sorry for me, and I had the stronger feeling that the guy in the avocado blazer did not. Whether that translated to his not *believing* me was another issue altogether, yet either way I was not really worried about him. Sometime during the questioning, somewhere in the middle when there were a lot of interruptions and different representatives posing different versions of the same basic five or six routine queries, I heard him say six key words to a fellow officer in the hallway.

The dead make for poor witnesses.

Besides, the guy didn't even really look at me during his part of the inquisition, and this I recall better than all the questions, bright rooms, rattling key rings, standard forms, and long hallways that could very well have led to my destruction.

Avocado kept staring at my mother.

I think he liked the way she looked in that low-cut white summer dress.

The new construction is going live at 7:00 A.M. tomorrow morning.

I rolled over and set my alarm for 6:30. If anything was going to be found it was to be soon, and for that I was thankful. At least I would know. I would be spared days, weeks, months, wondering when the hardhats would settle in, fire up the engines, and possibly unearth the "mistake" at the base of the rooted path.

The dead make for poor witnesses.

Yes, unless the equation added another dead body. Suddenly, the dead started talking loud and clear and people started looking back at the one left standing, wondering how he got that way.

If she was found it changed everything.

This line echoed in my head and became a numbing chant of sorts that I whispered out loud. Soon the combinations of the words gave in to the sounds of the letters, accenting the soft *shhh* in "she," the tender *fff* in "found," and the smooth exchange of syllables in "chhh . . . ai . . . ngggged" that floated over each other like silk.

My eyes drooped closed, gently shutting down the sight of my second set of clothes rumpled on the chair in the semi-darkness, next to a light blue Frisbee. The night in my mind spread and I curled down. In a far-off way my stomach ached, and in a further sense I felt myself weeping as I began to drift off. The tears felt distant and cold and I did not understand them because they seemed so disconnected. More familiar was the mild fragrance of cedar woven deep in the pillowcases and the whispery drone of the night bound cars on the overpass coming through my half-open window.

It all smelled lovely and tasted like tears. The strange flavor in my mouth painted the way. It forged a path, thickened the air, and kept me foggy right up until the dead ones came to visit me in my dream.

In my nightmare I was sleeping when I heard the strange noise. My eyes blew open and I jolted up in bed.

It was Kyle Skinner sitting on my chair.

He was shirtless, his body covered with circles of matted filth that grew outward in succession like rings you would see on the top facing of a sawed-off stump. The stump of an oak tree to be exact. There was a void in the back of his neck gushing sheets of blood against the wall behind him in rhythm with the beat of his heart. The place on the wall being doused was where my crucifix had hung. With the exception of a few splatters that dotted and sprayed up to the ceiling, the stains of fluid made more horizontal patterns that were spreading to the other walls. They looked like a row of mountains, or from another perspective, piles of backfill that were positioned a few feet above eye level from my place on the bed. He was painting my room in a manner that put me back in the pit.

The noise had been a crunching sound.

Kyle was holding my crucifix and chewing on the head of Jesus.

"It's hot down here in hell, Jimmy," he said. "Wanna see?"

His voice echoed off and he melted. His skin rippled, swam, dripped off, and gave way to a taller form, dark, a silhouette that gained shape and texture as if being brought into focus by some unseen artist of the grave.

It was the woman from the Honda.

Knees apart, she sat on the chair and rubbed searching hands up and along her bare thighs. She squeezed at her breasts. She ran a sneaky finger against the triangle shape her shorts made between her legs, and worked her face to a coy, questioning pout.

"Wanna go for a ride, Jimmy?" she said. "In my car?"

Her face broiled and changed. Wounds ripped open on her forehead and burst with wriggling worms. Bugs jumped out of her ears. Her teeth broke off and she spit them to the floor. Both of her eyes exploded and smoked.

"Give me back my blood," she rasped.

I snapped awake with a holler caught up in my throat. I clenched my teeth and mashed my lips with my hand to lasso the scream. I darted anxious eyes across the darkened room to relearn the old familiar shapes which now seemed menacing and strange.

Everything was ringing.

I breathed heavily and let the dream's aftermath settle into the reality of my heartbeat, the soft sounds of night outside of the window, the ticking of my clock. Gradually the surrounding gloom loosened, worked itself off, and waned to the pale intrusion of a low moon.

I swallowed dryly. I tried to cry and could not. I breathed through my nose, stared ahead, and wondered how long these ghosts would own the shadows in my darkened corner of the world.

Possibly a lifetime, depending on whether or not the construction men found something in the dirt tomorrow.

I closed my eyes and fell asleep wondering which of the scenarios was ultimately worse.

11.

I heard the sounds of chainsaws the minute I hit the bottom of the gully and shuffled across the rusted sewer pipe.

The alarm had blasted into a cheap, tinny rendition of Rod Stewart bitching to Maggie that he couldn't have tried any more, and I jumped up to dial down the volume. Mom's room was a door down past the den. I crept over to my chair and put on the same clothes I had worn to the police station the night before.

Mom's door was closed and there was nothing stirring around in there that I could hear. I padded past to the kitchen and out to the patio. I half expected Lucy to be waiting for me out there, cold in the crisp morning air, wet with dew, tail shaking so violently it moved her whole back end. Nothing but the yellow bowl still pushed to the side almost off the edge of the concrete. She was gone, so I put my hands in my pockets, pushed forward, and let the high grass of the woods take me in.

Going at my leisure made me realize how difficult the trip really was, and I had to be careful going down the first incline. At one point I misjudged the angle of the drop and slid about five feet, but I recovered without going ass over tea kettle. Once at bottom, I paused a moment to search for Kyle's blood in the general area that I'd head-butted him, and then I heard the machines.

It sounded like chainsaws, but there were other sounds too, like big engines. Come to think of it, I could feel the ground rumbling as well, and I tried to discern exactly how it made me feel. I had gotten the start time wrong and woken up too late. On the one hand, I had missed their initial progress, and this was bad. They could have found the woman already and called in the boys in blue for an assessment. On the other hand, those sounds on top of the rumbling engines were definitely chainsaws, and if they were cutting down trees they were not worrying about what was lurking down in the rabbit holes, so to speak. On the other, other hand, I wondered if they had gotten to the oak yet and if anyone had noticed the fresh gash. I started up the other side of the gorge with almost the same urgency that I felt one short day before.

I almost stumbled right into them because they had already changed the configuration of the woods. The glen that had contained the footer and the rooted path had been cleared of all machinery and foliage both in front going up to the original site and about forty feet back. I took a position behind a cluster of trees on that far side, and peeked from underneath the hood of a long, low-hanging branch of a maple endowed with a wealth of fluttering leaves.

Everything looked bald, and I was relatively high up. When I had raced after Kyle into the woods to protect Lucy, I had not realized how steep the initial climb out of the clearing had been. Now with so many of the trees gone from the original rear end of the grove, I was even with the top of the rooted path across the way. It was now merely a short hill that looked almost no different from the rise naturally cut into the ground to the left of it. The trees in that patch of earth had already been removed, and you could see the jobsite clear to the over-pass. The oak was gone. So were the construction trailer, the fencing, the dozers, the dumpsters, and the scatter of old tools for the most part. What stood up there now was a highly organized line of flatbeds seemingly putting the finishing touches on removing all traces left by the failed workers of the past. Men with hard hats moved and snaked all around in pockets of activity, and the loudest sounds came from the three dull-yellow, pitted tree-shredding machines parked in a line at Reed Road's dirt road entrance that we had originally come through on our bikes yesterday.

And the footer? I briefly had to search for its location with the surroundings altered so, but after a couple of seconds I saw it. It sat smack in the middle of the larger, tilled crater, rooted path and rise on the far side, little green flags all around the perimeter (I was close enough to one of the flag-stakes to reach down and steal it if I wanted to). What was so recently a hole now had a slightly darker face than the rest of the soil around it. Otherwise, it was uniform with the broader surface, and looked like a huge empty dish. They had filled in the dead woman's grave the rest of the way.

I was just starting to wonder what purpose the crater would serve, and what part the hole within the hole might play, when I saw the dump trucks, big ones, sounding their beepers that warned they were coming in reverse and backing up to the ledge of dirt between the upper site and the lower one. The gargantuan steel tubs started rising on their front hydraulics, and the new dirt started cascading out from under the heavy back tailgates pushed out and squeaking on their mammoth hinges.

They were filling in the crater, evening the ground from the rise, probably all the way to the green flags at my feet. The overpass ramp would now have a huge landing pad. There would be no more drilling or digging into the dead one's resting place.

I walked home with mixed feelings.

My pain was to be of the longer, slower, more internal type. Option number two.

When I came back through the kitchen door Mother was slicing up fruit for breakfast on a cutting board by the sink. We looked at each other expressionlessly and I went back to my room to change into fresher clothes.

12.

Feared. Shunned. Wall-shadow. Forgotten. What else is there to say about my social existence through the balance of my career in West-ville's fine institutions of learning? It was a rough ride from the day I entered eighth grade to the moment I dropped out of high school in the middle of my junior year, but I do not think it is appropriate in this kind of communication to dredge up those details. First, it is all pretty obvious (with the small exception of whether or not some girl with a wild side actually got close enough for me to sniff during those diffi-cult years, and the answer would be, not unless they had to) and sec-ond there is really no point. Does one really, finally care if a boy-murderer got a passing grade on his critical analysis of the structural issues in *The Catcher in the Rye,* or whether or not it was fair, or funny, or sad that he couldn't get laid?

I also do not wish to take up too much valuable time retelling all the little facts about the trial that one could look up in the back issues of newspapers. It would be more than easy to discover that Mom asked for and got a speedy trial for me in front of a judge, *"Only the guilty ask for juries, Jimmy."* It would be just as simple to find documenta-tion proving that Mr. Skinner tried to file a civil suit to protest my ver-dict of innocent, and ran out of money before it really got going.

What is not in the papers or online is a measure of how difficult it was to live in the same town with such a hateful enemy. I never quite shed the fear that I would run into Skinner or his small, plump wife on the express line at the Acme, or while sitting in the waiting room at Dr. Bransen's. That fear turned out to be a valid one, and this little thread of the tale has two halves, the first an incident that unfolded in May of 1975 just after the civil suit was dropped, and the second in the dead of winter, 1984. Here, however, I must split those two events and reveal but one now with the hope that you will patiently wait for me to unveil the other just a bit later. I know. Timelines are a bitch.

The first Skinner sighting occurred right after one of my key visits to the dead one.

Right around the time the man was dropping his civil suit and I was thanking God school was almost done for the year, the construc-tion specialists had shored up the east edge of the landing area from the Route 79 overpass, done the primary and secondary pours, and gated it off with Dura Flex safety rails. By Christmas of 1976, they would finalize the new construction of Reed Road, complete with overhanging streetlight poles every two hundred feet through Scutters Woods with a merge onto West Main Street five miles down. At the end of May 1975, however, right about the time when they were putting in the white shoulder lines on that wide landing, I had a horrifying experience.

I found her "spot."

I had wanted to do this for months. I had recurring dreams of her exploding eyeballs, and on some level I thought showing the courage to stand right over her again might help. I also had a constant fear that they would find some reason to dig and check out what was really down in that hole within the hole after all, and I had taken regular afternoon visits to the site all that year, hanging off in the cover of the trees to make sure they did not bust out the pneumatic jackhammers and put a whooping party on the cement and dirt fortress she was lurking under. Up until May, however, I hadn't had a chance to actually walk onto the cement platform because the space was always crawling with workers. And I hadn't dared make a night-time attempt. The darkness was her playground, and the dreams were bad enough in the safety of my bedroom.

It was a Wednesday afternoon. I walked my famous path over the sewer pipe, and when I pushed aside the leaves of my hiding tree I saw something that filled me with a sick kind of excitement. The landing was empty. There were surveyors marking off what would be the road paved through the thick part of the woods about a hundred yards away, but their backs were to me.

I approached the guardrail, climbed over, and had a moment of *déjà vu* when I crossed the threshold. It was hot and windy on the platform and I gave a quick study to the ground. I walked a few paces and then I saw it. About twenty feet from the guardrail, and fifteen feet south of the front end capped off with a three-quarter round cylinder painted in black and yellow stripes like a barber pole, was a small pair of grooves cut into the concrete. I looked up to get my bearings, and though it was difficult without the old landmarks, I was pretty sure someone had marked off where they had filled in that strange hole the rest of the way, now better than twenty-five feet below surface.

An arrow of fear went between my shoulder blades. If someone marked it, someone had a question about it. I would never be safe, not with these hidden ghosts always floating just out of the reach of my experience and authority, in boardrooms, with complicated plans spread across their drafting boards like tablets of fate.

"Hey!" I heard. One of the workers had seen me, and he was pointing a rolled-up piece of paper in my direction.

My face went suddenly red hot and my heart started palpitating. My hands felt like stones and I almost dropped right there on the hot top. This was not the fear of getting caught by the surveyor, now jogging toward me with his partner just behind, struggling to stick his sunglasses behind his pocket protector while on the move. This was different. The breeze came up around me in what felt like a whirlwind. At first it sounded like huge, beating wings, and then it moaned. It raced by my ears and made what could have been just an undeterminable gust like the one you would hear if you let down the back seat window of a car moving at a high rate of speed, or it could have been perceived as a couple of words.

"My blood," I heard.

My nose was bleeding.

I felt the liquid run out and drip down the top of my lip, but it did not quite feel like a drip. It felt like a pull. A dot of it splatted on the concrete, right into one of the little grooves, and I crumpled.

The voices of the men came to my ears. Then the temperature felt different, and I knew there were shadows over me blocking the sun.

"Hey, Doug," one of the shadows said. "Here's another one."

"C'mon, son," the other said. He helped me to my feet. I opened my eyes. They walked me over a few feet and then I ran for it.

"Hey! You!" they were calling. I scrambled for the guardrail, crawled over it, and sprinted for home. Ghosts didn't just hide in boardrooms. I suppose I could have interpreted *"Hey, Doug, here's another one"* as an acknowledgment that I was just one more kid who was dared by another to sneak onto the site, but that version didn't feel right to me. *"Hey, Doug, here's another one that passed out"* seemed more the fit. I knew it in my bones.

It was the first time she had spoken to me in the waking world, and she had been speaking to others before me.

I came through the weeds, trudged up the back lawn, and looked up at the face that came into the kitchen window. I didn't really feel the pull of those shock-blue eyes anymore, and it was easy to break the glance first. I turned and sat on the edge of the concrete patio, drawing up my knees to my chin. I stared out into the woods. What was going to become of me? What would I do if it became public knowledge that you passed out if you stood directly above the burial place of the neglected dead? I bumped my lips gently against my forearm. Maybe growing up was all about the ability to handle loneliness while living with the fact that there were possible outcomes, some horrific, that you could not control.

The doorbell rang inside.

I jerked my head up. It was a strange sound. Since the incident I had not been afforded the opportunity to invite over many "friends," and it was rare we had a caller. I pushed up and moved to the kitchen window. There was a wash of glare on it so I went up on my toes and made a hood with my hands for my eyes to peer through. I moved over to the left a couple of inches. I could not see the whole exchange because of the corner of the hall archway, but I had most of the front doorway in view. It was Mr. Skinner. He was wearing his Sunday best, reddish-orange plaid flood pants, a collared shirt, and a tan leather jacket that went down a bit past the waist. He removed his hat and held it before him. His hands were sort of wringing it. I could not really hear what he said even with the kitchen door standing open, but I could hear that his tone was soft.

I wondered what he could possibly want. An apology? A heart-to-heart? The civil suit had caved weeks before.

Suddenly I saw Mom's elbow pop into view. Her hands were obviously on her hips. Her voice was also unintelligible for all but the tone, but the pitch was of a sharper nature than that to which she had responded. She closed the door, came around the corner of the living room, and went down the far hall toward the garage.

I walked into the house and followed her steps. I walked past the refrigerator, into the utility hallway, and down the two wooden stairs. I stood outside of the screen door and peered into the garage.

It was a woman's space, filled with gardening tools thoughtfully placed on nails in the walls, lawn furniture, a couple of mulch bags neatly piled on top of each other, and a spiffy workbench. There were soldering tools, shears, strips of lead arranged across the surface, and colored glass pieces stacked at the right front corner. Dead soldiers. The stale remains of Mommy's little stained-glass hobby that got ditched when I started having my "problems."

She was by the utility sink. Her long fingers were making the prayer shape, her thumbs tucked under her jaw and her nose pressed between her index fingers. Her shoulders were gently shaking up and down.

"Mom?" I said. I pushed the screen door half open and it squawked.

She ripped her hands from her face and jerked her eyes to the wall in front of her. She was wearing faded jeans and a white cotton shirt that had blue stripes across it. It made her look both cold and fragile. There were tears on her face, but she had cut that particular faucet off to the quick. Rain on marble.

"What is it, Jimmy?" Her face was still looking off at the wall in profile.

"Ma?" I said. I came forward an inch or two, then stayed in the doorway. "Mom, do you love me?"

She looked over slowly.

"I'll always love what you could have been, Jimmy. We'll always have that, I suppose."

I went back to my room and turned up my radio as loud as it could go.

13.

Before I give the violent details of my second and final run-in with Mr. Skinner nine years later, I think it is necessary to talk for a moment about Maryanne. The woman buried in her car, twenty-five feet under the concrete apron at the base of the Route 79 overpass. Maryanne McKusker.

I found out her identity four days after her death.

Mom had not yet begun to drift from me, and we were in that mute aftershock that held loved ones together until the dust settled and they could really think things through. We were also still running on autopilot, our wheels in the grooves of our established patterns and habits. News had always been an absolute requirement before dinner so the both of us could go through life "informed," and with the hoopla surrounding my own case dying down just a bit, we had on NBC, the rabbit-ears antenna thrust all the way over to the fireplace that had on its mantel a picture of me and Ma smiling together at a church picnic last year.

I was watching Ted Johnson shift from one pile of notes to the other, thinking that his fake-me-out voice was more annoying than professional, when he said,

"This just in . . ."

He disappeared and a photograph took his place.

Good legs. Halter top. A woman in her back yard hanging up laundry. The white basket was perched on her hip. The sheets on the line, military gray, were frozen in time, furling around her in swells. Her expression was alluring in its gentle, girlish sarcasm, saying over the shoulder, *"Oh yeah?"* in a wry smirk.

She had straight blonde hair.

"Pictured here is Maryanne McKusker, a kindergarten teacher from Unionville who has been missing now for four days. The daughter of Minister Charles McKusker, she was last seen leaving her home in a rust orange '73 Honda Civic, enroute to Concord University for a training seminar in child psychology. Miss McKusker never made it to her destination, and her father claims she seems to have 'disappeared from the face of the earth.' The Unionville police have not yet officially made a statement confirming that there has been foul play, yet welcome any information leading to this young woman's whereabouts. Maryanne McKusker is five feet, three inches tall. She has green eyes. She is twenty-nine years old."

I glanced over at Mother without turning my head. She was staring at the television with the same general indifference as when Ted Johnson had talked about a four-alarm warehouse fire on Grant Avenue half a minute ago. If she suspected some sort of connection between Maryanne McKusker's last four days and the time elapsed since my confession, she was not letting on.

The good thing was that Unionville sat four towns over from Westville, up the Pike about twenty miles due east. The better thing was that Concord University happened to be three towns due east from Unionville, thirty or so miles in the opposite direction of where she'd made her final resting place.

She sure as hell was not going to any lecture.

And even though I was fairly convinced at that point that it would be amazing if they actually traced her here, this was an intellectual deduction that did not take into account my instincts and emotions.

I never felt safe.

And the nightmares did not get any gentler just because I knew her name. They continued once or twice every night with a horrid, almost mechanistic regularity. She haunted me in the dark and, in return, I decided to stalk her during the day. It was a defensive move. A coping device. I would *know* why she was headed in the wrong direction. It became a hobby, but I figured it out long before it could become a lasting obsession. In fact, I learned the truth before I even completed my first ninth-grade research paper. Of course, I had the advantage over everyone else in that it was far easier to unveil the set-up when I already knew the punch line.

As the summer wound down and I awaited my "trial" before the honorable Rita Moskowitz a few months later, I collected newspapers in my room and followed the investigation. Over a period of weeks the biggest piece of evidence that the Unionville police had uncovered was, in fact, a newspaper. In her room, on the bed, there had been a copy of the *County Gazette,* left closed and folded at the bottom edge of the mattress. The local police had dusted the paper and done every kind of test imaginable, but had come out with nothing but the statement, "At this point we have a number of possible leads, but we have so far found them to be inconclusive." Evidently, it would have been easier if the newspaper had been left open to a certain section, or something had been circled in magic marker, or she had left more of a wrinkle in the corner of a certain page. The inserts and leaflets, however, had been put back and rearranged in perfect order. And Maryanne McKusker's fingerprints were on every single page, all with the thumb on the front, top right corner, and the index finger on the back. Whatever she had been looking for had been mentally noted and passed. She was a subtle, yet thorough reader.

I went to the library on a Saturday in late September when the place was relatively empty, and aimed straight for the periodical room. I found the thing, and placed it beside the most current copy they had of the

Westville Herald. I kept looking over my shoulder. The last thing I needed was some librarian to wonder why Kyle Skinner's killer was so interested in the sole piece of evidence in the Maryanne McKusker case.

I scanned the more current paper first. The article on the progress of her case was shorter than the one I read at home the day before, and it was obvious that the police were letting this one fade to the unsolved file without much of a fight. They had completed their interviews up at Concord University, and were now "entertaining other leads."

In other words, the newspaper evidence had led them nowhere, and they were moving on to other cases.

I opened the copy of the *Gazette,* and spent a good while with it. There was only a couple of pages of real news—"Penny Becomes Scarce Commodity," "Amax Strike Drags On," "Local Industries Claim Coal Supply Will Withstand." I went through the various sections, spending most of my time with the advertisements and pullouts. Nothing. All dead ends. There were nature walks available in a national park, there was a special on the Johanson Company's supply of backyard pools, there were five pages of personals. I worked out some scenarios in my head, and though there were possibilities, like a female selling a used stereo, none of them made a straight line with Maryanne McKusker's place in Unionville and the Route 79 overpass. I made a second sweep of the *Gazette* and widened my focus to goofy stuff not so "evident." I came up with little else. In the back of my mind I had just noted the futility of the exercise considering the fact that the Unionville police had already made these deductions, when I ran across Rolling Joe's advertisement.

I had initially passed it over because it seemed so silly to be put even in the same paragraph as the person I had imagined Maryanne McKusker to be. Still, the place was local, so I took another look at it.

Rolling Joe was a Sixties dropout going on forty, who thought himself a visionary. He was balding and still holding on to a ponytail. His dingy shop was crammed with nudie posters, bongs, and other various no-no's, like rolling papers and canisters of nitrous oxide commonly known as "whippets." It was all perfectly legal, and most around these parts thought of Rolling Joe as the perfect asshole.

Business was limited, but Joe kept his little business going by feeding on teenagers. I had heard lots of high school kids tested the waters of rebellion and believed for at least a short period of time that it was cool to hang at the head shop.

Clearly, Joe was thinking bigger nowadays. His advertisement read,

"Rolling Joe's Shop of Dreams. Grand Opening Tomorrow! Monday Will Be YOUR Day of Psychedelic Rest. New Flotation Tank. Appointments Only."

Evidently, he came upon the new technology that wound up being later popularized mostly in myth by the William Hurt film titled *Altered States*. Oh yes, Rolling Joe was a trend setter!

Did Maryanne McKusker actually sign up for an appointment for this thing? I was about to wander out to find a phone booth so I could call and ask him to check his log book from a couple of weeks back, but I didn't. First, the police would have done this already, and second there was something about the ad that bothered me. Then I saw it. He called "tomorrow" Monday. We killed her on a Monday.

I turned the paper over to the front page. Of course. I didn't notice it before because the date at the top, just under the slightly perforated edge, had the month and day solely represented by numbers. This was a Sunday paper. That's why it had so many extra flyers. Maryanne had thumbed through it and failed to find what she was looking for. The next day she picked up Monday's paper, saw what she needed or wanted and went directly to it. She was already on the road and either tossed the paper out or left it in the car.

The police probably didn't jump to the conclusion I did because of those extra flyers. Everyone knew the Sunday paper had all the promotional stuff. Was it possible that whatever attracted Maryanne did not make the weekend deadline? Did they or he or she get a discount for having the ad or announcement or bid first shown in an edition with less circulation?

I twisted around and took a look through the doorway. The librarian was in the main lobby, half-cut bird's eye glasses on the end of her nose and a pile of file cards a foot high in front of her. There was a small girl with her mother way over by the children's section, and a guy in an army jacket asleep at the long table by the window. I crept over to the rack and slipped the next day's edition of the *Gazette* off the curled wire. I found what I was looking for in about two minutes.

It was an advertisement as subtle as the side of a cereal box, but to me, it was more than obvious.

NO NAMES NECESSARY
DR. GOLTZ GYN. M.D.
112 BYLINE RD., DEGGSVILLE
555-3865

She had been going to get an abortion. A kill of her own, and the more I thought of the ways that this might not be possible, the more assured I became that it was.

The father? Yes, where the hell was he in all this? Why had he not come forward to claim his right as a player? Was he a secret, ongoing fling, still under cover now because the disappearance would implicate him? Had Maryanne been on her way to see him in stealth? That did not play right somehow. First, why the secret, and second, someone at either end of it, his work buddy or her little phone-gossip friend or someone like that would have known. They would have come forward by now.

It must have been what they called a "one-nighter," or what Kyle would have referred to as a "pump and dump." They probably met at some crowded bar or some lecture she had attended in the past and gone and gotten a room. I understand and believe this now as an adult, and even at thirteen I had my imagination. It was not too difficult a stretch.

Maybe they had been drunk. Maybe recently he even recognized her picture on the news and had remained silent, ignorant of the pregnancy, sure of his innocence, and unwilling to arouse suspicions that would swallow his time, mar his reputation, and prove answerless anyway.

The fatal ride of Maryanne McKusker came to me with a hideous clarity. She did not want Dad the minister to know she was pregnant, so she anonymously called for directions from a mall or gas station telephone.

"Interstate 7 to Crum Creek Parkway. Make a right onto Exit 3 and follow the curve to Jukins Cross. Bear left at the 'Y' and continue on Byline Road. It is unmarked at that point, but you will see us a mile up on the right hand side."

Hell, Rolling Joe's was *on* Crum Creek Parkway and she probably passed it. But soon afterward she must have gotten lost. I do not believe, in fact, that she ever got to the clinic or much past Rolling Joe's, for that matter. I think she took a wrong turn at the "Y."

At the end of Jukins Cross there was a "Y" in the road all right, but it was not really a "Y." It was a three-pronged fork that had two major, unmarked arteries and an offshoot to the far left that looked more like a private driveway than a real street. Byline was definitely at the left of the "Y," but to the newcomer it would have appeared more as the center path of three, if you counted the little side-chute.

Maryanne McKusker's directions had specifically stated "bear left at the 'Y,'" and she did just that, even though the avenue in question looked generally untraveled with a center line of crabgrass sprouting between the dirt-worn tire marks.

The small patch of unmarked country lane was actually called Mulberry Street.

Mulberry Street led one way to the Route 79 overpass.

Maryanne McKusker had bumped along Mulberry Street, maybe fearing she might run over the amount of time she allotted herself for the false appearance at the lecture in Concord, fretfully searching for the clinic a "mile up." What she got was an ongoing, lazy panorama of seemingly deserted horse farms, barns, and meadows back dropped by dustings of trees. No gas stations, no general stores, just a confusing wind of back road stretching farther and farther to nowhere.

She was probably relieved when Mulberry Street curved suddenly and opened out to the overpass.

Civilization at last!

She would have passed under the big green overhead road sign that announced "Westville" in friendly white letters. She would have immediately understood her mistake at the "Y," regrouped, and opted for the first possible left turn allowing her to double back and try it again.

It was a mere fifty feet between the Mulberry street on-ramp and the fatal left turn. It is entirely possible that she, for that short period of time, was the lone motorist on the overpass and unobserved. It is fact that the triple guardrail kept her from knowing exactly where the left turn was about to take her, and it remains my own speculation that at this particular moment it felt right to her. At least it was a turn in the right general direction.

Considering the "alibi" she told her father, the time was getting tight. She was probably pressing on the gas a bit harder than usual. She swung down that ramp and onto the dirt road faster than you could say *"death trap."*

She wanted an abortion and she got one.

Kyle and I killed two birds with one nail.

14.

The toll booth did not go up until the summer of 1978. There were legal snags, and Runnameade's proposals that received initial local approval were put on hold at the state level. For a year and a half cars simply came into Westville off the turnpike for free. Then in late '75 there were questions about the integrity of the original exit ramp, and they closed off the turn on the overpass for another twenty-three months.

Of course, I did not know of these details until years later when I could access all the documents, transactions, and bureaucratic maneuverings online. As a developing adolescent I was left to my own assumptions. I therefore took it upon myself to continue going regularly to the jobsite as I had begun doing as a thirteen-year-old, so as to hide in the cover of the trees and see if today was the day the hardhats started poking around again.

I meticulously read what the papers gave away, but the information back then was spotty at best. It was old news that Runnameade Construction had won the bid with a simple, low-risk scheme to put a single toll booth in at the base of the overpass. In the Nineties, many referred back to this as "The Blair Witch Plan," not only because Runnameade's booth wound up being haunted, but more so to compare it with the miniscule cost the creators of "Blair" put forth to make their blockbuster in the first place.

The Siegal people always questioned the integrity of that original footer, but those protests were really trivial to them, more footnotes in fine print than the dollar signs that came across in bold. They wanted the powers that were to shoot the moon. Still, neither the "petty" technical angle nor the lofty financial one ever got past City Hall. These mavericks wanted the government to spend big, and plain and simple, the Siegal vision had a higher cost than what many believed would turn a profit. Through the years, as the running debate wore on, interested parties on both sides did traffic volume evaluations and Siegal's independent firms always seemed to come up with different results than those hired by the government. Go figure.

And when the single booth did go up in the summer of 1978, as predicted, it began turning that slow, faithful profit, like a low-risk, low-interest savings bond. Every time Siegal got to the table through the years, their bid was rejected for the same basic reasons.

The booth started turning a profit the minute it was put up.

We are a small town.

Your plan will cost millions in exposed funds that will take years to show dividends. As long as that booth stands, and continues to come up in the black on the quarterlies, there will be no plaza. Period.

That is why I dropped out of school in 1978, a year before graduation. Runnameade installed the booth and could not get anyone to stay in it, at least not after the sun went down. I do not recall the names in the succession of those who tried to work nightshift there throughout that critical month, but I know it was more than twenty. The reported physical symptoms were "lightheadedness, heart palpitations, and minor bleeding for no apparent reason," but it was the psychological symptoms that really captured everyone's imagination. It was bad enough that some actually recognized Kyle Skinner's fleeting image just at the periphery of vision, laughing silently and snapping his head back and forth on that flap of neck-skin. The one that really scared me, however, was Maryanne's image, hair flying behind her in slow motion, eyes crawling with worms, a baby in her arms that she reportedly first caressed, next scratched, then bit into, and finally snapped back and forth in clamped jaws like a frenzied dog tearing at meat. Supposedly you couldn't really "see" her, since the minute you fixed your eyes on the particular glass pane she was occupying she switched to a neighboring panel, but I could not afford to take the chance that someone would actually recognize the face (or worse, take a photograph of it) and connect it to Maryanne McKusker.

When the trouble in the booth started there were also reports in the newspapers and the *Construction Times* (of which I had become a regular subscriber by then) that Siegal had heard about the complication and were stirring around again, going back to the footnotes in small print concerning the integrity of the otherwise unexplored footer where that boy died years ago. Suddenly not so trivial.

I actually read an article about that while goofing off at school, and remember walking straight out of chemistry class and Westville High for good. When I told my mother later that day, she accepted the news with quiet defeat. She brought the collar of her robe up under her jaw in a fist and slowly went back into her bedroom. No shock-blue eyes. She had kept them down to the floor. The blue jean queen had lost her power over me some time ago.

I was hired immediately. And while many initially saw it as some sort of sick prank that I earn my living literally standing directly above the spot where Kyle Skinner was killed, there were others who came to understand (or thought they understood) that this was my duty, my way to mourn, my method of healing that allowed me to give something back to society.

And I did give back. The trusty low-risk savings account. I was never told exactly where the money was filtered off to after I took the weekly take in fifty-pound strongboxes and helped pack them onto the armored GM van they also used for prison transport, but I suppose a portion was put right back into the city. I never came up with the cure for cancer, but we erected a huge bandstand down in the Common back in '83. I never discovered a way to solve world hunger, but I would bet dollars to donuts that the war memorial they put in the grove behind the recreation center in '95 was sponsored at least in part by some cash that came from my strongboxes.

Of course this is all well and good, but I am not trying to fool anybody. If you are reading this you know exactly who I am, what I have done, and where it has left me. Working the booth has been no picnic, and I am not immune to the spirits that dwell there. I am forty-six years old and I feel like I'm in my seventies. I eat poorly, on purpose, and have been loading up on daily doses of F9 Blood Liquescence ever since it became possible buy your own smorgasbord of drugs on the Internet. As I said, I am a walking time-bomb, a guaranteed candidate, no, an *elected official* for a heart attack or stroke, but before I pass there are two more things I am obligated to disclose.

First, please know that my mother was always innocent of all this. For your information, she developed osteoporosis, broke a hip when

she took a header off the stairway in front of the Staples on Willow
Street, and died in the hospital of pneumonia last year. She was always
ignorant of the breadth of my sins, and for that I am thankful.

Second, understand that it was not just the supernatural that tar-
geted this booth. Through the years I was attacked a total of twenty-six
times on the job. Most were drunk teens chucking empty bottles or
rocks at the booth for a laugh, but there were some incidents born of
more serious motivation. I was shot at three times. Two of the occur-
rences were random acts of hate by those in vehicles I could not identify, but the one in the winter of 1984 was anything but random.

I was reading an article in a teen magazine that discussed the dif-
ferences between Eighties sleaze hair metal and New Wave, when I
heard a vehicle screech up to the gate. By the time I looked out, Mr.
Skinner had already exited his vehicle. His hair was matted with sweat
and he was shirtless. He called something to me but the fierce wind
swallowed the words. I was lucky he was so drunk. The other assaults I
experienced during my tenure in the booth were drive-bys, but here he
really wanted to get his hands dirty. There was a double-plated bullet-
proof sliding glass unit above the half-door I exchanged cash out of,
but I had left it up. Skinner only needed to walk four feet to have a
clear, frontal shot at me.

He didn't. He staggered, took a position at an angle to the booth,
spread his feet, aimed, and fired his weapon. It smoked and banged
louder than I thought it would have. I had covered my face, and now
slowly brought away my hands. The bullet had dented the safety glass
and glanced off into the roadway. Skinner was not visible.

I got out of my chair and opened the portal door. Skinner had slid
down to his butt. He had on dirty overalls with the straps down. He
had snot coming out of his nose, and the wind blew it away in threads.
He was propped up, back against the front right tire. He had one leg
splayed out straight and the other bent at the knee, untied boot against
the bottom of the booth. He looked at me with squinting, tearing eyes.
He smiled crookedly, and brought the gun to his temple.

I just watched, hands dangling at my sides, breath coming out in
steady little puffs that made clouds on the night air.

He started laughing. He laughed as he brought the weapon down,
and laughed as he pushed to his feet. He offered me the gun, butt first.

"Eh?" he coaxed.

I just cocked my head a bit to the side and stared.

He turned and tossed the thing into the woods beyond the edge of the concrete deck. He started laughing for the second time, and I could still hear it as he drove off into the darkness. I never saw him after that night. He moved out of state and no one I knew ever heard from him again.

And so that concludes my story. When I am gone, the booth will inevitably fail and Siegal/Tri State Industries will finally control that section of roadway. They may even go back to the fine print, bust the shit out of that dirt-and-concrete tombstone and finally exhume Mary-anne McKusker. It will be poor closure for her. She will be remembered as a vengeful spirit and sensationalized as worse.

As for me, I suppose this story is my closure, but one must be human to feel that kind of thing. My soul was erased years ago. I was a boy with dreams and I made a horrible mistake. I do not for a minute think myself more innocent than Kyle Skinner because I only threw one of those nails, and do not consider myself pure because I was unaware of the baby. I do not even feel there was righteousness in bringing fatal consequences to an unfeeling hoodlum who threatened a defenseless animal, even though the law would disagree with me.

When you strip this down to its bare bones, I am the worst kind of sinner. From everything I read about her, Maryanne McKusker was a wonderful person. I turned her into a monster. I could have told somebody before now. I could have at least told somebody.

Maryanne, please forgive me. And in my last days, when I see you rise from the dead looking only to take back what is yours, please know that I understand.

For I have always been the horror here.

I have always been the horror.

MICHAEL ARONOVITZ is an author and English instructor with a Masters in Education and a Masters in Literature. He has published short fiction in *Midnight Zoo, Slippery When Wet, The Leopard's Realm, Crimson and Gray, The Nighthawk Magazine, Philly Fiction, Scars Publications, Demonminds, Fiction on the Web, Metal Scratches,* and *Studies in the Fantastic.* He teaches twelfth grade language arts in a Philadelphia charter school. He lives with his wife and son in Wynnewood, Pennsylvania.

LaVergne, TN USA
18 November 2009
164536LV00005B/53/P